SEPTEMBER SONG

Recent Titles from Colin Murray

AFTER A DEAD DOG
NO HEARTS, NO ROSES *
SEPTEMBER SONG *

* *available from Severn House*

SEPTEMBER SONG

A Tony Gérard Thriller

Colin Murray

This first world edition published 2012
in Great Britain and in the USA by
SEVERN HOUSE PUBLISHERS LTD of
9–15 High Street, Sutton, Surrey, England, SM1 1DF.

British Library Cataloguing in Publication Data

Murray, Colin, 1949-
  September song.
  1. London (England)–History–1951–Fiction.
  2. Suspense fiction.
  I. Title
  823.9'2-dc23

ISBN-13: 978-0-7278-8110-6 (cased)

All Severn House titles are printed on acid-free paper.

Severn House Publishers support The Forest Stewardship Council [FSC],
the leading international forest certification organisation. All our titles that
are printed on Greenpeace-approved FSC-certified paper carry the FSC logo.

Typeset by Palimpsest Book Production Ltd.,
Falkirk, Stirlingshire, Scotland.
Printed and bound in Great Britain by
MPG Books Ltd., Bodmin, Cornwall.

Vous êtes un beau ciel d'automne, clair et rose!
Mais la tristesse en moi monte comme la mer,
Et laisse, en refluant, sur ma lèvre morose
Le souvenir cuisant de son limon amer . . .

From: 'Causerie', Charles Baudelaire (1821–67)

ONE

Pete's Place isn't the ritziest club in London. Come to think of it, it isn't even the ritziest club in Frith Street. But it does play my kind of music. So I wasn't too dismayed when the slim, good-looking young man I was following stumbled down the steps next to the Acropolis restaurant, waving a creased and flaccid ten-bob note, and disappeared into the smelly corridor that led there.

I stood for a few seconds as a taxi hissed past, its dim headlights casting a yellowish beam on the gleaming road. Soho glistened and glittered damply after the first rain in weeks, and the cool, damp air felt good.

The gloomy passage reeked of stale fat from the Acropolis and unwashed bodies from Pete's Place and I wondered whether I might not prefer to wait outside. Then the resident quartet started to belt out 'The Sheik of Araby' and there was no question where I wanted to be. I waved my membership card, smiled at Bill, the amiable ex-pugilist on the door, dropped half a crown in the jar on his card table and went on in.

The atmosphere was what the French call *intime* when what they really mean is hot and sweaty. The dense fug from dozens of cigarettes and the whiff of spilled beer almost made me turn around and head off out, but the driving sound had that magical something.

Peering through the gloom, I could just make out Philip Graham, the 'star' I'd dutifully babysat from pub to pub for the past two nights, slumped at one of the twelve round tables in front of the little raised stage, a glass of whisky already in front of him and two of his latest best friends on either side. The newspapers had Graham down as a hellraiser, and he certainly did his best to live up to that soubriquet, but, in truth, his best wasn't up to much. I didn't care for the look of his two sharply dressed companions though. Nasty little oiks in expensive suits hanging around someone nearly famous and very drunk never appealed to me.

I ambled over to the bar and ordered a glass of lemonade. I was just in time for Peter – no one ever called him Pete to his face – Baxter to drop the trumpet to his side and croak out a boisterous vocal. As a singer, he was a very good horn player, but it was raw, it was fast and it was fun. He raised the trumpet to his lips, and they went for one final, frenzied chorus, piano, bass and drums all frantically pushing the pace beneath Baxter's harsh, breathy melody. They finished more or less together, and, sweating profusely, they stumbled off, to ragged applause.

Peter Baxter grabbed a pint from a table in the wings and then shuffled back on stage. He was a big, florid, bad-tempered man in a shabby, brown suit. Bill the bouncer claimed to remember when the suit had been new and fashionable but no one believed him and his efforts to place it 'before the war' only had wags vying with each other to find a conflict early enough to explain its antiquity. The general consensus was that it predated the Crimea but was probably not quite as early as the American War of Independence.

'Let's have some hush, you horrible shower,' Peter said. When he asked for quiet, he usually got it, and everyone duly shut up. 'Tonight's special. We're being graced by one of America's rising stars, and I want you all to put your hands together and give a real Pete's Place welcome to Miss Jeannie Summers.'

The crowd of fifty or so clapped in a desultory way as a pretty, slim, youngish woman in a dark-blue evening gown glided up to the microphone and the light faded to a single spot. Her pianist had already taken his seat, and he tinkled an intro. She closed her eyes and started to sing.

She opened with 'Smoke Gets in Your Eyes' and followed it, without a pause, with 'These Foolish Things'. One song followed another seamlessly, and everyone in that shabby little club was transfixed. Miss Jeannie Summers had the kind of rich, deep alto voice that broke your heart. When she sang that she couldn't help loving that man of hers, you knew it to be true, and when she told you that she died a little every time she said goodbye, you believed her. She didn't perform the songs – she lived them.

Her set was about thirty minutes long and went by in a whisper. She finished with 'September in the Rain', and then she simply lowered her head. There was a long silence and then a single cry of 'Bravo!' and Philip Graham stood up, clapping wildly. Everyone joined in. Miss Summers didn't appear to notice. Then the spot died. When the floods came on, she'd vanished. After a moment or two, Peter Baxter lurched on, clutching his pint pot and trying to clap at the same time. He only succeeded in slopping beer over his brown, suede shoes. He leaned in to the microphone, said, 'Wow,' and shook his head before taking a great slurp of beer. Then he came close to looking happy.

'The lovely Jeannie Summers will be back later,' he said, and I swear he very nearly smiled. 'In the meantime, we'll all take a short break. Time to charge your glasses and visit the facilities, ladies and gentlemen. Fifteen minutes.' Then he shuffled off into the wings.

People started milling around, talking loudly: some rushed the bar, others slipped out into the dank corridor to find the loo. Through the crowd, I saw Philip Graham, still on his feet, looking longingly at the stage. I picked up my glass, drank warm lemonade and swayed to my left to allow a pasty-faced man access to the bar. When I looked for Philip Graham again I couldn't see him, or his companions. I didn't think they'd sneaked past me, but I poked my head around the door and looked out, just in case. He wasn't waiting outside the Gents, and I had a bad feeling.

Young Philip was a good-looking boy, and he fancied himself a star. That meant he reckoned the ladies found him irresistible and all doors were opened to him. And that might, I suppose, have been true, if he hadn't also been a nasty, graceless, boorish drunk.

I put my glass down on the nearest table without too many feelings of regret – there's only so much lemonade a man can drink in one evening – and wandered closer to the little raised area that masqueraded as a stage. I was standing right by it when, even above the hubbub in the club, I heard the ugly sounds of an altercation.

One step took me on to the stage; three more and I was in the wings.

Typically, Philip Graham was several feet away from the ruckus.

Jeannie Summers' piano player was backed up against a brownish-red door, and Philip's two companions were yelling at him. One of them was holding his right arm, and the other was jabbing a finger into his chest. As I approached, the jabbing finger turned into a fist and hammered into the pianist's stomach.

I ran the couple of yards that separated us and gave the puncher the kind of solid shoulder-barge that a beefy centre forward would use to bundle a goalie into the net. He was lighter than he looked and crossed the goal line by a good distance before falling to the ground in an untidy heap. I turned and grabbed Graham's other mate by the collar of his jacket, hauled him off the piano player and shoved him hard in the same general direction. He was much heavier and bulkier and only back-pedalled a pace or two before standing his ground. I placed myself squarely in front of him, making it clear that the only way to the panting ivory tinkler was through me.

'That's enough,' I said, just as Peter Baxter came out of another door further along. He was carrying a battered cricket bat. I turned to Hoxton Films' latest toerag of a star. 'Mr Graham,' I said, 'you'd best get out of here and take your mates with you.'

He took a step towards me, and the heavier of his companions threw a roundhouse right at the same time. I stepped inside it, took it on the shoulder and smacked a short right jab into his chin. For all his bulk, he had a glass jaw, and he just obligingly sat down, a vacant look on his acne-scarred face. His friend was still on the floor, with Peter Baxter's cricket bat pressed into his midriff. It isn't often that you can talk about seeing the blood drain from someone's face, but Philip Graham certainly turned an unhealthy, pale colour while I watched.

I pointed a finger at him.

'I really think you should go,' I said, 'to your bed.'

He didn't move.

'Now!' I barked, and he looked like the little kid he really was, thin, white-faced and scared.

'You've got no right,' he started to whine.

'Mr Graham,' I said, laying heavy emphasis on the Mr, 'you have a contract with Hoxton Films. I suggest you think about honouring it by going home, setting the alarm and climbing into that make-up chair by six o'clock tomorrow morning. Don't you?'

'I know people,' he said.

'Yes,' I said, 'and I'm sure you can make my life a misery. Just do me a favour and grab a cab, get some sleep and start plotting your revenge tomorrow.'

'What about my friends?' he said.

'They'll be following you out in due course,' Peter Baxter said, leaning on the cricket bat and forcing a grimace from the smaller of the two, 'if they know what's good for them.'

'All right,' Graham said, 'I'm off. But I'll be back.'

'No, you won't,' Peter Baxter said, shaking his head emphatically. 'You won't.'

Graham looked as if he was about to cry but did the sensible thing and left.

The piano player straightened up and coughed.

Baxter stepped back and allowed the man he'd pinned to the floor to stand up. 'Give me your membership card,' he said.

The man looked at him for a moment and then fumbled in his pocket for a wallet. He produced his card.

'Right,' said Baxter, 'I'm confiscating this.'

'Oh, come on, Pete, you can't—' the man started to say, but he broke off when Baxter brought the bat down on to his toes. Hard. 'Bloody hell, Pete!' he said.

Baxter prodded his foot again. 'Don't call me Pete,' he said. 'And now, get out and take him with you.' He pointed the bat at the guy sitting on the floor, nursing his jaw.

'I'll remember you,' the big man said to me as he struggled to his feet. 'I'll definitely remember you.'

There's always a certain amount of bravado after a ruck – even one that didn't really amount to much – and I ignored him and turned to the piano player.

'You all right?' I said. I was aware of the other two men walking away, giving me ugly looks as they did so.

'Sure,' he said. I don't know why, but it hadn't occurred to me that he was American, but that one drawled word emphasized his nationality. He was very thin and tall, and good-looking in a lean, pale, haggard way. The wide, garish, pink tie shimmering against his dark-blue shirt emphasized his pallor. 'Thanks.' He rapped on the door he'd been pressed against. 'It's OK, Jeannie,' he said. 'They've gone, honey.'

I awoke to the rich scent of Paris: the ripe, strangely sweet, cloying smell of drains fluttering past the heavy curtains; the heady intoxicating aroma of coffee drifting from the sunny kitchen where Ghislaine was carefully preparing it, using her grandmother's elegant old dark-wood grinder, as she gazed out of the window at the rooftops of la Ville-Lumière.

Then I did wake up, in Leyton, to the distant, mournful sound of the Caribonum factory hooter, booming out along Church Road, sounding hauntingly like a cross-Channel ferry in the fog, sadly warning its employees that they were about to be docked pay for their late arrival. And the smell, harsh and acrid, from the miasma of smog and smoke that always hovered over London, stinging my eyes and souring my mouth.

I lay there for a moment or two, sweating, eyes firmly closed against an incipient headache. I always knew that lemonade wasn't good for you. A trolleybus slid to a halt outside Enzo's café before grumbling and rumbling slowly away. A steady stream of bikes, carrying Caribonum workers who were cutting it fine, hissed by.

There was no noise from downstairs which meant that Jerry, my young landlord and owner of 'Jerry's Records', the shop above which I kipped, wasn't up yet. Dickie Valentine fans might have to wait an hour before he would be in a mood or a state to sell them any of the great man's records.

Not that that would bother Jerry all that much. Or me.

Dickie Valentine's kind of romantic balladeering was not to my taste. And I'd discovered recently that Jerry could afford to be sniffy about popular taste. Most of his income from the shop came from acquiring specialist jazz recordings from America for a select group of customers from all over London who shared his taste for bebop and what had become known as cool jazz. He stocked and sold the popular stuff under sufferance. He regarded it as charity work.

I rolled out of bed and lurched into the scullery, my bare feet slapping on the cold, worn lino. The gas ring exploded into flame, and I put the filled kettle on to boil.

I'm a great believer in old adages, particularly ones involving looking expectantly at household utensils, and so I slip-slapped my way back to the sink and splashed cold water over my face and rubbed a toothbrush over my teeth. The kettle still wasn't showing any sign of life so I returned to my bedroom (which was also my living room) and rummaged around for some clothes.

The kettle started to whistle, and I realized I'd been thinking about Paris and Ghislaine again. Well, not thinking, really, more daydreaming, and my trousers were in my hand rather than flapping loosely around my legs.

I sighed, pulled the trousers on and then padded back into the scullery where the kettle was shrieking like one of the more avant-garde trumpet players Jerry was so keen on.

Not even Jerry could sleep through that, and I brewed a big pot of Typhoo and put it on a tin tray with a picture of the coronation coach painted on it. I noticed that the gold of the coach was dull and stained as I dumped two cups, a bag of sugar, a teaspoon and what remained of yesterday's bottle of milk on it and carried the whole lot into my office, sat down at the kitchen table I used as my desk and waited for Jerry to appear.

I was halfway through my second cup, still wishing I was sitting with Ghislaine and drinking café crème and eating *pain beurré* at the little place on the corner of rue Saint-Sulpice, when I heard him clumping up the stairs.

He slipped around the door, yawning hugely, running a hand through his unruly, curly hair. He looked as if he was wearing the same clothes as he'd had on the day before, but with Jerry it was difficult to tell, since he always dressed the same: black trousers, black shoes, black socks, grey shirt, yellow waistcoat, bright tie.

'Thought I heard you making tea,' he said. 'Any chance of a cup?'

I poured him one, and he sat on the wooden chair I always borrowed from him when I had a client and usually forgot to return. He yawned again before heaping sugar into his cup.

'I hope I didn't wake you up,' I said.

He shook his head. 'No,' he said, 'the Caribonum hooter did that most effectively.' He looked queasily at the deep-brown liquid and stirred it languidly for a few seconds. He steeled himself, closed his eyes, tilted his head back and swallowed the tea in one long gulp. Then he thumped the cup back down. 'That's better,' he said, smacking his lips. 'What you up to today, Tony?'

I shrugged. 'Haircut, shave. Might pop in to the Antelope.'

Downstairs, the telephone in the shop started to ring, but its shrill insistence was dulled by distance. I looked at Jerry. He made a little moue. It stopped ringing. We both knew it was too early for the call to be about shop business, and neither of us had much of a social life so we knew it was most likely Les Jackson ringing to ask me how his current matinee idol had behaved on his night on the town. I didn't much want to tell him. Les was the unfortunate managing director who had the wayward Philip Graham under contract. And I was the unfortunate minder who Les was currently paying quite well to ensure that young Philip didn't get into too much trouble when he went on the town.

'When I was in Paris . . .' I began.

Jerry held up his hand. 'Tony, my friend, I love you dearly, but I do know that you spent the first two weeks of August in Paris. You really don't need to preface every statement with those words.'

'Sorry if I'm boring you,' I said. 'If you don't like the conversation, you can always risk Enzo's tea and bacon sandwiches.'

'Don't get tetchy,' he said.

'I'm not,' I said. But I was. 'All I was going to say was that I went to a jazz club you would have liked. There was a saxophonist, Bobby Jasper, played your kind of stuff.'

'You know your problem?' he said.

'No,' I said. 'What's my problem?'

'You've got the post-holiday blues. You've been away. It was exotic and different. Now you're dissatisfied with your lot. Well, get used to it, my friend. This particular lot –' he looked around the dusty bare room with something close to disdain flickering around his lips – 'is all you've got.'

He was, of course, right.

I, too, looked around the room and shared his almost-disdain. It wasn't much to show for nearly thirty-three years of life.

And I was getting boring about Paris.

Downstairs, the phone started ringing again. Jerry and I stared at each other gloomily. The sharp lines of his pale, lean face were accentuated by the black stubble and the dark circles under his eyes. Even so, he still looked very young to me, without his goatee. I remembered why he'd shaved it off, and my thoughts drifted back to Paris and Ghislaine.

'We'll have to answer that damned phone eventually,' Jerry said, getting to his feet. 'It might as well be sooner rather than later.' He paused at the door. 'Thanks for the tea, Tony. No offence intended.'

I shook my head. 'None taken,' I said, which wasn't strictly speaking true.

I sat slumped at the table, listening to him thump his way down the stairs and then waited to hear what music he'd play. It was usually Charlie Parker these days, but he occasionally surprised me.

This morning was one of those occasions. The joyous sound of Louis Armstrong, Kid Ory, Johnny Dodds, Lil Armstrong and Baby Dodds launching exuberantly into 'Muskrat Ramble' bounced up the stairs.

I smiled. It's simply impossible not to when you hear that. Anyway, it was Jerry's way of apologizing for any upset his uncharacteristic, early-morning crankiness may have caused, and, as an apology, it was completely acceptable.

I stirred myself and drifted back into my other room. It was time to prepare for the day.

*   *   *

I was just leaving my flat when the phone rang again and Jerry answered it.

He poked his head out of the door that led from the passageway at the foot of the stairs into the shop and saw me. 'It's Les,' he said.

I nodded and ran down and into the shop. The big, black phone was on the counter by the cash register on top of an unstable pile of invoices. I picked up the receiver. 'Les,' I said, 'how are you?'

'I'll be honest, Tony, I've been better. The thing is, I'm missing a leading man.'

'Les,' I said, 'the last time I saw him, he was heading out of a jazz club with specific instructions to go home. He wasn't happy about it, but I couldn't force the issue because I was tidying up after him. In short, doing what you pay me to do.'

There was a long silence that sounded very like a sigh.

'I'm not blaming you, Tony. There's only so much you can do with some of them. But he wasn't answering at his flat when the car went to collect him this morning. He's not picking up the phone, and he hasn't shown up at the studio. It's costing money. Serious money. And most of it is mine. Find him, Tony. Please. You will not be out of pocket.'

'I'll do what I can, Les,' I said. 'But I'm not promising anything. If he's decided to take a little holiday, he could be anywhere.'

'I know,' he said. 'Just give it your best shot. You've never let me down yet.'

Oddly enough, that was more or less true.

'I'll try,' I said.

'Thanks,' he said. 'By the way, can you come over to the office later?' He lowered his voice. 'There's something a bit personal I'd like to discuss.' He sounded a bit hesitant, almost embarrassed. That wasn't at all like Les.

'Will half two be OK?' I said.

'Fine. And if you've got the Brylcreem queen in tow, so much the better.'

'He's not a queen, Les,' I started to say, but he'd already hung up.

I put the receiver back on the cradle and sniffed.

Jerry wandered into the shop. 'Trouble?' he said.

'My boy's gone AWOL,' I said.

'Hardly your fault,' he said.

'No,' I said, 'no one, not even Les – surprisingly – is suggesting that I could have done much about it. But, all the same, it is my problem. Les has asked me to find him.'

'Good luck,' he said. 'Where are you going to start?'

'Where I was always going to start,' I said. 'With a haircut and a shave at Vic's.'

'Well, good luck with that too. I hope the DTs are under control this morning.'

'Vic doesn't have the DTs,' I said. 'It's just a slight tremor . . .'

Jerry laughed and patted my shoulder condescendingly. 'Of course,' he said, 'just like the slight tremor that reduced San Francisco to rubble back in 1906.'

Jerry had received the rudiments of a good education back when I was fighting for king and country, but I don't hold that against him. Much.

'By the way,' I said, 'there's a terrific singer at Pete's Place. Jeannie Summers. Fancy going there tonight?'

'Not heard of her,' he said, shaking his head.

I wasn't sure whether that meant that he was open to the experience or if he was dismissing the idea. I shrugged and left the shop. He'd probably come.

TWO

I t was another lovely morning, and I walked in bright sunshine along Church Road, past the green-grassed slope that led to the London Electrical Wire Company, past the dull brick of Church Road School where the low buzz of dull rote-learning sighed from open windows, past Etloe House, behind the tall walls and solid gates of which the grey-robed Sisters of the Sacred Hearts of Jesus and Mary discreetly cared for destitute girls, and past the looming presence of the big Caribonum factory, with the wonderful sound of The Hot Five still bouncing around in my bonce, until I arrived at the little row of shops where Victor Cardew snipped hair – and, just occasionally, ear lobes.

I walked a little further and stood in among the cracked concrete bristling with stinging nettles, dandelions and dusty convolvulus of one bomb-site and looked across at another, the one where my parents' house had stood. I thought of Mama, Papa and Grand-père for a moment or two. I'd been in France when they died, drinking *vin baptisé* in sufficient quantities to be very drunk, celebrating the liberation of Paris, and I hadn't seen them in nearly two years. Like so many others, we'd never had the chance to say goodbye. I'd thought that the pain of missing them would have dimmed after eleven years. It hadn't. But then neither had the memories. It seemed that in order to keep the one, I had to keep the other.

Having paid my respects, I retraced my steps back to Vic's.

I was sweating slightly, but the harsh, nose-wrinkling smells of the lotions and powders Vic applied to hair, faces and necks would mask any odours emanating from me.

Vic was a sour, dapper, little man whose accounts I'd look over for him, to make sure they would make sense to Her Majesty's Inspector of Taxes. Vic didn't like me knowing that much about his business affairs, but I was cheaper than a legit accountant.

He looked up from the neatly trimmed grey head he was fastidiously pecking at with the scissors. 'Hello, Tony,' he said. 'Is it that time of year already?'

'Don't come it, Vic,' I said. 'I was in here not three weeks ago.' I remembered what Jerry had said and bit off the 'after I got back from Paris'.

He gave me a bleak smile. 'It was just, from the state of your hair, I thought it must have been longer,' he said.

I ignored him and took a seat next to the thin-faced young man who was idly flicking through an elderly copy of *Reveille*, paying particular attention to the pictures of young starlets that graced its grubby and torn pages. There was something familiar about him, but I couldn't place him. He probably just reminded me of someone.

Vic stepped back from the chair, appraised the haircut he had just wrought and, seeing that it was good, swished his razor up and down the leather strop a few times. He stepped back to the haircut and carefully stroked the razor along the back of the man's neck. Then, in a cloud of magical barber's powder, he flourished a mirror so the customer could see the back of his head and nod appreciatively.

The old boy stood up and pressed silver into Vic's hand. Vic took a clothes brush to the man's suit jacket and trousered the money. Clearly, he couldn't see any point in troubling his till.

After the ritual pleasantries had been grunted and the pensioner marched briskly out of the shop, the young man settled noisily into Vic's creaking and complaining red leather-ette and chrome chair, waiting for the white cloth that Vic was flourishing to cocoon him.

As my thoughts drifted back to the night before and Jeannie Summers, I was dimly aware of the hollow-cheeked, pasty-faced youth waving his left hand at Vic and sniggering.

'Blimey,' Vic said, 'that's a wedding ring, ain't it? So, you're getting it regular now, you randy little devil.'

The youth sniggered again. 'Yeah,' he said, 'she loves it.'

'Mind you, that'll cramp your style with all the others,' Vic said.

'Nah,' the boy said, 'I'm wearing it on me finger, not me

prick. And, anyway, it's good to have a reserve at home.' He paused. 'Especially one who's always ready to play – in any position.'

Something about the way they both laughed, in an unpleasant, sleazy, conspiratorial way, really cheesed me off, and I stood up. 'You know what, Vic?' I said, aware that I was about to sound like a complete prig. 'I think I'll find somewhere else to get my hair cut.'

He looked at me, his eyes narrowed. 'Just for now?' he said.

'No, something more long term,' I said.

'Any particular reason?' he said.

'I don't much care for the conversation,' I said.

He looked puzzled and then shrugged. 'Fair enough,' he said. 'I can probably stand the loss of your custom. Sling your hook.' And he jerked his thumb at the door. The boy sniggered again.

I took one step towards the chair and stared down at the lad. 'You,' I said, 'should show some respect to your wife.'

The boy's mouth turned down in an ugly sneer. 'Bugger off, mush,' he said. 'How I talk about my wife is my business.'

'Not when you do it in front of me,' I said. 'In front of me, you show her some respect.' And I turned and left, feeling a little bit foolish but, when I thought of Ghislaine, of Mrs Williams, the widow I'd been spending pleasant Saturday evenings with for a few years, and, finally, of Jeannie Summers, unrepentant. In fact, I almost wished he'd given me cause to wallop him. It occurred to me that, for someone who liked the quiet life, I hadn't been keeping my head down anything like enough over the past twelve hours. Philip Graham would have blood in his eye the next time he saw me, and I'd just seriously cheesed off Vic, and a kid I didn't know, for no good reason.

I felt better out in the sunshine – although I still needed a shave, badly, and a haircut, less urgently – and I started walking briskly towards the tube station. Then I remembered who the boy reminded me of and some of the spring left my step.

*   *   *

I'd come across Dave Mountjoy before the war. I'd just left school, so it must have been the summer of 1937, when I was fourteen. My dad's painting and decorating business was a one man and a dog affair, and, for a month or two, I'd been the dog, mixing plaster, stirring paint, preparing walls, making tea and carrying ladders.

Mountjoy was a scrap-metal merchant with a biggish house in Woodford Green, and for four weeks Papa and I had cycled there at eight o'clock in the morning and stayed until six o'clock in the evening, except on Saturday when we knocked off at four. We decorated the kitchen, lounge, dining room, hall, bathroom and three bedrooms and never got paid a penny. Mountjoy found fault with the plastering, with the colour of the paint, the quality of the paper-hanging and so on. In fact, about the only thing he didn't object to was my tea-making. Of course, he'd never tasted my tea. But his reasons for not ponying up had little to do with the job we'd done and more to do with deep-seated and strongly held beliefs.

Mountjoy didn't believe in paying for anything, unless he could help it, and, because he was a villain, and a fairly nasty one, he could be very unpleasant. My dad reckoned that we'd done the work and bought the paint so we ought to be recompensed. And Papa, unfortunately, could be very obdurate. He finally went to confront Mountjoy at the scrapyard off Temple Mills Lane, thinking to embarrass him in front of his father, uncle and brothers. As a tactic, it didn't work out too well. It turned out that not only was Mountjoy unembarrassable but the entire clan held the same basic philosophy on paying bills. It could have been worse. They knocked Papa about a bit, but he was only laid up for a couple of weeks.

It must have been about then that my mother decided I should be articled to a small accountancy firm, where my experience as a qualified tea-maker really came into its own.

Now that I thought about it, Mountjoy had a couple of boys roaring about the house at the time. The younger one had been a toddler, which would make him about twenty now, so it could have been him. He had the same thin face as his father, the same lank dark hair, a similar wiry build – though he was slightly taller and heavier – and he certainly seemed to be every bit as charmless. It occurred to me that he might have been away, either doing time or his National Service. I was suddenly very glad I hadn't thumped him.

I found a barber close to Hoxton Films' office in Wardour Street, and he only charged me twice as much as Vic would have done. Still, the shave was a good one and the haircut more than passable. And my ears and cheeks escaped unscathed, without so much as a nick. I didn't even smell quite as poncey as I would have done emerging from Vic's. All in all, apart from the odd shilling or two, it wasn't a bad result. I didn't even mind losing the fiver Vic slipped me for cooking his books for him. In fact, I wasn't altogether sure that I had. When he discovered what a legit accountant would charge him, he'd probably remember that he was a thoroughly unprincipled individual and suggest that bygones be bygones. Whether I'd agree was, of course, a different matter.

I strode up Wardour Street, signally failing to turn any heads. Still, I felt better about my appearance.

The dingy reception area of Hoxton Films was unusually quiet. One scrawny messenger lad tapped his foot on the worn carpet and took long, greedy drags on his cigarette while he waited for someone to notice he was there.

I slumped down on the lumpy, brown sofa, content to sit for a few minutes until Daphne reappeared from her trip to the Ladies. I shouldn't have been there anyway. I was more than two hours early for my two thirty appointment with Les. But, of course, I wasn't there for that. I wanted to hear what Daphne made of the summons. As Les's ex-wife and in-house nemesis, she made it her job to know what he was up to and she'd happily tell me what it was all about. She'd also know if Philip Graham had appeared on the set yet and so save me a trip to his flat and a whole lot of unnecessary grief if he had.

After about ten minutes, the messenger was getting decidedly antsy. The drags on his second cigarette were shorter, and the rhythm of his tapping was faster and erratic. He'd never make a decent drummer. I decided to put him out of his misery and stood up.

'If you're in a hurry,' I said, 'I'll sign for that. Who's it for?'

'Er . . .' He looked down at the package. 'Mr Leslie Jackson,' he said. He looked at me. 'You work here then?'

'Sort of,' I said, picking a pen off Daff's desk and advancing on him with malice aforethought.

He thought about it for a few seconds and then put the package on the desk and thrust a crumpled docket at me. I scrawled my name, and he snatched the scrap of paper from me, murmured, 'Cheers,' and was gone.

I stood by the desk for a minute or two and then picked up the package, negotiated my way through the door that led to the offices and strolled down the corridor, whistling 'Let's Face the Music'.

Les heard me coming and was standing by his door when I arrived. He looked anxious and was rubbing his eyes which were a little bloodshot.

'Tony,' he said. 'Thanks.'

'You're welcome,' I said, handing over the package.

'No,' he said, 'no. I meant about the other thing. I just got the call. Phil Graham arrived on the set ten minutes ago.'

'Oh, that,' I said. 'Good.'

'Well, thanks.'

I shrugged nonchalantly. He'd find out I hadn't done anything soon enough.

'Overslept, apparently. No one phoned him. Or knocked. Lying little . . . Everyone's fault but his,' Les said. 'Sometimes, Tony, I swear I think Walt Disney's got the right idea. Cartoon characters only go on benders when it's part of the plot in the film.' He took me by the arm and steered me into the comfortable armchair he'd put in his office a month or two back, then he carefully closed the door. 'Since you're here already, I can tell you about the other matter. The private one.'

'Sure,' I said. 'But, Les, there's no one on reception. Daff isn't out there—'

'I know,' he said. 'That's the thing, Tony.' He paused. 'Listen, how about we grab a bite? Fancy Bert O'Reilly's?'

I nodded. I'd only ever eaten in Bertorelli's with Les, and then only the once, but I certainly fancied it. He'd probably let me choose the wine.

He did. And, since he'd said, 'Something meaty,' when I'd asked him what he fancied, he'd find himself forking out a few bob for a Barolo.

We'd walked up Wardour Street, crossed Oxford Street and made our way to Charlotte Street without saying a word. Les had looked uncharacteristically morose, and that, combined with the empty reception, gave me a bad feeling. I felt that I would probably be grateful for a substantial wine.

I was, too, when he told me.

'Daff's got a cancer,' he said. 'It's the size of a cricket ball. In her lung.' He pushed his prawn cocktail around a bit and then gulped down some wine. 'She ain't going to make it, Tony.'

I didn't know what to say, so I said nothing. But that kind of news takes your breath away and stings the eyes a bit.

'We don't know how long she's got, but it's not too long. The thing is, she wants a favour.'

He looked at me, and I realized that something in Les was going to die with her. I'd never understood their relationship since their divorce, but then I hadn't known them before, when they were, I assumed, all lovey-dovey.

I sucked minestrone soup far too noisily from my spoon and nodded at him. 'What?' I said. 'You know I'll do it if I can. I'm very fond of Daff . . .' I was a bit wary. I always am when people want favours.

'I dunno,' he said. 'She won't tell me. Just asked me to ask you.'

'OK,' I said, reaching for my glass, 'I'll go talk to her. Which hospital is she in?'

'She's at home at the moment. And expecting you this afternoon. Well, more hoping that you'd agree.' He paused. 'The thing is, Tony, she's not at all well. Even if you can't do it, say you will.' He was almost pleading with me.

'I'll do what I can, Les,' I said. 'You know I will.'

He looked relieved. 'Thanks, Tony. I knew I could rely

on you. I don't know what it is, but I do know it's important to her.'

He gulped down some more wine and pushed his uneaten food to one side. For a moment, I thought he was going to cry.

THREE

Daphne's gaff is the old family home in Leytonstone, very close to Wanstead Flats. She kept it after the *decree nisi* came through. It isn't all that posh, of course, but it is a couple of rungs up from Hoxton where Les hails from, and it's the sort of decent three-bed terraced house you'd hope for as your first (and, in their case, only) marital home if you were raised in a couple of rooms in a rundown, overcrowded house in Beaumont Road in Leyton, like Daff.

It was about a quarter to four when I hopped off the fifty-eight bus at Cobbold Road and walked past the new Secondary Technical Commercial School, Headmaster P. Claydon BA (Commerce). It was called Tom Hood now, but I couldn't, for the life of me, remember what it had been called when it was still one of the old Central schools. I could hear the frantic clack of typewriters and the discordant dings of the little bells as the carriage return was slapped and the sound of a male teacher's raised voice. A sad-looking boy in a grey blazer, grey shorts, grey shirt and red tie dawdled across the playground towards the toilets. Apart from that, the place could have been deserted.

I found myself dawdling, as the edge of Wanstead Flats came into sight and the prospect of meeting a very sick Daff came closer. I stopped to watch a couple of placid cows dropping some impressive pats on one of the football pitches. The players would be cursing the laws that still allowed grazing on common land. Not that the cows would care: the cricket season was over, so the chances of being struck a resounding blow by one of those nasty hard red balls had diminished to nothing.

I checked the address, adjusted my tie and stepped up to Daff's dark-blue front door, coughed nervously, seized the black lion's-paw knocker and beat a little tattoo on the plate beneath.

Les had said that Daphne's older sister, Betty, was staying

with her, so I was taken by surprise when Daphne herself opened the door, and I stood there in silence for a few seconds.

'Come on in, you silly bugger,' Daphne said. 'It's not catching, as far as I know.' She clocked the sad bunch of flowers – the last one there – I'd hurriedly picked out of the vendor's bucket at Leyton tube station and smiled. 'They for me?' she said.

I nodded, and she took them from me as we entered the little hallway.

'Betty,' she called, 'can you find another vase, love?'

She pushed me into the front room and then disappeared with the flowers. I heard her coughing harshly in the back of the house.

She hardly needed my few wilted blooms. The room looked like Kew Gardens at the height of summer. Six white roses in a crystal vase were flanked by yellow chrysanthemums on the mantelpiece, and there was a potted geranium on the window sill, still trailing red flowers.

Daphne came in carrying an earthenware jug with my drooping dahlias and freesia thrust in it. She plonked it down on the sideboard, next to the small alabaster child with its arm wrapped around a large Alsatian dog, and then slumped wearily on to the sofa, pulling a shawl around her shoulders.

'Sit down, you great useless lump,' she said.

I perched myself on one of the hard, wooden chairs and coughed nervously. 'How are you, Daff?' I said.

'Apart from dying, you mean?' she said. 'Very tired, Tony. Very, very tired.'

I cleared my throat again. 'It's a bit of a shock, Daff,' I said. 'Is there really nothing they can do?'

She harrumphed. 'It's too late,' she said. 'Already spread. Liver. And brain, probably. They think. Still, they give me happy pills for the pain. At least I can stay at home for the moment.'

'I'm really sorry, Daff,' I said.

'It's all right,' she said. 'To tell you the truth, I never fancied growing old, anyway. Mind you, I did think I might have a few more years to get on Les's wick.'

'He's really upset,' I said.

'Crocodile tears,' she said. 'He can't wait for me to drop off me perch.'

'I don't think that's true,' I said.

She flapped her hand at me dismissively. 'Enough about Les,' she said. 'I'll be dropping off to sleep soon, so let's talk about why you're here.'

'Les said you wanted to ask me something,' I said. 'A favour.'

She leaned forward, and I suddenly saw how thin and tired she'd become. I tried to think how long it had been since I'd seen her. It was only six or seven weeks.

'Yeah,' she said, 'and I want you to promise that you won't breathe a word of this to Les.'

'I'll try,' I said, 'but you know he's going to ask.'

'Yes he is, and he can be very persuasive. So I want your promise.'

'Sure,' I said. 'I promise.'

'And make sure you keep it. Otherwise I'll come back to haunt you.'

'Scout's honour,' I said, putting both hands up in a Churchillian victory salute.

She sighed and leaned back. 'All right, then.' She paused and sighed again. She looked dreamily over my shoulder, out of the window, at Wanstead Flats, but she was really staring into the past.

And then she told me her story.

It was a bleak little tale and not an uncommon one. If the telling hadn't been quite as flat and matter of fact, it would have made a nice old-fashioned melodrama. Young girl, who is poor but honest, meets charming gent who, after he's had his wicked way, turns into moustache-twirling villain and leaves her in the lurch and, of course, in the family way. As Daff told it, she might have been young and poor, but she was far from honest, and the charming gent, the son of the owner of the laundry she worked in, was neither all that charming nor much of a gent. The baby, though, was real enough. Born in July 1928, named after her grandmother, Eugenia Higgins, and dumped without any ceremony into an orphanage somewhere. Daff thought it might have been run by a local convent. I could only think of one.

'How—' I started.

'I know what you're going to say, Tony. How could I? Well, I didn't have much to do with it. It was a hard pregnancy, a harder birth – in fact that was the reason Les and I never had children – and I was very ill and weak and in no state to stop it.'

'Actually,' I said, 'I sort of understand that. What I was really wondering was how you could call her Eugenia.'

She gave me a good, old-fashioned, Daphne look and sniffed dismissively. 'That wasn't up to me either,' she said. 'Mum took care of everything: registering the birth and all that. I hardly saw the little mite.' She paused. 'I'm not much of a one for sentiment, Tony, but I've always wondered what happened to her. And I'd like to say sorry for not looking after her.' She paused again. 'Do you think you can find her for me? Before I . . .'

'I can try, Daff,' I said. 'I can try.'

She sighed and leaned back on the sofa. She looked exhausted. The bags under her eyes were green. 'Thanks, Tony,' she said. 'What will you tell Les?'

I shrugged. 'A little bit of the truth,' I said.

She sat up again, looking anxious.

'That I'm looking for a long-lost relative. He doesn't have to know any details. If he presses, I'll tell him it's a cousin or something.'

'That'll do,' she said and fell back again. 'Now bugger off, before I fall asleep on you.'

Les hadn't really done justice to the Barolo at lunch, which meant that I had, so I decided to walk from Daff's back to the Antelope to clear my head a bit. It also meant I could drop in at the Osborne Arms on the way and have a chat to someone.

The Osborne is a big, old barn of a boozer on the corner of Crescent Road and Church Road, a hundred yards or so from where my parents' house had stood. The bomb that took them must have rattled a few windows and smashed a few glasses there. It's not a particularly notorious pub or anything. Nobby Clarke, the local bookie, hangs out there with a few other local rascals, but the real villains drink a little further west, up Whitechapel way.

It was just after six when I pushed open the big, old green door and went into the almost empty bar. Nobby was already sitting in a dark corner, a glass of whisky in front of him, reading the *Evening News*. He'd carefully folded it over and wasn't so much reading it as annotating the sports pages with the stub of a blunt pencil, which he occasionally licked. He looked up when I came in and nodded, but we hardly knew each other and I had never been a client. His gold pinkie ring glinted, his bronze sharkskin suit gleamed in the gloom, and his bald, pink head reflected the dull yellow electric light.

I stood at the long wooden counter, by the glass partition that separated the bar from the Ladies' Snug, and peered around it. When Derek, the morose landlord, came over, I ordered a whisky and a bottle of Mackeson. He disappeared behind the jars of arrowroot biscuits and pickled eggs. When he reappeared with the drinks, I told him the Mackeson was for Mrs Norton in the Snug. He nodded and took it to her.

'She says thanks,' he said, slowly walking my ten-bob note to the old wooden till. I remembered that he'd taken a machine-gun bullet in the knee in Sicily in 1944. Standing up behind a bar, serving drinks for a living, with a gammy leg must have given him cause enough to be miserable. I thanked my lucky stars, again, that I'd come out of the war pretty much unscathed. I lifted my glass to the memory of some of those who hadn't.

Derek handed me my change just as Mrs Norton's big, round, florid face peeped around the glass from the Snug.

'Tony Gérard,' she said. 'Long time no see.'

'It can't be that long,' I said. 'How are you keeping?'

Mrs Norton moved into number five Crescent Road when I was about ten. Her little yard backed on to our garden. Come to think of it, her back windows must have gone in the blast too. After her initial hesitation about having foreign neighbours, Grand-père's theatrical Gallic charm and generosity in the pub had won her over. Papa had been the really good neighbour, though, decorating her house and dealing with the regular infestations of mice from the rag and bone shop (my mother called the owners *les chiffonniers*) next door to her. Mama had remained cool, but even I'd run errands for her to the local shops.

'Mustn't grumble,' she said. 'The legs are playing up, but that's nothing new.' She paused to take a swig of thick, black stout. 'What brings you down here? You drink at the Antelope, don't you?'

'Not always,' I said. 'Anyway, I just wanted to pop by and see you.'

'Really?' she said. 'What d'you want?'

'Must I be after something?' I said.

'You usually are,' she said and sniffed.

I sipped a little whisky. I don't know why I order it. I like it no more than I like beer. But it does at least have the virtue of coming in considerably smaller measures, and it isn't so unusual, or effeminate, as to draw unpleasant and unwelcome attention.

'Before you moved into Crescent Road,' I said, 'you lived in Beaumont Road, didn't you?'

She nodded. 'What's that got to do with the price of fish?' she said.

'I just wondered if you happened to know the Bakers back then,' I said.

'Bert and Mavis Baker?' she said.

'Daughter called Daphne,' I said.

'Three daughters. And a boy. Lived next door,' she said. 'Nice family. Good neighbours. Decent people, not common or nothing, but one of the girls – I think it was young Daphne – got into a spot of trouble, I remember.'

'Really?' I said.

'Yeah, she got in the family way and wasn't wed. Poor Mavis was at her wits' end.'

'What happened?'

She swigged some more stout. 'Oh, the usual,' she said. 'The baby was put out for adoption. As a matter of fact, I seem to recall that they handed the poor thing into that convent place over the road there. You know, the one up by the school: run by the Sisters of the Sacred Hearts of Jesus and Mary. At least it wasn't to anything to do with the Immaculate Conception.' She gave a little shriek of laughter. 'Wouldn't have been appropriate in this case, would it?'

I smiled politely at her slightly risqué joke.

She paused. 'Someone told me the grandparents – the other ones – took the little mite.'

'Oh?' I said. 'Who were they?'

'I don't know. Someone said it was that big scrap-metal merchant. You know, the one lived up Grove Green Road. He had an interest in the laundry the girl worked in. They said it was one of his sons had his wicked way with her. Though, from what I heard, she was no better than she ought to be.'

I did know who she meant and found myself thinking about the Mountjoys for the second time that day.

'How's Albert, by the way?' I said.

'Don't go changing the subject by asking after my useless son. What do you want to know about the Bakers for?'

'Oh, no reason,' I said. 'Just happened to hear someone mention them.'

She harrumphed. 'Well, good to see you,' she said, 'and thanks for the drink, but I can't stand up here much longer. Not with my legs. I've gotta go and sit down.'

And she pulled her head back, like a tortoise, and I watched her shadowy, bulky figure, distorted by the dimpled glass, heavily resume her seat.

Behind me, the door banged open and four men came striding in. They saw Nobby and made their way over to him.

I recognized the young lout from Vic's and turned away as he thrust his betting slip out and Nobby wearily reached into his pigskin satchel for the money to pay him his winnings.

I reluctantly swallowed down my whisky, thinking that it might be better if English pubs served it in the tumblers that French cafés used for red wine, rather than in the little bowls with stems they used, and carefully placed the glass on the bar. I nodded a farewell to Derek, who was completely engrossed in counting the pickled eggs in the jar in front of him and clearly unaware of the illegal transaction taking place on his premises, and headed for the door.

The kid stepped back from Nobby's table at just the same moment and moved in front of me, a surprisingly large number of soiled pound notes clutched in one hand.

'Hello, again,' he said and smirked.

I nodded and made to step past him.

He moved in the same direction, blocking me again. I stood still.

'I been asking about you,' he said. 'You're the frog, ain't you?'

'No,' I said, 'you've been misinformed.'

His three companions had drifted away from Nobby's table, towards the bar. He looked across at them, his tongue flicking quickly across his thin lips. He really did look a lot like Dave Mountjoy.

'If you'll excuse me,' I said, indicating the door, 'I have somewhere to go.'

'Do you?' he said, looking down at my feet.

'Yes,' I said, 'and I'm going to be late.'

'I don't want to see you in here again,' he said.

'You probably won't,' I said. 'I don't often drink here.'

'You'd better not,' he said.

'Why's that?' I said.

'Because I don't want you to and I'll hurt you if you do.'

'You think you can do that, do you?' I said.

By way of answer, he slipped his hand into his jacket pocket and brought out a nasty-looking cut-throat razor.

I looked at him as evenly as I could but my pulse rate had gone up a little and I was aware of a slight trembling in my hands. I was fairly certain I could take him, but I was aware of his friends looking at us and I really couldn't see any point in raising the level of hostility. I decided to beat as gracious a retreat as possible.

I smiled at him pleasantly. 'I'll bear your request in mind,' I said. 'Now, if you'll excuse me . . .'

He slipped the razor back into his pocket and ostentatiously, if gracelessly, stepped aside.

'Good riddance to bad rubbish,' I heard him say before the door closed behind me. I wasn't sure, but there could have been an unpleasant expletive included in there somewhere as well. There was certainly a little bark of muffled laughter from his friends.

The atmosphere in the Antelope was altogether more welcoming. For a start, Jerry was standing at the bar, a pint

of wallop in his hand; there was the reassuring click of domi-
noes being laid down triumphantly and the phlegmy chuckle
of the victor; and big Mickey Morgan was over at the dartboard, looking for someone to trounce. I smiled and shook
my head when he waved the arrows at me and made my way
through the blue-grey fug from a dozen Woodbines over to
Jerry.

'Tony, my friend,' he said expansively, 'what are you
having?'

I looked up at the big clock behind the bar, set ten minutes
fast. It was saying ten to seven. Obviously, this wasn't Jerry's
first pint, but he couldn't have sunk all that many in forty
minutes.

'I'll just have a lemonade, thanks,' I said, thinking of the
whisky still roiling about in my guts.

'You heard the man,' Jerry said to Henry, the cadaverous
barman who had silently materialized as I'd approached the
bar. Henry sniffed, put his cigarette down on the scarred wood
and reached down for a glass and a bottle.

'So,' I said to Jerry, 'you coming to Pete's Place?'

'You paying?' he said.

'No,' I said, 'this is pleasure, not business. I'm not babysit-
ting young Philip tonight, thank God, so I'm not on exes.'

'Pity,' he said. He took a pull at his pint. 'She's good, this
singer, is she?'

'Yeah,' I said, 'very.'

'All right, then.' He lifted his glass again. 'By the way, a
package arrived for you in the four o'clock post.'

I raised my eyebrows. No one sent me packages.

'Addressed to "Antoine",' he said. 'So I'm guessing that it
might just have come from a certain lady in gay Paree.' He
paused and sipped beer. 'And that policeman, Rose, phoned.
He said to tell you he was still on the case, following up a
new lead.'

I groaned. It was obviously a coincidence, but the two things
were related. The package was, as Jerry guessed, almost
certainly from Ghislaine. And, although I hoped he didn't
know it, she was who Inspector Rose was looking for. Since
the two men whose premature demise she had been responsible

for had been giving a damned good imitation of strangling me at the time – well, I'd certainly been convinced of the authenticity of their performance, and Daff's chicken soup had been all that my bruised oesophagus could cope with for nearly two weeks – I was more than a little grateful to her and intended to do everything I could to keep her out of it. This mainly involved keeping my mouth shut and playing ignorant, both of which came very easily to me. I told myself that Rose calling on the same day as a package arrived from Paris really was just coincidence. He didn't know anything. He didn't even know about her. He couldn't. He was just winding me up.

Very successfully.

I drained my glass.

R. White's finest tasted flat, bland and unappealing. Mind you, ever since the first time my mother had made *citron pressé* for me, when I was five, I'd found English commercial brands of lemonade disappointing and had always suspected that their relationship to lemons was tenuous at best. So maybe the image of Inspector Rose thoughtfully, and very irritatingly, filling his pipe with Golden Virginia and puffing contentedly on it for a few seconds before quietly asking some pertinent question that I didn't want to answer hadn't been responsible. Maybe.

Jerry looked at me with raised eyebrows. At first, I thought he might have been wondering what was bothering me, but then I noticed that his glass was empty.

'Another?' I said.

'Why not?' he said.

And, just as I raised my hand to beckon Henry over from the end of the bar where he was hunched over his cigarette, Mickey, with the impeccable timing he was known for, appeared next to me.

'What you having, Mickey?' I said.

'That's very good of you, Tone,' he said. 'I'll have a brown ale, thanks.'

A short coughing fit wracked Henry's thin frame, and I waited quietly for it to subside before placing my order. I decided on a brandy for myself.

'Tone,' Mickey said, 'I don't want to worry you, but Dave

Mountjoy's youngest, Ricky, has been asking around about
you. Just thought you ought to know. He's been away, for a
two stretch. Attacked some geezer with a knife was what I
heard. Anyway, he got out a couple of months back. He was
in here at dinner time.'

Henry plonked glasses down on the bar. He coughed again.
'Yeah,' he said. 'He was real interested in you.'

'What did you tell him?' I asked.

'Nothing,' he said, taking my ten-bob note. 'I don't know
nothing about you.' The till dinged dully as he thumped some
keys. 'Or anybody else.' He pushed some silver and coppers my
way. 'But I'll tell you what: I'd watch meself, if I was you.' And
he ghosted back to his corner for another quiet smoke.

Mickey picked up his beer. 'Cheers, Tone,' he said, took a
huge swig and looked over the rim of his glass and inclined
his head slightly in the barman's direction. 'Henry did happen
to mention as how you was a war hero and a tough nut.'

I groaned. That'd really scare young Ricky off, and all the
other would-be James Deans, looking to make names for
themselves.

'Mickey,' I said, 'I'm not—'

Jerry reached out a hand and gently patted my shoulder.
'Yes, you are,' he said.

'Anyway,' Mickey said, 'Henry's right. You should watch
it. He's a right sneaky one. My eldest was at school with him.
Vicious temper.' He drank more beer and nodded at the dartboard. 'Fancy a game?'

'Not tonight, Mickey. And thanks for the heads-up.'

He nodded and plodded back to the board, looking around
for a victim.

'What you been up to, then?' said Jerry. 'And who's this
Mountjoy?'

'Nothing much,' I said, 'and he's the son of someone my
dad had a run-in with years ago. A not very nice someone . . .'

Jerry looked serious, said nothing and supped ale.

FOUR

I brooded on Ricky Mountjoy as Jerry and I rattled along deep under London and the Central Line train squealed and screeched its way into Bank station.

I wasn't overly bothered by the threat posed by young Ricky, although I didn't much fancy getting striped by his razor. It was more that his antipathy might complicate matters. It seemed likely that I'd have to have a word with his grandpa if I was going to find out anything for Daphne, and it wouldn't be easy to talk to the old boy in the best of circumstances. I was beginning to wish I'd kept my mouth shut in Vic's. It wasn't as if I even knew his wife, although she had my deepest sympathy.

As we slowly lurched and shrieked our way out of Bank, I remembered another vicious, little rat-faced sod. All the NCOs in basic training had been unpleasant bullies, but there had been one lance-corporal who'd been particularly nasty. The fact that he'd been a Geordie, and pretty much incomprehensible to me and Bernie Rosen and all the other London lads, had not improved matters. Bernie, of course, had been a professional soldier's nightmare. Unkempt, uncoordinated, uncooperative and uncommonly clever, Bernie was not cut out to be cannon fodder. He was always on a charge of some kind, but, whether he was spud-bashing or scrubbing the parade ground with a toothbrush, he smiled sweetly and bore it all with the patience of Job. Which drove Corporal Geordie Patterson wild. Our basic training was almost up when he finally cracked and decided to use Bernie as a punchbag. He got four or five good pokes in before I and two other lads dragged him off and quietened him down.

The quietening down, of course, was what got us into trouble.

Corporal Patterson lost two teeth, suffered a cracked cheekbone and three broken ribs. The other NCOs were not happy, although one of them did admit that he had it coming. As he also said, though, they couldn't pretend it hadn't happened, and they decided that all of those involved would spend three rounds in the ring with Sergeant Philip Harrison, who just happened to be regimental champion at middleweight and, we were told, a bit of an animal.

In fact, the anticipation turned out to be far worse than the event itself.

None of us survived the first round. I didn't survive the first half of the first round, but even that was about a minute more than Bernie managed. Harrison was good and fast, and he more than punched his weight.

We didn't see Patterson again, though, so we reckoned we just edged it on points.

Oh, and Bernie took us all back to his mum's for a proper Jewish momma's nosh. She fussed over our bruised mugs and kept on ladling out the chicken soup and other delights till we could hardly move. The other two lads weren't too keen on the food, being more your roast dinner sort of chaps, but I developed a real taste for potato latkes. And, for some reason, the Rosen family developed a liking for me.

I don't know why I thought of Lance-Corporal Geordie Patterson, although I suppose he did share a sly and unpleasant look with Ricky Mountjoy. I couldn't help but think that he'd been a lucky boy. He'd have suffered a bit more than a few cracked ribs if he'd encountered me after the commando training I'd undergone for Special Ops had toughened me up. Harrison would still have given me a good hiding, though.

Jerry and I walked from Tottenham Court Road station down to Pete's Place. Charing Cross Road sparkled under the street lights and the headlamps of the buses and cabs after a little shower had rinsed the tarmac and the paving stones. Two girls wearing tight-fitting blue jeans caught Jerry's eye, but they just giggled at him when he tried to start a conversation.

He shrugged, sighed theatrically, blew them a kiss and then told me enthusiastically that he'd tracked down some French records of Sidney Bechet and asked if I'd write to the recording company for him, to place an order. I suggested that, if he was paying, I could jump on a ferry and do the deal in person. He sniffed dismissively. I decided to take that as a 'maybe'.

The band was enjoying a cigarette and beer break at Pete's Place and chatting in a desultory fashion with the half dozen customers who had beaten us to it. Peter Baxter himself was standing with his back to the bar, a pint in his hand, gloomily surveying the empty wilderness of his club. His trumpet gleamed dully on the dark wood of the counter, next to him, among the sticky puddles of spilt beer. He nodded at me and smiled bleakly.

'Not many in tonight,' I said.

He cleared his throat. 'Not now,' he said. 'There were quite a few more in earlier.' He sighed and turned to the bar. 'Let me buy you a drink,' he said. 'For helping out last night.'

'That's all right,' I said. 'Let me get 'em. I'm having a short.'

'In that case,' he said, 'come back to my office. I've got a bottle of brandy there and I could do with a proper drink.' He looked at Jerry. 'Will your mate be all right here?'

Jerry shrugged.

'Sure,' I said. 'I'll just get him a pint.'

Peter sank his own beer and picked up his trumpet while the barman poured Jerry's drink and took my money. Then Peter put his hand on my shoulder. 'Jeannie's back there too. We wouldn't mind a quiet word.'

I slid Jerry's drink over to him. 'I'll be back in a minute,' I said.

'Take all the time you need, my friend,' Jerry said. 'A jug of beer, a bag of crisps and thou . . .' He smiled contentedly, and Peter gave him a puzzled frown before the two of us ambled over to the stage and slipped quickly along the narrow, dingy corridor where the dressing rooms and the office lay.

The heavy, dark-brown door with 'Office' stencilled on it in black jogged unpleasant memories of loitering outside the headmaster's study at school, gloomily anticipating the inevitable consequence of the summons. He liked to keep us waiting, knowing, I suppose, that there was no punishment he could administer that was so bad it wasn't made much worse by being thought about. However, Peter and I didn't hang about outside the door.

Jeannie Summers looked up from her glass when we pushed past it, and she offered us a wan smile. But then she immediately resumed studying the glass of warm gin and tonic her hands were wrapped around.

Peter Baxter shaped up to pat her tentatively on the shoulder as he bustled by her, but he seemed to think better of it and his hand hung awkwardly in the air for a second or two before he moved behind his desk, put his trumpet down and fussed with a bottle of Hennessy's and two smeared tumblers. He handed me one of the tumblers and absent-mindedly splashed a large measure of brandy into it.

'Her piano player's gone AWOL,' he said, pouring an even bigger slug into his own glass. After slurping at his drink, he continued: 'Thing is. We were wondering if you could help.'

I couldn't think why he was asking me. I'd never even mastered the comb and tissue paper.

'I don't see how,' I said.

'Oh, nothing to worry about,' he said reassuringly, his brandy threatening to slop over the edge of his glass as he waved it about, 'just make a few enquiries, ask around a bit. He can't be too far.' He glanced down at Miss Summers, his look a strange combination of affection and exasperation. 'Jeannie, love, perhaps you could explain . . .'

Jeannie Summers looked at me in the same heart-melting way she'd done the previous night. She wasn't as young or as pretty as I'd thought when I'd first seen her on the stage, but there was a fragility about her that made you want to hug her, to tell her that everything was all right, and if it wasn't, you'd make it so. She was wearing a green, full-skirted dress that left her pale shoulders bare, making her seem that little bit more vulnerable.

'Lee has a need,' she said quietly, and she lowered her gaze to her drink again. 'An illness, really, an addiction. It's not uncommon in our line of work.'

I wanted her to look at me again, but she didn't. Instead, she continued staring at the clear liquid in her glass. Her voice, though, soft, rich and low, still touched me. But something about it nagged at me.

'Will you help find him?' she said.

I realized that she didn't look at me because she was expecting me to say no and didn't want me to see the hurt in her eyes.

'How long has he been missing?' I said.

'I haven't seen him since our second set last night. He didn't come back to the digs.'

'Do you know where he went?'

She shook her head.

'Did he leave with anyone?'

Again, she gave a little shake of her head. I wasn't quite sure if that just meant that she didn't know.

Twenty hours wasn't a long time in a junkie's life. I hadn't come across very many – only one, in fact – but I did know that he could stare in languid fascination at the sole of his boot for hours.

'He's probably just lost track of time,' I said.

'Yes.' She nodded her head. 'He does that.'

I looked at Peter Baxter. 'Anyone here I should talk to?' I said.

'No,' he said. 'We're completely clean here.'

'And you don't know anything?'

'No, and I don't want to.'

I raised my glass to Peter and tossed down the brandy. 'OK,' I said. 'I know a few places close by where I can ask. I'll try and be back in an hour or so.' I looked at Peter. 'You won't try and charge me to come in again, will you?'

He laughed. 'If you come back with Lee, you've got free entrance for life,' he said.

I put my glass down on the desk. 'Deal,' I said.

As I passed her, Miss Summers put her hand on my arm and breathed, 'Thank you.' The wedding band on her third finger suggested that she and Lee perhaps had more than a professional relationship.

I walked back into the club to tell Jerry I was disappearing for a while, and I realized what I'd been missing. Digs! Jeannie Summers wasn't American at all. She was English.

As I ran up the steps to Frith Street, I ruminated on the fact that my day seemed to have filled up with missing persons,

and I ran through the few places in the immediate vicinity
that Lee might have gone to. There were only three I could
think of, and one of those was a very long shot. But it was
the nearest. And the sleaziest.

Rainer, the German addict I had come across in Berlin when
I was stationed there as a bean counter after hostilities had
ceased, told me that junkies had no self-respect and no shame
but they did have an amazing ability to home in on junk. I
remembered his pinched face as he shivered in spite of the
vast army greatcoat that enveloped him, his hands shiny with
dirt, as he pleaded with me for money. He couldn't have been
more than seventeen and almost certainly didn't make it to
twenty, and he had the look of an elderly monkey, but he was
clever and spoke excellent English. I let him sleep in the living
room of the dusty, decaying apartment that had been requisi-
tioned for me for a few weeks and tried to help him a little.
But he didn't want food or a bed. He wanted junk, and I
couldn't give him that, so one day he went out and never came
back. Funnily enough, he didn't take anything of mine with
him. A few of my colleagues wondered why I'd given him
house room, and, to be honest, I don't really know the answer
to that. Certainly, I never got any thanks. But I did get a small
insight into the ways of the drug addict.

So, it was to the nearest and sleaziest place I went.

The Frighted Horse is just a hop, step and a jump from
Pete's Place and is not a pub for the faint-hearted or weak-
stomached. I've always assumed that there are only two reasons
the landlord keeps his licence. The first is that half of the
police in Soho are completely bent and money changes hands.
The second is that the less corrupt members of the force are
well advised to be complicit.

The bar itself, though not exactly inviting, is not, if you
ignore the sad, careworn whores, the stick-thin, seedy alco-
holics and the cold-eyed, over-the-hill toughs all waiting for
something to happen, that much worse than some other Soho
hostelries. But it's the two upstairs rooms where the action is.

Nobody looked up when I went in. Eye contact is not
encouraged in the Frighted Horse. The smell of unwashed
bodies, old urine, sour beer, bad feet, stale cigarette smoke

and harsh cleaning fluids caught at the back of my throat, but I fought back the desire to gag and marched swiftly to the counter.

I risked a surreptitious look around. There wasn't much of a crowd in. There were a couple of craggy-faced low-life villains, nursing pints of Guinness and pinching out roll-ups after five or six puffs, slumped over a table in one corner.

Unusually, and sticking out like the proverbial sore thumb, there were three expensively dressed black guys tucked away behind the door, which was why I hadn't seen them on my way in. They all seemed to be drinking white rum.

Two elderly, fat white brasses were trying to strike up a conversation. The men politely and silently ignored their repeated suggestions that they be bought a drink.

I turned back to the bar before it looked as though I was paying more attention to the other customers than was polite, or good for my health.

I hadn't seen the barman before. That wasn't too surprising. I'd only been in the pub three or four times in my life and avoided it if I could. He wasn't an old man, but he had the sunken cheeks of someone who'd long since lost his back teeth, and his thin, lined face suggested a very hard life. Or a few nasty habits. He sniffed and ran the back of his hand and the frayed cuff of his shirt across his mouth and nose before shuffling over to me. I decided not to ask for a drink.

'I was just wondering,' I said, 'if you've seen a tall American in here.'

The barman coughed and spat on the floor. 'When?' he said.

'The last twenty-four hours.'

'Nah,' he said and spat again.

'You sure?' I said, reaching into my pocket for my wallet.

He watched me slowly pull the wallet out of my inside pocket, running his tongue around his lips. 'Well,' he said, 'there might have been a Yank in. He didn't say much. But he might have been a Yank.'

'When?' I said, sliding the edge of a ten-bob note out of my wallet.

'Well after hours,' he said. 'Late last night.'

'And?' I said.

'And what?' he said.

'How long did he stay? Where is he now?'

'Are you stupid? How am I s'posed to know that?'

'Did you see him leave?'

'No.'

'Was he with anyone?'

'No.'

I put my wallet away. 'All right,' I said. 'Thanks.' I put my hand in my pocket, took out a shilling and put it on the damp bar. 'Here. Have a drink.'

He looked at the shilling, and then he looked at me. His eyes were red rimmed. He tilted his head slightly, indicating the stairs.

I nodded and pushed the shilling towards him. He snatched it and pocketed it.

'Thanks,' I said very quietly. 'You get the ten bob when I come down.'

His rheumy eyes lost what little interest had greedily and briefly flickered in them. He was a man who had long ago reached an accommodation with disappointment.

I pushed through the door to the left of the bar that led to the stairs. As it banged behind me, I pulled my wallet out from the inside pocket of my jacket and slipped it into my front trouser pocket. I didn't need to look behind me to know that one of the semi-retired toughs would have slid off his seat and be following me.

The smell on the dark stairs was even worse than in the bar.

I clumped carefully up, trying to avoid tripping on the worn and loose carpet, into the gloom of the first floor.

I heard the door to the bar open and close and someone shuffle through just as I reached the landing. I reckoned whoever it was would probably wait for me to come down. At any rate I didn't hear any stairs creak.

There was a room directly opposite me, and I thought I might as well start there. The old wooden knob on the door was loose and turning it didn't get me anywhere, but a gentle push did.

The room didn't smell any worse than the landing. But it

didn't smell any better either. Apart from two beaten-up and heavily stained sofas and a small table with a lamp on it, the place was empty. The lamp gave off a dim, yellow light, and most of the room was in soft shadow. The old, rotting red carpet was worn away by the door and looked as if some medieval edict against the use of brooms had never been revoked. I was reluctant to step further in for fear of what I might tread in, but there was a splash of colour on one of the sofas that looked familiar. I tripped across to it as daintily as Jerry's big, ugly cat negotiating the narrow fence in our back-yard and managed to avoid most of the debris sticking to my shoes.

The bright, pink tie was twisted and tied into a ligature, but it definitely looked like the one the piano player had been wearing. The *Brooks Bros, New York* label offered more than a little confirmation. He'd probably been here then.

I slipped the tie into my jacket pocket and wondered where to look for him next. Where would an American jazz musician addict go after getting his junk or his fix, or whatever it was he'd picked up here, if not back to the woman who loved him? Fortnum & Mason and Harrod's would both have been closed. So would the British Museum. Trafalgar Square? Buck House? Another jazz club, perhaps.

As I stood there, my thumb pressed against my lips, I heard a noise behind me.

'Well, well, look who it isn't,' said a thin, reedy voice, just as something hard and blunt hit me on the back of the head and I fell into the black, treacly, spinning vortex of semi-consciousness.

FIVE

There's an old saying about what goes around, comes around. Unfortunately, after my head stopped whirling, I came around on that disgusting carpet, with grit pressed into my face and the whiff of damp and rot deep in my lungs. I coughed – well, spluttered – into consciousness.

Oddly, there was no one else in the room. The owner of the thin, reedy voice had gone. And so, too, I thought, had my wallet. Then I remembered I'd moved it to my trouser pocket. I tried sitting up and felt slightly sick. I touched the swelling on the back of my head. It hurt. But at least the skin wasn't broken, and there was no blood. A sock full of sand will raise an impressive lump and give you as nasty a headache as a proper, lovingly hand-stitched, lead-weighted life-preserver, so I could have been hit by an amateur.

I risked rising to my feet, but that didn't make me feel any better, and I stumbled over to one of the rat-nibbled, lumpy sofas, fell back on to it and closed my eyes for a few seconds.

When I opened them, there were two other men in the room.

I recognized Ricky Mountjoy immediately. It took me a moment or two to recall the other one as the lightweight from the altercation in Pete's Place the previous night. I remembered him whining at Peter Baxter about the loss of his membership. It must have been him who'd socked me.

'We really must stop meeting like this,' Ricky Mountjoy said, putting down the brown-paper carrier bag he was holding. He affected a slight lisp, but the narrow-eyed look he gave me undercut any humour.

'That's fine by me,' I said. 'I've got a bit of a headache, anyway, and I thought I might head off home.'

I stood up, swayed a bit more theatrically than necessary and blinked away some pain that was just a little more imaginary than real.

'Not tonight, Josephine,' he said. 'Or, at least, not yet.'

He was still giving me that wary, hostile look, so I hadn't completely fooled him into thinking I was in a worse state than I really was.

When I thought about it, I couldn't blame him. I hadn't exactly convinced myself that I was feeling better than I really was.

'We need to talk,' he said.

'What about?' I said. 'I have no business with you.'

'Then what are you doing here?' he said.

'Looking for someone,' I said. 'As a favour to a friend.'

'Who?' he said.

'No one you know,' I said. 'This doesn't concern you.'

He took a step towards me. 'But it does,' he said. 'You're on my turf.'

'Really?' I said, looking around at the seedy room. 'Moving up in the world, are you? I'd've thought this was a bit too far West for you. A bit out of your territory, a bit too classy.'

'Don't try to be funny. Just tell me who you're looking for.'

'I'm not trying to be funny, Ricky,' I said. 'Just making an honest observation. And, like I said, I don't think it's anyone you're likely to know.'

He took another step towards me and so, slightly hesitantly, did the lightweight with the cosh.

'Ricky,' I said, 'I don't want any trouble with you, and I'm sure you don't want blood splashed all over that sharp suit or those nice shoes. It can be a devil to get out, it really can.' I paused and looked hard at the lightweight. 'And you've already had your free hit. You're not getting another one.'

Gratifyingly, he stopped and looked questioningly at young Mountjoy. Unfortunately, young Mountjoy was made of sterner stuff and kept on coming. He reached into his jacket pocket, and I knew what he was going to pull out and didn't hang about.

One stride took me right up to him, and I slammed my forearm into his throat. It might not have been in the spirit of the Marquess of Queensbury rules, but it would have warmed the cockles of my old commando trainer's heart, and it certainly had the desired effect on young Ricky, who collapsed in a gurgling heap, the razor still in his pocket.

I turned to face the lightweight, just in case he needed a salutary clip around the ear, but he was already on his knees, shuffling to the aid of his stricken colleague. I grabbed him by the collar of his jacket and hauled him to his feet.

'He'll be all right,' I said. 'In an hour or so, he'll be swallowing beer with the best of them.'

I marched the kid – he wasn't much more than that – over to the nearest wall and leaned him up against it, not too gently, holding him by the lapels, shirt front, tie and, probably, some skin.

'Now,' I said, 'tell me what you know about the piano player you had the rumble with last night.'

He looked like he was going to pee his pants. 'I don't know,' he stammered out.

'Yes, you do,' I said. 'You followed him here, didn't you?'

He said nothing, just stared over my shoulder.

I tapped my finger against his nose to get his attention. 'Didn't you?' I said.

He nodded.

'And what happened?' I said.

'Nothing,' he said. 'Honest. He bought his stuff, he shot up and just sort of slumped. Over there.' He waved his arm at the sofa I'd been sitting on, the one where I'd found the pink tie.

'And what did you do?'

'Went downstairs and had a pint.'

'With?'

'Del, Phil and Ricky.'

'And then?'

'I went home.'

'The others?'

'Stayed in the bar. It was a shut-in. After hours.'

That would explain why Philip Graham hadn't been cavorting with the lark that morning.

I let go of the lad, and he smoothed down his lapels, straightened his shirt and tie and brushed at his chest.

'Who sold him the stuff?' I said.

He looked uneasy, but he glanced over at Ricky Mountjoy and said nothing.

'Where's Del now?' I said.

'Haven't seen him tonight,' he said, shaking his head vigorously. 'Nor Phil neither.'

Ricky Mountjoy was coughing harshly, and I turned towards him, just in case. He was sitting up but in no shape yet to try to stripe me. I'd expected the lad to try and make it to the door, but he hadn't. He was still standing against the wall. Maybe he was waiting for my permission to leave.

'What's your name?' I said.

'Billy,' he said. 'Billy Watson.'

'Well, Billy Watson,' I said, 'I don't want to know what you do for a living that means you can afford that fancy Italian suit, but I'm willing to bet it isn't working as a hod-carrier on a building site. And I bet it isn't legal. I just hope it isn't quite as illegal and ugly as I suspect it is.'

He looked down at the floor and flushed an angry red. 'You can't talk to me like that,' he said.

'Listen, son,' I said in my best avuncular manner, 'a word of advice. Forget the tough-guy stuff. You're not cut out for it.' I shook my head. 'You're not hard just because you've got a sock full of sand in your pocket and you're happy to hit someone with it from behind. That's just sneaky. So, as long as you're just sneaky, I reckon I *can* talk to you like that.' I shrugged. 'I hope that you don't grow up to be vicious with it. That'll get you into all kinds of trouble.'

Some more gagging and hoarse coughing and a little shuffling suggested that Ricky Mountjoy was stirring behind me. Now, he was already vicious and I was in no doubt about how cheesed off with me he'd be. Not only had I hurt him but I'd also humiliated him in front of a subordinate – Billy Watson was just a runner, and Ricky was something more than that – and he'd be after revenge. Ah well, it couldn't be helped.

I turned around and made my way over to him. 'Ricky,' I said, 'I'm sorry that I had to hit you, but you didn't give me any alternative.'

He looked up at me with real malice. 'You've made a bad enemy,' he said. 'I'll get you for that.'

I shrugged. 'I'm sure you'll try, Ricky,' I said.

'You bastards,' he said. 'You're all the same. Just because

you've got a few medals, you think you're heroes. Better than the rest of us.'

'No one I know thinks that,' I said. I shook my head and stared down at him. 'I'm trying to find someone,' I said. 'There was an American in here last night, looking to be . . . accommodated. He's gone missing. I assume you arrange for people to be accommodated here, so I wondered what you know.'

'I wasn't in here last night,' he said. 'I don't know nothing.'

Mrs Wilson, my white-haired old teacher at Church Road School, would have tutted over his grammar there, but I let it go. I was more bothered by the fact that he was lying, but I decided to let that go too.

'Fair enough,' I said. 'If you hear anything, let me know.' I started to walk out and then turned back. 'You don't know where I might find Del, do you? I fancy a chat with him.'

He ignored me, and, after a few seconds of uneasy silence, I walked out of the room and down the stairs.

I hoped that Lee had stumbled back into Pete's Place during my absence, but one glance at Peter Baxter's gloomy face as I was waved back in by Bill was enough to confirm that he was still resolutely AWOL. There were a lot more people standing around now than there had been before, and the other three members of Peter's quartet were shuffling around on stage as if preparing to play.

I joined Baxter and Jerry, who was cheerily slurping a pint, by the bar and admitted that all I had to show for my efforts was a lump on the head, the lasting enmity of a member of one of the nastiest families in my neck of the woods and the knowledge that Lee had been in the Frighted Horse the night before. Actually, I left out the stuff about the bash on the bonce and the sworn enmity of Ricky Mountjoy as being of no interest to him, but I told him everything else.

Peter Baxter looked even gloomier. 'I'd better go tell Jeannie and then explain to this lot – again – that she's going to be a no-show tonight,' he said, heaving himself away from the bar.

Jerry looked up from his pint and beamed at me. 'Can't someone else play the joanna for her?' he said.

'With no rehearsal?' Peter said.

'Why not?' Jerry said. 'Or maybe she can sing a cappella . . .'

'Do what?' said Peter.

'Unaccompanied,' Jerry said.

'Don't be daft,' Peter said.

'Just trying to be helpful,' Jerry said.

'Well don't,' Peter said.

Jerry shrugged and sipped a little of his beer. 'If you like,' he said, looking up again, 'I could have a look at some of her arrangements while you and the band play a set.'

'You?' Peter and I said more or less together.

'I had a lot of piano lessons when I was a kid,' he said. 'I take it you've got a piano back there. We might be able to cobble a few songs together. You never know. I'm not saying I'm any good, but I can play a few chords, get her in the mood . . .'

'Nah,' Peter said. 'She's a pro. She won't sing with a rank amateur.'

Jerry shrugged. 'If she's a real pro, she might give it a whirl,' he said. 'It's worth asking. Isn't it?'

'Not really,' Peter said, 'but I'm desperate enough to try anything. Come on.'

Peter was right, of course. And, of course, he communicated his unease brilliantly.

Jeannie Summers sat and listened politely as he stuttered and stammered his way through Jerry's suggestion, then she frowned as though considering it. After maybe thirty seconds she spoke.

'It's very sweet of you to suggest it, love,' she said, looking at Jerry, 'but it won't fly. Lee and me, we have a musical . . . understanding. It's not a simple thing. It's taken years.' She looked away as her eyes filled with tears.

Peter Baxter stood up, cleared his throat, murmured something about getting on stage and shuffled off to the door.

'He might still turn up,' Miss Summers said very quietly.

Peter stopped, cleared his throat again. 'Yeah,' he said. 'Yeah. Well, he's got about three quarters of an hour.' He stood awkwardly in the doorway for a few seconds and then stomped off. After a few minutes we heard the band launch into 'The Sheik of Araby'.

'Do you think he will?' I said. 'Turn up, that is.'

Miss Summers looked up at me. 'He always has,' she said, 'in the past.'

'Does he often go missing?' I said.

'Not often, no.' There was an edge to her voice. 'No more than two or three times a week.'

I was relieved that the edge wasn't directed at me. For some reason, I didn't want her mad at me.

Jerry stood up. 'Well,' he said, 'if you'll excuse me, I've got a warm beer waiting on the bar, and it's probably getting cold.'

Miss Summers smiled at him. 'Thanks again for the offer,' she said, 'but I'm just not comfortable singing with anyone else at the piano.'

'That's copacetic,' Jerry said and strolled out, carefully shutting the door behind him.

I was still wondering what he meant when Miss Summers spoke again.

'And thank you for looking for Lee, Mr Gérard. I really must apologize for inconveniencing you.'

'Not at all,' I said. 'I'm just sorry I didn't find him . . . And it's Tony.'

She looked down at her lap where her pale hands rested. 'Well, thank you, Tony,' she said.

The faint American accent I'd detected the night before had evaporated completely. She now sounded like a regular London girl.

'Where did you meet him? Lee, I mean,' I said.

'Here,' she said, 'during the war. March 1944. I was sweet sixteen and he was on leave, playing the piano in a pub in Camden for his mates. Don't ask me how a bunch of Yankee soldiers found their way to Camden because I don't even know what I was doing there. Betty, one of the girls from the factory, probably suggested it.' She sighed. 'It was probably Betty who persuaded me to sing as well. Which was why Lee told me how much he liked my voice. I thought it was just a line and he was just another glib, charming, handsome, feckless American, but, after the war, he came back and whisked me away. I was a GI bride.' She paused and smiled wanly. 'He wasn't ill then, of course. That came later, when we started playing the jazz clubs in Kansas City and Chicago . . .'

I tried to find a few words of reassurance, but I didn't have any. All I could offer her was an awkward silence.

The distant, raucous sound of Peter Baxter and the boys struggling with 'I Got Rhythm' drifted along the corridor. She had the grace not to wince, but she raised her eyebrows and smiled sadly at me. 'It's just as well Lee isn't here,' she said. 'He loves Gershwin. He's been working on arrangements of "Someone To Watch Over Me" and "They Can't Take That Away From Me" for us. He thinks they'll suit my voice.'

'He's right,' I said. 'Not that I'm an expert or anything.' After a long pause I asked the question that had been on my mind for a while. 'Has he ever been gone for this long before?'

She leaned forward and reached for the glass of warm gin that was still on the desk. She sipped it. 'Only once,' she said. 'Six months ago, in New Orleans. The stuff had been cut with something very bad. He nearly died.'

'Perhaps,' I said, 'it's time to contact the police . . .'

She sipped some more gin. I found myself wondering how long she'd been drinking.

'Or I could try some hospitals . . .'

She looked up. 'I'd rather the police weren't involved,' she said. 'A junkie jazz musician? He'd be deported, and me with him. It might make it difficult to get back into the country.'

I nodded. 'Of course,' I said. 'You must have family here.'

'No,' she said. 'I don't have any family, except Lee. I just don't want to burn any boats. Or is it bridges?'

'It depends on whether you want to stop the enemy advancing or your own lot retreating,' I said.

Peter Baxter's office had a small, grubby window which looked out on to a narrow alleyway. A few patches of dull, yellow light spilled out from the upstairs windows and glinted on half a dozen bashed and dented bins and piles of boxes overflowing with rubbish from the Acropolis. Something large moved sinuously in the shadows. I hoped it was one of Soho's cats.

The raw, gutsy sound of Peter Baxter and the boys belting out 'Chattanooga Choo Choo' drifted along the corridor.

Jeannie Summers stared dreamily at the dirty, smeared panes. She obviously hadn't heard what I'd said. I started to suspect that she'd had more than the one gin.

I watched her for a moment or two. She was one of those women who really have no idea just how attractive they are.

And even if she was a bit older and more worn than she looked on stage, she *was* very attractive. Her pale, bare shoulders added a touch of vulnerability to the sadness in her eyes, and I found myself wanting to hold her. But I didn't. I'm not impulsive, I'm not God's gift to womankind and it was her husband who should take her in his arms, not me.

Anyway, there was a certain *froideur* in her gaze when it settled on me that told me she knew what I was thinking and that such intimacy would not be welcome. I suddenly realized that I was wrong. She did know how attractive she was.

I coloured slightly. At first, because I was a bit miffed that she thought that I was as obvious and predictable as every other man she'd ever been alone with, and then because I realized that she was right.

I consoled myself with the thought that at least I wasn't as crass or as crude as Ricky Mountjoy and never had been. Not that that would have meant anything to Jeannie Summers.

Something about young Ricky had been nagging at me for a while, and I suddenly realized what it was. A lad (however likely) from a Leyton family on one of the bottom rungs of criminal activity wouldn't just have strolled out of Pentonville or Wandsworth and started up a nice little business in the West End. Even Leyton's most important villains (a category that certainly included the Mountjoys) wouldn't make it into the robbers' version of *Burke's Peerage*. This was lucrative stuff. And it was dangerous. It was turf that was fought over. Maybe his dad or one of his uncles had moved into the big time and was employing him. But it was far more likely that he'd made some interesting friends on the inside. Either way, there were grown-ups behind him.

It also crossed my mind that Les Jackson wasn't going to be too happy to hear that one of the actors he was grooming for success had been slumming it in the Frighted Horse, in the company of some seedy purveyors of little bags of powdered happiness. And it occurred to me that he might blame me. After all, I was supposed to be looking after the little toerag.

A door banged somewhere above us, abrupt and startling, and then there were heavy footsteps on the stairs that led from the kitchen of the Acropolis down to the alley. We both tensed slightly and stared at the window.

Miss Summers nervously glugged down enough mother's ruin and tonic water to slake the thirst of a Welsh front row.

It'd be one of the Greek kitchen staff with a bucket of potato peelings and fish heads to add to the cats' cornucopia.

I attempted a reassuring smile. But my heart wasn't in it. I wasn't feeling very reassuring because I counted three pairs of feet clanging on the iron stairs and I doubted that the Acropolis boasted more than one kitchen boy to wash up and dump the rubbish. On the other hand, maybe it was just the management using the back exit, or the council investigating complaints about the sanitary arrangements.

I guess that the bash on the head had me looking for people creeping up behind me.

If that was the case then I definitely had something to thank young Billy Watson for because these guys shuffled around for a moment or two at the bottom of the steps, muttering, and then opened the back door to Pete's Place. They strode steadily along the corridor, past the office and then stopped and knocked on the next door, which was, I realized, Jeannie Summers' dressing room.

She looked at me with wide eyes, and I held my hand up to indicate that she should stay put and moved to the door.

I listened for a moment, but all I heard was some more muttering and another knock. I remembered all that stuff I learned in the army about never volunteering for anything, always keeping your head down and how discretion is very much the better part of value, then I gave a little mental shrug and, as I'd done so often before, ignored any good advice I'd been offered and slipped out to see what was going on.

A quick glance confirmed what I already knew. There were

three men standing outside the dressing-room door. Well, two, who I didn't recognize, were standing there, and one, who I had seen before, was propped up against the wall next to it and looked as if he was about to slide down it.

The two who I didn't know were hard-looking guys about my age in nice suits, clean white shirts, neat blue ties and were recently shaved. The other one had close on two days' worth of stubble, had clearly slept in his crumpled suit and wasn't wearing a tie.

At least my record on finding missing persons was looking a lot more impressive. Two found in one day wasn't bad, especially as I hadn't lifted a finger to find Philip Graham and had only sustained one bump on the head to locate Lee the piano player, who now did begin to slide gently down the wall.

At this rate, I could expect Daff's long-lost daughter to bring me my early morning cuppa along with the *Daily Herald* on Monday.

Always assuming the two tough-looking gents were a lot friendlier than they looked and I survived until Monday.

SIX

'**H**e all right?' I said, waving a hand in Lee's direction. Both of the tough guys turned to face me. They were silent for a few seconds, and Peter Baxter's strident trumpet filled the little corridor with a shrill, and not altogether successful, attempt to reach something very high as the climax to 'St James Infirmary'. The man nearest to me allowed a slightly pained and puzzled expression to soften his battered face. His nose had been broken a couple of times, and there was scar tissue around his eyes, suggesting mixed fortunes in a long career in the ring.

When Peter finished and applause broke out like sporadic gunfire, the man flashed me an amiable smile and jerked a thumb at the almost recumbent piano player. 'He yours?' he said.

'Sort of,' I said, with a dismissive shrug. 'Is he all right?'

He ran his tongue around his lips. 'About as all right as a beaten-up junk fiend coming off a bender can be,' he said.

'Beaten up?' I said.

'Yeah, someone's given him a bit of a seeing to. Quite professional. Left the face alone. Lots of body shots. He'll probably find it a bit painful to pee for a few days.' He paused to rub his damaged nose. 'Anyway, we've delivered him. He's all yours.' He nodded at the other guy and they both moved towards me.

'You didn't happen to find him upstairs in a pub?' I said.

'Maybe,' he said.

'The Frighted Horse?' I said.

They stopped.

'What makes you ask that?' The second man spoke for the first time, and there was an edge of suspicion, and a touch of Yorkshire, in his voice.

'Oh,' I said, 'I was over there looking for him an hour or so back.'

The first man looked at his companion and the amiable smile became a very wide grin. 'You didn't,' he said, 'by any chance meet up with a couple of young lads, did you?' he said.

'Might have done,' I said cautiously, taking a step back.

'Because I heard that someone did some very nice things to the Mountjoy boy,' he said, 'and, if that was you, I'd like to shake your hand.'

To prove it, he held out one of his large, misshapen paws. The thick, blunt fingers looked as if they'd all been broken once or twice, and none of the knuckles appeared to be where they should be. What could I do? I took the hand and we shook.

'Malcolm Booth,' he said.

'Tony Gérard,' I said. 'What's your interest in Lee here?'

'None at all,' he said. 'But our employer has some businesses around here, and we were looking out for them when we came across him in the course of our duty, as it were. He gave the club's address, and we thought it would be a neighbourly act to bring him back.'

'That's good of you,' I said. 'Very. I appreciate it. And I know his wife will.'

Malcolm raised his eyebrows. 'Think nothing of it. And if you see young Mountjoy, or one of the other little oiks he hangs out with, tell him Malc would like a word.'

'I'll do that,' I said, 'but, to tell you the truth, I was hoping not to run into him again.'

'Oh, you will,' he said. 'Believe you me, you will.' And he patted me gently on the shoulder, jerked his head at the other man and the two of them left the same way they'd arrived.

I listened to them clang up the iron staircase, heard the heavy door of the Acropolis's kitchen bang shut, wondered which particular villain they worked for, and which of his 'businesses' they had been 'looking out for', and then I reached down to help haul Lee to his feet. He towered over me by perhaps six or seven inches, but he must have weighed a stone and a half less. He was painfully skinny. I gripped his upper arm. It felt like a pipe cleaner.

He winced as he stood up, then he staggered slightly and doubled over, clutching his stomach. For a few seconds I thought he was going to vomit all over me, but I was worrying unnecessarily. He was responding to some heavy bruising rather than an urge to retch.

He straightened up and leaned against the wall again. 'Thanks,' he said so quietly that I almost missed it as the door behind me squeaked open and then closed with a little tut of exasperation and Jeannie Summers slipped into the corridor.

The band started an uncharacteristically subdued version of 'Lover Man'. I couldn't decide whether this counted as an ironic coincidence or not. The mellow sound of Peter Baxter's trumpet echoed hauntingly in the drab, brown, damp and smelly corridor. I stood quietly and listened for a moment or two as Miss Summers reached up and stroked her husband's clammy forehead, then I helped her manoeuvre him into their dressing room.

He slumped into a battered but comfortable-looking old armchair, his long legs thrust out in front of him, taking up most of the available space. She knelt beside him and gently rubbed the back of his hand.

The room was dark and cramped. It was painted the same drab brown as the corridor and Peter Baxter's office, and its one small window was covered by a dusty-looking dark-red curtain. An old upright piano occupied all of one wall, and the stool was covered in music. There was a table with Miss Summers' shiny black handbag sitting on it and some make-up – a lipstick, a compact – scattered about. An old, smudged mirror with an unhealthy, brown-spotted complexion leaned back from it, resting precariously against the wall. Miss Summers' street clothes were neatly folded on the only other chair in the room, her sensible flat-heeled shoes tucked carefully underneath it.

She looked up at me and forced a sad, little smile. 'Tell Mr Baxter to give us twenty minutes,' she said. 'We'll be ready to go on then. Or maybe half an hour.'

I must have looked unsure. I certainly felt it.

'Really,' she said, nodding her head decisively. 'He'll be fine.'

'That's . . . good,' I said. 'I'll go and tell Peter.' I paused at the door and turned back to face her, but she was busy wiping a handkerchief across his face, just as my mother had done to me when I'd been a nipper with a dirty mug. The difference was that Lee wasn't complaining about it and trying to pull away. The harsh smell of cheap eau de cologne irritated the lining of my nostrils, and I sneezed noisily. She turned her head towards me, and I sneezed again. 'I'd be interested to know what happened to him,' I said, choking down a third sneeze and rubbing my hand across my nose. 'When he's up to talking about it. Who gave him the lumps and so on.'

She nodded, doused the already grubby handkerchief with more perfume and scrubbed at Lee's forehead. I quietly left her to it.

I closed the door behind me and stood in that dimly lit corridor, trying to ignore the smell of old cabbage water, listening to the band storming towards the end of 'Mississippi Mud'. I didn't know if they started together, but they were making a pretty good fist of finishing together. Applause crackled around the hall like there was a serious skirmishing action going on in there. Then I heard Peter make an announcement that I didn't catch. As he and the others, sweat-drenched and beaming, then bounced down off the stage, I assumed he had declared a drinks and pee break.

When he saw me, his expression changed to one of grim anxiety and he strode down the corridor, trumpet in hand.

'He's back,' I said quickly, 'and she seems to think they can go on in twenty minutes or so.'

He looked at me for a moment or two. 'You don't seem so sure,' he said.

I shrugged. 'He's not looking too well,' I said. 'But Miss Summers seemed certain.'

The other band members were mopping brows, smiling and talking quietly together. It must have been a good set.

'Hey, Peter,' Danny the tubby bass man shouted out, 'is it all right if we go and sink a pint or two? I've got a thirst on me like a dehydrated camel.' I assumed that he meant he was very dry indeed. Danny knew something about camels. He'd been in North Africa during the war.

'Sure,' said Peter. 'Tell whoever's on at the bar that the first one's on me.'

'Cheers, Peter,' Danny said. He waved his hand at the dressing-room door behind Peter and lowered his voice. 'What's the score?' he said, conspiratorially. 'We on again after the break, or what?'

'They're on in twenty,' Peter said, looking at me sceptically. 'Apparently.'

I'm not a great one for omens. There were blokes in the war who saw them in everything: that it was raining; that, for once, it wasn't; that the sergeant-major had nicked himself shaving; that the huge brown cow in the nearest farm mooed. It all meant something for them. I remember dear old Mrs Wilson at school telling us about the Romans, or some lot, who used to disembowel a chicken and read the entrails in order to see how things would turn out. Well, that was fairly rational compared to someone like Bernie Rosen, who saw stuff in the shapes of clouds, or Big Luc, one of the Frenchmen I found myself working with during the war, who once told me quite seriously that a particular operation couldn't possibly be successful because my socks were an inauspicious colour. Since they were the same drab colour I always wore, that puzzled me.

I've never believed in them myself. I've always preferred to look at facts and make judgements – if I really have to – accordingly.

Lee the piano player had long since come off his chemical high, and, to add to his general level of *joie de vivre*, he had been knocked about quite a bit as well. I also suspected that Jeannie Summers was well on her way to being more than a little sozzled. The facts, as I saw them, all led inevitably to one conclusion.

I gloomily joined Jerry at the bar, fearing the worst. He smiled at me cherubically, bought himself another pint and reluctantly forked out for a brandy for me. I felt I needed it.

'Why so morose, my glum friend?' he said as I knocked back most of the brandy in one fiery gulp and slumped against the bar. 'It may never happen.'

I shrugged helplessly. 'I'm afraid, Jerry,' I said, 'that I've concluded that the omens are not good.'

I swallowed down the rest of my brandy and looked for the barman to refill the glass. Jerry looked at me owlishly over the rim of his pint glass. I suddenly realized that the round-eyed gaze indicated surprise. His surprise didn't noticeably diminish when I ordered a double.

'What are the omens not good for?' he asked amiably.

'Tonight's main attraction,' I said.

He shrugged. 'So what?' he said.

'Well,' I said and stopped. He had a point. Peter had his club's takings to worry about. Lee and Miss Summers had their reputation to worry about. But why was I bothered?

'Well what?' he said.

'The piano player's turned up, but he's not in much of a state to perform.'

'He'll still be better than me,' Jerry said. 'What was I thinking?' He laughed. 'Do you know how long it is since I played the piano in semi-public? Two years and eight months. It was at what your mate Bernie would call a knees-up and what my mother would call a cocktail party. I was adding a bit of class to her at-home. I tinkled those ivories like my life depended on it. And all I got for my pains was a glass of lemonade, one small, triangular, meat-paste sandwich, two crackers with some Cheddar and a smidgeon of Branston's pickle on top and my father asking if I'd mind playing something "a bit more traditional". I told him that "Smoke Gets In Your Eyes" was as traditional as I got, and he went off in a huff, muttering, "There's nothing wrong with Stephen Foster."' He sighed. 'The vicar did give me a consoling pat on the shoulder, though, so the evening wasn't a complete waste of time.'

He sought further consolation in his pint as Peter Baxter shuffled on to the stage, tapped the microphone and announced that the delightful Jeannie Summers would be on in five minutes. There was a smattering of applause and one amiable, muffled shout of, 'About time,' followed by a leisurely stampede for the bar.

Jerry and I moved away from the front line and sat at a suddenly empty table.

'So,' I said, 'what's the difference between a cocktail party and a knees-up?'

Jerry looked up at the ceiling, which at one time had probably been a delicate primrose but had matured into a fetching smog colour. After carefully contemplating this masterpiece wrought by time and nicotine – mainly nicotine – for a few seconds, he nodded. 'At a cocktail party,' he said slowly, 'the sherry is Amontillado and pretends to be Spanish.' Having made this, as far as I was concerned, completely baffling pronouncement, he thoughtfully sipped more beer. Then he looked up again. 'Oh,' he added, 'and your bank manager never goes to a knees-up.'

Clearly, Jerry was drunker than Jeannie Summers.

As it turned out, the set was not the disaster I'd been expecting, and nowhere near as embarrassing. But it was close. I was relieved. I wasn't sure why.

Miss Summers and Lee both stumbled on to the stage and then stumbled into their first number. They stopped 'Stormy Weather' twice, very apologetically, before managing to synchronize their efforts. Fortunately, they improved a little over the next couple of songs, and by the time they came to the end, they even managed to make a pretty good fist of 'Can't Help Lovin' Dat Man'. There was some enthusiastic applause. But that might have come from Peter and the band, standing at the bar.

Jerry wasn't as impressed as he would have been the night before, but he didn't say anything, just pursed his lips and concentrated on his beer.

When the lights came up, Miss Summers had disappeared but Lee was still slumped at the piano. After a few seconds he looked up, blinking, saw me and pulled himself to his feet. He was clearly stiffening up, and the bruises were throbbing. Then, very gingerly, he walked very slowly over to our table.

'Jeannie told me that you came looking for me, and I want to thank you,' he said. 'I appreciate it, sir.'

'It was nothing,' I said. 'I just wish I'd found you.' He was holding his stomach, and I nodded at it. 'By the way, who gave you the beating?'

He sniffed. 'Just some kids,' he said. 'I don't rightly know why. But they could have been the fellers who were in here last night.' He shook his head. 'Maybe. I'm not sure.'

His uncertainty was unconvincing. He knew. I wondered why he wasn't saying.

In the sickly, yellowish light, his gaunt face was all sharp angles and fierce bloodshot eyes. He rubbed his hand over the stubble on his cheek. Miss Summers had done her best, but he hadn't cleaned up that well. Fortunately, the poor lighting on the stage hadn't revealed the full extent of his disarray.

'Say,' he said, 'you don't know where I can get some protection, do you?'

'Protection?' I said.

'Yeah, you know,' he said and made a gun out of his right hand, his first two fingers forming the barrel and his thumb the hammer. 'A shooter.'

'No,' I said, 'it's not easy to acquire firearms in this country.' I now had a very uneasy feeling about his reasons for not telling me who had beaten him up.

He sighed. 'Pity. I guess a blade will have to do,' he said.

'I wouldn't,' I said, 'go looking to get your own back.'

'It's just for protection, man,' he said. 'Just for protection.' He chuckled.

'All the same,' I said, 'it wouldn't be a good idea.'

He smiled in a mean, ugly sort of way. 'Anyway, thanks again for looking out for me,' he said and shuffled back on to the stage. He went to the piano and picked out the opening notes from 'The Funeral March', then he grinned at me before stumbling out of the rear exit.

Thanks to Bernie Rosen and a dodgy little deal from a few months before that was still haunting me in the unusual spectral form of sporadic telephone calls I received from the inspector at Scotland Yard, I was in funds and, blissfully, the cost of the taxi back to Leyton was not a concern.

Jerry's case of hiccups, however, was. It was clearly touch and go whether he would make it back to the little shop on the corner of Lea Bridge Road and Church Road in Leyton without a gallon or so of beer making its considerable presence felt.

Still, my worries diminished into insignificance beside those of the cabby, who spent more time looking at us than he did at the road. When he wasn't inquiring solicitously after Jerry's health, he spent the time muttering darkly. I didn't make any real effort to hear what he was saying. It probably wouldn't have made me happy.

In the event, Jerry made it back without any serious spillage, but he was still hiccuping helplessly. He stood on the pavement and swayed gently in the non-existent breeze while I overtipped the driver, who did have the grace to look a bit sheepish and thank me twice – 'Very kind of you, guv. Very kind' – before rumbling off in a cloud of grey exhaust fumes.

I negotiated Jerry into his flat and left him lying on his bed, still threatening to erupt at any moment. I removed his shoes but left it at that and then made my way out into the dark passageway that led to the stairs to my own flat.

Jerry had thoughtfully left my post – the parcel from Ghislaine – on the top step where I was bound to trip over it. This had the advantage that I wouldn't miss it.

And the decided disadvantage that I did indeed trip over it. Fortunately, I didn't break anything important, just bruised my knee painfully.

Fluffy, Jerry's large and bad-tempered cat, eased his way languidly around the door to my office and dispassionately watched me hopping about on the landing. He wasn't noted for his compassion towards others' suffering. His eyes glittered like broken glass in the light from the lamp post outside the window. With a dismissive meow, he brushed past me and loped silently down the stairs.

I rubbed at my knee, picked up the parcel and felt for the light switch in my office as I went in.

I sat in my grandfather's old leather chair and looked at the brown-paper package: the exotic stamps, Ghislaine's handwriting, my name appearing as 'Antoine'. Only Ghislaine called me Antoine these days.

The scorch marks on Grand-père's chair reminded me every day that Papa and Maman never would again.

It would be a book. I knew that. This was only the second gift that Ghislaine had ever given me, and the first had been a book. It sat in splendid isolation on the old, scrubbed kitchen table that pretended to be my desk: *Les Fleurs du mal* by Charles Baudelaire.

I unwrapped the parcel as carefully as an archaeologist unwinding the bandages around an Egyptian mummy and finally unveiled *Alcools* by some geezer called Guillaume Apollinaire.

Like her previous present this was also second-hand: the pages had already been slit. It was another collection of poetry. Ghislaine had evidently decided that it was time for me to be educated in the finer things of life.

Racy poems about malevolent flowers and strong spirits seemed like an odd way to go about it.

The accompanying letter was bland and formal enough. She sent her *felicitations* and said how much she had enjoyed spending time with me in Paris. There was a sting to it, though. At the end she said she was thinking about getting back together with her husband, Robert, and asked what I thought about that.

I didn't really know what I thought about that. As Robert was a noted womanizer and had, on one occasion that I knew of, beaten her, I wasn't sure that making it up with him would lead to happiness, but it wasn't my decision. In any case, the date on the letter suggested that she'd sent it the day after I left, so she'd probably done whatever she was going to do already. My reply would tax my limited French diplomatic vocabulary.

I picked up the volume of verse and started to read.

SEVEN

I don't sleep well. According to friends, I worry too much. I think that may be true. It certainly doesn't take much to wake me up.

And the thumping on the front door before the sun had risen was definitely *de trop*. I was up and pulling on my trousers at the first bang, but the hammering continued as I ran down the stairs. Whoever it was seemed determined to put a dent in solid wood and wake up everyone in the building. Well, they may have splintered a plank or two, but Jerry, the only other occupant of the house, resolutely refused to be roused.

I have to admit, I was expecting a couple of burly law-enforcement officers. I don't know why policemen have such a liking for seeing the unshaven cheeks and chins of known felons, or the hair curlers and face cream lathered faces of their spouses, but predawn visits have long been their idea of a good time. I also couldn't think why they would be calling on me. (Well, I could, but I didn't want to dwell on what I regarded as ancient history. Although, to be fair, Inspector Rose preferred to think of it as an ongoing investigation.) So it was with some misgivings that I opened the door.

Not enough misgivings, though.

The two burly men standing on the pavement were far too smartly dressed to be on-duty policemen. From the recently brushed hats down to the highly polished shoes, via the sharp, double-breasted suits and the crisp white shirts and neatly knotted ties, they oozed villain. Thugs like to look nice.

'Mr Tony Gérard?' one of them said. His accent was pure East End, but he was polite enough. And, clearly, he was keen to ensure that he only knocked lumps off the right person. So, a decent sort, then.

I nodded.

'Would you be so good as to get in the car.' He indicated, with a flick of his head, a flamboyant, two-tone Ford Consul in red and white parked just down the road, motor running quietly. 'My employer would like to see you.' He was a very big man, and I was grateful that he was asking nicely. I don't think that he and his equally large companion would have had too much trouble picking me up and carrying me.

'Any point in asking who?' I said.

'All will be revealed in the fullness of time,' he said, tossing his cigarette butt on to the pavement and grinding it out with his heel.

'Do you mind if I shave, wash and finish dressing?' I said, thinking that it wouldn't be a bad idea to apply a cold, wet flannel to the bump on the back of my head that was starting to throb like a good 'un.

'Be my guest, Mr Gérard.' He looked at his watch. 'Shall we say five minutes?'

I nodded and went back up the stairs.

I didn't have time to boil a kettle so I shaved, painfully, in cold water. Then I dressed in record time and went back down the stairs. I'd been gone for slightly less than four minutes.

He smiled at me warmly when I reappeared. For some reason that made me wish I'd taken the extra minute and gone for a pee. I realized I had no idea where we were going.

'Is it far?' I said.

'No,' he said, putting his hand gently on my back and guiding me towards the waiting car.

It's not very brave or resourceful of me, I know, but I've always found that some things just can't be resisted and it's better not to waste time or energy fighting them. At school and in the forces I was occasionally accused of dumb insolence, but it isn't that at all. Sometimes it really is best just to let events unfold and see how they develop and wait for an opening or bow to the inevitable.

These two gents looked pretty hard and fairly inevitable to me so I slid meekly into the car. It smelt of new PVC and stale cigarettes. The politeness and courtesy I'd been offered so far indicated that things might turn out all right, but I wouldn't have been human if I hadn't had a bad feeling fidgeting away in my guts about it all. I recognized the bad feeling for what it was. I'd been scared before.

I did hope that the banging on the door and my to-ing and fro-ing had roused Jerry, and that, even in his befuddled state, he'd had the presence of mind to make a note of the car's registration plate, which was more than I had, but I wasn't overly optimistic that he'd even woken up.

The car was parked on the wrong side of the road, facing Lea Bridge Road, and so described a beautiful arc as the driver executed a perfect U-turn, the headlamps sweeping across the pale-yellow wall of the Gaumont cinema and, for a brief moment, lighting up the window of Enzo's dark and deserted café.

Then the surprisingly powerful motor accelerated smoothly along Church Road, empty at this time of the morning, swiftly passing all the old familiar landmarks made eerie and alien by the early morning light and silence. We glided past the bomb site where Maman, Papa and Grand-père had met their fiery end; past the Oliver Twist pub, where the road made a harsh left, and St Mary's Church; past the congregational church and the hall where the 1st Leyton Boy Scouts meet every Friday night; and then we turned into Leyton High Road at the cavernous Lion and Key pub.

Within minutes, we'd swung into Grove Green Road and I had more than an inkling of where we were going. I started to feel a little less scared, even relieved. Anyone wanting to do bad things to me would probably have taken me off to a secluded glade in Epping Forest, rather than whisking me off to their home. This was going to be a warning, at worst.

We swished to a halt outside one of the only houses with any lights on. In fact, it was lit up like a Christmas tree. Once again, the driver parked on the wrong side of the road, facing the non-existent traffic, and, once again, he stayed in the car, with the engine running, lighting up a cigarette as we slid out and the big man gently eased me in the direction of the wide steps that led up to the front door, his hand on the small of my back. His companion bounded up the steps and rattled the knocker. The door was opened instantly.

I was manoeuvred into the standard working-class-made-good front room. There was a lot of gleaming dark wood, a thick, fitted carpet with a headache-inducing, swirly pattern in dark greens and browns, and some cut-glass vases. There was also the same alabaster Alsatian dog with a small child wrapped around its neck that I'd seen at Daff's perched on the sideboard. It made me smile.

There were also a number of hard-looking men scattered about the room, sitting stiffly on high-backed dining chairs, all smoking furiously. Even through the fug, I recognized two of them, and two of the others shared a family resemblance. The smile was short-lived.

Dave Mountjoy got up from his chair and walked towards me. He'd put on a little weight since I'd last seen him and lost some of his hair. He looked more like the older man who was sitting on the only comfortable-looking armchair in the room than like the sour-faced Ricky, who was sprawled untidily on his chair. Something decidedly unpleasant inside me took great pleasure in the discovery that I wasn't the only one suffering after last night's little fracas. Ricky had a very nice Technicolor bruise just under his jawline.

'Thanks for agreeing to come at such short notice, Mr Gérard,' Dave Mountjoy said. He extended his hand, and I saw no choice but to take it. We shook perfunctorily. 'Cup of tea?'

I nodded, and he jerked his head at the big man who had steered me into the room. He left silently. I was now far more intrigued than scared. We were going to drink together. What could be friendlier?

'Sit,' Mountjoy said, and he indicated a vacant seat by the window. It was starting to get light outside. What I could see of the sky, as I stepped to the chair, had some pale-pink streaks sketched across it.

When I was sitting, Mountjoy beamed at me. 'Good, good. Tea won't be a minute,' he said. He seemed nervous, and I couldn't understand why.

'Maybe you could tell me what you want to talk about,' I said. 'I'm very curious.'

'Yeah, of course,' he said. And then he stood silently for a few seconds, apparently lost for words.

'I won't beat about the bush,' he said, beating about the

bush. 'I'll get straight to the point.' He then signally failed to get to the point, either directly or by some devious route, because the door opened and my tea arrived.

The small, delicate teacup and saucer looked tiny in the big man's big hand. I wondered if there was more than one swallow in it.

'I didn't know if you took sugar,' he said, handing me the cup that looked considerably more substantial when transferred to my hand, 'so I put two spoons in.'

'That's fine,' I said, though it wasn't. 'You were saying, Mr Mountjoy?'

'Yeah, the thing is we heard – well, Ricky told us – that you had a run-in with him last night, and Ricky just wanted to say he was sorry. You know, like, all forgotten, water under the bridge, no hard feelings.' He looked across at Ricky and encouraged him to speak.

'I was out of order last night,' Ricky said in a flat monotone, staring at the floor. 'And I'm sorry for having a go at you. I shouldn't of.'

His father nodded at him again.

'Yeah, I'm really sorry. I apologize.' He was squirming like a puppy on a leash being taught to walk to heel.

This was decidedly odd but welcome all the same. If I wasn't entirely convinced by his sincerity, well . . . I smiled in his direction, anyway. He still wasn't looking at me. I decided this was probably not a good moment to tell him that Big Malc wanted a word.

'That's fine by me,' I said. 'There are no hard feelings on my part. I told you that last night. I never wanted to take this thing any further.'

'That's good,' Dave Mountjoy said. 'So we're all kosher here. All forgiven, eh? I don't want any misunderstandings about unfinished business or assumed vendettas. I just wanted it clear that there's none of that.'

'Sure,' I said. 'I'm happy to hear that.' I was really puzzled now, but I suspected I was going to have to be patient. I wasn't going to find out what this was all about here. I slurped as much sweet tea as I could stomach and then stood up. 'Well, thanks for the apology, which really wasn't necessary, and for the tea, which I really needed.' I looked around the room. 'All right if I head back home now?'

'Yeah, yeah. Benny'll give you a ride back,' Dave Mountjoy said.

'No, you're all right,' I said. 'I'll walk back. It'll do me good.' I made for the door and then stopped and clicked my fingers as though something had just occurred to me. 'Actually, this is quite a coincidence. I needed a word with Mr Mountjoy senior.' I looked at the old boy, who was still sitting in his comfortable chair, puffing on a pipe. 'In private. If that's possible.'

The room fell silent, and Dave Mountjoy looked at his brother who looked at Ricky who shrugged. He had dumb insolence down to a fine art. I almost wished that I had mentioned Big Malc. It would have been a real treat to watch the little oik turn an even sicklier shade of pale yellow.

'That all right with you, Dad?' Dave Mountjoy said.

'What?' the old boy said. He was wearing a flat cap and had a sturdy walking stick by his side. He had a truculent air about him that suggested he used it more as a weapon than an aid to getting about.

'Mr Gérard would like a word with you.'

'What about?' the old boy snapped.

'It's just about something that happened a long time ago,' I said. 'Before the war, back in the late twenties.' The clarification was in case they thought I was going to bring up the beating they'd administered to my father.

'That's a long time ago,' the old boy said. 'All right. I'll see if I remember anything.'

'Thanks,' I said and waited for the others to leave.

It took them a long time to cotton on. Eventually, Dave Mountjoy looked embarrassed. 'Right,' he said. 'Right. We'll leave you to it then.' And he ushered everyone out.

When they'd gone, Mountjoy the elder looked at me balefully. 'What do you want then?' he said, chewing on the stem of his pipe, which, mercifully, had gone out.

'Oh, it's nothing important,' I said and told him the story I'd heard about Daphne and his son and how I understood that he and his wife had adopted the child.

When I'd finished, he looked at me like I was a piece of dog poo on the sole of his shoe.

'Never happened,' he snapped.

'What didn't? I said.

'None of it,' he said. 'None of it.' He paused. 'Well, Joe might have knocked the little bint up, and we might have bunged her a few quid, but we never even saw the little girl. Kid. We certainly didn't adopt the brat. Nah. Never happened. You've been misinformed.' His grip on his stick had tightened, and he looked like he wanted to start wielding it.

'Well, thanks for putting me right,' I said. 'I appreciate that.' And I started to walk towards the door just as he spoke again.

'Life's nothing without a woman,' he said. 'Nothing.'

'Sorry?' I said, turning towards him.

But he was lost in his thoughts, and he clearly hadn't been talking to me.

As I closed the door behind me, I wondered what ancient memories I'd dug up.

I was also as sure as I could be that he'd been lying to me. Just as young Ricky had been when he'd said he was sorry and that our little contretemps was at an end.

I walked slowly back along Grove Green Road in the cool, early morning and turned into the High Road as the first bus busily breezed past, lights blazing. It was empty apart from the driver and conductor. I hummed a few notes of 'St James Infirmary' and then let Louis Armstrong take up the tune, in the concert hall of my mind.

I stood on the corner for a moment before dawdling towards home, thinking of the old boy, pipe clenched fiercely between his teeth. I wondered what ghosts from the past were haunting him, just what had 'never happened'. I glanced at my watch as I passed the imposing red brick and Portland stone of the Victorian town hall. There was something solid and reassuring about it. And I needed reassurance. Twenty to seven on a fine Saturday morning. A fine Saturday morning that could well turn into a very ugly day indeed.

Clearly, something very worrying had happened. Something that involved Ricky Mountjoy. And me. I couldn't think of much that connected us, and I kept coming back to Lee the piano player.

Coronation Gardens wasn't open yet, so I couldn't sit there and contemplate what to do. Not that there was much to contemplate. I could either do nothing and wait to find out what had occurred, or I could ask around. The first course of action (or inaction) was very appealing. As far as I could see, its only drawback was the likelihood that something could come out of nowhere and completely floor me. The second was much less appealing. It would mean that I wouldn't be able to potter about in the garden or watch Orient play that afternoon. The fact that I didn't have a garden and that Orient were playing at Southend did take the edge off that argument, but it might mean that I wouldn't be able to schlep out to Ealing to see Mrs Williams – Ann – that evening, and I really wanted to see her. It might also see me blundering into matters that were nothing to do with me and were way beyond my control.

There seemed only one way forward.

Fortunately, Enzo had opened Costello's Café by the time I reached the corner where Jerry's record shop and home nestled, and the shiny coffee machine that was Enzo's pride and joy (if such a lugubrious person could ever be said to exhibit pride or joy) was hissing like a seriously cheesed-off and deadly snake.

Enzo performed a very impressive double-take when I entered and, a bit too theatrically, I thought, checked his watch three times.

He wiped his hands on a grubby tea-towel and then leaned on the counter. 'So,' he said, 'it must have been some night, you get home this late.'

'Just up a bit earlier than usual, Enzo,' I said. 'How about some coffee and a couple of slices of toast?'

'Sure,' he said. 'When do you ever get up before Sunday on a Saturday?'

I was hurt and would have showed him a very unhappy face if he hadn't turned his back on me to shove a couple of pieces of bread under the grill and align a cup under a steaming nozzle on his gleaming machine.

Since the unhappy face wasn't going to cut any mustard, I felt I had to speak.

'I'm hurt, Enzo,' I said, 'that you should think I slug around in bed all the time.'

'I don't think that,' he said over his shoulder. 'I just think that you keep very strange hours for an accountant.'

'I'm not really an accountant, Enzo,' I said for the umpteenth time.

'Then why you do my books?' he said, turning around and plonking my coffee on the counter.

'I don't do your books, Enzo,' I said. 'I just check your figures.'

'I bring your toast in a minute,' he said.

I shook my head, picked up my coffee and went to find an empty table. That wasn't difficult, as there was no one else in the place. Well, it was ten past seven on a Saturday morning.

The coffee tasted better than usual. Well, maybe it didn't. Perhaps I just needed it more than I did on most mornings.

I couldn't really argue with Enzo about this being a particularly early start to Saturday for me. Basic training, back when I was first called up, had persuaded me that five o'clock reveilles were not events to relish. And, later, when I was in France, working with Ghislaine's husband, Robert, Big Luc and the others, I developed a hearty distaste for sneaking around before dawn. Particularly when it involved wet fields, irritable, raucous crows and armed men. Which it so often did.

Still, it was beginning to look as if I'd been up in time to see the best of the day. After Thursday's drop of dampness, Friday had been very hot, but it had rained overnight and it appeared that the spell of good weather had broken. Some cloud was coming in, and it was a lot cooler.

'Weather's changing,' I said to Enzo when he brought my toast.

He looked forlornly through the window. 'Bloody country,' he said. 'It's going to rain again.'

He was so distraught that I couldn't bring myself to trouble him for another cup of coffee. Instead, I joined him in staring silently out of the window.

As I watched, a beautiful old black Rolls-Royce sailed

around the corner from Lea Bridge Road and shivered to a halt outside Jerry's shop.

Now I knew something really serious was up because Charlie Lomax, Les Jackson's driver, jumped smartly out (well, as smartly as a fifty-two-year-old, slightly overweight ex-boxer could – perhaps 'lumbered smartly out' would be more accurate) and opened the back door and allowed the man himself, Les, to slide off the leather seat and step on to the pavement, straightening his jacket as he did so.

Now Les is not a lazy man, and it is not unknown for him to be up and at his desk by eight o'clock, but he has never paid me a call before half past seven. In fact, I was struggling to remember an occasion when he had paid me a call at any hour of the day.

'Excuse me, Enzo,' I said. 'I'll be back in a minute. With a rich customer for you.'

I walked to the door and called to them. 'Les, Charlie. Over here. I'll buy you a cuppa.'

It was still cool, and it didn't look as if the sun was going to break through the increasing cloud. I found I preferred this to the high seventies of yesterday. My new wool suit felt right for the weather.

Les looked up, saw me and stalked across the road, followed by a serious-looking Charlie.

'No time for that,' Les said. 'Get in the car.' The dark bags under his eyes were a fetching shade of green, and he looked decidedly irritable.

'And good morning to you too, Les,' I said.

'Sorry, sorry,' he said, shaking his head. 'I didn't mean to be rude.'

'That's all right,' I said. 'Have a cup of coffee, calm down and tell me what's up.'

He rubbed his eyes, stroked his chin and sighed. 'Yeah, that's not a bad idea.' He turned to Charlie. 'I don't suppose you had time for any breakfast, did you?'

'No, guv,' Charlie said.

'Let's grab some now, then. While we've got the chance.'

I led the way back into Costello's.

Enzo nearly smiled when Charlie ordered bacon, egg, fried

bread and beans, but normal service was soon restored and he was back to his miserable self as soon as Les just ordered tea.

'So, what's up?'

'Philip Graham is what's up,' he said.

'Disappeared again?' I said.

'No,' he said. 'Holed up in his flat. Won't come out. Sounds shit scared.'

Another one, I thought. 'What's he scared of, Les?' I said.

'Buggered if I know,' he said. 'He wouldn't say. He mentioned you, though. And I thought . . .' He trailed off and looked at me appealingly.

Les at his most appealing is a cross between an old basset hound and the Cheeky Chappie himself, and difficult to resist. He also pays my wages.

'That I might know something, or squeeze something out of him,' I said.

'Perzactly,' he said.

'Well, I don't know anything,' I said, 'and I can but try to find something out. Where's he live?'

'Somewhere in Ladbroke Grove,' he said.

'Really?' I said.

He nodded.

'Les,' I said, 'you really have to start paying your stars properly. Shouldn't he be living in Mayfair?'

'No, he bloody shouldn't,' he snapped. 'He's an oily rag, and I don't like him. The camera does, though. Mind you, it doesn't love him half as much as he loves himself . . .' He trailed off again and sighed. 'I'm getting too old for all this. I'm fed up with it, Tony. The unions, the stars, the distributors, they're all getting me down.'

I took a deep breath. 'You're worried about Daff, Les,' I said. 'That's what's getting you down.'

Enzo brought over tea for Les and Charlie and another coffee for me. Les stirred a spoonful of sugar into his cup and took a sip. I lost count of the number of spoonfuls Charlie put in. He would have saved time by pouring his tea into the sugar bowl.

'I know,' Les finally said, 'and the toothache doesn't help either.' He paused. 'All the same, it's a miserable bloody business at the moment. It's just one damned thing after another. Someone's always trying to stitch me up.'

'Must make a change from you stitching them up,' I said.

'Very funny,' he said and sipped some more tea. 'But, yeah, I do miss having Daff around the place.'

Charlie stared steadfastly into his tea. Clearly, he didn't miss having Daff around. Fortunately, Enzo arrived and slapped a plate of fried food down in front of him and he set to with a will.

'She always kept me on the straight and narrow,' Les said.

I laughed. 'I doubt even Daphne could do that,' I said.

Les gave a phlegmy chuckle. 'I suppose not,' he said. 'But she tried harder than most.' He paused. 'Ah, I wish you'd known her before the war. Handsome woman. Smart, too. Sharp tongue on her, mind.'

'She's not gone yet, Les,' I said. 'You never know.'

'The forecast's not good,' he said. 'Not good at all, Tony. The quack says there's not much hope.' He paused again. 'By the way, what did she want with you?'

'Oh, nothing much,' I said. 'There's just a little family matter on her mind. From way back. Well before she met you.'

He sniffed. 'You going to be able to sort it out for her?'

'I'll do me best, Les,' I said. 'But the mists of time and all that.'

'Mists of time!' he said. 'I think me memory's going. Remembering the past is like trying to look through a pea-souper these days. You know something's out there somewhere, but you're blowed if you can see what it is.'

'Come on, Les, you're not that old,' I said, thinking of old man Mountjoy.

He finished his tea and stood up, looking impatiently at Charlie, who was busily mopping up the last of his egg yolk with a piece of fried bread. There was a little dribble of bean juice on his chin.

'Ready when you are, Mr J,' Charlie said through a mouthful of soggy bread, scraping his chair back across the floor and bending over to swill down the last of his tea.

I left half a cup of coffee. I'd been wrong. It wasn't that good.

Characteristically, Les waved aside my offer to pay and rummaged in his pocket for a few half crowns. Enzo thoughtfully put the cigarette he'd just lit into the scarred ashtray on the counter and, once again, in another rare moment of peace and happiness, came close to smiling.

Les was misinformed. Philip Graham didn't live in Ladbroke Grove at all. His flat was at the top of a big, old house in Bayswater. It was pretty rundown though, and there were a lot of stairs. Les looked like he'd just climbed the north face of the Eiger by the time we stood outside the flimsy-looking blue door. He was huffing and puffing like a pressure cooker about to blow. As he said himself, he was getting on a bit. Still, so was Charlie, and he didn't look too bad. It was all those 'spots of lunch' Les treated himself to and those expensive cigars and cheap women that were slowing him down. Come to think of it, though, I hadn't seen him light a cigar lately, and he hadn't drawn my attention to the charms of his latest secretary for a month or two. Perhaps he really was feeling his age.

He nodded to Charlie, who rapped on the door. The door shivered.

We heard someone shuffling about inside and then a muffled and wary, 'Who is it?'

'It's Mr Jackson, Mr Graham,' Charlie said.

There was a long silence.

'Why don't we just huff and puff and blow the door down?' I said, hoping that Les wouldn't take the comment personally. 'It's what the bad boys would do, if that's who he thinks we are.'

Les shook his head irritably. 'Just open up, Phil,' he said. 'I've brought Tony to see you.'

The door shook a bit more and then swung to and there was Philip Graham.

Unshaven, in grubby vest and pants and with his hair awry and rubbing at sleep-encrusted eyes, he didn't much look like a matinee idol, more like a scrofulous and unpleasant young man, thin, pale and malicious. Which is, I suppose, what I'd always thought he was.

He stepped back and beckoned us inside. Then he looked quickly out on to the landing and firmly pushed the frail door to when we were in. I don't know who he thought that was going to keep from getting at him, if that's what he was afraid of. He was certainly afraid of something.

We stepped straight into the living room. There was the usual stale, young-man smell about the place – feet, sweat, unwashed clothes and bodies – and it was dark and untidy in there.

Home, not-so-sweet home.

It reminded me of the war. And, I was sadly forced to admit, it was just a little bit like my own flat, above the record shop.

'So,' I said, keen not to stay in that fetid atmosphere any longer than was necessary, 'what's up?'

In the half-light and shadows of the room, the venom in the look he flashed me shone brightly. I thought it was uncalled for.

'You telling me you don't know?' he said.

'Er, yes,' I said, 'I'm telling you that I don't know. If I knew, I wouldn't have to ask, would I?'

'Can we have a light on? Or draw the curtains?' Les said. 'This place is like a bloody tomb. And an open window wouldn't hurt. It smells like something died in here, weeks ago.'

Charlie pulled the curtains to one side and forced the sash window up.

The light didn't improve noticeably, but some cool, sooty air sneaked in and disturbed the *ambiance* a little.

I looked out of the window at the higgledy-piggledy rooftops of west London while I waited for Philip Graham to talk. There were a few gaps in the roofline here, but not as many as in the East End. The light was the colour of a dirty net curtain. I thought of the blue sky of Paris and felt a brief but overwhelming spasm of regret. I wasn't sure what for.

I turned away from the gloom of a London morning, back to the gloom of a seedy flat in west London.

Les had lit a cigar. It wasn't quite of Churchillian stature, but it was heading in that direction. Charlie was lighting a Woodbine for Philip Graham. Graham was looking worried and furtive. I glared at him unsympathetically.

'Well?' I said. 'What's the story?'

He drew nervously on the cigarette, then blew smoke out through his nose. 'Last night,' he said and then stopped.

I sighed. 'Yes,' I said, 'last night . . .'

And then it all came out in a breathless rush.

The gist of it was that he'd gone slumming again and had visited the Frighted Horse way after hours. It was the usual lock-in scenario, and he'd met up with Del, one of his 'friends' from Thursday night, and then Ricky and Billy had turned up. Billy had seen Lee ('that piano-playing bloke we had the run-in with'), and Del and Billy had decided on a pre-emptive strike. They were only gone about five minutes and came back, grinning and full of it. Apparently, Lee'd pulled a blade on them, but Billy had wielded his little cosh and they'd given him a bit of a seeing-to and he'd collapsed like a soggy newspaper. They'd left him in a crummy alley round the back of the pub. Then Ricky had handed them some envelopes and sent them off to make their deliveries. And they hadn't come back.

I shrugged. 'So what?' I said. 'They probably went to a club.'

'No,' he said grimly. 'They were supposed to come back. But they couldn't. When Ricky and me went out, we found them. Lying in the alley they'd left your mate, the pianist, in. They'd both been knifed.'

'Dead?' I said.

'Don't know,' he said. 'Ricky and me ran for it. But I suppose so.' He paused. 'They didn't look well.'

Neither did he, but I didn't say anything. As for the other two, I didn't feel anything much tugging at my heart strings. A lot of good, decent young men died in the war. These may well have been stupid, pointless deaths, but, somehow, I couldn't think of Del and Billy – short though my acquaintance with them had been – as good or decent. But I was worried for Lee. Well, if I was honest, I was worried for Miss Summers.

'And you think . . .?' I said.

He looked at me like I was an idiot. 'I think that your mate Lee did for them and you know all about it,' he said.

I shrugged again. 'Why would you think that?' I said as mildly as I could manage.

Judging by the look that crossed his face, either I'd been a lot more aggressive than I'd intended or he really was a shrinking violet.

'He was there,' he said. 'Waving this bloody great knife. Why do you think we ran?'

'Are you sure it was him?' I said. 'They'd dealt with him a couple of times before without much difficulty. What would have been different this time?'

He looked at me warily, not saying anything. The accusation was in the look.

'For the record,' I said, turning to Les and Charlie, 'I wasn't there. And knives are not my style.' But I was thinking back to what Lee had said to me the night before. It had sounded suspiciously like knives might be *his* style.

'No one's accusing you of anything, Tony,' Les said.

'I rather think they are,' I said.

It wasn't just Philip Graham. The Mountjoys obviously thought I was involved too. And they, equally obviously, thought that I was connected, and that a corrective punishment was therefore not advisable. My thoughts strayed to Big Malc and his boss. I wondered who that might be.

'What are you involved in, Philip?' I said.

'Nothing,' he said.

'Oh, come on. Why didn't you call the police?'

'Ricky didn't think it was a good idea,' he said, looking past me.

'And why do you think that was?' I said. 'What do you think was in those envelopes that Ricky Mountjoy was doling out? Fairy dust?'

He blushed and stared down at the floor. He looked like an overgrown schoolboy caught out in a lie.

'What's this, Tony? What are you saying? What's he mixed up in?' Les looked genuinely perplexed and more than a bit angry.

'I didn't know, Mr Jackson.' Young Philip was still staring

guiltily at the floor, and he was mumbling. 'Not really. Ricky had some contacts, but he didn't have any cash. He said he'd double my money in a week. It was a business opportunity.'

'Give me strength,' Les said. 'Tony, can you sort it?'

'It's what you pay me for, Les,' I said. I nodded at Philip Graham. 'He ought to take a holiday. Somewhere bracing, perhaps.'

'He's got a film to finish,' Les said.

'All right. A strict curfew, and put him in a quiet hotel. Get him a minder. Charlie could do it. For a week. I'll see what I can do.'

Charlie didn't look too thrilled, and neither did Philip Graham.

'What?' Philip Graham looked up pugnaciously. 'What's this all about? All you've got to do is warn your mate off and everything's fine.'

We ignored that. Though there was an outside chance he was right.

'Get washed, shaved and dressed,' Les said to him, 'and where's your phone?'

He shook his head. 'There's a phone box on the corner.'

'Charlie,' Les said, 'phone the office. Tell whoever's there to sort out a hotel room for this one.'

'I don't think I can mind him, Mr Jackson,' Charlie said.

'It's all right, Charlie,' Les said, 'he won't need minding.'

Charlie nodded and left.

Philip Graham slouched off to his bedroom and Les wearily rubbed at his eyes.

'What is with youngsters these days, Tony?' He shook his head sadly. 'Remember the cosh boys a few years back? In the big smog?'

I remembered a cosh boy from a few hours back. The bump on my head throbbed at the memory. 'Wasn't that a newspaper thing, Les?' I said. 'I didn't bump into any.'

He shook his head again. 'Nor did I, but there were a lot of reports, Tony. And now there are all these Teddy boys.'

'I'm sure I'd have been in just as much trouble. If I hadn't had a war to fight.'

'That's the thing. We had a war to fight. Put 'em in the army, I say.'

'We do, Les,' I said. I left it at that. Reminding him that he hadn't actually done any fighting seemed a little harsh.

He stared moodily out of the window, chewing listlessly on his cigar, listening to the muffled sounds of Philip Graham splashing water about and rummaging in drawers for clothes. Graham coughed a lot for a young man.

Les had a lot on his mind, and most of it had nothing to do with his young star. He would be content if I could keep Philip Graham and Hoxton Films out of the papers. That could probably be managed if the little toerag stayed out of harm's way. And if the old bill didn't sniff him out and decide to feel his collar. But I couldn't see Ricky grassing him up. Unless he used him as an alibi. Of course, a lot was hanging on whether Graham had told me the truth about what had happened. I supposed that he might have done.

As we waited for the young heart-throb to emerge, I found myself remembering something someone had once said: 'No, no, no: game is hung; men are hanged.'

EIGHT

I t was close to ten when Charlie stopped the Rolls in Frith Street. I nodded to Les and told him I'd be in touch, and then I thanked Charlie for the ride and slid along the seat and stepped out into a cool, overcast September morning in a seedy and hung-over Soho. I didn't have anything to say to a sheepish Philip Graham.

I waited until the big car had swished away before looking for another cup of coffee. I didn't want Les thinking that I was swinging the lead.

As it chanced, Charlie had dropped me outside the Moka.

The dumpy, middle-aged waitress looked up, reluctantly abandoned her cigarette and the *Daily Mirror* she was flicking her way through, and clumped over to me. She had a number of things in common with Enzo: a nationality, a similarly gracious manner and a shiny, gurgling coffee machine. The Moka claimed that their machine was the first in the country, and they had certainly flown Gina Lollobrigida in to declare it open a few years before. They probably had a photograph of the momentous event on the wall somewhere, but I couldn't see it.

Enzo didn't openly dispute anything, just sniffed dismissively if anyone mentioned the Moka in his presence.

The coffee was better than Enzo's, and I sipped it gratefully. A late night and a very early morning awakening had left me feeling decidedly dozy. I yawned mightily.

'Someone needs his beauty sleep,' a soft, low voice I recognized whispered out of the deep shadows at the back of the coffee bar.

I stood up. 'It's a while since beauty sleep could do anything for me, Miss Summers,' I said.

'Join me? Please,' she said. 'And it's Jeannie.' She looked at me thoughtfully as I sat down opposite her. 'I don't think that's true,' she said and smiled a little enigmatically. 'Everyone needs their beauty sleep.' She paused, and her lips quivered into that little smile again. 'Though you probably need it less than most.'

'Because it can't do anything for me?' I said.

She shook her head. 'No, that's not what I meant.'

I wasn't sure if she was teasing me or not. She certainly wasn't flirting with me.

She looked tired, which probably explained her concerns about beauty sleep and her decision to sit away from the light – such as it was – of the windows.

I sipped some coffee. 'Where's Lee?' I said.

The large, black handbag lay on the bench next to her, and she reached down and fussed with it, eventually taking out a cigarette case and a box of matches. She lit a cigarette and puffed on it, then carefully put everything back in the bag and replaced the bag. Then she looked at me bleakly.

'I wish I knew,' she said. 'But I don't.' She put the cigarette into the ashtray and watched it smoulder away. She really wasn't a smoker. 'He's been even more unpredictable ever since we got to London. He told me he was just going out for a breath of air after that fiasco of a set. He knew we hadn't been good, and he didn't want to talk about it.' She looked at the thin, greyish smoke curling up from the cigarette towards the ceiling. 'So I waited for him. I slept in the dressing room. But he didn't come back.' She sat up straight and looked at me fiercely. 'I'm really worried about him.' She paused before adding, 'Tony.'

'Did he say anything, before he went out?' I said.

She gave a little shake of her head. Her hair waved gently in a faint echo of the gesture. It wasn't firmly lacquered in place. 'Just that he needed a breath of air.'

'Did he pick anything up to take with him? I said.

'Like what?' she said.

I shook my head. 'I don't know,' I said airily. 'Just anything.'

She looked at me suspiciously. 'Do you know something?' she said.

I didn't want to lie to her, but I didn't want to tell her what I knew either, so I shrugged and shook my head in a dismissive, non-committal sort of way. 'He may be back at your digs,' I said. 'Perhaps you should go back and wait there.'

'We're supposed to be going to Glasgow tomorrow,' she said and laughed. 'He pronounces it to rhyme with glass cow. It always makes me laugh.'

She picked the cigarette up from the ashtray. It was half burnt down, and a long line of ash drooped from its end and fell on to the table. She angrily mashed the cigarette out and swept the ash to the floor. Then she looked directly at me again, and I saw tears in her eyes.

'I'm lost without him,' she said.

'I could get you a cab,' I said, 'to take you back to your digs. And I could ask around . . . I can't promise anything . . .'

She fumbled in her bag again, and this time she took out a little handkerchief. She dabbed at her eyes. 'I'll take you up on the cab,' she said, 'but I can't possibly ask you to spend your Saturday chasing after Lee.'

'It's not a problem,' I said. 'I've things to do around here anyway.'

She reached across the table and put her hand on mine. 'That's very kind of you,' she said. Again there was a little pause before she added, 'Tony.'

After settling Jeannie Summers in a taxi and sending it on its rumbling way to her digs, I strolled past Pete's Place. Well, I walked past the Acropolis restaurant and peered down the greasy steps at the dark and decidedly smelly basement that housed the club.

A louche figure in a crumpled brown suit was hunched over a cigarette at the foot of the steps. He looked up at me, took one last drag on the fag cupped in his hand and then tossed it aside. It glowed weakly on the gloomy paving stones for a few seconds.

Peter Baxter's tired face was nearly as crumpled as his suit. He nodded at me and wearily climbed the steps.

'You don't look like you got to bed,' I said.

'Just thinking about it,' he said. 'I'll manage a few hours before tonight's show.' He paused. 'Have to find a replacement act first though. That junkie piano player is a liability.

But she won't perform without him. And he's disappeared again.'

I nodded but said nothing.

'Still, there's always someone who needs a spot. Not that they're anywhere near as good as her . . .'

I nodded again.

'She's pissing her career away on that no-hoper,' he said.

I shrugged. 'She loves him, I suppose,' I said.

'Love, schmove,' he said and took a step back down before turning to me again. 'By the way, watch yourself round the corner. There's a swarm of rozzers about. Something's up, but I don't know what.'

'Thanks,' I said, 'I'll avoid them, if I can.'

He nodded and trod carefully down the steps.

He was right. The police were out in force by the Frighted Horse. Most of them were just standing around, stopping honest citizens like myself from going about their business, but three or four in plain clothes were rummaging around in an alleyway thirty yards or so from the pub. I recognized one of them, and unfortunately, before I could turn and bolt, he recognized me.

Inspector Rose was wearing a very becoming lime-green bow-tie that went well with his brown Harris Tweed jacket, natty brown trilby and fawn twill trousers. He was, in short, as dapper as ever. He clutched the bowl of his old pipe in his right hand. He pointed at me with the chewed stem. 'Tony,' he said, strolling over to me, past the uniforms, 'fancy seeing you here.'

'Just passing, Inspector,' I said.

'Really?' he said.

'Really,' I said.

'So you can't tell me anything about what happened here last night, then?' he said.

Rather than openly lie, I just shook my head.

'Come on, Tony,' he said, 'let's have a cup of tea and you can tell me all you know.' He put a hand on my shoulder and steered me back towards Frith Street. 'You do have an uncanny knack for turning up at murder scenes, don't you?'

'Only after the event,' I said. 'Well, usually.'

He laughed. 'And before. Sometimes. Like last night,' he said.

I wondered who had been talking. The barman in the Frighted Horse. It had to be. Oh, well, I'd better come clean. Well, cleanish. 'It's a fair cop, Inspector,' I said. 'I'll come quietly.'

He laughed again. 'I've always wanted to hear some villain say that,' he said.

And I've always wanted to say it. I can just see the look on the judge's face when the copper reads from his notes. But I didn't mention that to the good inspector. I probably didn't have to. He's a clever man. And he wasn't taking any notes.

'Let's skip the tea,' he said, stopping. 'I'm quite busy at the moment. I'm looking at a double murder here. I'm sure you're only peripherally involved. So just tell me what you know. I should tell you that I know you had a vigorous discussion with a young lad in the pub and it appears that two of his mates then ended up skewered. What do you know about it?'

I took a deep breath. 'That's true,' I said. 'I went to the Frighted Horse looking for someone. Someone coshed me for some reason, and when I came to I was threatened with a razor. I took exception and, as you say, responded vigorously. Then I left and the person I was looking for turned up where he should have been and I went home.'

The inspector started fussing with his pipe, stuffing the bowl with long, golden-brown strands of tobacco in it from a leather pouch and tamping it down with his finger. 'Who were you looking for?' he said.

'A piano player called Lee,' I said.

'And why were you looking for him in the Frighted Horse?' the inspector said amiably.

'Come on, Inspector,' I said. 'You know as well as I do.' I paused. 'He's a jazz player.'

'So?' he said.

He filled the silence by lighting his pipe and puffing on it contentedly.

'And that's all you know?' he said.

I nodded.

'Fine, Tony, fine,' he said. 'And you can still be contacted at the same address in . . . Leyton, was it?'

I nodded again.

'Only, there are developments on the other thing. The other double murder you were, shall we say, less peripherally involved with. I'll need to be in touch.'

'That's good,' I said.

'Is it, Tony? Is it really?' he said.

'Must be, if you're about to solve it,' I said.

He looked at me benignly and puffed on his pipe again. He was bluffing. He was nowhere near solving that one.

He nodded to me and walked a few steps back the way we had come; then he stopped and turned towards me. 'By the way, Tony,' he said, 'did you enjoy your little holiday? Gay Paree, wasn't it?'

'That's right,' I said. 'I visited a few old friends. From the war.' How did he know about that?

'That must have cost a few bob,' he said. 'Come into some money, have you?'

'It's not that expensive,' I said defensively. 'Half a crown goes a long way in France.'

He looked thoughtful. 'Never fancied it much myself,' he said. 'Abroad.'

'Well,' I said, 'each to his own.'

He nodded. 'As you say, each to his own. I'll stick to the allotment, I think. Maybe a trip to Chalkwell with the missus.' And, apparently lost in thoughts of prize runner beans and the delights of the stony beach at Chalkwell, he wandered off.

I wondered what he did know. Probably a great deal less than he hinted at. But what he suspected was another matter altogether.

Obviously, the Frighted Horse was out of bounds, so I ambled aimlessly towards Soho Square.

It was cool and cloudy, in contrast to the last few weeks, but pleasant enough, and I stood for a moment on the corner, lost in my own thoughts. They didn't include any green veg or deck chairs and rolled-up trousers.

'Penny for 'em,' someone behind me said.

I sighed. 'I thought this only happened in Trafalgar Square,' I said.

'What?' Big Malcolm looked genuinely confused.

'Never mind,' I said. 'It's just that this morning I seem to have run into everyone I've ever met.'

'Well,' he said, 'I was just going to give you a friendly warning.'

I waited.

'Your mate,' he said, 'the Yank. He's in a spot of bother.'

I laughed. 'You could say that,' I said.

'No,' he said. 'Really. You could do worse than have a spot to eat in the Acropolis at dinner time. There'll be someone there who wouldn't mind a word.'

'And if I'm not hungry?' I said.

'I were you, I'd be there,' he said, and he patted me on the shoulder hard enough to hammer me three inches into the pavement.

I stood there for a few more minutes, thinking about my mother and wondering if she'd ever been just here in the sleazy centre of the great city she'd been brought to as a young bride. I'd never know.

The one thing I did know was that she would have disapproved. And that I would have been a disappointment to her. Shabby suit, badly shaved, hatless in Soho, mixed up in things and events that brought me to the attention of policemen . . .

I remembered that Papa used to take her up West sometimes, to see a show when one of the French stars came to the Palladium or the Hippodrome, which wasn't often. And then she'd fuss with his tie and fuss with his hat and fuss with his suit, and Grand-père would tease her: 'Mireille, he's in the audience, not on stage.' And she would look hurt and ask what was wrong with being smart. She didn't come from the bourgeoisie, but she had standards and aspirations, and here was I leading what she would have thought of as '*la vie bohème*'. No, she wouldn't have approved.

In the Antelope once, Mickey Morgan had not been in his accustomed place by the dartboard but had been sitting at the bar, looking thoughtful and uncharacteristically morose. 'You

know, Tony,' he said, 'that war cost me the best years of my
wife.'

I sympathized, but at least he'd had a wife to come back
to, and, as far as I knew, she hadn't been playing around with
Eytie prisoners of war or rampant GIs. Coming home had
been hard for everyone. Even Mickey Morgan. I was nothing
special.

I tried to shrug off *le cafard*, but the music that played in
my head as I strolled slowly around Soho Square was a sombre,
sedate New Orleans funeral march I'd once heard, and,
although the music was full of a subdued exuberance, it still
filled me with a profound melancholy.

But, funnily enough, I was no longer thinking of Maman,
Papa and Grand-père. I thought of Daphne. Losing a child
must be the hardest thing to bear.

The Acropolis restaurant was a gloomy place. Even in the middle
of the day, very little light from outside penetrated the large,
grimy, greasy window because of the faded blue-and-white
awning, the function of which in Greece, presumably, was to
protect the three outside tables from the strength of the
Mediterranean sun. Quite what it was doing on a murky
September day in London is anyone's guess. Inside, the only
illumination came from candles flickering on two tables at the
back of the long, thin room.

I waited for a moment next to the door, partly for my eyes
to adjust to the darkness and partly to see if anyone acknowl-
edged my presence.

No one did.

The only other person in there seemed unaware of me. He
sat at one of the only tables with a lit candle, a creamy *serviette de table*, as my mother would have called it, tucked neatly
into his collar and splashed across his dark jacket. He was
sawing away valiantly at a large slab of meat, pausing occasionally to sip white wine from a small glass. During one of
these pauses, he finally noticed me, put down his fork and
glass and beckoned me to him.

He indicated the chair opposite him, and I sat. Almost
immediately, a white-jacketed waiter bustled through the door

from the kitchen and set a place for me, complete with glass and my very own beautiful *serviette de table*. While he quietly fussed around, I looked at my new-found companion.

He wasn't much older than me, maybe thirty-five or thirty-six, but he was clearly much more prosperous. His chubby, boyish face and the large corporation that he was carrying around his middle suggested a sedentary life and a willingness to indulge his appetites. His mean little eyes suggested that he didn't indulge anyone else's. Oddly, his suit, though much better cut than mine, was worn, shiny and shabby. I suspected that this was because such things didn't bother him too much. Petty vanity was obviously beneath him. Even in the poor light in the restaurant, I could see an unhealthy sheen on his face, as though the act of cutting into his meat and then consuming it was physical activity enough to raise a sweat.

He dismissed the waiter with an airy wave of his small, plump hand. 'I've taken the liberty of ordering for you, Mr Gérard,' he said, beaming at me. 'I hope you don't mind.' His cultured, public-school pronunciation surprised me. I'd been expecting a thick European accent. 'Can I offer you a glass of Retsina?'

He lifted an almost empty green bottle and waved it at me.

I nodded, and he poured a dribble of yellowish wine into my glass before replenishing his own rather more liberally.

He beamed at me again. It wasn't a completely reassuring sight. His little eyes almost disappeared completely, and there was a flash of stained, crooked teeth. He raised his glass to me. I picked mine up, and he clinked his against it before taking a great swallow of wine. I sipped a little. The taste surprised me.

He laughed. 'It takes a little getting used to,' he said. 'It's resinated, and, to be honest, that means it doesn't travel well, but it is the perfect accompaniment to Greek food. It cuts right through the grease.' He chuckled as though he'd just cracked a great gag. And, when I thought about it, I supposed there was a pun or something in there somewhere.

I offered him an appropriately weak smile and took another sip of wine. I tried not to shudder. He was wrong. It was going to take a lot of getting used to.

He leaned back on his chair, drank deeply again and contemplated me thoughtfully. 'Mr Gérard,' he said, 'may I call you Tony?'

'If you like,' I said, 'but what do I call you?'

'Forgive me, Tony,' he said. 'James. James Fitzgerald. No relation, alas, to the famous American writer.'

'I'm pleased to meet you, Mr Fitzgerald,' I said, although I wasn't being entirely honest. I made a mental note to ask Jerry about American writers called Fitzgerald.

'James, please. I'm sure we are going to become firm friends.'

I nodded slightly and tightened my lips into a thin smile. I was sure of no such thing. 'James,' I said.

'You know,' he said, waving his hand around expansively, 'I got a taste for all this during the war.' He paused and leaned forward conspiratorially. 'I was in Crete. SOE and all that. Just like you, I believe.' He tapped the side of his nose. 'Not supposed to talk about it and so on, but it was all a long time ago now. No harm, eh?'

I shrugged in a non-committal sort of way. I was wondering how he'd come by his knowledge of my background.

The waiter bustled out of the kitchen carrying some small dishes, which he set down on the table.

'Aristotle,' Fitzgerald said, 'would you be kind enough to bring another bottle?'

The waiter nodded deferentially, whisked the empty bottle from the table and slipped away.

'His name really is Aristotle, you know. The Greeks still have a sense of their ancient culture, however far removed from it they are these days.' He leaned across the table and pointed to some pink sludge. 'That's one of their specialities. Cod's roe, olive oil and lemon juice. Delicious.' He pointed at another dish of dark mush swimming in oil. 'Aubergine dip,' he said and almost smacked his lips. 'In fact, I'll join you if you don't mind.' He took a piece of bread from a basket, tore off a piece and dipped it in the dark mush.

I watched him suspiciously as he ate. Then, very tentatively, I picked up a small piece of the bread, brushed it against the dip and brought it to my lips. This time he was right. It *was*

delicious. I found myself wondering what sort of beast aubergine was and why I'd never come across it before. I risked a
small sip of wine to wash the bread down and had to repress
another shudder.

Fitzgerald smacked his lips and sank back against his chair
again.

Aristotle swept in with another bottle, which he opened. He
poured a glass for Fitzgerald, who nodded at him. Aristotle
vanished again.

'Enjoy,' Fitzgerald said, lifting his glass. 'I'll talk for a
while. You just have to listen.'

I dipped some bread enthusiastically into the pink sludge
and munched on it while I waited for him to talk.

'I'm a businessman,' he said. '"In trade", as my sainted
mama puts it.' He chuckled. 'She's not that proud of me.
Wanted me to go into the City, like my big brother. Imagine!
I've told her that the Square Mile is home to the biggest crooks
in the country, but she won't have it. Anyway, I import goods,
I export goods, and I distribute the goods I import through
my, er, agents here.' He finished his wine and refilled his glass.
'You have come across some of my agents recently.'

I looked up, but I didn't need to ask.

'A few of my Young Turks,' he said. 'In fact, "come across"
hardly comes close to what happened. There was what we
used to call at school "a rumble", I understand.'

'Not of my making,' I said.

'Of course,' he said, 'that goes without saying. Some of my
younger employees can be very hot-headed. Impulsive. The
indiscretions of youth, eh?' He put down his glass, leaned
forward, placed his hands together as though praying and
adopted a decidedly ecclesiastical manner. 'I understand that
matters went beyond a mere rumble, though, and that is a very
serious matter.'

'I'm afraid,' I said, 'that I can't help you there. I know very
little about what happened after I came across your, er, "agents"
in the Frighted Horse.'

'That's most unfortunate,' he said. 'I was hoping for some
cooperation. A little assistance. You see, some important items
went missing after the "events", and they have caused me

some financial loss.' He paused. 'I understood that you might, at least, know the whereabouts of the missing items, or the whereabouts of the person who has occasioned me that loss. I would be most grateful for any information. Naturally, I am also very keen to see the full force of the law take its course, but I would like my goods returned to me first.' He paused again and gave me a long, hard look through his mean eyes. 'I hope you understand me.'

'I understand you perfectly,' I said. 'But, as I've already said, I'm unable to help.'

'That's a great pity, Tony,' he said, 'a great pity. But thank you for stopping by.'

I realized that I'd just been dismissed, dabbed my lips with the fine *serviette de table*, pushed back my chair, nodded at him and walked towards the door. Before I reached it, Aristotle, the waiter, came bustling up and presented me with a bill. It seemed that I was liable for James Fitzgerald's meal as well as for what little I'd eaten.

Aristotle looked so nervous and embarrassed, continually glancing to the back of the restaurant where the fat toad sat, that, rather than add to his obvious discomfort, I carefully counted out the money and added a modest *pourboire*. I had no beef with the sad-looking and anxious waiter.

I glanced back at the table and saw James Fitzgerald still sitting in the gloom, still drinking his – well, mine really – filthy wine, dipping bread into the exotic dips. He was staring straight through me. I realized that there was something I needed to ask him about and walked slowly back. When I was standing just in front of him, casting a slight shadow over him, he deigned to look up.

'I think you'll find, Tony,' he said, 'that our business is concluded for the day.' There was no threat in his voice or any more meanness than usual in his eyes.

'There's just one thing,' I said. 'I was wondering what Philip Graham has invested in.'

'Philip Graham?' he said.

I nodded.

'Never heard of him,' he said and turned his attention back to the dips and his glass of wine.

Clearly, information was a commodity, like everything else, to be bought and sold.

I turned and left. I haven't met many public-school boys. There had been a few officers in the army, though, and, for the most part, they could have come from a different planet to me and the other enlisted men. James Fitzgerald inhabited a world much closer to mine, but he had done nothing to improve my general view of posh boys who oozed privilege, a sense of entitlement and a complete indifference to other people's well-being. In my experience, blokes like that get you shot at.

Malcolm Booth was hunched over one of the tables outside the Acropolis, smoking. The cigarette was cupped in his hand, giving the distinct impression that he was engaged in something furtive. He lumbered to his feet when I emerged.

'Seeing me off the premises?' I said.

He gave a phlegmy chuckle. 'Something like that,' he said.

We both stared at Frith Street and the waifs and strays who hurried past. Most of the lean men with hollow cheeks were looking to cadge a few drinks before closing time. What the few worn-looking women were doing was a mystery. Maybe the same thing.

'Listen,' Malcolm said, 'I don't know about you, but I'm not much of a one for this foreign muck. Fancy some fish and chips? There's a very decent chippie just off Leicester Square.'

'Is there?' I said. 'I didn't know that.'

'It's tucked away.' He patted me on the shoulder and smiled knowingly. 'Come on. I'm buying.'

How could I resist? After all, someone owed me a bite to eat.

As we walked away from the restaurant, I glanced back and saw three big, well-dressed black men pause outside and light cigarettes.

We mooched around the shabby little garden in the centre of Leicester Square silently eating our cod and chips, not quite oblivious to either the pinched-faced people in their Sunday clothes loudly making the most of their afternoon off or the bright lights of the giant picture houses. Sunday clothes on a

Saturday afternoon? Maman would not have approved. The, according to Les, quite risqué film *The Seven Year Itch* with Marilyn Monroe was playing. I thought I'd wait for it to come to the Gaumont. Though I supposed I might have to take the bus up Lea Bridge Road to the Bakers' Alms to the Ritz or the Plaza.

In fact, we were not entirely silent – Malcolm chomped quite noisily on his crisp wally – but we didn't speak. Malcolm was right. It was a good chippie. I couldn't believe that I hadn't come across it before.

Malcolm smacked his lips when he finished and then licked some of the grease off his fingers, balled up the newspaper wrapping and dropped it by a sad stunted bush, on the bare earth, among a group of mean-eyed and ill-favoured pigeons. I rather pointedly sought out one of the rubbish bins so thoughtfully provided by the municipal authorities. Sometimes there's something of my severe, rather proper mother about me. The bin was, of course, full to overflowing.

'Well?' I said.

'Good fish and chips, yeah?' he said, running his tongue around his back teeth.

'Yeah,' I said, 'thanks.'

He was a big man, but his dark-brown suit hung well on him, and his shoes were nicely polished, his brown trilby recently brushed.

'Listen,' he said, 'I hope you didn't get the wrong idea last night.'

'Sorry,' I said, 'I'm not sure I know what you're talking about.'

'Last night,' he said, 'when I said I'd like to shake you by the hand for thumping Ricky.'

'Oh,' I said. 'How could I have got the wrong idea?'

He shrugged and scuffed the ground with one of his expensive shoes. 'I don't know,' he said. 'You might have thought I didn't like young Ricky.'

'Well, I didn't get the impression that you were best mates,' I said.

He looked at his watch. 'I could murder a pint,' he said. 'We've got time. What about it?'

'All right,' I said, 'but I don't really like beer.'

He looked worried. 'Well, if you don't want a drink, you can always have lemonade or something.'

'I said I didn't like beer,' I said. 'I didn't say I didn't like a drink.' After the horrible Greek wine that Fitzgerald had forced on me, I needed something. 'Come on, I know somewhere.' And I led the way out of the scruffy little park, past the foul-smelling toilets, to the French.

As always, there was a thin crowd at dinner time on a Saturday, and we had half an hour to closing so there was plenty of time for a couple of drinks. Which was just as well, as the bottle of dark beer I bought for Malcolm went down in one great glug. The 'decent little Burgundy' recommended by Gaston turned out to be rather better than decent, and it completely washed away the unpleasant memory of the wine at the Acropolis. I sipped at it and looked around the little bar while Malcolm went back to the counter 'for the other half'. Gaston, his big soup-strainer moustache suggesting that he was more French than was really the case, efficiently poured him another glass. Malcolm brought me another glass as well which was very decent of him.

'So,' I said, 'what's on your mind?'

He leaned in closer, conspiratorially. 'What you have to understand,' he said, 'is that I've been with Mr Fitz for a long time now. I've worked hard to get where I've got.' He looked around to make sure that no one was listening. 'And so it's only natural that I'm worried about where I stand when he brings in the youngsters. Isn't it?'

I shrugged. I really didn't know.

'The thing is, though, I wouldn't want Mr Fitz hearing that I'm cheesed off or anything.'

'Your name didn't come up, Malcolm,' I said.

'Well, you know, what with what occurred,' he said, 'I wouldn't want any suspicions being raised.'

'Of course not,' I said.

'The thing is,' he said, 'Mr Fitz, he has an odd way of running things. He likes to keep us all on our toes, you know. So, every so often, he brings new people in.'

I nodded. Les had explained something similar to me. He

called it the 'cats in a bag' approach. When things in the
sack quieten down, you open it up, chuck another cat in and
see what happens. 'Supposed to stop the hired help becoming
complacent,' Les had said. He didn't approve. 'Life's aggra-
vating enough as it is,' he'd explained, which seemed true
to me.

I sipped some wine and looked around the little bar. It was
emptying rapidly, and, Gaston and Malcolm apart, there wasn't
a soul in there who I knew.

Malcolm glugged down his second beer and wiped his mouth
with the back of his hand. He pulled a pack of Woodbines
and a box of matches out of his suit pocket and lit up.

'So,' I said, 'what's going to happen now? To the distribution network that Mr Fitzgerald's Young Turks ran.'

Malcolm took the cigarette out of his mouth, still cupped
inside his big hand, and shook his head.

'I don't know,' he said. 'Ricky's still running things, I guess.'

I nodded, but I didn't see Ricky running anything, except
scared, for a week or two.

'Do you know what happened last night?' I said.

'No,' he said. 'Course not.'

He looked at me so honestly and frankly that I couldn't
quite bring myself to believe him. I wasn't entirely sure that
I liked Malcolm Booth. I certainly didn't like the man he
worked for, and I knew I wouldn't like what he did for a
living.

'The piano player,' I said, 'the Yank. Where did you find
him?'

He took a long drag from his cigarette and looked at me
through eyes half closed against the rising smoke.

'We was on our rounds,' he said, 'collecting the rent, you
know, from the girls. One of them asked us to help her with
him. She'd dumped him on her sofa the night before.'

I raised my eyebrows, and he shrugged.

'Feeling sorry for him, I guess,' he said. 'She's always been
a soft touch, Viv.'

I sipped at my second glass of wine. 'Where's her gaff?' I
said.

'Just round the corner. Why?'

'I thought I'd have a word with her. She might know where he went when he left the club last night.'

'Doubt it,' he said. 'She's a working girl. In any case, we know where he went, don't we?'

'Maybe,' I said. 'All the same, I wouldn't mind a little chat with her.'

He picked up his glass, drained it, put it back on the counter, sucked cigarette smoke deep into his lungs and sighed. 'Sure, I can take you there, if you like.'

'Thanks,' I said. 'I appreciate it.'

I sipped some more wine and watched Gaston busy himself behind the bar as closing time approached. The pot boy shuffled over and collected our empties. There was none of the 'time, gennulmen, please' nonsense from Gaston.

The photograph of a rugged, handsome Robert Rieux in his black beret and bulky leather jacket in a field in Normandy, brandishing a captured German Luger, was lost in shadow to the right of the bar. But I knew that I was still there, in the background, looking impossibly young and callow, with Big Luc towering over me and the Blier brother who was picked up in Caen a few days later standing to my right, looking like an overgrown schoolboy playing soldiers.

I sipped some more wine, the words from the original French version of 'Autumn Leaves', the ones about life gently separating those who love without making a noise, whispering in my head, and I thought of Paris in the summer: clear, blue skies, warm sunshine, the smell of drains and strong cigarettes, crusty bread and café crème. And I wondered if Ghislaine had, as she'd said in her letter, gone back to Robert.

She probably had.

Then I wondered if I really cared.

I probably did.

NINE

Malcolm Booth and I ambled out of the French, looking for all the world like we were bosom friends, and strolled along Old Compton Street for a little while. He stopped outside a seedy bookshop that probably stocked the sort of title that Foyle's didn't, and he nodded towards a beaten-up old black door suffering from what looked like an advanced case of eczema.

'Top floor,' he said. 'Don't bother to ring. The door's always open.'

Sure enough, pinned to the panel above the little buttons for the bells was a handwritten card. 'Artist's model, top floor.'

I nodded to Malcolm. 'What's her name?' I said.

'Viv,' he said.

'Viv what?' I said.

He looked puzzled.

'I don't know. Viv.' He snapped his fingers and nodded vigorously. 'Laurence. That's it. With a "u".'

'Thanks,' I said. 'For the fish and chips as well.'

'You're welcome,' he said. 'And thanks for keeping me straight with the gaffer.' He paused and looked uneasy. 'I'll leave you to it then. I've got to get back to Mr Fitz. He'll be wondering where I am as it is.' He raised his eyes to the top floor. 'You'll be all right?'

'I'll be fine,' I said.

He nodded thoughtfully and looked down at the pavement. 'Be seeing you then,' he said but didn't move.

'Yeah,' I said, 'be seeing you.'

'Do you think she knows something?' he said.

'No idea,' I said. 'And I won't until I speak to her.'

'Of course,' he said, 'of course. Well, I won't keep you. If she does know something, I'd appreciate you getting in touch. Just leave word at the Acropolis. They'll know where I am.'

'Right,' I said and stepped to the door, aware that Malcolm Booth was still standing there, still watching me.

I pushed with a fingertip, and little flecks of black paint, like tiny, sooty snowflakes, drifted slowly to the ground as the door swung open. I turned to Malcolm and held up my hand in final farewell, hoping that he'd take the hint, and then I walked into the narrow, dingy hallway, sidling past the two solid bicycles leaning against the right-hand wall without barking a shin, and reached the staircase.

The stairs must once have had a carpet because the central eighteen inches of each was paler than the outer six inches or so, but it had long since been ripped up and thrown away. Still, that was probably for the best as, although the place didn't exactly smell sweet, at least it didn't fill the nose with the fragrance of rotting Axminster, and the steep steps may have creaked alarmingly but there was no treacherous frayed fabric to catch at the heels and trip you up.

It was quite a climb to the top, but I eventually arrived at the final landing. I had a choice of two doors, but one was open and showed a stained WC and a sink so I opted for the other one and knocked. It was a flimsy affair with just a plywood face which gave alarmingly when I rapped on it. Nothing happened, and I knocked again.

I was about to give the door some more grief when I heard sounds of movement inside and then a pleasant, sleepy voice that I assumed belonged to Viv.

'All right, all right, keep your hair on. I'm coming.'

The door opened, Viv peered around it and I was assailed by masses of brown, curly hair, about a gallon of cheap scent and a cleavage that Jane Russell would have been proud of.

'I'm not open for business yet, dear,' she said. 'You'll have to come back later.'

'I'm not here for business,' I said.

'Doesn't matter what you call it, dear – business or pleasure – I'm still not open for it.'

I laughed, and she chuckled.

'You must be Miss Laurence,' I said.

She nodded, and then looked at me suspiciously. 'You a

copper?' she said. 'Only, I heard about them boys last night, but I don't know nothing.'

'No,' I said, 'I'm not a copper.' I reached into my wallet and took out one of the posh cards that Hoxton Films had supplied me with and handed it to her. 'That's me,' I said. 'Tony Gérard.'

She held the card delicately between her forefinger and her thumb, narrowed her eyes and peered at it myopically.

I took the opportunity to peer at her.

She was still quite pretty in a tired, worn sort of way, with a longish nose, neat little mouth and a pointed chin, and she could have been anything from twenty-five to thirty-five, but I settled on late twenties.

She looked up from the card and frowned at me. 'Films?' she said.

'Yes,' I said, 'I work for a film company but—'

'No.' She shook her head violently, and her hair flew about and the impressive bosom heaved. 'I don't do stags.'

I held up my hands to calm her down. 'No.' I said, 'I'm not here for anything to do with the company. It's a private matter. You helped out an acquaintance of mine the other night.'

She looked at me suspiciously. 'Yes, dear, that sounds like me. Heart of gold. The original tart with a heart.' She paused and chuckled again. 'Well, not the original. That would have been that Nancy in *Oliver Twist*, wouldn't it?'

'I wouldn't know,' I said. 'I haven't studied the matter.'

She sighed. 'I have,' she said sadly. 'So, what do you want?'

'Like I said. I wanted to say thanks for what you did for Lee, the American bloke you brought here the other night.'

'Oh, him. Poor lamb.' She shook her head dismissively. 'Anyone would have done it. He was helpless, and those horrible little oiks were just taking advantage.' She paused. 'I don't like to see anyone being bullied. And that Ricky . . . I really don't like him. Just seeing him gives me the willies.' She paused again, looking thoughtful, then she shook her impressive tresses and laughed. 'I gave them a right mouthful, I can tell you, sent them off with a flea in their ear. Couldn't leave him there, could I? They'd be back and start again. So I brought him here.'

'I don't know that anyone would have done it,' I said. 'And Lee is really very grateful.'

'I know,' she said. 'He came back last night to tell me.'

'Did he?' I said. 'Is he still here?'

She avoided my eyes and looked down at the worn wooden boards. 'No, he left a couple of hours ago,' she said.

'Pity,' I said. 'You don't know where he went, I suppose. People are keen to find him.'

She shook her head. 'He didn't say where he was going,' she said.

We stood on that cramped, dark landing in silence for a few seconds. Viv Laurence stared at the floor. I stared at a patch of damp on the discoloured ceiling by the bare light-bulb.

'Are you really his friend?' she said very quietly.

'No, I'm just an acquaintance, like I said. But people who are his friends have asked me to find him.'

She looked at the card that was still in her hand. 'Is there really a film studio in Leyton?' she said.

'No, that's just where I live,' I said. 'There used to be one in Walthamstow, though. My grandfather worked there.'

'I didn't know that,' she said.

We stood in another awkward silence. My mother wouldn't have approved of her, but Viv Laurence seemed to me to be a fundamentally decent sort. I found that I wanted her to like and trust me.

'I'm really sorry to have bothered you,' I said. 'If you do hear from Lee or see him, perhaps you could call the number on the card. There are people who are very worried about him.' I don't know why, but I decided not to mention that one of them was his wife.

She tapped the card against the door jamb. 'I'm sure he'll turn up,' she said. 'He's like a bad penny, that one.'

I smiled at her as reassuringly as I could and turned to go.

'Wait a minute,' she said and slipped back into the flat. She emerged a moment later holding the tie Lee had found some-where before last night's performance. It was a very sudden pea-green. 'He forgot this,' she said, holding it out.

I took it, and her warm, soft hand briefly brushed mine, and then she shut the flimsy door.

I stuffed the tie into my jacket pocket, where the other one still lurked, and I realized that if I didn't find him soon, I'd have quite a collection of the ghastly things.

There was a little welcoming committee waiting for me when I emerged on to the pavement on that dull afternoon. Malcolm Booth hadn't taken the hint and shoved off and was now accompanied by the bloke he'd been with the night before and by Dave Mountjoy and two other little Mountjoys. Well, not so little, really.

They were huddled together to the left of the doorway, all puffing away furiously, giving off smoke like the Flying Scotsman at full pelt.

Malcolm saw me and shrugged apologetically, as if to say that it was nothing to do with him. I smiled back an 'of course not, how could you think that such a thing had entered my head?'

I then nodded brusquely to Mountjoy and strode off to the right, in the direction of Wardour Street, in a decisive, 'important things to do' sort of way. I had no great desire to talk to Dave Mountjoy. I strongly suspected that a little *tête-à-tête* would do nothing for my *joie de vivre*.

I must have surprised them because I'd gone about ten yards before the first, 'Oi,' reached my shell-likes, twenty before I heard the sound of pursuit and thirty before a meaty hand dropped on my shoulder and Mountjoy's large, out-of-breath henchman, as I'd come to think of him, came alongside me.

I stopped, smiled sweetly at him and then looked meaningfully at his hand, which rested on my shoulder like a pound of pork sausages. It took him a few seconds to cotton on, but then he lifted it off gratifyingly speedily.

'Can I help you?' I said. 'Only, I'm expected, and I'm late already.'

'Dave,' he said, still panting, 'would like a quick word. It won't take a minute.'

I shrugged. He was woefully unfit, but then cigarettes aren't called gaspers for no reason. However, he was a very big man and I didn't want him to take umbrage so I waited for Dave Mountjoy to saunter up.

I glanced down at the wristwatch Mrs Williams – Ann – gave me a couple of years ago.

'Do you mind if we talk while we're walking?' I said. 'Only, like I just said to your mate here, I'm a bit late for an appointment and they'll worry about me.'

'Sure,' he said. He turned to the big man. 'George, you can have a cuppa at the caff round the corner. I'll see you there in twenty minutes.'

George looked at me suspiciously, and then nodded to his boss and turned back the way we'd come.

Dave Mountjoy snorted and indicated the big man with a backward jerk of his head as we started walking.

'George doesn't much like you. He still thinks you know something about them kids getting cut up. Thinks you're connected. Thinks you might do the same to Ricky.' He snorted again. 'But I know who you are. I remember your dad. I did wonder for a bit if you was perhaps made of tougher stuff. But I asked around. So I know you're not, and I know you don't know nothing about it. Or very little. I don't know what we was thinking, treading on eggs with you.' He sniffed. 'Your dad was a waste of space. A lousy painter and decorator who had to be taught a lesson when the job he done was so bad that I wouldn't pay him for it. Bloody frog.' He took the cigarette out of his mouth and a harsh, racking cough shook his entire body. He hawked up phlegm and spat into the gutter.

The years hadn't been kind to Dave Mountjoy. He still had the same shifty look in his eye and the same rodent's features. But he'd developed a flabby belly and heavy jowls, and there was a yellowish tinge to his skin. A little lock of his white hair hung over his forehead and was stained brown from the constant stream of nicotine that wafted up from the cigarettes that were always clamped between his lips. His shabby, brown suit was a size too small for him, and his white shirt had seen better days too. It had the same faint yellow look as his skin. Maybe the scrap-metal business wasn't holding up as well as it once had.

I was surprised to discover that my indifference to him was profound. I couldn't even be bothered to get angry on my father's account.

We'd nearly reached Wardour Street before he spoke again.
I could see the scruffy old Duke of Wellington on the corner.

'I want to know what you said to my old man this morning.
He's been odd ever since, muttering away about things
forgotten years ago,' he said.

'Oh,' I said dismissively as we turned into Wardour Street.

'Come off it,' he said. 'What did you talk to him about?'

'I just asked him about one of his granddaughters,' I said.

'He doesn't have any granddaughters,' he said.

'Yeah he does,' I said. 'Your brother, he knocked up one
of the laundry girls. Would have been about 1928.'

'What's that got to do with you?'

'Nothing much,' I said. 'Someone asked me to see if I could
find the girl. That's all. I said I'd ask around.'

'Well, don't,' he said. 'You've upset Dad, and I won't have
that. He's not been well, and that Jean wasn't nothing but grief.
She ran away during the war, and we've not seen her since.'

'Jean?' I said.

'That's what we called her. She had some fancy, old-fashioned
name.'

'When did she run away?'

He shrugged. 'Late forty-two, early forty-three? Dad was
really worried about her. But he got over it, and I won't have
you raking it all up. All right? George would like nothing
better than to be let off the leash, and one word from me . . .'

'Why'd she run away?' I said.

He was quiet for a moment and looked down at the pavement. 'I wouldn't know,' he mumbled. He suddenly stopped
walking and looked straight at me in what I'm sure he thought
of as a menacing manner, a finger raised. 'I'm telling you to
leave it alone. For your own good. All right?'

'Understood,' I said, 'understood.' And I raised both hands,
palms out, in a gesture of surrender, to reassure him of my
good intentions. Although he would have been fooling himself
if he thought he'd scared me off. The only thing about Dave
Mountjoy these days that would make you take a step back
was the smell of stale sweat, sour beer and old cigarette
smoke.

He stared over my shoulder for a few seconds, threw a very

terse, 'Good,' at me, turned and walked back towards Old Compton Street.

As I watched him, I thought of something Jerry said whenever someone came on a bit stronger than was, strictly speaking, necessary.

No one, I'm fairly sure, would mistake Dave Mountjoy for a lady – he wasn't, for a start, anything like as fragrant – but, for someone who was just concerned about his father's welfare, he was certainly, if I understood Jerry aright, protesting a bit too much. I wondered what there was to find out.

I also wondered if our meeting had been completely coincidental. I assumed it must have been, as it would have been much easier to seek me out on home territory. Then I wondered what he'd been doing up West anyway. George didn't look like the sort you'd take to the pictures on a Saturday afternoon. But, Ricky apart – and look how well things had worked out for him – the Mountjoys didn't do business in Soho. They were strictly a local firm.

Dave was probably just taking in the sights. And trying to find out which way the wind was blowing.

TEN

I was still pondering the mystery of Dave Mountjoy's appearance in the West End when I pushed my way through the glass doors into the empty lobby of the building where Hoxton Films had its offices.

There was that quiet, Saturday afternoon, musty feel about the place, the hustle and bustle of the morning long past. I stood there for a moment or two, grateful for the calm, before climbing the stairs to the second floor.

Hoxton Films' reception area was just as deserted as downstairs had been. Well, it was if you ignored the piles of large envelopes scattered haphazardly around the place. I pushed a few to one side and sank down on to the muddy-coloured battered old sofa.

The desk didn't look right without Daff sitting behind it, simultaneously swilling tea, smoking, barking into the telephone and imperiously handing out and receiving bulky packages from elderly delivery boys. Sadly, I realized that I would have to get used to her absence.

I was beginning to feel the effects of my early-morning call. Lee's ties were an unsightly bulge in my jacket pocket, and I pulled them out, before they bagged the material too much, and laid them on the sofa next to me.

Les always reckoned that he got more done on a Saturday afternoon than he did throughout the week. Everyone else thought that he was just banging his secretary. As I lay back and closed my tired eyes, the distant sound of his voice drifted on the stale air. He was probably talking on the phone.

The back of my head, where I'd been walloped, was throbbing, and I was working on developing a monumental headache. Closing my eyes helped, and I was soon dozing, not quite awake and not quite asleep, with a riot of chaotic thoughts roaring around.

Jean Mountjoy, as I suppose she must have been known,

was on my mind. I'd have to tap Mrs Norton again, to see if she knew anything about her disappearance. There was something odd there. The old boy didn't strike me as the sort who got sentimental or upset about the past. Though I suppose he could just be going doolally.

I should have been playing football with the lads out in Ealing, but I hadn't gone to any of the August training sessions because I'd been in Paris. And I'd contrived to miss the first two (now three) games as well. I wasn't high on Reg the manager's 'most reliable players' list so far this season. Fences to be mended there.

Mrs Williams – Ann – would be expecting me that evening as well. I wasn't sure that I'd be much use to her in my knackered state. She was suspicious of my visit to Paris. Not that she had any reason to be. But there were fences to be mended there as well.

And then there was Jeannie Summers. I had a few questions for her. And Lee. Ah, those God-awful ties. At least I wasn't in bad odour there.

Inspector Rose, though, was a different kettle of stinking fish altogether.

And when I opened my eyes he was standing in front of me, a sly smile on his face, tapping his pipe into the big, solid glass ashtray that was usually full of Daphne's fag ends. Les was standing just behind him, and so was a roly-poly sergeant I remembered from earlier in the year. He was scowling. I assumed at me.

'Hard night, Tony?' Inspector Rose said.

'Not especially,' I said, trying, unsuccessfully, to stifle a yawn. 'Bit of an early morning, though.'

'Hmm,' he said. 'How is the head now?'

'Fine,' I said, touching the tender lump. 'Never better.'

'Hmm,' he said again. 'I hope the conscience is in the same condition.'

'Why wouldn't it be?' I said.

'Oh,' he said, slowly stuffing his pipe with strands of sweet-smelling tobacco, 'just that you forgot to tell me that you'd been keeping a fatherly eye on Philip Graham for the last few nights.'

'I didn't know that would interest you,' I said.

'I'm always interested in people who may be material witnesses in a nasty murder, Tony,' he said. 'You know that.' He clamped the pipe between his teeth, but he didn't light it. 'My sergeant here has a good mind to arrest you for obstructing a police inquiry or some such crime.'

The sergeant, whose name I still couldn't recall, moved forward a little menacingly. He was someone else who didn't like me much. He had very bad breath, I remembered.

'I've told him there's no need for that,' Rose continued. 'You're a reasonable man, and you'll cooperate without all that. You'll give us a helping hand with our inquiries if we ask nicely, won't you?'

I shifted uneasily on the sofa, unsure what to make of this. 'Of course,' I said. 'If I can help . . .'

The inspector took the pipe out of his mouth, pointed the stem at his sergeant and positively beamed. 'You see, Sergeant,' he said. 'I told you that Tony was an upright and law-abiding citizen, keen to do his bit.' He nodded benignly. 'Well, now we know, thanks to Mr Jackson here –' he inclined his head at Les – 'where Mr Graham is currently, and we'll be having a word with him later. In the meantime, it would help enormously, Tony, if you could let us know his whereabouts over the last couple of days.'

I was acutely aware of his keen gaze. 'Well,' I said, 'where do you want me to start? Thursday he was filming first thing in the morning at Shepperton. He turned up at the Coach and Horses for a swift half at about half one, and that's where I caught up with him.'

'Hold on a minute, Tony,' Rose said. 'That your tie?'

I looked down at Montague Burton's finest dark-blue *cravate*, put my hand on my chest and patted it. 'Course it is,' I said, more than a little nonplussed.

'No, no, no. Not that one,' he said. '*That* one.' The stem of the pipe shot out, swift and sharp as an assassin's stiletto, and pointed to the badly crumpled pea-green strip of material by my right leg.

I shook my head. 'No,' I said. 'It's a bit sudden for my taste.'

The inspector looked me up and down thoughtfully, as though he was trying to guess my weight.

'Would you describe yourself as a tall man, Tony?' he said.

'No. Your sergeant there is tall. I'm not,' I said.

'No,' he said, 'I wouldn't call you tall. Not tall enough to be a policeman.'

I waited for him to say something else, but, infuriatingly, he put the pipe back in his mouth, took out a box of matches, struck one and applied the flame to the tobacco in the bowl. He made a few popping noises as he sucked on the pipe, and then puffed out a cloud of fragrant grey-blue smoke. He placed the spent match in the ashtray on Daff's desk, then, still taking his time, turned, picked up Lee's tie and examined it carefully.

'That's an interesting stain, Sergeant,' he said, pointing it out. 'Do you think that's blood?'

'Could be, sir. Very likely,' the sergeant said.

Inspector Rose folded the tie neatly and then looked at me. 'The thing is, Tony,' he said, 'a couple of witnesses saw someone in the vicinity of the Frighted Horse last night. About the only things they agree on were that he was tall and skinny. And that he was wearing a particularly 'orrible tie of lurid green.' He paused and puffed contentedly on his pipe for a few seconds. 'I'm sure that it's entirely coincidence that such a tie is found close to your person, but I'd love to hear about that coincidence from your good self.'

I took a deep breath, stood up and told him most of what I knew. It didn't take very long. After all, there wasn't that much to tell. Lee the piano player was tall and skinny, and he'd been wearing that tie, and he'd been heading to the Frighted Horse. The boys who'd been carved up had knocked him about a bit, so it was probably his blood (if it was blood) on the tie. I even told him how I'd come by the tie.

I admit that I didn't tell him that Ricky Mountjoy and Philip Graham claimed they'd seen Lee brandishing a bloody big knife later, but that was only because I didn't entirely believe it.

I did, though, offer my opinion that Lee was not physically capable of overpowering two young tearaways and slicing them up. The fact that I thought that if he'd had a firearm he

might well have shot them didn't seem to me relevant so I
didn't mention it.

After I'd finished, there was a long silence in which the
sergeant, whose name, worryingly, I still couldn't remember,
did a lot of scowling, Inspector Rose puffed on his pipe
thoughtfully, Les Jackson looked at his nails, and I sweated
copiously.

Eventually, Rose took the pipe out of his mouth. 'So, where
is he now, this piano player?' he said.

I shrugged. 'No idea,' I said.

Rose nodded and replaced the pipe in his mouth and bit
down on it. The sergeant sighed and folded his arms.

'So,' the inspector said through clenched teeth, 'where is
this –' he paused as if ransacking his memory for her name
– 'Jeannie Summers?'

'At her digs, I imagine,' I said.

'And where might that be?' Rose said.

'I'm afraid I don't know,' I said.

Rose took the pipe out of his mouth again, cleared his throat
and then sighed. 'No,' he said. 'I can't imagine why I thought
you would.'

The portly sergeant coughed, and I found it difficult to
repress a smile as I imagined him looking at me dolefully and
saying, 'Here's another nice mess you've gotten me into,'
while the inspector sheepishly scratched his head. But he
didn't. Instead he looked at the inspector, and he smiled. 'What
shall I book him for, sir?' he said.

'Preferably something that carries a very long sentence,' the
usually amiable Rose said.

'Come on, Inspector,' Les said. 'He hasn't done anything.'

Rose held up his hand in a fist and flicked up one finger at
a time as he rattled off, 'Wasted police time. Obstructed an
inquiry. Withheld information. How's that for starters?' He
shook his head. 'And I'm sure we can come up with something
like "accessory after the fact" if we can get anything to stick
to this Lee character.' He turned to me. 'How do you feel
about that, Tony?'

I shrugged. Neither of them had cautioned me, so I wasn't
yet under arrest. I wondered if I was going to be. It would

cause a few problems with Mrs Williams – Ann – if I was in chokey instead of with her.

'Hang on a minute,' Les said. 'Suppose Tony finds this bloke for you. Couldn't you drop all that? He's good at finding people.'

The inspector sniffed. 'Not in my experience,' he said. 'Still, I suppose we could turn a blind eye.' He looked at me. 'What would you rather, Tony?'

'I'd rather be in Southend, watching the Orient, actually,' I said, 'but I don't suppose that's on offer, is it?'

The inspector shook his head.

'And you don't really think that you could get any of those charges to stick, do you?'

He smiled wryly.

'But your sergeant –' Radcliffe, that was it – 'would like to have a try, because he doesn't like me.'

'It's nothing personal, Tony,' the inspector said. 'Andy doesn't like anybody. It's part of the job. You spend so much time dealing with rogues and villains, you start to think everyone's a rogue or a villain. And they usually are. Me? I like you. But I'd like you a lot more if you could tell me where this piano player is.'

I stood up. 'All right,' I said. 'I'll see if I can find him. I have a tie to return to him, anyway.'

'Uh-uh,' the inspector said. 'The tie stays with us. It could be evidence.'

'Not that one,' I said and picked up the pink tie. 'This one. He leaves them all over the place. I think he uses them to mark out his territory. Must cost him a fortune.'

I nodded to Les and mouthed 'thanks' at him. He shrugged and thrust his hands into his trouser pockets. He looked even more lugubrious than ever.

The inspector followed me to the door and put his hand on my shoulder. 'Tony,' he said, 'I meant what I said about liking you, but that only goes so far. You know that.'

'I understand,' I said.

'If you're not honest and above board with me, I will have him arrest you.' He looked over his shoulder, back at Sergeant Radcliffe, then he spoke very quietly. 'We both know those boys were supplying illegal drugs, and we both know that piano player was a customer. While it's not unheard of for unhappy and dissatisfied customers to turn on their suppliers, it's unusual. Most gang members – and these boys belonged to a gang – are attacked by other gangs. I don't think this Lee is our man, but I do need to talk to him. Frankly, I don't have time to go looking for him. I'm too busy following other leads. I'd like to, as we say, eliminate him from our inquiries sharpish. Andy Radcliffe may not appreciate your help, but, funnily enough, I would. It's bad enough having to waste time talking to people like Philip Graham. But at least we know where he is.' He sniffed. 'You know you owe me a favour or two, Tony.'

I nodded politely and went down the stairs.

Flocks of high-pitched-twittering starlings blackened the sky above Charing Cross Road, swooping, whirling and soaring in their hundreds from one soot- and smoke-stained building to the next as I wandered slowly, and fairly aimlessly, down towards Trafalgar Square. Those in the late Saturday after-noon crowds not used to it stopped to gawp at the spectacle, making progress even more difficult than usual. The racket the birds made inhibited thinking a little as well. But that rather suited me.

I had absolutely no intention of trying to track down Lee or Jeannie Summers until they were due to perform at Pete's Place later. They'd either be there or they wouldn't.

All I wanted to find at that moment was a telephone. There was one outside the National Portrait Gallery in St Martin's Place, and I didn't have to wait too long for the woman inside to finish her call and come out. I felt sorry for the bloke in the queue behind me because I was planning on making two calls.

The cries of the starlings were a little muffled inside the box, but I still had to put my finger in the ear that wasn't to the receiver to hear Mrs Williams' dulcets when I told her I'd be over in an hour. She didn't sound too displeased. Jerry sounded perfectly relaxed, and I could hear something spiky and modern that, of course, I didn't recognize playing in the background. Jeannie Summers had called to tell me that everything was fine ('Copacetic,' Jerry said, but I asked for clarification). I took that to mean Lee had turned up. I wondered for a moment, but only for a moment, if Mrs Williams – Ann – would care to visit a jazz club later, but I decided not even to ask her. After all, a refusal often offends.

I asked Jerry what he was listening to, and he murmured something incomprehensible about a felonious monk, so I left it at that.

'I have, though,' he said, 'just located something you'll love. A recording from a few years back from a trumpet player called Bunk Johnson. He was really big thirty or forty years ago but he lost his front teeth in a brawl, but then – and you'll love this – Sidney Bechet's brother, who's a dentist, fixed him up with dentures. He plays your sort of stuff like a dream. The New Orleans revival . . .'

While he spoke, I peered through the smudged glass of the telephone box at the passers-by and loiterers, the stale smoke of a thousand cigarettes leaving a bad taste in the back of my mouth.

'The radiogram is primed and ready,' Jerry said. 'Just waiting for your return.'

'That's great, Jerry,' I said. 'Something to look forward to. I've gotta go now. I'll see you when I see you.'

'In a while . . .' he said and hung up.

I'm not what you would call a religious man. Like everyone else, I had my moments during the war, of course, calling on a divine being for preservation during the occasional ticklish moment and promptly forgetting any implied bargain immediately after the danger had passed or been survived. These days I'm more your traditional christening, wedding and funeral sort of church attender – although none of the first two for a long time and not so many of the last for a bit. So, it would have surprised most of those who know me quite well to see me push my way out of the box and, after politely holding the door open for the decidedly cheesed-off bloke standing waiting to use the phone, scampering across the road, past Edith Cavell – who would, devout Anglican that she was, surely have approved – and nipping quickly up the steps and under the portico into St Martin-in-the-Fields.

It was dark and musty inside the little antechamber to the big church. After my eyes adjusted a little to the gloom, I moved away from the door to the right and, lost, I hoped, in the shadows, waited. Then I stepped through into the bright and busy church itself and stopped by the back wall.

I tried to look suitably pious, but I probably fell short by a nautical mile. The suit was crumpled, the tie awry, the hair, though so recently barbered, unruly and the morning's perfunctory shave was no longer standing me in good stead. Maman would have been mortified that I could even contemplate entering God's house in such a state.

I didn't really expect him to follow me inside the church, but people do strange things.

I'd first noticed him lumbering after me at Cambridge Circus, but I hadn't really been absolutely sure he was following me until I'd stopped at the phone box and he'd failed miserably to conceal himself behind the railings surrounding the entrance to the subterranean public conveniences about thirty yards back.

Flushing him out was a bit childish, but then so was tailing me.

I hadn't really decided whether to lose him, confront him or just let him follow me out to Ealing. Losing him had its appeal – it was neat, for a start – but then I wouldn't know what he was after. Of course, confronting him didn't necessarily mean that I'd find that out, but it might. I was against letting him follow me to Ealing on principle. The principle being that the less men like James Fitzgerald knew about me the better, and I assumed that his man – who I recognized as Malcolm's mate – would be reporting to him. I had no great liking for Mr Fitz learning about my relationship with Mrs Williams. No good could possibly come of that.

As I leaned against the wall, feeling the cool stone through my jacket, watching the steady procession of people going about whatever business it is people who bustle about churches go about, I saw a figure I recognized.

She was wearing a baggy brown cardigan buttoned up to the neck and a green scarf over her hair and was tidying up a stack of dark-green prayer books, but, even performing such an apparently unlikely act, with her impressive cleavage hidden and her shock of hair under wraps, she was unmistakable.

'Miss Laurence?' I said. 'Viv Laurence.'

I don't think I've ever before seen someone, as Jerry sometimes says, start like a guilty thing upon a fearful summons, but I think, if I understand the phrase aright, that Viv Laurence did exactly that. She turned big, startled eyes on me and dropped one of the prayer books on the floor.

I bent down and picked it up. 'Can I help you with those?' I said, nodding at the pile of books.

She shook her head fiercely and clutched those still in her hands tightly. She looked warily around, but there was no one else near us. 'Are you following me?' she whispered.

I shook my head. 'No, no. Of course not,' I said, holding the book out towards her. 'I just happened to come in here. I'm sorry.' I looked around for a suitable surface to plonk the prayer book. There was a straight-backed old wooden chair up against the wall next to me. I dropped the book on to the seat with a little bump. 'Sorry,' I said again, 'I'll, er, leave you to it.'

I offered her a wan little smile and turned towards the door. I'd walked about five paces when I felt her hand on my shoulder.

'I'm the one who should be sorry,' she said. 'It's just . . . I don't know.' She paused. 'Listen, I could do with a ciggy.' She placed her pile of books carefully on top of the one I'd deposited on the chair, and then she walked with me out of the door and on to the steps outside the church.

I stood looking across at Trafalgar Square while she fumbled in her shiny black handbag for a pack of cigarettes and a box of matches.

She dropped the match, tilted her head up and breathed smoke into the sky with a sigh. The starlings were still tearing about up above us, raucously criss-crossing the air in immaculately choreographed manoeuvres.

'I've been a bit jumpy ever since last night,' she said. 'And this –' she inclined her head back towards the church – 'is a sort of refuge for me. I do a bit of work around the place: cleaning, that sort of thing. It's somewhere I can go and forget

about those parts of my life I want to forget about. I couldn't
bear it if that was all ruined.'

'I promise that I wasn't following you,' I said. I looked
around nervously for the man who'd been following *me*. I
didn't spot him. 'And I promise that I won't mention to anyone
that I've seen you here.'

'Thanks,' she said and rested her hand on my forearm for a
few seconds. 'The thing is, what happened to those boys was
horrible.' She looked around nervously. 'It's got me worried.'

'It's all right,' I said, as reassuringly as I could manage.
'Nothing's going to happen to you.'

She took her hand from my forearm, removed the half-
smoked cigarette from her mouth and threw it to the ground.
She watched it smouldering there and then delicately stretched
out her right foot and stepped on it very gently.

'You don't understand,' she said, still looking down at the
step.

'No,' I said, 'I don't. What's bothering you?'

She looked bleakly out at Trafalgar Square and then across
to the bottom of Charing Cross Road. 'I can't talk now,' she said
abruptly. 'I have to finish up in here.' She turned hurriedly back
towards the door of the church and then glanced at me again.
'Perhaps if you could come and see me tomorrow morning?'

I nodded. 'Of course,' I said.

'Can you come to my place about eleven?'

I nodded again, but she'd already moved under the portico
and was almost through the door.

I wondered where the guy who'd been following me was.
I thought he'd be loitering outside somewhere – under the
portico, probably – unless he knew I'd spotted him. In that
case he'd be hanging about in Trafalgar Square, discovering
a hitherto unsuspected, but nonetheless engrossing, fascination
with pigeons. But I still couldn't see him. Maybe he hadn't
been following me. I couldn't think what Mr Fitz would hope
to gain by knowing my movements, anyway. Except that he
seemed to think that I knew where his merchandise was. Or
knew someone who did.

The starlings swirled around, making a terrible din, and I
stood for a moment or two at the top of the steps looking up

at them, fiddling with my tie in a futile attempt to make myself more presentable. I even patted at my hair.

Then I saw my shadow.

He wasn't under the portico or in Trafalgar Square with a pigeon on his shoulder. He was leaning against the railings outside the National Gallery opposite, peering over the top of the late edition of the *Evening News*. I considered wandering over and asking him how the Orient had got on at Southend, but he might have thought that I wasn't taking him seriously and got ratty about it.

Mind you, I couldn't be too sure how seriously he was taking things himself. As soon as he saw me looking at him, he folded the paper and stuffed it into the side pocket of his suit jacket, unpeeled himself from the railings and started to walk briskly in my direction, swaying as neatly and effortlessly as a matador avoiding a maddened bull to dodge a taxi as he crossed the road. For a moment I thought that he would walk right up to me, but he stopped at the bottom of the steps and waited for me to do something.

What I did was look at him and worry away at a chip in one of what my National Health Service tooth doctor calls my anterior teeth with my tongue.

When I'd exhausted the possibilities that offered, I walked down the steps and plonked myself right in front of him. OK, it was a change of plan, but I'd've felt silly leading him off to Embankment station.

'Hi,' I said.

He stared at me fairly phlegmatically. 'Do I know you?' he said.

'We were never introduced,' I said, 'but we ran into each other last night. And then again an hour ago. In Old Compton Street.'

'Did we?' he said.

I nodded and smiled at him. 'Bit of a coincidence, running into you again here,' I said.

He sniffed. 'Is it?'

'No. I'm not sure that it is,' I said. 'I think you're following me. And not making much of a fist of it.'

There was a short silence, full of possibilities.

'All right,' he finally said. 'I am.'

'What for?'

He shrugged. 'Something to do?' he suggested.

He was a big man, maybe five years younger than me, and he looked useful. He certainly didn't appear to be at all concerned at me calling him out.

I worried at the tooth again and watched the people hurrying by and the buses throbbing past.

'I'll tell you what,' I said. 'I'll make it easy for you. I'm just on my way out to Ealing to see an old friend. After that, I'm coming back into town. I'll drop in to Pete's Place on Frith Street and listen to the band there for a while. Then I'm heading home for a decent night's kip.' I looked up at the darkening sky. 'If you want to schlep all the way out to Ealing, wait out in the rain for an hour or two while I eat my meat and two veg, schlep all the way back in, spend another couple of hours listening to some jazz and then spend half an hour on the Central Line, that's up to you, but I imagine you can think of better things to do with your Saturday night.' I paused and waited for him to respond but he didn't. 'The other thing is,' I said, 'that I might get browned off with being followed.'

That got his attention. He looked me up and down and sneered. 'You reckon you can stop me, do you?' he said.

I shrugged. 'I don't know, but if I get browned off enough we might find out.'

He reached forward and grabbed me by the shirt and tie. I lost buttons. He leaned in to me, and his harsh, sharp cologne stung the lining of my nostrils.

'Don't threaten me,' he said, 'unless you intend to follow through.'

I hit him once – a short right jab just under the heart. It wasn't my best shot by a long way, but it did the business. He let go of me and stepped back, allowing me a much better punch to much the same place. That one travelled the requisite six or seven inches and really sank in. He fell to his knees, gasping for breath like a gaffed fish, surprise widening his eyes. A couple of passers-by looked at us long and hard, but I shook my head at them and they gave us a wide berth.

'There was no need,' I said, 'to ruin a perfectly good shirt.'

I held my left hand cocked and ready to strike if he looked like coming for me. I was actually a bit disappointed that he didn't. I thought he was made of sterner stuff. In fact, he sat back on the steps, very pale and wan.

Oh, well, someone else with a grudge against me. I'd add him to what was becoming a long list.

I saw the paper poking out from his pocket and pulled it out.

It could have been worse. Orient had held Southend to a nil-nil draw.

ELEVEN

Pete's Place was about as full as it ever gets on a Saturday night by the time I arrived. And that's pretty full. The sharp tang of spilt beer, sweaty bodies and cheap aftershave and scent cut through the thick fug of cigarette smoke. No wonder our lords and masters call us the great unwashed.

I elbowed my way to the bar as the Peter Baxter Band played what was rapidly becoming their signature tune, 'The Sheik of Araby'. The boards of the little stage were bouncing alarmingly as Peter and the others thumped out the time rather too enthusiastically, Peter's battered old brown suede shoes leading the way. They must have been the same vintage as his suit, bought back when Edward VIII was still the Prince of Wales and a fashion leader rather than the Duke of Windsor with some dodgy allegiances.

Brimming with Mrs Williams' – Ann's – good roast beef dinner (meat and *three* veg as well as Yorkshire pudding), two glasses of Berry Brothers & Rudd's best claret (specially bought for me by Mrs Williams now that she accepted that I really didn't drink beer), and apple crumble and custard, I was prepared to drink warm, flat lemonade for what remained of the night and still beam at anyone and everyone. Ann had even sewed three buttons back on to my damaged shirt, while she had worried away at the unfairness of hanging Ruth Ellis when, ten years ago, Cyril Patmore had only got five years for manslaughter after returning from the war to find his wife pregnant and stabbing her to death. It had been on her mind for a few months. I'd agreed with her. It had been a couple of hours of the nearest I'd ever come to domestic bliss.

But then I saw Philip Graham on the far side of the room, and my mood soured. He was sitting with Ricky Mountjoy, and that could not be good news.

I assumed that young Ricky had got over last night's little

fright and was looking for whatever goods he'd lost. Or for revenge. Probably both.

Whether Philip was in the same frame of mind was difficult to tell. He was certainly scowling into his drink when he wasn't fidgeting on his seat or nervously drawing on a cigarette.

I wondered if they'd come mob-handed – little Ricky didn't seem to me the sort for one-on-one combat, and Dave had appeared to have real paternal feelings for his boy – so I looked around for obvious muscle, like George, but I didn't see anyone.

I thought it might be a good idea to lose myself in the crowd, and, as Peter and the boys basked in the warm applause, I eased myself to the rear wall. By the time the band had started 'Moonglow', in what sounded to me like the Benny Goodman arrangement, I had put most of the room and about a hundred and twenty people between me and them. I couldn't see Philip or Ricky because of the dimmed lights, the largish audience and the smoky fug, so it was a fair bet that they couldn't see me either. But I had the advantage of knowing they were there.

'Moonglow' finished, and the band roared straight into a barnstorming account of 'Nobody's Sweetheart Now'. What they lacked in finesse they more than made up for in enthusiasm and noise, and, in fact, they weren't bad. I found my foot tapping along. And I applauded along with everyone else.

The band sauntered off the stage while Peter, trumpet dangling from his hand, sweat dribbling down his face, breathing heavily, waited for the applause to die away to make his announcement.

He kept it short. 'Ladies and gentlemen, the very wonderful Miss Jeannie Summers.'

The stage lights dimmed to a single startling spot, and there she was in a shimmering blue gown. The woman more than a hundred people had come to see. And there, slouched over the piano, in shadow, tinkling an introduction to 'Smoke Gets in Your Eyes', was the man three of us had paid our entrance money in the hope of seeing.

I suddenly wondered how Philip Graham had managed to get in. When Peter barred people, they usually stayed barred.

Perhaps that particular piece of information hadn't made it to Bill on the door. Or Bill just hadn't recognized him.

And I wondered at Lee turning up as though nothing had happened. He probably reckoned he was safest in a crowd. And, just maybe, he thought that by acting as though nothing had happened he could make it so. I'd seen men try that in the war.

The smell of unwashed bodies, including my own, seeped through the thin overlay of Brylcreem, Evening in Paris, Amami, Old Spice and the reek of ancient cooking oil from the Acropolis. It was hot, and I took off my jacket and leaned back against the cool wall, letting Jeannie Summers' rich, warm voice wash over me. She wasn't as affecting as Lady Day. But who is? And her phrasing wasn't as perfect as Ella's. But, again, whose is?

All the same, she definitely had that something special that could move you.

I closed my eyes and listened.

I must have dozed off because all kinds of jumbled thoughts came into my head: sharp, jagged images of France during the war – creeping up behind a young German sentry guarding a goods yard; Ghislaine and Big Luc picking up windfall apples in an orchard – and bleak memories of aimlessly wandering through London in the cruel winter of '47, treading warily across treacherous frost-bitten bomb sites for no reason, chilled to the bone even through the big smelly greatcoat I'd come home in.

I jolted awake as Jeannie Summers soothed and swayed her way to the end of 'The Man I Love'. She looked across at Lee briefly, and when she turned back to acknowledge the applause her eyes were full of tears.

They both left the stage, and the lights came up.

I still couldn't see Philip Graham or Ricky Mountjoy through the crowd. People were standing up, stretching or heading for the bar before Peter and the boys came back on.

I yawned and put my jacket back on. It was time to make my way backstage and give Lee the good news that Inspector Rose of the Yard would love to see him. I glanced around for Ricky and Philip. Puzzlingly, they didn't seem to be around.

I pushed my way apologetically through the crush at the bar until I was standing by the stage. I had one long last look. The lads had clearly left. Ah, well. One less thing to worry about.

I made a mental note to suggest that Les have a word with his boy. It might have seemed a bit harsh to young Philip, but Les definitely wanted him tucked up in bed in the nice hotel Hoxton Films was paying for, with a nice polite Agatha Christie mystery at this time on a Saturday night, not gallivanting around Soho jazz clubs with a nasty little razor-wielding hooligan.

Over the hubbub at the bar, I heard the unmistakable sound of the band arriving back on stage: a cymbal singing, a few bluesy chords on the piano, a rumble from the double bass.

'Any requests, Tony?'

I turned to see Peter Baxter beaming at me. Well, it was the nearest Peter ever gets to beaming at anyone. It was more of a scowl really.

I shook my head. 'I could live without "The Sheik of Araby",' I said.

'Duly noted,' he said, 'but you've just brought my premature retirement from the music business that much closer.'

'Sorry,' I said, not meaning it. 'Listen, is it all right if I go backstage for a word with Lee? The *gendarmerie* would like him to turn up and give a statement. They've asked me to convince him.'

Peter shrugged and scowled (or beamed) at me again. 'Sure. Why not? That was their last set for us. They can keep him in overnight for all I care now. Might do him some good. Keep him off the junk. That would be a consummation devoutly to be wished.'

Sometimes, Peter sounds very like Jerry. But then they did go to the same kind of posh private school.

I nodded at him and ambled across the stage to the dingy corridor beyond, just as the lights in the club went down and the band started belting out 'Chattanooga Choo Choo'.

I knocked gently on the door of the dressing room and announced myself.

The quiet voice of Jeannie Summers drifted out. 'Just a minute. I'll make myself decent.'

I turned away from the door and started tapping my foot to the rhythm. They really were quite a good Saturday night band. In one of the big cathedrals to dance, the kids would be out on the floor, jiving and jitterbugging – or whatever they did these days – away. Of course, to fill one of those places with sound, Peter would need a lot more of a brass section to back him up. It probably suited him very well to be soloist and vocalist in a small club.

I heard the door open behind me, and there was Miss Summers wearing a dressing gown and looking very tired.

'That was a great set,' I said. 'Really very good.'

She lowered her head modestly. 'Thank you,' she said. 'I'm glad you enjoyed it.'

I started to feel a little guilty about nodding off and hoped she wouldn't ask me to expand on my comments.

'I'm afraid that I need a word with Lee,' I said. 'About last night.'

'Oh,' she said but didn't move. Then she looked up at me and gave me a fake, bright smile. 'I'll send him out.'

The door shut behind her, and I heard the low murmur of conversation.

The band pleaded to be carried home and then stopped dead, more or less at the same time. There was some enthusiastic clapping and whistling before a sprightly up-tempo account of 'Someone To Watch Over Me' echoed down the corridor.

The door to the dressing room swung open, and Lee stepped out, wiping his face with a grubby towel. He pulled the door to and then leaned back against the wall. He jerked his head towards the club. 'Doesn't have much of a left hand, that piano player,' he said.

I shrugged. 'Ah, he does for us,' I said. 'We're not that sophisticated an audience.'

He nodded. 'I guess not,' he said. 'You put up with me playing like I've got arthritis in my hands.'

He held out his right hand. The long, slender fingers were about as removed from the gnarled and knotty digits of an elderly arthritis sufferer as I've ever seen.

'I've not been at my best the last few days,' he said. 'Need to get clean.' He mumbled like he was talking to himself.

Maybe he was, because he suddenly looked across at me. 'Jeannie says you got something you want to talk about.'

'Yes,' I said. 'The police here would really like to talk to you about last night. They know you were in the alley where those boys were killed.'

'Yeah,' he said. 'Pity I can't tell them anything on account of being unconscious at the time because "those boys" had just roughed me up.'

'All the same,' I said, 'they need a statement. Just tell them that. The inspector in charge is a good egg. He wants to ascertain whether you know anything or not.'

'Sure he does,' he said. He stood up straight, shook his head and made to go back into the dressing room. 'I don't know anything.'

'I think you should go to see him,' I said. 'Voluntarily.'

He paused with his hand on the door knob, but whatever he was about to say was lost as the outside stairs to the Acropolis rang with the sound of many feet and the door that led on to the yard where the dustbins nestled was flung open with a crash.

Malcolm Booth and his mate, the bloke I'd tangled with that afternoon, strode into the corridor, followed by three other tough-looking guys. As I suppose I should have expected, Ricky Mountjoy and Philip Graham were nowhere near the vanguard but sauntered in, well to the rear, like staff officers keeping an eye on the troops, don't you know.

'We need a word with your mate,' Malcolm said.

'What about?' I said, stepping in front of Lee.

'Come on,' Malcolm said, 'you're not stupid.'

'He doesn't know anything,' I said.

'Look, I don't want to have to sort you out,' Malcolm said, 'but you protect him and I will.'

'You can try,' I said.

His mate stepped forward and swung the sort of roundhouse punch you only ever see in Westerns. I stepped back and watched it labour past. He was completely off balance, with his back to me, so I just gave him a little dig in the right kidney and then pushed him into the other members of his team.

Malcolm neatly stepped around him and came towards me, fists cocked. He looked useful. 'This isn't personal, Tony,' he said. 'I hope you understand that.'

He pushed out a straight left which caught me on the temple and stung a bit, but not as much as the big right he followed it up with, which felt like it might have cracked a rib. All the same, he knew I wasn't out of it yet and followed me as I backed off down the corridor. He also knew that I was no boxer.

What he didn't know, though, was that I'd been taught how to hurt people during the war, and some of it had stuck.

Go for whatever's unprotected had been one of the maxims drummed into me. And, perhaps the most important piece of advice, don't be half-hearted, always do it like you mean it.

So, when Malcolm planted himself in front of me and prepared to knock seven bells out of me, I tapped him quite hard on the left ankle. I wasn't wearing battered old brown suede shoes but decent black English Oxfords, and I felt the impact all the way up my leg, so it must have, as Bernie Rosen was very fond of saying, hurt like a bastard. The ankle all but gave way under him, and he lurched to the side. As he did so, I swung a left down into the side of his head, and he fell heavily against the opposite wall, banging his head again.

'Nothing personal, Malcolm,' I said, rubbing the bruise that was already coming up on my chest. The rib didn't give at all so maybe it wasn't broken.

I looked across and saw that the other blokes hadn't hung about and were holding Lee pretty much immobile. Jeannie Summers had appeared at the door to the dressing room, and, to my surprise, she wasn't screaming hysterically but beating at the back of one of the bigger men roughing up her lover man. Her blows were pretty much ineffectual, but at least she was doing something, unlike Lee. The thug who I'd thumped earlier grabbed her and pulled her away none too gently, and I decided I'd better intervene. But I'd underestimated Malcolm, who wasn't out cold, as he should have been. As I moved past him, he lashed out a leg, which caught me on the shin. I stumbled to my knees, and one of the guys I'd never seen before peeled away from the melee around Lee and, closely followed by Ricky Mountjoy, came towards me. Then they were on me like jackals.

I rolled up into a ball, and as the first blows came in I was only too aware that Peter and the band were still playing at full volume. It would be just my luck to take a kicking to the sound of 'The Sheik of Araby'.

In the event I didn't.

They were playing 'Tiger Rag'.

And, just like in the pictures, the Seventh Cavalry turned up in the nick of time.

The first I knew of it was Ricky Mountjoy haring off towards the rear exit as if Bill the doorman's yell of, 'What the bloody hell's going on?' was the starting gun for a hundred yard dash.

There must be something catching about a panic-stricken retreat, because Ricky's flight out the door and up the Acropolis's stairs took two others with him.

Which left only four – including Philip Graham, who didn't count, and Malcolm, who was still lying on the floor – and that was reduced to three by an impressive left and right combination from Bill that left the bloke assaulting me lying next to Malcolm. At that point, the last bloke holding Lee, Malcolm's oppo, reflected on the situation, decided that discretion was the better part of valour and hopped it double quick too before Bill could get to him.

Philip Graham was looking to sneak out when Bill's stentorian bark of, 'Oi, you! Come here!' stopped him in his tracks. Jeannie Summers hugged Lee tightly, but he looked very uncomfortable about such a display of marital affection. And he definitely didn't reciprocate. She was holding him, but he wasn't holding her.

Malcolm Booth stirred, started to get up but stopped and held up a placatory palm when Bill took a step toward him, fist cocked. 'It's all right,' he said. 'It's all over now. Finished. Done with.'

'You're right,' Bill said. He pointed to the slumped heap next to Malcolm. 'Now get out and take him with you.'

For a bloke thickening round the middle and nudging up towards fifty, Bill's a daunting prospect – he has the look of someone who knows he can take your best shot and still be standing – and Malcolm scrambled to his feet, shook the bloke next to him into something approaching consciousness and helped him down the corridor, out into the yard, and we heard them clanging their way slowly up the stairs.

Philip made to go after them.

'Not you,' I said. 'We need to have a chat.'

I could see the start of a monumental sulk coming on.

'I've nothing to say to you,' Philip said, 'and I'm going now. If you try to stop me, Mr Jackson will be informed.'

Bill looked at me and smiled. 'You want me to give him a slap, Tone?' he said.

'I don't think that'll be necessary, Bill,' I said. 'Because I'm going to slap him myself, if he doesn't start to behave.'

Well, after we'd taken up residence in Jeannie Summers' dressing room, with Bill firmly planted outside the door, young Philip did start to behave, after a fashion, but not until I explained the facts of life to him. I don't know that in his heart of hearts he believed me – the boy had a very high opinion of himself – but when I told him that Les Jackson didn't like him any more than I did and Les might well decide to suffocate his career before it had really got off the ground he did sober up a bit, calm down and at least pretend to be cooperative. But it was all with a very bad grace. And it may have had something to do with the fact that he could see that I really would have given him a slapping.

Lee, on the other hand, agreed with some alacrity that maybe going to the police wasn't such a bad idea after all. The little set-to had certainly shaken him up, but his acquiescence probably had more to do with Miss Summers' worries for his well-being and her insistence, I think, than any fears he had about his safety. He was really focused on getting out of town the next day and up to 'glass cow' for their next engagement. I had a sneaking suspicion that Inspector Rose might well have a view on that, but I thought it wiser not to give voice to it.

Apart from the bruised rib, I had a rather unattractive little red lump coming up on my left temple, and neither injury was doing anything for my mood. But I tried to be patient with Philip Graham. I really did.

The dingy little room felt cramped and crowded. Probably because, although there were only four of us in there, it was.

Lee stood near the door, fizzing like a bottle of Tizer, desperate to prowl up and down while waiting for Peter Baxter to come off stage and give him access to the telephone in his office.

Jeannie Summers sat quietly, occasionally murmuring to Lee, telling him to relax and that everything would be all right.

Philip Graham sat in the only other chair the room boasted, his legs crossed, holding his cigarette well away from his body in an oddly affected way that I found annoying. But then everything about him irritated me, from his carefully cut and brilliantined hair to his beautifully shined Church's shoes.

Although she wasn't talking to me, I listened to Miss Summers, took a deep breath, calmed down and asked young Philip, again, what it was all about. And, I told him, this time I wanted as much detail as he could give me.

'Just a little business venture that Ricky and I had going,' he said offhandedly. 'Buying and selling stuff. At a considerable profit, natch. I never knew the ins and outs of it,' he said. 'I was just the man who financed it.'

I sighed. 'So,' I said, 'you handed cash over to Ricky Mountjoy, he did the deals and handed you back your cash and the profit and you never asked any questions and knew nothing about it.'

'That's about it,' he said, flicking ash ostentatiously on to the floor.

I sighed again, yawned and stretched. 'We have a small problem here and a large problem,' I said.

He looked at me expectantly, managing to combine insolence and patronization in one open-eyed expression.

'The small problem,' I said, 'is that I don't believe you. The big problem is that if I don't know what this is all about I can't do what Les Jackson pays me to do, which is to look after his assets – of which you are one – when things threaten to turn nasty. And this has more than threatened. It's already gone sour.' I paused. I really wanted to knock the faux-innocent look off his face but I knew that wouldn't get me anywhere. 'I'm going to take a two-minute turn out in the corridor now, and while I'm gone I'd like you to see if you can recall the nature of your business with Ricky Mountjoy. If you can't, I'm going to call Mr Jackson, tell him that I'm washing my hands of you and then I'm going to call my favourite detective inspector and tell him what I think was going on.' I paused again. All this talking was exhausting. 'Do you understand me, Philip?'

He offered a cautious nod.

'More importantly, do you understand the consequences of that course of action?'

'Yes,' he said. 'I'll make sure that you lose your job.'

I smiled at him in what I hoped was a suitably menacing way. 'I don't really have a job to lose, Philip,' I said. This time the pause was for dramatic effect. 'You do.'

My swift and effective exit was somewhat ruined by having to manoeuvre my way around Lee and mumble an apology for standing on his foot, but I hoped that young Philip had got the point. I wasn't convinced, though, and stood in the corridor reflecting that the boy's arrogance knew no bounds. I could remember being twenty-one. My arrogance had been limitless too. But it had been a substitute for confidence, like, I suspected, Philip's. There had been nothing much behind it.

The band was still playing. But they were well into 'The Sheik of Araby' again, so I guessed they were into encores and about to finish the set.

Bill marched briskly back from a quick recce in the yard. 'Nothing going on upstairs, Tony,' he said. 'I reckon they've called it a day for the night.'

As it were, I thought. White-haired old Mrs Wilson would have loved that back at Church Road School when I was ten. She'd been a great teacher.

'Thanks, Bill,' I said. 'That's good to know.'

He leaned against the wall next to me. 'Fancy the Orient for promotion this year?' he said.

I shrugged. 'Who knows? Good chance, I suppose, but they flatter to deceive. Here, you've got your ear to the ground. What's young Ricky Mountjoy been up to?'

'Ricky Mountjoy?'

'The boy who ran when you came riding to the rescue tonight,' I said.

He looked blank and shook his head.

'Young lad from my neck of the woods. Hangs out at the Frighted Horse. Runs some sort of drug distribution service for one of the big gangs.'

'Oh, him. I don't know, really. He turned up a month or two back, working for Fitz's lot. Word is he's very ambitious and he and his boys have set something up on the side. Don't know what. You know what the gossip's like around here. Could be something or nothing.'

'And Fitz knows?'

Bill rumbled a deep laugh. 'Tony,' he said, 'I ask you, if I've heard something, what are the chances that Fitz hasn't?'

Not very high. I nodded in a sage sort of way.

He took out a pack of Woodbines and offered it to me. I shook my head and he took out a cigarette, rasped a match across the abrasive edge of its box and lit up with a deep satisfied breath.

I smiled at him and went back into the dressing room just as the band came to an abrupt stop to what sounded like thunderous applause. Of course, everyone was well oiled by now and having a great time. Lee and Jeannie Summers passed me on the threshold. They'd obviously decided to wait for Peter in the corridor where Lee could pace to his heart's content.

I stepped aside to let them by and then took the two steps that placed me directly in front of Philip Graham. I looked down at him sternly. He looked at the carpet.

'Hashish,' he said, '*kif*. Ricky met a Moroccan when he was in jail. He came here to avoid all the trouble but got done for something. Anyway, he and his mates have a regular supply from the Rif Mountains. And a lot of the Africans and the other darkies from the West Indies, they like it. They call it ganja. There's a real demand in some of the clubs and pubs. Ricky wasn't looking to go in big, but he needed some money to start up. I gave him a hundred quid. He gave it back with another hundred on top within a week and we were up and running.'

I asked why they'd thought I'd been involved in the attack on the two other boys. He just shrugged and said something about 'bad blood'. When I asked why they'd come after Lee tonight, he just said that they wanted their 'goods' back. When I asked if Malcolm Booth and Mr Fitz's other boys knew what they were after, he said he didn't think so, that they just thought it was Mr Fitz's 'goods' they were looking for. And some summary justice. Of course.

'Lee doesn't have your stuff,' I said. 'And I really don't think he knifed Del and Billy. Do you?'

He shrugged dismissively. He obviously felt differently. I suppose if he really had seen Lee holding a knife when he and Ricky went past the alley, I couldn't blame him. And, of course, there was the matter of 'bad blood' there as well.

This time my sigh wasn't born of exasperation but of deep and unmitigated gloom. I could think of a few people whose toes they'd trodden on. James Fitzgerald probably wasn't pleased with them. He wouldn't like his boys going freelance, and he'd definitely want his cut. And the Maltesers who ran some of the seedier streets of Soho, where a few of the black clubs had taken root, could have been cheesed off. But, as a warning, carving up Del and Billy into something suitable for a kosher wedding seemed a bit excessive.

I wondered if Ricky Mountjoy and Mr Fitz were still upstairs, because after I'd put Les Jackson's would-be matinee idol in a taxi there were a few questions I needed answers to. And those two just might be able to help.

I couldn't for the life of me think of a single good reason why Les Jackson should be forking out serious moolah to keep Philip Graham in a hotel out of harm's way when the boy didn't appear to have the sense to take advantage of Les's generosity and keep a low profile. But then I couldn't think of a single reason – good or bad – why I was going to do my best to extricate the unpleasant little oik from any brown and sticky substance he was immersed in, but I knew I would.

TWELVE

Robert Rieux, Ghislaine's husband, serial adulterer, heavyweight trades-union leader in France and one-time communist resistance fighter, had certain rhetorical flourishes masquerading as rules for confronting the enemy. The first of which, roughly translated, was: 'Be swift, be deadly.'

That was certainly sound advice when dealing with the sentry at a goods yard you were planning to blow up, but it didn't offer me much for what I had lined up.

One of Robert's other maxims is easily translated as: 'Surprise!' I guess I had that going for me.

As I clanged my way up the back stairs to the Acropolis, I was half-hoping that there wouldn't be anyone home. After all, it was very late. Peter and the band were doing one final sweaty set, otherwise Bill would have been very happy to accompany me, but, he said apologetically, he just couldn't leave the club in case he was needed. I did think about waiting, but decided I needed to get this sorted and out of the way.

I braved the puzzled looks of the kitchen staff as I strolled past and pushed my way through the swing doors that led to the dining room, feeling a bit like the mad major I'd seen in 1944 walking straight at a German machine-gun emplacement with nothing but his Webley in his hand. Robert, Big Luc, Ghislaine and I had all watched him with mounting disbelief. If he'd waited, we'd have dealt with it, as we'd dealt with four or five others. But he'd seemed to think that a sneaky attack involving hand grenades was unsporting.

Still, I'd got a very good Webley out of the action.

I rather wished I still had it when I saw James Fitzgerald and a few of his men sat at what I assumed was his usual table, but I was (slightly) relieved to see that Malcolm Booth wasn't there. His bruised – possibly cracked – ankle would have reminded him that he had a genuine grudge. I noted that Ricky Mountjoy wasn't there either.

Gratifyingly, Mr Fitz himself looked very surprised to see me. He gave his world-famous impression of a fairground goldfish waiting to be won, mouth opening and closing a few times. Two of his boys, including the one I'd thumped outside St Martin-in-the-Fields, half rose, looking a bit belligerent, if confused.

'It's all right,' I said, extending my hands out, palms towards them in what I hoped was a placatory gesture. 'I haven't come to make trouble. I just need to have a few words with his nibs here.'

All three of the men with him turned to James Fitzgerald. He stopped gulping and actually smiled.

'Tony was kind enough to buy me luncheon earlier today,' he said. 'The least I can do is hear him out.' He looked at one of his bruisers. 'Find him a chair, Harold,' he said.

There was a certain amount of shuffling around the table as room was made for another place. Mr Fitz himself, though, looking like a cross between a boyish and benign Chinese Buddha and an impish Alfred Hitchcock, did not so much as twitch a buttock. Eventually, enough space was found, and Harold rammed a chair into the back of my legs. I didn't have much choice. I sat. Harold remained standing behind me. I can't say that I felt entirely comfortable. Especially as I hadn't really thought through what I was going to say. All the scenarios that had flickered across the silver screen of what I think of as my mind hadn't got me as far as sitting down. Most had ended in fisticuffs before a word had been spoken.

I heard Harold light a cigarette behind me. I was reminded of the bad boys sitting behind me in the picture house before the war, blowing smoke into my hair so my mother would think I'd taken up smoking. Which, in spite of my protestations and explanations, she did.

I also remembered a hairy moment in a café in Pontorson when three German soldiers had decided to examine my documents. I should never have been there, but Ghislaine had talked about Mont St Michel and I'd wanted to see it. The moment wasn't as nasty as some that had followed, but it was tense enough, and one of the soldiers, who was probably even younger than me, had stood behind me, puffing away nervously.

I never did get to see Mont St Michel.

James Fitzgerald took a sip from his brandy glass, smacked his lips and smiled at me. 'I'd offer you a glass,' he said, 'but Greek brandy is, like Retsina, an acquired taste, and I didn't gain the impression over luncheon that the wine altogether met with your approval. Perhaps a light ale or a Mackeson?'

I shook my head. 'No,' I said, ever polite. 'No, thank you.'

He put his glass on the table, leaned forward slightly and placed his fingers together in a vaguely ecclesiastical gesture. 'Well then,' he said, 'what can I do for you?'

'First,' I said, 'you can promise me there will be no repetition of what happened half an hour ago.'

He raised his eyebrows and leaned further forward. 'What happened half an hour ago?' he said.

'Oh, come on,' I said. 'Some of these boys, and a few others, came down to lift the piano player from the jazz club. There was a bit of unpleasantness.' I paused and stared into the mean little eyes that glittered in his bland milk pudding of a face. 'You must have heard about it.'

His expression as he fell back against the cushioned wall behind him was all innocent surprise. He looked at the men around the table, who suddenly had a somewhat sheepish appearance.

'Is this true?' he said. He turned to the man who had followed me only six or seven hours earlier. 'What do you know of this "unpleasantness", Stanley?'

Stanley said nothing, just stared at the tablecloth.

'You could also,' I said, pointing at Stanley, 'tell him to stop following me. Apart from anything else, he's not very good at it.'

Mr Fitz shook his head sadly, like a man disappointed in those around him. 'Tony,' he said, 'what can I say? I knew nothing of any of this. You and I have broken bread together. We have shared our wartime experiences. Why, we are practically comrades-in-arms. You have my assurance that nothing like this will occur again, if I can possibly stop it.' He sighed and spread his hands. 'Of course, even the most experienced and in-touch officers can't make absolute promises . . .'

I know when I'm being lied to, and I know when I'm being patronized. But I also know when there's no point in taking umbrage. I've been lied to and patronized by much better men than James Fitzgerald.

'That's most reassuring . . . James,' I said.

He smiled smugly and picked up his brandy glass again. He swirled the dark spirit around, twitched his nostrils over the rim and then drank deeply, emptying the glass.

'I think,' I said, 'I know some of what's been going on, but it doesn't make much sense.'

He suddenly looked a bit more interested and alert. 'Oh?' he said. 'Do go on.' He handed his glass to Stanley, who stood up and walked to the little bar that ran along one wall of the restaurant. I watched him pour a stiff measure from a squat bottle on the counter.

I suddenly realized that there was no one else in the place: no adulterous couples furtively holding hands, lingering over an exotic candlelit dinner; no waiters picking their teeth, waiting to make their weary way home to Turnpike Lane; no proprietor adding up bills. I could hear some clattering coming from the kitchen, but that was it. Apart from me, Mr Fitz and his boys. I started to feel even more uncomfortable. Ah, well, in for a penny and all that.

'I think it's about the ganja market,' I said.

Fitzgerald widened his little eyes a fraction. 'Drugs?' he said. 'Gosh! What makes you think that?'

I again thought it wiser not to rise to the tone. I can live with someone being sarcastic at my expense. 'I'm afraid it probably is about drugs, James. Drugs, and an ambitious young man.' I paused and took a deep breath. 'I should explain that my only interest is in protecting my client's interests. He has an asset who has become mixed up in all this. I'd like to be able to reassure him that his asset is safe. If that reassurance is forthcoming, then I'm out of this and you and your –' I spread my hands to encompass everyone around the table – 'colleagues won't see me again.'

Mr Fitz looked slightly puzzled, and I wondered if this

could be genuine. He shook his head. 'I'm afraid,' he said, 'that you will have to elucidate.'

'Philip Graham,' I said, 'a young actor contracted to Hoxton Films, has inadvertently got involved. My boss would like him out of it.' I paused. 'It's that simple.'

Mr Fitz nodded slowly. 'I'm more than happy,' he said, 'to assure you, and the estimable Mr Jackson of Hoxton Films, that *I* have no quarrel at all with that particular rising star of the silver screen.'

I made to stand, but Harold put big meaty hands on my shoulders and I remained seated. 'In that case,' I said, 'I need take up no more of your valuable time.'

There was what felt like a long silence before Fitzgerald nodded to Harold and spoke. 'Just one proviso,' he said. 'Convince that young man that dabbling in things he wots not of is hardly conducive to a long and peaceful life.'

'Understood,' I said and stood up after Harold removed his mitts and moved a foot or two back from my chair.

I stepped away from the table and peered through the gloom at the front door to the restaurant.

'I think,' Fitzgerald said, 'that you may have to leave via the kitchen, Tony.' His small, pale hand indicated the double doors. 'And just one other thing, before you go.'

I stood still and looked down at him.

'The other gentleman,' he said, 'the musical one. What's your interest there?'

'None,' I said. I wasn't washing my hands of him, or throwing him to the wolves. Smugly, I assumed that Lee was already on his way to Scotland Yard. Or was about to be. And then he'd be off to bonny Scotland, safely out of the way. 'None at all.'

Mr Fitz sucked in his cheeks and then flicked the tip of his pink tongue around his lips. There was something dismayingly obscene about the sight. 'I'm delighted to hear that, Tony,' he said. 'Have a pleasant journey home. To Leyton, isn't that right?'

'Yes,' I said, wondering how he knew and if it mattered, 'that's right.'

He nodded and smiled sweetly. It was, of course, a warning. *I know where you live.*

I smiled back and pushed my way through the swing doors into the kitchen. The bright light was blinding after the shadowed gloom of the dining room. Two tired-looking middle-aged men in grubby white jackets stopped smoking and stared at me. I nodded at them as I passed and strode out on to the staircase.

It had been a very long day. I stood on the top step for a moment and looked down at the dingy, cluttered little alley. Something large squirmed past an overflowing bin. The ripe smell of rotting vegetables drifted up on the gritty bitter air. The authentic smell of London: coal smoke and rubbish. A few vehicles rumbled past in the distance, and I could just hear the band downstairs working up a real sweat with 'Way Down Yonder In New Orleans'. Jerry has a record of the immortal Bix Beiderbecke playing it. I thought of that lovely mellow sound.

Then I ambled slowly down the stairs, my footsteps ringing out in the night air. I got down to the yard and yawned mightily. I was really looking forward to tumbling into my pit.

Then an arm reached out from the shadows under the staircase, grabbed my arm and dragged me back there. I just had time to think about Fitzgerald and perfidious Albion before something hit me very hard on the side of the head. I fell to my knees, took another couple of punches and a kick or two before collapsing completely into semi-consciousness. Thankfully, the two of them (there were definitely two of them) stopped thumping me at that point and moved on. So it wasn't a punitive beating they were administering. They just wanted me out of the way. Well, for the moment, I was happy to oblige. I stretched out on the cold, damp ground. The ugly black cat – the one that had been rummaging in the bins – swayed cockily past, tail erect. I was so much of a threat it couldn't even be bothered to hiss at me.

I heard some muffled yelling in the distance and tried to sit up, but my head didn't feel quite right about that and I slumped back down just as people emerged from the back entrance to Pete's Place.

Two men were dragging another, and a woman – Jeannie Summers – was pulling at them in a vain attempt to stop them. As they came to the foot of the stairs in front of me, one of the men – Ricky Mountjoy – turned and viciously backhanded her. Then he punched her in the stomach. She went down as heavily as I had done and started sobbing.

I struggled to get up, but this time it was my legs that weren't having any of it. I did, though, manage to reach out from under the stairs and grab Ricky Mountjoy's ankle. He completely lost his footing and crashed and slithered back down the four or five steps he had climbed and lay in a heap at the bottom.

Lee the piano player took his chance. He pulled away from the man holding him, jumped down the stairs, hared off to the back of the yard, clambered up on to a bin, leapt over the wall and was away. I couldn't help noticing that he was pretty good at this running away stuff. I assumed he'd had a lot of practice.

Malcolm Booth limped down the stairs and hobbled off in pursuit. I don't suppose that, even at his best, he was anything like as nimble, and with one ankle out of use it was a bit like watching a tubby, crocked right-back trying to catch Tom Finney.

Ricky Mountjoy was altogether sprightlier, and after one vicious glance at me and a quick rub of his barked shins he dashed to the rear of the yard. There was the clatter of a falling bin, and he was over the wall. I hoped that Lee had enough of a start.

As I slid over to Jeannie Summers, Malcolm Booth, favouring his left leg, came back from the rear wall. The look on his face suggested he'd been sucking on a bag of lemons.

I was feeling a bit better after pulling Ricky Mountjoy back to earth, and I stood up, fists at the ready. When Malcolm was about five feet away I put up my guard. 'All right, stop there,' I said. 'Another step and I will really hurt you.'

He stopped, but he didn't speak. The voice came from behind and above me.

'No you won't.'

I didn't look away from Malcolm. I knew who it was. I recognized the voice.

'No,' I said, 'I won't. Not if he stays where he is. But I have to tell you, Stanley—'

'It's Stan,' he snapped out. 'Only Mr Fitz calls me Stanley.'

'Fine,' I said. 'I have to tell you, *Stanley*, I am not a happy man. I don't like being ambushed after *James* and I came to an agreement. I am very browned off with Malcolm here. And I do assure you, *Stanley*, that I will break his arm or his leg – I haven't decided which yet – before you or anyone else can fall down those stairs.'

Applause chuckled out from Pete's Place, and Jeannie Summers sobbed a little more.

'Now,' I said, 'there's an injured woman here, and I am going to take her inside the club. If anyone follows me in, he is going to regret it for a good month or two. I really am that browned off.' There was no response. 'Do you understand me?'

Stanley coughed. 'Yeah, I understand,' he said. 'No one's coming after you. Take her in. Mr Fitz has no interest in you or her.'

'Thank you,' I said. 'All the same, I think I'll wait until Malcolm is safely upstairs before I move.'

Malcolm Booth looked at me like I was a smelly mess his cat had just vomited up as he passed me and made his slow, halting way up the stairs. Although I thought I detected a touch of regret in his eyes as well. Regret that we were no longer the firm friends he thought we could have become. But then I'm an old sentimentalist. He was probably just sorry he hadn't fractured my skull.

What with all my bumps and bruises, I'd thought I would be relieved when the taxi drew up opposite the Gaumont. But I wasn't.

It was very late, and the cinema was dark and had been for many hours. I looked across to Jerry's shop for any sign of light as I handed the cabbie my last pound note. He counted out my change in that slow, careful way cabbies have. I'm sure it's so that you have time to do the mental arithmetic and come up with the tip.

There wasn't even a glimmer leaking from Jerry's place, so Jerry was asleep. Since Jerry didn't go to bed much before Monday on a Saturday, that meant it was very late indeed. I handed back some of the silver the cabbie gave me, said goodnight and, picking up her suitcase, led Jeannie Summers across the road.

We'd sat in Peter Baxter's office for a while, swallowing Aspro and brandy, holding cold-water-soaked flannels to our faces, and she'd expressed a desire to be anywhere but in her digs waiting for her feckless husband to show. She said she'd had it, with him, with her life with him, even with singing. Peter had looked helpless and murmured something about the missus not being the understanding sort, so I'd felt I had to offer my 'umble abode. I'd told her not to expect much, that it was shabby and dirty, had an outside loo and no running hot water. She'd just said that she'd spent most of her life in places like that and, as long as it didn't contain her worthless husband, it would do fine. It was then that I'd stopped looking forward to falling into my bed. I'd be on my grandfather's old chair, sleeping in my office for the few hours before dawn broke. Not that it was likely to be a glorious sunrise. The occasional spatter of rain as we crossed Church Road suggested that this Sunday would not be one of cloudless skies and bright sunshine.

I apologized to her again for the state of the flat as I waggled my key around. The new lock was still a bit stiff and took some turning.

The dank little corridor that ran alongside the shop smelt damper than usual, and the stairs that led to my couple of rooms creaked and groaned louder than ever. The dim, unshaded light bulb threw weak shadows on the brown, scuffed walls and mice scurried noisily under the floorboards.

Jeannie Summers didn't seem to notice. Or she was too polite to comment.

She stood in the middle of my living room, which is also my bedroom, looking a little *distrait*.

The livid mark on her left cheekbone, where Ricky Mountjoy's wedding ring had struck her, showed no sign of fading yet and emphasized her pallor and the greenish tinge to the bags under her eyes.

'I think I'd like to go to bed now,' she said, turning a weary smile on me.

'Of course,' I said, putting her case down. 'I'll just find some clean sheets.'

She sighed. 'Oh, I'm too tired to worry about fresh bedding,' she said.

'It won't take a minute,' I said.

She yawned hugely. 'All the same,' she said.

I shrugged and pointed to the sad-looking heap of sheets and blankets that hid the narrow cot I slept on. Fortunately, and unusually, Jerry's monster of a cat, Fluffy, was nowhere to be seen. I wondered where he was. He wouldn't be mousing. Mice offered him no challenge. He'd never been known to stir for anything less than a foot-long rat.

'There's the bed,' I said. 'I'll just pop out the back.'

I left her to it and drifted through the scullery and down to the backyard and the loo. The rain was still pit-pattering down in little flurries, and I didn't hang about. Fluffy wasn't out there either. Perhaps he was spending the night with Jerry. Or a lady friend.

I splashed water over my slightly battered face – two small bruises coming up nicely, one above and one below the left eye – and then brushed my teeth.

Jeannie Summers was still standing in the middle of the room. It wasn't that she hadn't moved. She clearly had. She'd removed her shoes, stockings and her dress. She was holding the copy of *Alcools* that Ghislaine had sent me and looking puzzled.

'Miss Summers,' I said.

She looked up and smiled at me again. 'I think,' she said, 'that, since I'm standing in your bedroom in my underwear, you can probably call me Jeannie, don't you, Tony?'

'I suppose so,' I said. 'Is there anything I can get you, Jeannie?'

'No,' she said, 'I'm fine.' She held the book out to me. 'Is this yours?'

I nodded. 'A friend sent it to me.'

'You speak French?' she said.

'Yes, I do,' I said.

'What a surprising man you are.'

'Not really,' I said. 'My mother and father were French.'

'Of course,' she said. 'Your name.'

I nodded again and smiled.

'Were you in France? During the war,' she said.

'Yes,' I said, 'I was. For quite a while.'

'So was Lee. The D-Day landings.'

'Pretty hairy by all accounts,' I said.

'Were you not there?'

'I was already there,' I said. 'Before. I did some behind the lines stuff. Being able to speak French has only ever got me into trouble. At school, in the army . . .'

She sighed. 'Lee was OK when he first came back,' she said. 'Never spoke about it much. He had his dark moods, but I guess every soldier who'd seen what he'd seen has those. But he seemed fine. Then the dark moods got worse, and about five years ago the drug-taking started. And he became unreliable and started to lose weight.' She paused and sighed again. 'This was going to be a new start for us. He promised me he'd kick the habit. We'd come to Europe, and he'd go clean. He wouldn't know where to score.' She threw her hands up in the air. 'But a junkie always knows how to find drugs, I guess, like a lemming always knows how to find a cliff.'

'Let's get some sleep,' I said. 'Things will look different in the morning.'

'No, they won't,' she said. 'He'll still be a junkie. I'll still be unhappy.'

Yes, I thought, I suppose that's true. But I managed to keep my big mouth shut for once and just stared past her left shoulder at one of the damp stains on the wall.

She smiled sadly and stepped towards me, leaned forward and kissed me on the cheek.

'I think you're a dear man,' she said very quietly, 'and I think I'm making you uncomfortable. I'm sorry.'

I didn't know what to say. She was right. I felt awkward. The kiss was cooling on my cheek.

'Miss Summers,' I started, but she gave me a disapproving, school mistress's look, all pursed lips and furrowed brow. 'Sorry. Jeannie. I've been meaning to ask. Where are you from? You're London, I can tell, but you're not from around here, are you?'

'Nah,' she said, smiling broadly as she turned on a terrible Cockerney accent. 'I shouldn't even be talking to you, really.

I'm from sarf of the river. I'm a Lambeth gel I am. What you asting for?'

'Just wondered,' I said. 'Listen, I'll grab that chair, a blanket and get out of your way.'

She put her hand gently on my forearm. 'Thank you, Tony,' she said.

THIRTEEN

Sunday slid slowly into my office, as bleak and wet as promised.

I'd managed a few hours of fractured sleep, but I felt far from refreshed. The bruise on my rib and the couple on my back made it difficult to find a comfortable position on Grand-père's old chair. Every time I dozed off, one of the lumps would complain and I'd wake up with a start.

Still, no one had burst in or banged at the door, so it had to count as a peaceful night.

I hoped that Jeannie Summers had slept the sleep of the pure at heart.

I lay there and thought of her.

I was disappointed that she came from Lambeth. I'd entertained hopes . . . Well, that's pitching it a bit strong. However, I'd have to admit that I had briefly fantasized that I'd found Daphne's long-lost daughter without even looking for her. Not that I would have wished the Mountjoys on Miss Summers. Or on anyone else for that matter, though some poor sod had had to suffer them. The coincidence of the name – Eugenia, Jean, Jeannie – had been the straw that I'd clutched at, but it had been just that. A coincidence. How could I have thought it was anything else?

Still, it was a pity. She'd have been a good daughter for Daff. Someone she could have been proud of.

I thought of her standing by my bed last night, in her lilac slip, sad and ground down by life with Lee. There had been something touchingly vulnerable about her.

I realized that I'd wanted to take her in my arms and tell her that everything would be all right, make her believe it, even though I knew it would probably turn out not to be true.

I thought of her slim, pale arms and legs, her slender neck and naked throat, her white shoulders and the hint of swelling breasts, and I wished I hadn't.

I lay there for a moment or two listening to the wind shaking the window against its frame, the rattle of the little spatters of rain against the panes, the steady drip of the leak in the roof, the hiss of the tyres of an early morning bus going through the puddles on the road, and the gurgle of the blocked drain. Then I heard the more unusual sounds of someone moving quietly about in the next room and decided to get up.

My aches and pains hadn't improved over night, and I creaked more than a bit as I eased myself out of pyjamas and into shirt and trousers. I folded the blanket and placed it carefully on the table before dropping back into Grand-père's chair. I dozed while I waited a suitable time for Miss Summers – whatever she said, I found it difficult to think of her as Jeannie – to wash, dress and so on.

I wondered if Jerry had anything I could offer her for breakfast. I knew that my cupboard was bare, and Costello's wouldn't be open. Enzo never worked on a Sunday. She might have to make do with just a cup of tea. Assuming I could find some milk that hadn't curdled.

I listened to the sound of Sunday morning. The rain had eased off, and I heard a bicycle slither past, then a bus throbbed and rumbled along Lea Bridge Road. And that was it. Dead. Teams of footballers would soon head off to Hackney Marshes; gnarled old men would tend their gardens and allotments and smoke pipes; churchgoers clutching big, black Bibles would head purposively for their respective places of worship; the pubs would open at twelve, the Gaumont some time later. The caffs, pie and chip shops and the Co-op would remain resolutely shut.

I levered myself away from the doubtful comfort of the old, scorched chair and stood on the landing outside my other room for a few seconds, unsure whether to knock. Eventually, I rapped lightly on the door. 'Miss Summers,' I said quietly.

A few seconds later the door opened, and she stood there, looking tired but composed. She'd covered the bruise on her cheek with make-up. She offered me a wan smile. 'Tony,' she said, 'how are you?'

'Oh, just a few aches and pains,' I said. 'You? How did you sleep? I'm sorry about the state of the place—'

'It's fine, Tony,' she said. 'I've slept in much worse flop-houses than this. And I'm fine. I had a good night.'

I nodded. 'I'm just going to pop down to Jerry to see if he's got anything for breakfast,' I said. 'You remember Jerry?'

She nodded. 'The sweet boy who offered to play the piano for me,' she said.

'That's him,' I said.

'Can he play?' she said.

'I really don't know,' I said. 'I've never heard him.'

I turned to go, but she put her hand gently on my arm.

'I'm sorry if I bent your ear too much last night,' she said. 'I just needed to sound off. I didn't mean what I said. Not those things about Lee.' She paused. 'In spite of everything, I do love him.'

'It's all right,' I said. 'And I'm sure he knows.'

We stood in an embarrassed silence for a few seconds. Finally, I managed a smile.

'I'll see about breakfast,' I said and pulled away and scamp-ered – well, scampered in a gingerly sort of way – down the stairs.

Jerry had bread. Jerry had margarine. Jerry had milk and tea. Jerry even had marmalade. And Jerry had the Bunk Johnson records he wanted to play for me.

I was on my third cup of Typhoo, and Bunk Johnson – and, according to Jerry, George Lewis, Jim Johnson and Baby Dodds – were wishing they could shimmy away like someone's sister Kate when the telephone rang.

Jeannie Summers sat at Jerry's table munching toast and gulping down tea with the best of us. She'd even seemed to enjoy Jerry's potted biography of Bunk Johnson. Whether she enjoyed the music she didn't say.

Jerry answered the phone, and I heard him say, 'I'll go get him,' so I knew it was for me when he came back. He indi-cated the direction of the shop with his head and his thumb, and I stood up and swallowed my tea.

'It's Les,' he said.

The shop was the usual chaos of piles of sheet music, boxes of records and musical instruments – for some reason, Jerry had decided to stock some guitars as well as the odd piano accordion, the harmonicas and the recorders for school kids – but I managed to find a path to the counter without disturbing Jerry's incomprehensible to anyone but him filing system.

It was, indeed, Les, and he was in sombre mood.

Philip Graham had gone AWOL from the hotel, and Les wondered if I might care to look for him. It seemed that he hadn't made it back there last night. Les said he'd send Charlie round with a motor in about an hour. I asked if Charlie could bring a few exes, as I was a bit short. Characteristically, Les didn't give me a lecture on hard times, just said he'd give Charlie a few quid. He sounded so down that I had to ask, and it turned out that Daff had taken a turn for the worse and had been rushed to Whipps Cross Hospital. It didn't sound good.

That put paid to our morning of domestic bliss. Jeannie Summers remembered Lee and telephoned her digs to see if he was there. He was another one not snapping out 'Present' at the roll-call. Jeannie looked at me sadly, and I knew I'd be looking for him too.

I visited the loo, washed, shaved, brushed my teeth and changed my shirt and socks. I felt a lot better until I put my suit on. Suits can only take so much rolling about on the ground. Mine was very much the worse for wear, but it would have to do.

I snaffled two quid from Jerry from his float, just in case Les forgot about the exes, and we sat and waited for Charlie.

I was glad Charlie would be with me. He's a good bloke, and, in spite of having left the ring more than fifteen years ago, he's still more than useful to have around. He knows how to throw a punch. You get hit by Charlie and you stay hit for quite some time.

It was getting on for half past ten before he arrived, not, sadly in Les's Roller, but in the old Wolseley, which sat, engine running, pointing down Church Road. I thought I'd have time to drop Jeannie Summers off, call in on Viv Laurence, as I'd promised, and still make it to the Frighted Horse – which had to be my starting point in the search for either of the absentees – just after opening time.

I've always found it best not to over-complicate things, so the plan was simple. Check out the Frighted Horse, lift a few stones and see what crawled out. The other half of the plan was that I'd call Inspector Rose at Scotland Yard and hope that Lee had shown up there.

To be honest, if nothing wriggled at the Frighted Horse and if Lee wasn't safely banged up, I wasn't sure what I was going to do. After all, I'm just a failed accountant, not a copper.

One of Robert's other dodgy maxims was: 'Sometimes, having no plan is a plan.' And that should have given me occasion to think, because it had certainly landed us close to the brown and sticky stuff on a couple of occasions.

Still, if I didn't have much of a plan, it did seem like a workable approach at the time. And no one else was going to come up with anything better.

Charlie stood smiling on the pavement at the door, but he raised his shaggy eyebrows up towards his seamed forehead when he saw Miss Summers. I frowned at him, and he rearranged his features into something suitably bland.

'Charlie,' I said, 'this is Miss Jeannie Summers. The singer. We'll be taking her back to her place before we go anywhere else.'

Charlie dutifully raised his finger to his brow. 'Pleased to meet you, miss,' he said. 'So where's that then, Tone?'

I realized I didn't know and looked across at Jeannie Summers.

'Oh,' she said, 'it's off by Marble Arch. I can't remember the address, but I'll know when we get there.'

'Righty-ho,' said Charlie. 'All aboard. Sorry, it's not the Rolls, but Mr Jackson felt you'd be more comfortable riding in this, Tone.' And he winked at me.

I wasn't sure if he meant that I was used to riding in police vehicles or if he was hinting that the Rolls was not altogether safe around me. The first wasn't true, but there was an unfortunate incident in the recent past that meant there was an element of truth about the second.

Miss Summers and I settled down in the back of the Wolseley happily enough. After all, I can't even drive, let alone afford to run a motor car, and beggars can't really expect to be choosers.

Charlie put the car into gear and smoothly pulled away from the curb, turning the car around so that we pulled alongside the Gaumont before turning left on Lea Bridge Road.

Jeannie Summers sat in complete silence until we were driving along Oxford Street.

'Will you,' she said, 'look for Lee for me?'

'Of course I will,' I said. 'I can't promise, mind.'

She nodded sadly. 'This will be his last chance,' she said. 'He has to sort himself out. I just can't take much more.' Then her *sangfroid* finally deserted her, and she wept. There was a quiet desperation about her tears, reflecting what must have been a very long hurt.

I reached into my pocket, recognizing that the clean handkerchief I'd so sensibly furnished myself with earlier wasn't going to be clean, or even in my possession, for very much longer. Ah, well! What were clean handkerchiefs for?

She sniffled her thanks as I handed it to her and then sniffled and snorted copiously straight into it. She wiped her eyes and tried to smile. I waved the soggy snot rag away when she offered it back. She held it tightly, squashing it into a small, wet ball.

As we passed Selfridges, she sighed deeply, and I could almost see the effort she put into getting her emotions under control before she leaned forward and quietly explained to Charlie more or less how to find the building she'd been staying in for the past week.

Charlie nodded his understanding and deftly executed a few left and right turns before pulling up outside a neat-looking red-brick building that I couldn't help thinking of as a mansion block. Though I couldn't for the life of me begin to put a meaning to those two words. It seemed to me that something was either a mansion or it wasn't. And this didn't look like a mansion to me. Still, it seemed to be the place Jeannie Summers was staying.

Charlie and I both helped her out of the car. I carried her suitcase for her to the door.

She held my hand for a moment or two and then kissed me

lightly on the cheek. Then she opened her handbag, dropped my handkerchief in and took out a small notebook. She scribbled an address and two telephone numbers on a page, then tore it out and gave it to me.

'That's the telephone number here –' she pointed at the house behind her – 'and that's the number of the club in Glasgow we're supposed to be playing from Tuesday night. And that's our address in the US. Ring me when you know something.' She paused. 'And write me sometime. I'd like to keep in touch.' She kissed me again and then turned towards the black front door behind her.

Charlie and I stood on the pavement and watched until she was safely inside.

'What's that all about?' he said.

I shook my head. 'It's a longish story, Charlie,' I said, 'but I think I'm in love. Only with her voice, of course.'

He laughed. 'She's a bit out of your league, Tone,' he said and jumped back in the car.

I knew he was right, of course, and I slipped into the passenger seat next to him. 'Old Compton Street, James,' I said, sounding a lot more chipper than I felt.

There was no answer when I pressed the bell to Viv Laurence's gaff.

It didn't matter. The battered old door swung open when I gently put my hand against it.

I didn't hear any noise from the flat, and I peered into the gloomy hallway. 'Miss Laurence,' I called quietly, but there was no reply.

Charlie clocked that the door was open and started to walk in, but I held my arm out in front of him and he stopped and looked at me. I put my finger to my lips and then pointed at him and then at the landing to indicate he should stay put. He nodded his understanding and took up a solid position two feet back from the door. The floorboards under the worn lino gave a little as he adjusted his position. He flexed his muscles and his jacket bulged slightly, like a bulkhead under pressure. He'd put on a bit of weight since he bought that suit.

I was reasonably sure the place was empty, but there was no point in taking any chances. Any whisper of trouble and Charlie would come swooping in. Well, lumbering might cover it a bit better, but he'd be no less effective for that.

I stepped into the quiet hall. There was a strong smell of perfume, so strong that it irritated the lining of my nose. For a few seconds I fought back a monstrous sneeze.

When I describe my flat as a mess, I mean that it's a bit untidy, could do with a clean and maybe a lick of paint. Viv Laurence's place was a mess of a completely different kind.

The living room was one of those comfortable rooms with what's often called the woman's touch. There were three cushions embroidered with cheerfully coloured flowers on the sofa, and another one on the armchair. There were tastefully crocheted antimacassars on the sofa and the armchair; there were vases of flowers on the mantelpiece and table. At least, that's where they would have been, if they hadn't all been scattered over the floor. The many knick-knacks that should have been artfully arranged on the mantelpiece, window ledge and sideboard were similarly distributed across the rucked-up carpet. I trod carefully around the broken glass, wondering if anyone used Macassar oil in these days of Brylcreem and Brilliantine.

In the bedroom, all the drawers had been taken from the tallboy and the contents had been dumped on the floor in poignant heaps. The thin, stained mattress was leaning against the wall, stripped of its sheet, which lay across the board at the head of the bed. The bed springs quivered suggestively when I stepped on a loose board in the middle of the room. A few photographs, letters and some official-looking documents lay about like litter. I noticed that she'd kept her ration card. A broken bottle of scent explained the overpowering smell.

'Miss Laurence,' I called again, but I was sure she wasn't around.

I went into the little kitchen just in case, but there was no sign of her, just more evidence, in the tins of beans and soup that had been swept out of the cupboard, of unwelcome visitors.

I felt slightly guilty, and that made me angry. I strode out of the flat.

Charlie looked at me. 'Trouble, Tone?' he said.

'Yeah,' I said. 'Change of plan, Charlie. We'll leave the car.'

I marched along to Frith Street with Charlie wheezing away behind me. That extra weight and the fags were slowing him down considerably. Still, he was the wrong side of fifty and so wasn't doing too badly for an old buffer.

The Acropolis was closed for business, but I was sure I could see people in there.

I took the steps down to Pete's Place four at a time, leaving Charlie to follow me as best he could.

A bleary-eyed, broom-wielding Bill stopped his sweeping and looked up suspiciously until he saw it was me and he nodded amiably enough. 'Help you, Tony?' he said.

'Is it all right if we go out through the back, Bill?' I said. 'I'd like a word with some of the blokes upstairs, and I'd quite like to surprise them.'

'Course,' he said. 'It's not locked. Never is.'

I walked past him, but he called after me.

'Want some backup?' he said.

'That'd be good,' I said, working on the old maxim that two old bruisers were better than one.

I stormed through the kitchen, ex-pugilists trailing in my wake, eliciting the same lack of interest as before from the same grease-stained kitchen hands who were still sucking on cigarettes, and into the restaurant.

Gratifyingly, Mr Fitz was sitting at his usual table. It hadn't occurred to me until then that he might not always be there, that he might have a home in Highgate or Kensington with a wife and kiddies and a garden that he tended lovingly. Less gratifyingly, Harold, Stanley, Malcolm and two other thugs were gathered around him. They tensed when they saw me. I was happy to hear Charlie and Bill clump into the room.

I pushed past Stanley, leaned across the table and stared at James Fitzgerald. 'Where is she?' I said.

He swayed back a few inches, against the plush dark-green upholstery. 'I'm sorry, Tony,' he said, forcing a smile, 'but you will have to be more explicit than that. To whom are you referring?'

'You know perfectly well,' I said.

'I'm afraid that I don't,' he said. 'Now, why don't you sit down, calm down and tell me all about it? Can I offer you some refreshment?'

'No,' I said. 'Just tell me what you've done with Viv Laurence.'

'I'm at something of a loss,' he said. 'I'm afraid I really don't know who you're talking about, and, I have to say, I am rather fed up with you barging in here in what I can only think of as a most pugnacious manner. I'm toying with the idea of asking my colleagues here to teach you some manners.'

I straightened up, and there was a long silence while we all sized each other up. Harold took a step towards me, and even Malcolm had the kind of grim expression on his face that suggested he wouldn't mind having a swing.

'But I'm not going to do that,' Mr Fitz said. 'Just yet.'

His thugs froze.

'Now,' he continued, 'just who are you looking for?'

'Viv Laurence,' I said. 'She's—'

'A tuppenny ha'penny tart,' Malcolm said.

'Hush, Malcolm,' Mr Fitz said. 'Tony has the floor.'

'Sorry, Mr Fitz,' the big man said.

'Go on, Tony,' Fitzgerald said.

'She's disappeared from her gaff,' I said. 'I was just round there, and the place has been comprehensively turned over. If it wasn't your boys looking for the "goods" that you think Lee the piano player took and stowed there, then who was it?'

'That's a good question, Tony,' he said. 'Malcolm, Harold, have you been there looking for anything?'

They both shook their heads. 'No, Mr Fitz,' they chorused.

'Do you know if anyone else has?'

There was a general shaking of heads.

Mr Fitz held out his hands in a gesture that in French would say '*désolé*' and shrugged. 'You see, Tony,' he said, 'we can't help you.'

I knew they were all laughing at me, and I wasn't having it.

I leaned over his table again. 'James,' I said very quietly, 'someone here is telling me untruths, and I don't like that. Let me ask them. Individually. And I think I'll start with Malcolm.'

'Don't you think you've damaged Malcolm enough? He tells me his ankle is very sore.' He paused. 'I assume you have physical coercion in mind.'

We stared at each other in silence again. I don't know what he was thinking, but I was remembering an incident in France. Robert was convinced that he had tracked down a German informer in a small group of Breton *maquisards* that we had occasionally worked with. The commander of that group – an oily creep with, according to Robert, extreme right-wing views – refused to countenance the possibility. After some fruitless discussion, Robert smiled and made a few placatory remarks, then, as we left, he shot the man in the head. The *maquisards* were so shocked that they did nothing. We never went on a joint operation with them again.

I've often wondered if the *type* had been an informer.

'We appear to have reached an *impasse*,' Fitzgerald finally said.

'No, we haven't,' I said. 'We're still talking.' I'm nowhere near as ruthless or decisive as Robert. Or as effective.

Fitzgerald thoughtfully rubbed his nose with a finger. 'I'll tell you what,' he said. 'Forget this –' he waved his hand around airily – 'fanciful vendetta stuff with my entirely inno-cent colleagues, and I'll put out some feelers. I'll probably know something in an hour. In the meantime, you could stroll around Soho Square.' He smiled. 'Take in the sights.'

I'd been wrong. We hadn't been talking, we'd been nego-tiating. And, what's more, I just might have gained a small concession. I wasn't sure why.

I glanced at my watch. The Frighted Horse would be open in a few minutes.

I nodded. 'Thank you, James,' I said. 'I'd appreciate that. An hour then?'

'An hour should do it. Malcolm seems to know the girl, judging by his less than flattering description.'

He should do, I thought. She *is* one of yours.

I turned to leave.

'Tony,' he said, 'If I were you, I'd be a bit more careful

where you put that face of yours. Those are nasty bruises. They quite mar your handsome *visage*.'

I left the restaurant and entered the kitchen to the sound of quiet chuckling. But I rather doubted that Stanley and Harold knew what they were laughing at. *Visage* was unlikely to figure much in their vocabulary.

FOURTEEN

Charlie and I left Bill at Pete's Place and walked at a sedate place towards the Frighted Horse. Charlie was spitting nails on my behalf. He really is a lovely bloke – what the criminal fraternity would call a diamond geezer. I don't think he had understood much of what went on. He just didn't think they should laugh at me. Charlie thinks that because I have an Oak Leaf and a couple of campaign medals tucked underneath the shirts in my chest of drawers I'm some sort of war hero.

Not that Charlie hadn't done his bit. He'd been a fireman from the start, which meant during the Blitz. Now those blokes really were heroes. I saw some of the fires in 1940. And I've seen the newsreels.

A couple of small kids were hammering an old, ragged football against a wall. The ball was in dire need of the ministrations of a bicycle pump and hardly bounced when it hit the ground, but they were giving it a fair old leathering. Their mothers wouldn't be too happy with them kicking the toes out of their shoes. They stopped their game politely to allow us past. Though, on reflection, politeness may have had nothing to do with it. A hard hand administered to the back of the head leads to wariness and sullen obedience rather than courtesy. Still, I nodded my thanks to them, anyway.

From an open window on the opposite side of the street a wireless pipped its pips and the gentle reassuring voice of Jean Metcalfe announced that in Britain it was twelve noon, in Germany it was one o'clock, but home and away it was time for 'Two-Way Family Favourites'. We turned a corner to the distant sound of 'With a Song in My Heart'.

I didn't know where I stood with James Fitzgerald. I'm not a terribly subtle man, and I hadn't a clue what he was up to, but I was sure he wasn't playing straight with me. I also had the uneasy feeling that he might be using me for something, but I didn't know just how devious he was being. Perhaps our next meeting would give me some idea. Most likely it wouldn't. I wasn't even sure if I disliked him because he was genuinely dislikable or if it was just my prejudice against the public-school officer class. Probably a bit of both. That and the fact that he was a wrong 'un.

As we approached the Frighted Horse, I gave Charlie a couple of bob for a drink and told him to walk around the block before coming in. I just felt safer if no one in there clocked that I had any backup.

If anything, the place was more squalid than usual. A strong smell of Jeyes Fluid lay on top of all the other noxious odours, suggesting that the toilet had suffered its annual cleaning. The dull, overcast day meant that little light came in through the grimy windows, but, all the same, daylight wasn't kind to the place. A patina of dirt coated the bare boards on the floor, and decades of nicotine consumption had stained the walls and ceiling – once a fetching primrose colour, I suspected – a sludgy brown.

The few customers, as disreputable as ever, sat silently staring into pint glasses.

The barman was as thin and weasel-like as the one who'd served me the other night, but, fortunately, it wasn't the same man. This one was considerably older. Or maybe he just had more unpleasant habits that had taken even more of a toll.

I ordered a brandy and, after a quick look to make sure there was nothing too nasty in the smeared glass, sipped at it until Charlie came in. He took up a position at the opposite end of the bar to me and bought himself a bottle of stout.

I waited a couple of minutes and took another sip, then, when the barman ghosted past – he was so thin and frail that he hardly had a physical presence – I nodded to him. 'I'm off to the lavatory,' I said.

'What's that to me?' he said. He was a surly so and so.

'Just mentioning it so you don't take my drink,' I said.

He gave me the sort of look most people reserve for when they sniff a rotting fish. 'Lavvy's round the back,' he said, pointing with a jerk of his thumb.

I knew the way and went through the door and quickly up the stairs to the first floor. The first room – the one where I'd found Lee's tie and had such a close and personal encounter with the late, and probably much lamented by his mother, Billy's cosh – was empty, so I trod carefully along to the second and opened the door.

This one was just as foul-smelling and shabby but wasn't empty. It was positively crowded in comparison.

There were three men in it. Four, if you counted Philip Graham. But I've always thought of him as a boy, and he didn't present much of a threat as he was slumped in an old chair that had had the stuffing knocked out of it, much as he had, with his head lolling on his chest, giving a very passable impression of semi-consciousness. He'd been slapped about a bit and wasn't looking quite as pretty as Les would like. The drool leaking in a thin line down his chin was flecked with blood.

In any case, I wasn't doing too much counting because one of the three immaculately groomed and expensively dressed black guys was pointing a sawn-off shotgun at my midriff. It was all a bit strange and exotic for me.

'What ya doin' here, man?' he said in a curious lilting accent that I'd heard once or twice before, when I'd popped in to one of the black clubs in pursuit of an even less pleasant and more disreputable leading man than Philip Graham, and sort of recognized as coming from the West Indies.

'Whoa,' I said, 'I'm just looking for the toilet. I must have got lost.'

'Yeah,' he said, 'you lost.'

'Right,' I said, 'I'm on my way.' I paused. 'Do you know where the toilet is?'

And I might just have got away with it, if Philip Graham, with that immaculate sense of timing for which he is renown, had not chosen that very moment to swim back to something approaching consciousness.

'Tony!' he said. 'Tony, thank God.'

A sawn-off shotgun is not something to argue with – at that range and with the spread there's no way he could have missed me – and when the guy indicated that I should move away from the door and enter the room, I did just that. I even raised my hands, although he hadn't asked me to. I really did not want my liver, or some other useful organ, nicked by birdshot.

One of the others came over to check my pockets for lethal weapons. The tie he was wearing was pure silk, but the bright green and yellow stripes made it a bit flamboyant for my taste. Still, it probably cost more than my suit. He smelled of musky cologne, which was certainly better than the mouldy damp of the shabby room.

I've never been patted down before, and it was a strangely intimate and embarrassing experience. I didn't much care for it. Needless to say, he didn't find so much as a soggy handkerchief. I'd left that with Miss Summers.

The guy stopped feeling my waist and stepped back with a shrug. The one with the gun continued to point it unwaveringly in my direction as the third man spoke.

'You wit' Mr Fitz?' he said.

I shook my head.

'Only, I think I saw you wit' one of his men, yesterday,' he said.

He must have been talking about Malcolm. 'Just a casual acquaintance,' I said.

He nodded slowly. He had a toothpick between his lips, and he moved it from one corner of his mouth to the other. Then he took it out and smiled. It was a dazzling smile, not least because one of his front teeth was gold. 'So,' he said, 'who you wit'?'

'No one,' I said.

'No one,' he repeated. 'So, how you know James Dean here?'

'I do some work for a film company,' I said.

He started chewing on the toothpick again. 'What sort of work?' he said. 'Can you get me into pictures?' He laughed, and the other two joined in.

'No,' I said, 'I'm just a bookkeeper.'

He looked me up and down. He didn't give me the impression that he was impressed by what he saw. 'So, what you doin' here?' he said.

I decided to come clean. Sort of.

I pointed at Philip Graham.

'Looking for him. The studio's a bit worried. They don't like their assets going missing.'

He nodded slowly. 'Yeah,' he said, 'I can dig that.' He laughed again. 'I don't like my assets goin' missin' neither.' He took the chewed toothpick out of his mouth and dropped it on the floor. There were about a dozen more lying there. 'So,' he said, 'you ain't a party to the business?'

I tried to look suitably puzzled, and I probably overdid it. 'What business?' I said. 'Like I said, I'm a bookkeeper at Hoxton Films, so I suppose I am a party to the film business.'

He chuckled in what seemed like a friendly enough way. 'So,' he said, 'you don't know Ricky Mountjoy? Or where I can find him?'

I decided to answer only the second question. 'No,' I said, as innocently as I could. 'Sorry.'

He reached into his jacket pocket and took out another toothpick.

He stepped towards me and held the toothpick close to my left eye.

'I hope you telling me the trut',' he said. 'Cause if you ain't, I *will* take your eye out.' He paused, and we stood in silence, staring at each other. He wanted me to know that he meant it.

I believed him.

Thin, red threads ran across the whites of his eyes, and the dark-brown pupils were slightly dilated. His sharp eau de cologne didn't disguise the earthy, sweaty smell of him, or the strange, sweet smoky reek of his clothes.

Something about my response must have satisfied him, because he stepped back and smiled that golden smile. 'What's your name?' he said.

'Tony,' I said. 'What's yours?'

He laughed, and the others chuckled. 'I tell you what, Tony,' he said, 'you can call me Boss.'

He seemed to find this thigh-slappingly amusing, because he roared with laughter and slapped his thighs. The other two continued to chuckle.

Right, I thought, now that you've convinced them you're no kind of threat and they've dropped their guard, it's time to do the 'with one bound he was free' stuff. The only problem was that I couldn't think how to do it.

And then there was the only other problem: I didn't know how long Charlie would wait before he came looking for me. I really didn't want Charlie to walk into this. I couldn't be sure, but I rather thought that Charlie would come in punching, and that could end up with one or more of us with a gutful of birdshot, or whatever was in the sawn-off.

'I'll just get on my way then,' I said, 'if that's all right . . .'

The man who suggested I call him Boss cocked his head to one side, a bit like a budgie before it says something its owner thinks is cute. 'Now, Tony, I could let you walk out that door. And I could let you take this rassclart wit' you.' I assumed he was talking about Philip Graham, and I assumed he wasn't describing him as a nice young man. 'But I ain't gonna do it. You see, your friend here, he's been messin' wit' my business, and I can't be doin' wit' that.'

'I'm sure there must be some misunderstanding,' I said, going for the authentic bluster of the pukka white man. 'I'm sure that we can sort this out in a friendly fashion. And impress upon Mr Graham that interfering in your business – whatever that business is – is really not on.'

'Oh, we can sort it out, all right, and we can make sure he doesn't interfere in our business again,' he said. 'And the t'ing is, we don't need your help to do it.'

He beamed at his two companions. They both chuckled again. Though, worryingly, these chuckles edged towards the sniggering of playground bullies.

'Oh, I don't imagine that you *need* my help,' I said, still blustering away like a good 'un, 'but I thought I'd offer.'

They chuckled away again.

I could only see the one firearm, but I wasn't sure. There were no suspiciously large bulges in jacket pockets that suggested impressive handguns, but I assumed they carried knives as standard kit.

I suppose I heard the sound of light footsteps on the landing outside before they did because I expected to hear them. And they, of course, were busy wetting themselves with merriment at my expense at the time.

So I was ready when someone cautiously opened the door.

And, happily, they weren't.

All three of them glanced at the door as Charlie's tousled head appeared around it.

I charged across the stained and ragged carpet and slammed the heel of my hand into the top lip of the guy with the gun. I'd aimed at the base of the nose, but I missed. My old unarmed combat instructor would have been appalled. I could still see him, a wiry little bruiser in his singlet, shorts and plimsolls, all sinew and gristle and varicose veins, standing on a coconut mat in a freezing church hall, barking instructions on how to kill someone with a rolled-up magazine.

Still, I may not have killed him – as Sergeant Wilkinson would have desired – but the blow seemed to have done the job I wanted it to as the bloke clutched at his bleeding mouth and loosened teeth and forgot he was riding shotgun. I poked a decent short left jab into his now unprotected stomach, and as he doubled up I hit him hard in the side of his face with my right forearm. He went down, bleeding all over his expensive suit, and I wrestled the gun away from him and turned back into the room.

The guy who'd patted me down was sprawled on his backside, feeling his jaw, so I was guessing he had experienced Charlie's very impressive right hand.

Boss, though, was wielding a nasty-looking blade, swishing it about in front of him, and had Charlie backed up against the wall.

As I fiddled with the sawn-off, to my utter amazement, Philip Graham, who, it seemed, had not been tied to the chair, jumped up and grabbed Boss's knife arm – who would have thought he had it in him? – allowing Charlie a free hit. Which Charlie duly made the most of, following a left jab with a cracking right cross. Boss dropped with all the grace and dignity of a sack of potatoes. Philip Graham kicked him in the ribs, hard. I looked at the blood clotted around young Philip's nose and caked around his mouth, and I couldn't find it in my heart to chastise him.

The man who Charlie had taken out first, the one who'd searched me, was struggling to his feet, and I walked over and pointed the sawn-off at him. His tie was looking a bit more garish than before, as a little blood had dribbled down his chin and splashed on it. He was still a bit glassy-eyed and finding it difficult to focus and even harder to stand still. His legs wavered a little, as if he was too heavy to support.

I pointed the gun at the crumpled heap of tailoring that had called itself Boss.

'Tell him this is all over,' I said. 'There will be no more interference in your business from him.' I waved the gun vaguely in the direction of Philip Graham. 'I guarantee it. Do you understand?'

He nodded.

'You take this any further with him,' I said, 'and I will personally see to it that you regret it.'

He nodded his understanding again and dabbed at his mouth with his tie. His business must have paid a lot better than mine if he could treat a silk tie like that.

The nodding head did not reassure me. As I stared at him, he gave me the kind of hard-eyed, contemptuous look that left me with the distinct impression that he was more than prepared to risk my wrath. Then he spat bloody spittle on to the floor.

Charlie, Philip and I left that room at a trot, and we were down the stairs in a few seconds.

I took a detour to the cold, damp loo out the back where the only sound was the gurgle of running water. I broke the sawn-off and unloaded it, dropping the cartridges into the gutter of the *pissoir*. The steady trickle from the leaking pipes swept them quickly towards the drain. I then climbed up on the seat of the WC in the one cubicle and stuck the gun in the cistern there. Dirty-brown water slopped over the edge. Whoever risked sitting there in the near future would suffer a very damp bum.

'Blimey, Tone,' Charlie said when I emerged into the dull, grey, very ordinary afternoon, 'what was that all about? Who are those devils?'

'I'll explain later, Charlie,' I said. 'Let's get Mr Graham

back to his hotel and cleaned up. Better let Mr Jackson know we've found him. Can you handle that?'

'Course I can,' he said.

We started to walk briskly back to the car.

'Mr Graham,' I said, 'are you all right? Apart from the obvious . . .' I waved my hand in the general direction of his facial injuries. 'You don't need a doctor or anything?'

'No,' he said. 'I'm all right.'

We reached the car, and I opened the door for young Philip. He stood still and looked at me. 'Thanks,' he said.

I shrugged. 'Just doing what Les Jackson pays me for,' I said. 'No thanks necessary.'

'No,' he said, 'I understand that. But thanks, anyway. Especially for not giving me a lecture.'

'Think nothing of it,' I said, helping him on to the back seat. 'I imagine Les'll give you quite an earful when he sees you. You don't need me adding to your misery.'

He had the grace to hang his head sheepishly.

'It was my own stupid fault,' he said. 'Instead of going home last night, after . . . you know, I went to that bloody club where they play that Caribbean music. Do you know it?'

'Yeah,' I said. 'Blokes in bright shirts and gold jewellery and girls in very tight dresses.'

'That's where they found me. I didn't know . . .'

'It's all right, Mr Graham. It's all sorted,' I said, surprising myself with my confident tone. 'And what isn't sorted, I'm about to deal with.'

I watched the car disappear and then looked around for any sign of pursuit.

There wasn't any, and I walked quickly along towards the Acropolis, hoping that the dodgy reassurance I'd offered Philip Graham could be turned into something approaching reality.

I tried to shake off any forebodings by the kind of positive thinking advocated by some American minister I'd read about somewhere – possibly in an advertisement in a copy of Enzo's *Daily Mirror* – and there was much to be positive about.

After all, I'd done my job: I'd found young Philip, as Les

Jackson had requested, and rescued him from the bad guys. Young Philip was more or less intact, and I'd walked away from the rumble with nothing worse than a bruised forearm. The blood on my jacket wasn't mine.

Life was sweet.

FIFTEEN

Nothing much had changed in the restaurant. It still wasn't open, but James Fitzgerald now had a selection of small dishes in front of him.

He looked up when I came in, a piece of bread dipped in something white and squidgy held delicately an inch or two from his mouth.

'Tony,' he said, 'you're back rather earlier than I was anticipating. Surely an hour hasn't passed yet.'

'No,' I said, 'but I know who did your boys.'

Malcolm and Stanley, who were sitting either side of him, suddenly looked less bored.

'So do I, Tony, so do I,' Mr Fitz said. 'Do you mind?' He waved the piece of bread around, and something dripped off on to the tablecloth. Even in the poor light, I could see that the white dip was shot through with little green flecks.

I shook my head, and he popped the morsel into his mouth and munched contentedly. I was reminded of a big black and white cow I'd come face to face with in a field in Normandy, chewing away, more or less oblivious to me. I hoped that Mr Fitz wasn't going to completely replicate the memory by dropping a large brown cow pat. Happily, he didn't. He picked up his glass of wine and took a swallow.

'I've always known, Tony,' he said. 'Your lanky friend, the piano player.'

'No,' I said, 'it wasn't him.'

'Yes, it was, Tony. Think about it. What do the police look for?' He looked at me slyly. 'Motive and opportunity. He had both.'

'But he couldn't have done it,' I said. 'There were two of them.'

He smiled at me benignly. 'Ah,' he said, 'who can tell what a human is capable of? You must have seen things in the war, Tony, that are difficult to account for.'

'Of course,' I said, 'but this is different.'

He shook his head. 'No, I don't think so. And nor, I'm sure, do the police.' He indicated the chair opposite him. 'Sit down and I'll explain something to you.'

I paused for a moment, but then I reluctantly sat.

Mr Fitz leaned back and steepled his fingers in front of him. For a moment I thought he was going to invoke the Almighty.

'What you have to understand, Tony,' he said, 'is that Soho is a little bit like a medieval country; it's a collection of fiefdoms. Or, if you like, it's tribal. For the most part, the various tribes all rub along, but, occasionally, someone does something silly and treads on a few toes. That person has to be reprimanded, and then the status quo is restored and everyone rubs along again. I'll admit that I made a mistake. I thought that young Ricky was a likely lad who deserved an opportunity. I had no idea that he would set up on his own account – how could I possibly know that he would have access to a supplier and be able to find adequate financing? Nelson Smith and I have an agreement. He supplies the black clubs and pubs around here with what he calls weed and what the Dangerous Drugs Act calls ganja. I leave that market to him.' He shook his head sadly. 'Needless to say, he doesn't take kindly to his fiefdom being invaded. Or, if you prefer, to finding his prices undercut in his own market. If only young Ricky had spoken to me, all this unpleasantness could have been avoided. Of course, I would have had a stern word with him and instructed Malcolm or Stanley or Harold to keep an eye on him, but all would have been well.'

'So, let me get this straight,' I said. 'You know perfectly well that this Nelson Smith – I'm assuming he's the bloke with the gold tooth?'

Mr Fitz smiled his agreement.

'You know perfectly well that this Nelson Smith "reprimanded" those two boys. And you're not going to do anything about it.'

'I'm not going to do anything about it because I know nothing of the kind, Tony. In any case I much prefer a quiet life,' he said. 'I'm happy with the status quo, and I can't see much to be gained by doing something barbaric by way of misguided revenge. Anyway, your piano player gives us all an easy out, and Nelson knows he owes me a favour.' He rubbed his hands together. 'Anyway, lessons over for the day. If you'll excuse me, I'd like to get on with my lunch. Would you like to join me?'

I shook my head.

'Of course not. I was forgetting. You've things to do. A motor car was seen outside Miss Laurence's apartment earlier today. It was quite distinctive, which is why it was noticed, I suppose. Most vehicles around here are on the drear side, apart, that is from the buses, of course, which are rather gay and quite brighten the place up, don't you think? But this particular car was red and white. And it could have been her who was seen being "escorted" to it. I don't know if that's helpful to you or not.'

His eyes narrowed as he turned his attention to the food in front of him. He ripped a piece from the pile of flat bread in a chichi little wicker basket and plunged it into the white goo.

Stanley and Malcolm were both studying the wall away to my right. I assumed that was because they didn't want me to ask them any pertinent questions, but it could just have been that they had as little liking for Mr Fitz's table manners as I did.

I didn't bother to say goodbye.

There was a little rain in the air, and the breeze had picked up. I shivered as I stood on the pavement outside the Acropolis, wondering what to do.

No motor, no Charlie. I could grab a cab and be back in Leyton in half an hour. But what then? In any case, there was a strong chance that Malcolm or Stanley would have been on the blower by the time I arrived. Forewarned is forearmed and all that. And, in this case, armed could well be the operative word.

Still, neither Malcolm nor Stanley would have reason to suspect what I suspected. They didn't know that I'd seen a two-tone car in red and white lately. So maybe the call had not been made.

Robert Rieux always maintained that I was more than a bit

cracked. I didn't take it personally because I thought the same of him. We'd all been a little mad in the war. But, as I turned my collar up against the wind and allowed a plan of sorts to form, I wondered if he might not have been right.

Still, I'm a law-abiding person, more or less, and I did my best to ignore the daft 'plan' that bubbled away in the less rational part of my brain and headed off to a telephone box. A few were occupied and even had short queues, and so I found myself in the same one I'd used the night before.

After a few minutes of the usual 'just what is it concerning, sir?', a nice policeman told me that he didn't think Inspector Rose had come in today – I had a vision of him sat sedately on a folding camp stool, in wellingtons, smoking his pipe, surveying the muddy vegetables he had just dug out of the allotment – and offered me Sergeant Radcliffe. I hesitated for a few seconds and then thought I'd better get it off my chest, and the beefy sergeant came to the phone.

He was surprisingly affable and thanked me for convincing Leroy Summers to turn himself in. I asked him where Lee was now, and he told me he was 'safely banged up'. The 'safe' part sounded fine, but the 'banged up' bit bothered me.

So I told the sergeant what I suspected about Nelson Smith and his boys, and there was a longish silence. Then the sergeant coughed and adopted his more usual, and more hostile, manner.

'I might as well tell you,' he said, and there was a 'you're wasting my time, sunbeam' edge to his voice, 'that said Leroy Summers is being held on suspicion of murder.' He paused. 'There's too many of these Americans coming over here and killing people.' So poor old Lee was being held because one of his compatriots – a US airman – had gone potty the previous week and killed three residents of Broadstairs. Although there was, Sergeant Radcliffe informed me, the small matter of said Leroy Summers' signed confession to add to the 'overpaid, oversexed and over here' sentiment that Andy Radcliffe was exuding.

I bit down hard and didn't ask how many stairs he'd fallen down or how much the confession of a hurting addict could be relied on. Instead, I counted to five and then told the good sergeant about Viv Laurence's disappearance. He took down

a few details and said he'd get someone to look into it if she
hadn't turned up in a day or so, which didn't fill my heart
with gladness.

I put the big, black handset back on its cradle and sighed
so hard I probably blew all the candles out in St Martin-in-
the-Fields. If they had any alight.

Then I picked it up again, deposited more pennies in the
slot and made another call to Les to tell him that Philip Graham
was more or less all right but probably wouldn't be filming
for a day or two. I asked about Daff but learned no more. And
then I asked him if he could get a brief working on Lee
Summers' case. He said he would see what he could do. Which,
with Les, meant it was as good as done.

And then it was mad, hare-brained-scheme time.

I received a very odd look from the barman in the Frighted
Horse when I marched straight through, but he was the least
of my worries and I completely ignored him.

I stood on the seat of the WC and fished out the sawn-off
shotgun, holding it as far away from me as possible. The water
in that cistern really was rank. Then I patted the weapon down
ineffectually with a couple of shiny, non-absorbent sheets from
the meagre supply of San Izal. I gave up and let it drip for a
couple of minutes.

A tubby, red-faced regular came in, but he took one look
at what I was holding, dropped his fag and scuttled off to
find a nice safe wall to pee against instead. And I hadn't
so much as scowled at him.

When the gun was close to dry, I tucked it inside the waistband of my trousers, draped my jacket artfully over it and left
the lavatory, which still smelled fiercely of Jeyes Fluid. There
was no point in even thinking about retrieving the soggy
cartridges, and, in truth, I really didn't want to be carrying a
loaded weapon.

I stood outside for a moment, took a deep breath and then
headed into the pub and up the stairs.

I'd been gone for close on three quarters of an hour so I
wasn't sure they would still be there, but I hoped they would.
I doubted that any of them was so badly hurt that they needed

hospital treatment. They were just bruised and bloody. Well, the bloke I'd thumped in the mouth might have lost a tooth or two. But who hasn't? My tongue flicked to my chipped right canine.

They were still there, drinking now. To ease pain, rather than drown sorrows, I assumed.

Two of them were slumped on the battered old red velveteen sofa under the window, and Boss – Nelson, I supposed – stood looking out, a glass in his hand. They formed a very sorry little tableau, but my entrance snapped a little venomous life into them.

'Please don't get up on account of me, gentlemen,' I said, producing the shotgun. They all tensed but remained where they were. 'Listen,' I continued, 'I'd like to apologize for earlier. But you didn't give me any real option, did you?'

They all looked sullen and decidedly disagreeable.

'Apologize?' Nelson almost spat at me. 'Look at Clive!' he said, pointing to the guy I'd whacked. 'He goin' t' lose teet'.' He paused. 'Well, he goin' t' lose the one front toot' he had.' Then he laughed. 'Still, he won't be any uglier than he was before.'

Clive looked suitably affronted and glared at him miserably. If he'd known that Sergeant Wilkinson showed us that particular blow because it was supposed to shatter the nose and send bone fragments into the brain, but that I'd never had cause to use it and so had messed it up, he might have been slightly more inclined to thank his lucky stars and felt a bit happier, but I decided to wait until we knew each other better before explaining all that.

Still, I could look on the bright side. If Nelson Smith hadn't completely lost his, admittedly rather elementary, sense of humour, maybe this wasn't going to be quite as hard as I'd feared. On the other hand . . .

'Well, for what it's worth, I am sorry,' I said. 'Really.'

'You got a nerve. Comin' back here.' Nelson Smith shook his head. 'And some balls. What you want, man?'

'I've got a proposition,' I said slowly.

'Oh, yeah,' he said carefully. 'What you got to offer?'

'Ricky Mountjoy,' I said.

The sudden gleam from his golden tooth told me we might just have negotiated an uneasy truce.

I arranged to meet them outside their club in twenty minutes. That gave them time to, as Nelson put it, 'get tooled up'. I wasn't sure if I liked the sound of that or not. I hoped I'd be the only person with a firearm. Even if it was unloaded, it gave me some sort of edge and a modicum of comfort. Of course, neither the edge nor the comfort would last long if anyone else found out the cartridges were slowly disintegrating in the continuous and, I suspected, toxic stream of pee and water in the *pissoir* at the Frighted Horse.

I used the same twenty minutes to check that Viv Laurence hadn't miraculously turned up back at her flat, and to telephone Miss Summers at her digs from a telephone box in Soho Square that had a similar whiff to the Frighted Horse's loo, and for similar reasons. I told Miss Summers about Lee being in clink and suggested she ring Les to find out which smarmy brief she should be in touch with. Her relief at hearing that Lee was safe carried down the phone line in the warmth of her thanks. But there was more than an edge of anxiety when I explained that he was being held on suspicion of murder.

I left the telephone box with some relief. Eau de stale sweat, smoke and urine has never been my favourite fragrance.

I stood on the pavement and looked at the grey sky brooding above the little patch of green and wondered what I thought I was doing – although, in truth, I knew that thought had little to do with anything.

It wasn't my fault that thugs had invaded Viv Laurence's life. She'd brought that on herself when she'd salvaged what she could of Leroy Summers from Ricky and the boys. And, as the saying goes, in this particularly seedy neck of this wicked old world, no good deed goes unpunished.

All the same, I couldn't shake off a feeling of responsibility. I'd asked Malcolm Booth to take me to her, and then I'd had the chance encounter with her in St Martin-in-the-Fields, when Fitzgerald's boy, Stanley, had been following me. I felt I owed her something, and I wouldn't feel right if I didn't try to find her.

Whether I'd gone about things in a sensible fashion by enlisting Nelson Smith in the venture was a fish of quite a different odour.

I briefly toyed with the idea of sidling furtively off into the narrow little road on the east side of the square, the one that leads to the top end of Charing Cross Road, and plunging down into the dank and gloomy depths of Tottenham Court Road tube station. But I knew I wouldn't do it.

For some reason I thought of Big Luc, the bravest man I've ever known, sitting against an apple tree, sipping Calvados from his battered old flask, waiting quietly for the signal that the German patrol we were planning to take out was on its way. He was, of course, as anxious as the rest of us, as worried about taking a machine-gun bullet in the guts (which, eventually, he did), just as neurotically concerned that his weapons would function faultlessly, and anyone who thought him impervious to fear was wrong. Robert had faith in something he called historical inevitability, and Big Luc, also a communist, may have shared that. But Luc had, above everything else, an ironclad belief in his own competence. And that, I'm sure, was what sustained him in those final tense minutes before an operation and gave him the self-discipline to exude confidence.

I don't kid myself that I share Big Luc's self-belief – I know that I'm far too fallible for that – but, so far, I've never got myself into a situation I haven't got out of. And, while I recognize that could easily change, that knowledge does give me some comfort when I'm about to plunge into some foolhardy adventure. I'd survive. Unless, of course, I didn't.

So, I didn't run for the hills – well, shuffle towards the Central Line. I straightened my shoulders, turned my back on the noxious telephone box and marched down Greek Street.

At least I wouldn't have to neurotically check the sawn-off stuck in my waistband.

I knew it wasn't loaded so it didn't matter whether it was functioning or not.

Nevertheless, I still reached inside my buttoned-up jacket and ran my hand over its smooth, warm stock when I saw Clive sitting on the bonnet of a big, maroon Ford Zephyr parked outside the shabby, rundown building that housed the Sugar Cane Club.

Clive was preoccupied with his loose front tooth, holding it between the thumb and forefinger of his right hand, waggling it cautiously. He jumped off the bonnet of the car and glared at me as soon as I came abreast of him. I nodded amiably, but he didn't respond. I couldn't altogether blame him.

At least I wouldn't have to worry too much about reprisals until we'd found Ricky Mountjoy, and, I have to be honest, I hoped that Clive and his companions would have their hands full at that point and I could, like a *News of the World* journalist at a suburban tea party that was about to turn into something more *intime*, make my excuses and leave.

Clive sauntered across the pavement and into the little alleyway where the side entrance to the club could be found. He hammered on the flaking black paint of the door and yelled in a voice loud enough for Cliff Michelmore to hear over in Germany, at the other end of 'Two-Way Family Favourites'. Though whether the good Mr Michelmore would have found him as easy on the ear or as comprehensible as Jean Metcalfe is another matter altogether.

'Boss, yo' man here,' was what I thought he said.

A few minutes later, Nelson Smith burst out of the door and bestowed his wicked golden smile on me. 'So, Tony,' he said, rubbing his big hands together, 'where we goin'?'

'I'd like to get one thing straight before we go,' I said.

He looked at me expectantly, moving the toothpick he was chewing from one side of his mouth to the other.

'This is just about talking, right? I don't want any more killings.'

He stopped smiling. 'You t'ink we kill them boys? We didn't kill no boys. They hearts was still beatin' when we left them.'

I didn't say anything, but I must have looked sceptical.

'Anyhow, this is just to parley wit' the boy. Explain the ways of this wicked ole world.' He shrugged. 'Like wit' your friend, James Dean. We didn't hurt him none, did we?'

I spread my hands in an 'I suppose not' gesture, but I wasn't so sure what would have happened if I hadn't turned up.

'OK then,' he said. 'Let's get in the motor. Like I say, we

jus' goin' to have a quiet chat wit' him, like we was in a Joe
Lyons tea house.'

'Fine,' I said, looking around for his other companion. 'As
I told you, he's going to have some friends with him. Shouldn't
there be more of us?'

He laughed and patted me on the shoulder. His palm was
surprisingly pink.

'Victor ain't feelin' so good.' He rubbed his jaw. 'Your pal,
the big man, he knows how to punch. Anyway, we don't need
no one else. We got you.' He laughed again. ''Sides, we're only
talkin'.'

He patted me again, this time on the cheek, skipped around to
the other side of the car, hauled the door open and slid on to the
passenger seat. Clive sat behind the driving wheel.

I hesitated for a few seconds and then clambered into the
rear, where I sat in splendid isolation.

'OK, tough guy,' Clive said, 'where we goin'?'

By the time we turned off Leytonstone High Road into Cat
Hall Road and headed towards Grove Green Road, I was
feeling increasingly anxious.

Nelson Smith and Clive had passed a hand-rolled cigarette
between them for most of the journey, taking the smoke deep
into their lungs before exhaling and filling the car with a
distinctive sweet smell. And they had become more and more
relaxed and affable, laughing uproariously every so often at
some remark I either didn't quite catch or didn't understand.

I wasn't sure how much use they would be if things turned
ugly, as there was every chance of them doing. They were
even polite enough to offer the cigarette to me a couple of
times, but I declined on the grounds that I didn't smoke. Which
didn't matter, really, given how much of the stuff was wafting
about in the car.

At least one of my anxieties was allayed a bit though. I
didn't think that I had all that much to fear from them
afterwards.

And I did feel strangely exotic, sitting in a car with two
black, surprisingly cuddly, gangsters on a dull grey Sunday
afternoon.

I leaned forward and told Clive to pull over and park a few doors away from the house where the Mountjoys had entertained me on Saturday morning, a mere thirty-two hours before. The car gently bumped against the kerb and rolled to an uneasy stop with a little squeak of the brakes and a harsh, metallic complaint from the gearbox.

I poked my head a bit further forward into the gap between their seats and turned to Nelson. Since we were all getting on so well, I thought I might as well ask. 'Did you really not kill those boys?' I said.

'No, man,' he said. 'We gave 'em a warning and a little spanking, but we didn't kill 'em. We didn't even confiscate their goods. We don't kill people, man.'

Clive barked out a phlegmy laugh. 'Not unless we have to,' he said.

'No,' Nelson said, 'we don't kill people.'

'That's good to know,' I said. 'It puts my mind at rest.' Which it didn't. 'Stay here. I'll find out where Ricky is. I'll be back in two minutes.'

I climbed out of the car and walked to the steps that led up to the front door of the quite grand villa that Old Man Mountjoy lived in. I looked back at the big Ford.

The problem with being exotic is that you're also conspicuous. Black faces aren't that common in Leyton. There weren't many people around. In fact, I couldn't see anyone, but that wouldn't be the case for long. Someone would notice.

I bounced up the half-dozen steps and rapped on the door.

Nothing happened, and I was about to knock again when I heard someone shuffle along the hall and fumble with the lock. The door opened slightly, and the old man's face peered out. He looked at me blankly. 'Yeah?' he said.

'Remember me? I was here yesterday morning.'

He clearly didn't recall me, and the blank look turned suspicious. 'What you want?' he said, withdrawing his head slightly, preparing to slam the door.

'A word with young Ricky,' I said. 'That's all.'

'Ricky ain't here.'

'Oh, right. Do you know where he is?' I said.

'Ricky don't live here. I *told* him he couldn't bring her here.

Why would he bring her here? Anyway, I was listening to the wireless. I like Billy Cotton.' He looked up at the sky and smiled. 'Wakey, waaakeeeey,' he said very quietly. He started to hum something that might have been 'Somebody Stole My Gal'.

'Who was that, Mr Mountjoy? Who did Ricky bring here?' I said.

'Her, of course. The girl.' He ran his hand over the delicate silver stubble on his chin. 'Nothing but trouble, girls.'

'Right,' I said. 'So, where is he? Ricky, I mean.'

'The yard, I expect. They went to the yard. I told him he couldn't bring her here. Not now. It's too late.'

'How long ago was that?' I said.

'I don't know. Half an hour?'

'How many of them went to the yard?' I said.

He looked at me blankly again. 'I don't know. Dave, young Ricky, George. All of them. I'm off.' And, still muttering, he shut the door on me. I heard him walking back along the hall, his carpet slippers slapping against the wooden floor.

I stood on the top step and looked back at the maroon Ford. There still wasn't anyone around, but a few cars were chugging towards it from one direction, and a bus was bustling up behind it.

I couldn't be completely sure – he seemed more than a bit confused – but I guessed that the old boy had just confirmed that Ricky had picked up Viv Laurence. Again, I couldn't be sure, but I hoped he was right about there only being three of them at the yard.

I shivered. It was a bit chilly on the steps, and I ran down them and back to the car, where Nelson and Clive were sharing another fragrant cigarette. I slid into the rear seat and enjoyed the warm fug for a few seconds before telling Clive where to go.

The name Temple Mills goes way back to when one of the Henrys (the second, I think) had his steward, who was probably called William, give some land next to the River Lea to the Knights Templar sometime back in the twelfth century, and they, according to Mrs Wilson, put a water mill on it. It's changed a bit since those days – it even boasted a gunpowder factory at one time that – again according to Mrs Wilson, who knew all about these things – blew up, killing a French Huguenot, which may just be why that lodged in my mind. I don't suppose the knights would recognize the place now, with the acres of marshalling yards and engine sheds, and, of course, the Mountjoys' big scrap-metal business.

I instructed Clive to head off to Leyton High Road and turn left towards Stratford. The Ford backfired colossally and then lurched out into the middle of the road. Fortunately, nothing was coming. Another enormous backfire had Clive declaring that the car had the bottom burps. He and Nelson laughed uproariously, and then we roared off.

I remembered something Jerry had once sung when in his cups. It was from a pirate show he'd been in at school apparently. He'd played one of the pirates. A coveted role, unlike that of Mabel, he said, which one of the prettier first-formers had been forced to take.

'In silence dread, our cautious way we feel,' were a couple of the lines I recalled. No doubt others would spring to mind as we not so covertly approached Temple Mills Lane.

Funnily enough, I was nearly as relaxed as my two companions. For some reason, I wasn't too bothered about the confrontation to come. Dave Mountjoy didn't figure in my calculations as a problem. Ricky was a vicious little sod, and he had a razor, but I knew I could take him. George was the unknown quantity. He was certainly a big man, but I had him down as slow.

I just hoped there weren't any others there, but there was a fair chance there were. Dave's brother for a start.

I also hoped that they hadn't done anything to Viv Laurence. I assumed that Ricky thought she knew where his stuff was. I also assumed that she didn't know and he wouldn't believe her. And I suspected that, as he couldn't get at Lee, he might take out his spite on her.

I briefly wondered again why I was involving myself in this, but it was a bit late for such thoughts. In for a penny, in for a pound, and all that. I couldn't help but think that I'd committed myself the first time I met her.

We swept around a corner; the rear of the car fishtailed as it tried to catch up with the front, and I bounced around on

the big back seat, the sawn-off stuffed down my trousers
banging painfully against my hip and thigh. A vague memory
of Sunday school and someone or another smiting someone
else mightily, hip and thigh, roamed meaninglessly into my
mind. I guessed it was the Israelites doing the smiting. So that
would make me a Philistine. Which would be appropriate
enough.

As I don't drive I couldn't be sure, but it seemed to me that
Clive was being just a touch on the reckless side.

Some decisions turn out to be unwise. Enlisting Nelson and
Clive looked like it might turn out to be one of those. I didn't
even know how tough they were. They hadn't put up much
of a fight back at the Frighted Horse. Nelson had talked tough,
but he hadn't followed through. I was actually beginning to
believe him when he said he hadn't murdered the two boys.
Listening to the pair of them prattling away in the front, helpless with laughter at silly jokes, it was difficult to see them
as cold-eyed killers.

The only conversation we'd come close to having on the
journey to the old man's house had been about cricket and the
West Indies' chances against Australia. I imagine that there
must be a murderer or two who like cricket, but I've never
come across any. In fact, the only icy killers I've ever known
– two blokes in Special Ops and, of course, Robert Rieux –
would have only been interested in a cricket bat as a potentially
lethal blunt instrument.

Still, Nelson and Clive were all I had. I thought it was
possible that they might make so much noise that the Mountjoys
and their allies would think I'd brought an entire battalion
with me, tanks and all, and flee without waiting to engage us.
And there was always the chance, if they waited around and
saw us, they would laugh so hard they'd be a pushover.

We turned into Temple Mills Lane, with what I was beginning to recognize as Clive's characteristic flourish, and the gun
impressed another bruise on my leg as I bounced against the
door. I suggested that we pull over, next to a derelict warehouse,
a couple of hundred yards from the Mountjoys' yard.

I hauled myself out of the car with some relief and looked
around.

There was a little rain in the air, and gusts of wind were rattling the door of the warehouse. Chickweed and dandelions were sprouting up through the cracks in the paving stones that surrounded it.

Nelson and Clive tumbled out, still laughing boisterously. Nelson picked up a stone and threw it at the warehouse. It crashed against the rusting metal door. Nelson let out a great whoop.

Another couple of lines from Jerry's little song popped into my head.

'With catlike tread, upon our prey we steal.'

SIXTEEN

There was nothing remotely catlike about our tread as we crunched along the pavement to the yard. Clive spent a long time complaining bitterly about having to walk, and, in fact, for all the stealth we were generating as we advanced on the Mountjoys, we might as well have announced our presence by screaming through the gates in the Zephyr. There would at least have been an element of surprise involved in that.

Still, I reasoned that they could hardly be expecting us. The old boy was unlikely to have telephoned them to say I was on my way. He'd seemed to be even more out of things than he'd been on Saturday morning. And, anyway, it sounded as if his Sunday afternoon ritual was to listen, uninterrupted, to the Light Programme for quite a while. I looked at my watch. We'd only left him ten minutes ago. I imagined he'd gone straight back to his armchair by the wireless, a cup of stewed tea on the table next to him. With any luck he'd even forgotten that I'd bothered him.

While there was a Sunday afternoon calm about the whole area and the marshalling yards were relatively quiet, a few engines chuntered about, and there was the occasional mournful cry of a hooter as a train flew through on the main line.

Rain was spattering down now, adding to Clive's discomfort and complaints. As a litany of woe it didn't really amount to much, and I have to confess that my withers were unwrung. After all, I'd just discovered that I had a leaky right shoe and a damp sock.

Clive was really starting to get on my wick by the time we reached the gates to the yard. They were wide open, swinging a little in the brief gusts of wind, and I could see the red and white Consul gleaming brightly on the damp, hard-packed dirt road that threaded its way between the mounds of mangled rusting metal that seemed to stretch for miles, like so many treacherously jagged sand dunes. The car was parked, in a haphazard sort of way that suggested it wasn't expecting company, outside a prefabricated office, blocking access to two of the side roads that wove off to the right of the building.

There was a light on in the office.

I told Nelson and Clive to stay where they were for the time being. I ignored the groans from Clive and just told Nelson I'd yell if I needed them, otherwise I'd be out with Ricky in ten minutes. If I wasn't and they hadn't heard anything, they were to come with, in a manner of speaking, all guns blazing.

I walked through the gates, just as my father had done all those years ago. The prefab wouldn't have been there then, and Papa had gone armed with only a sense of what was right.

I had Clive and Nelson, an unloaded sawn-off, for what they and it were worth, and a determination not to be knocked about. I'd also received a certain amount of training – admittedly more than ten years before – in how to look out for myself.

I glanced back at the two West Indians, collars turned up against the drizzle, their shiny mohair suits not looking quite so expensive and well cut as the damp seeped into the fabric. They didn't look right here. Soho was their natural habitat. Gloomy old Leyton on a dreary Sunday afternoon, with the chilly wind and persistent rain sweeping across Hackney Marshes, was a place for less showy, duller creatures, like me. This was where I belonged – not in Paris, or even up West.

Before I got too introspective and morose, before *le cafard* took hold, I tried to bring something perky by Louis Armstrong or Bix Beiderbecke to mind, but nothing much came. Just a few snatches of 'Muskrat Ramble'. Still, that was enough to get me moving, and I took a few determined steps towards the prefab.

I hadn't thought about any plan of action, and I decided I'd better. The first thing to do was to find out how many of them there were and how they were dispersed. A quick recce was in order.

In this case, that meant covering the twenty yards to the office without being heard and then peering through one of the grubby windows without being seen. Easy-peasy! Unless

Nelson or Clive decided to yell out their encouragement or I picked the wrong window to take a butcher's through.

I was conscious of every soggy step I took, every dull splat as I lowered a foot, and every breath sounded to me like a faulty steam whistle, but I made it to the Ford Consul without any incident. I ducked down behind it and took a careful look at the low, grey, rectangular building in front of me. A certain awkwardness as I bent my knees to hunker down reminded me of the sawn-off stuffed down my trousers, and I pulled it out. It really was a very ugly, squat thing. I rubbed my thigh.

A narrow door bang in the middle of the office looked like the only way in, unless there was another one at the back, which I doubted. A window either side of it offered a view in, but I was too low down and too far back to see anything from my hiding place behind the bonnet of the car.

Happily, the rain had eased off, but I was fairly damp, and the wind, when it blew, had a real edge to it. The gentle yellow light issuing from the two windows and the glass in the door called to me. Inside was probably warm and dry.

I wasn't sure if I did it out of foresight or straightforward vindictive vandalism, but I pulled out the small souvenir-of-Paris penknife with a picture of the Arc de Triomphe on the handle and stabbed a hole in the tyre. If it came to a car chase, that should put the Consul at some disadvantage.

Then, still hunkered down, thighs complaining bitterly, I slipped away from the car and made my way to the side of the building.

I slowly raised my head level with the small window there.

I was in luck. Everyone in there had their back to me. Well, there was an exception. Viv Laurence was sitting in a chair, facing me, but the other four people were grouped around her, almost completely obscuring my view of her and hers of me. In any case, it looked like she had other things on her mind than waving her hand in greeting.

Dave Mountjoy was yelling and stabbing his finger at her, and Ricky Mountjoy was gently stroking her face. But he was doing it with his open razor. I couldn't see if he'd cut her yet, and I didn't wait to get a better view.

I waddled as quickly as I could in my bent position back to

the flimsy door, stood up, hefted the sawn-off and kicked the door open. I didn't hang about posing. I strode straight up to them and smacked Ricky across the side of the face with the barrel of the gun.

He crashed to the floor. Dave Mountjoy looked shocked and stooped down to his son. George and the other big ape who'd come for me the other morning both took a step towards me, but I pointed the sawn-off at them and they stopped and raised their hands.

'I don't want anything, except her,' I said. 'Let her go and I'm out of here with no more trouble. Try to stop me and you'll regret it.'

I waved the gun at them, indicating they should step back from the chair, and the two of them did so.

'You bleeding bastard,' Dave Mountjoy snarled at me. 'You've really hurt him.'

'Good,' I said. 'Maybe it'll stop him taking blades to women.'

'He wasn't going to cut her,' he said.

'Didn't look that way to me,' I said. 'Now, shut up.'

Viv Laurence stood up and moved quickly behind me and off to the door. As she passed, I noticed that her blouse had been torn and there were a couple of nasty marks on her neck and face, but they didn't look like cuts. When she was safely out of the door, I backed away, still covering George and his mate with the gun.

'Don't bother following,' I said. 'Oh, and by the way, there are some blokes out there who'd like a word with Ricky. Send him out, on his own, when I've gone.'

And I slipped out. It was as easy as that.

But, of course, it's never as easy as that.

Dave Mountjoy came barrelling out of the office as soon as I turned my back. I wheeled around when I heard his long, low, anguished cry of rage, and he crashed into me. My shoulder hit him in the chest, and the sawn-off shotgun caught him in the stomach. The impact was considerable, as he had built up some momentum, and he sent me sprawling on the wet ground. Happily for me, he'd bounced off and smacked into the side of the Ford Consul. The dull bang suggested that the services of a panel beater would be required to hammer out the dent. And a doctor might be needed to tend, a little more gently, to the crack on Dave's head.

Unhappily for me, though, I'd lost my grip on the gun, and it had slithered some yards from me. By the time I'd scrambled to my feet, George had it pointed at me, and a very angry, if still slightly groggy, Ricky was stumbling out of the office door, followed by the other heavy.

'Give me that shooter, George,' Ricky shouted.

'I don't know about that, Ricky,' George said hesitantly. The big man was having trouble deciding what was for the best. 'Have a look at your dad. Make sure he's all right.'

'Give me the gun.' Ricky was snarling now. 'I'm going to shoot his bollocks off.'

'I don't think that's a good idea,' George said, shaking his head.

'I think it's a bloody good idea,' Ricky said, and he walked up to George and snatched the gun. The other guy stood in the doorway of the office.

I looked around. There was no sign of Clive or Nelson. I assumed that they'd done a runner when things turned a bit ugly. But they might have just decided to shelter from the rain. Viv Laurence, though, was standing by the gate.

Ricky took a couple of steps towards me. He had a thin, tight smile and narrowed eyes. He also had an angry red mark down one side of his face about the shape and size of the barrel of the sawn-off that he was pointing at my midriff.

'I've had enough of you. I'm going to shoot your bollocks off,' he said.

'I don't think so, Ricky,' I said. 'I really don't think so.'

Guns are interesting things. There's something about them – an aura, I suppose you'd call it. It's as if they magically confer power on those who hold them, and in a way, of course, they do. But, when it comes down to it, they're only tools. Admittedly, they're tools that do a very ugly thing, but, like other tools, they're only as good or useful as the person wielding them. Ricky didn't impress me as a master craftsman. Perhaps if he'd done his National Service instead of time, and had actually handled a gun before, he'd have been more formidable, but even then I don't think I'd have been as impressed as he would have liked because I did have an advantage in assessing this particular situation.

I knew the sawn-off wasn't loaded.

The look of surprise on his face when I stepped closer to him was something to behold. The thin, tight smile widened into something resembling a circle as his mouth dropped open and the eyes stared in disbelief. I put my hand on the top of the barrel and forced it down until it was pointing at the ground while he struggled with the triggers, with no apparent understanding of how the thing worked or why it wasn't responding in the expected manner. Then I twisted it out of his grasp, and he stepped back in some confusion. He looked so pathetic that I couldn't be bothered to hit him.

Behind me, Dave Mountjoy groaned. I risked a quick glance at him. His false teeth had fallen out and were lying, like a strange pink and white crustacean, a few feet from him. He looked like an old, old man.

'George was right,' I said. 'You ought to make sure your dad's all right. That was a nasty fall.'

The boy looked uncertainly at George, who gave him an encouraging nod. After a few seconds of hesitation, Ricky moved slowly around me, going sideways like a crab, always with his eye on the gun, and knelt down by Dave.

'It might not be a bad idea to get him looked at,' I said. 'Bangs on the head can be quite unpleasant.' I looked at George. The quizzical expression on his face and the way he half-smiled at me suggested he had guessed that the sawn-off wasn't loaded. Or he thought that I was insanely brave. The smile, though, said that he wasn't sure either way and that he wasn't about to risk anything. All the same, I was aware of a slight tremble in my hands that I tried to disguise by moving them a bit. And there was a cold, uncomfortable trickle of sweat dribbling from my armpits. 'As far as I'm concerned this is all over.' I waved the gun in Ricky's direction. 'I'd advise you to make sure he knows that.'

George nodded, and I turned to go.

'Oh, there really are some blokes who want a word with him. About his "business dealings" up West. I don't know where they've gone now, but they will find him, you know.'

George nodded again. 'I'll keep an eye open,' he said.

I sauntered off, trying for a nonchalance I certainly didn't feel.

I joined Viv Laurence at the gate. 'Phew,' I said, 'you all right?'

'More or less,' she said. 'Blimey, you make a habit of this?'

'What?' I said.

'Rescuing damsels in distress.'

'Only in the silly season,' I said.

I gazed along Temple Mills Lane, but there was no sign of a maroon Ford Zephyr.

A long shrill whistle sounded as a locomotive screamed past in the distance, and a gust of wind slapped some cold rain into my face. This had once, a long time ago, been a bleak marshland, offering pasture for a few skinny cattle, and now, criss-crossed by railway lines, littered with featureless warehouses, vast engine sheds and scrap-metal yards, it was just as depressing and desolate. *Plus ça change, la plus c'est la même chose.*

The rain slapped me in the face again.

I looked back at the little group huddled by the car, around the prone figure of Dave Mountjoy. It didn't look as if any of them, even Ricky, had any appetite for following me. A damaged Dave and a deflated tyre seemed to have taken the sting out of them for the time being.

'Sorry,' I said to Viv, 'my taxi didn't wait. Are you up to a short walk to the bus stop?'

She looked down at her less-than-sensible high-heeled shoes and giggled rather charmingly, but then she looked back warily at the group of Mountjoys and I realized that she was frightened and nervous.

'Do you think they'll let us on a bus?' she said.

It was my turn to laugh. We were unlikely to pass as respectable citizens out for a quiet Sunday stroll down Leyton High Road. My shirt, shoes, suit, face and hands were stained with mud from the scrapyard. Her blouse was very badly torn, and a certain amount of flesh and bright-red underwear was on display. I tried not to notice that she really did have impressive thruppenies.

I took off my jacket and draped it around her shoulders.

And then, of course, I remembered that there was the small matter of a sawn-off shotgun. The banks (and pretty much everywhere else for that matter) may have been closed, so an armed robbery might not have been very likely, and I'd never heard of anyone using a bus as a getaway vehicle, but I still couldn't see the conductor being too happy about letting me on with that shoved down my trousers. On the other hand, he'd have to be a brave man to tell me to get off.

I decided to disable the damned thing as best I could by jumping on it or something and then dumping it in the disused warehouse we had to pass. I started walking along the road with Viv tick-tocking along next to me.

The rain had stopped, but it was too late for me. My shirt was soaked.

As we came up to the warehouse, a maroon Ford poked its bonnet out from beyond the far wall and then slowly lumbered over the weeds and broken paving stones, through the puddles and the mud, bounced heavily off the kerb on to the road and then rolled to a halt next to us. The passenger window was wound down slowly, and Nelson looked out at me. He pointed at Viv Laurence. 'Don' look much like Ricky Mountjoy,' he said.

'No,' I said, 'he's still in the scrapyard. You can catch him there.'

He stared through the windscreen. 'I remember you sayin' you was goin' to bring him out,' he said.

'I did,' I said, 'but you weren't there to greet him.'

'It was rainin',' he said. 'We decided to wait in the motor. You can go and get him now.'

'No,' I said. 'I've done my bit, and I've got what I came for. You want him, you go get him.'

The windscreen continued to fascinate him. 'That wasn't the deal,' he said.

I shrugged.

'OK,' he said, 'but I'll remember this. And I'll remember we owe you for Clive's toot' and Victor's headache.' I assumed he meant the bloke Charlie had biffed. 'And that's Clive's gun you got there. You gonna give it back or what?'

'Sure,' I said and dropped the sawn-off on his lap.

'Hey,' he said, 'be careful. You coulda hurt my marriage prospects.'

He hefted the gun and then pointed it out of the window, straight at me.

I leaned in towards him and pushed the barrel of the gun to one side. 'A word of advice,' I said. 'Be very careful who you point that thing at.'

'Why?' he said.

'It's a dangerous weapon,' I said. 'You point it at the wrong person and you'll find out just how dangerous. Oh, and you don't owe me a thing. We're straight.'

He didn't reply, and I stepped away from the car. He slowly wound the window back up. The light fell on its slightly convex surface in such a way that it was opaque. All I could see reflected in it was a dark, lowering sky.

Clive slipped the car into gear, and it pulled slowly away. I watched it roll up to the gate of the scrapyard. It paused there for a few seconds. I could hear the engine idling noisily, and I don't imagine it went unnoticed by George and the others. That was probably what Nelson had in mind. Make them aware of him. Give them something to think about.

They soon drove on past.

I shuffled over to a thoughtful-looking Viv Laurence, who had retreated a few feet. She took my arm, and we walked quickly off towards Leyton High Road, away from the Mountjoy boys and in the opposite direction to that taken by Clive and Nelson.

I did listen carefully for the powerful purr of a prowling Ford motor all the way to the bus stop and all the while we waited for a number fifty-eight.

But all I could hear was that strange, pounding sound in your head generated by the stress of unfinished business.

SEVENTEEN

J erry was just a bit bemused.

In all the time that I've rented the flat from him, I've only ever brought one woman back there, and now, having, it seemed, only just waved farewell to one after serving her breakfast, here was another, gasping for a cuppa and desperate for a custard cream.

Unsurprisingly, Viv had been very quiet after we'd plonked ourselves down in the warm fug of the empty top deck of the bus. We'd done nothing more than steam gently and stare gloomily out of the front window after the conductor had taken my coppers and punched our tickets. He'd looked at us suspiciously but said nothing.

I suspected that I had started to smell riper and more pungent than a piece of Big Luc's favourite Livarot cheese by the time the bus stopped outside the Gaumont and we stepped out into the cool, grey afternoon. To be fair to Big Luc and to Livarot, the cheese does taste a lot better than it smells, which is not something that I ever expect anyone to say about me.

Jerry was back from the Antelope and full of beer and *bonhomie*. He'd heard me open the door and had insisted we join him.

I'd been more than happy to do that. He had a very decent two-bar electric fire that could singe the hairs on your arm if you sat too close, and he didn't mind stuffing the meter with sixpences to keep it going. He would also play jazz all afternoon on his mellow-toned radiogram. What's more, he'd share his last tin of sardines with you. All in all, Jerry's a pretty good landlord to have.

I don't know that he's all that familiar with working girls, but I think that even he sussed pretty quickly that Viv probably didn't have gainful employment at the Matchbox Toy factory or at the Caribonum. But he didn't say anything or so much as raise an eyebrow. He likes to think he's something of a bohemian and very open-minded. There may be some truth in that, but the real reason he didn't say anything is because he's a complete gentleman where ladies are concerned and just an all-round nice guy.

He was still on a Bunk Johnson binge, and Bunk and the boys were still, as they had been that morning, wishing they could shimmy like someone's sister Kate when we dropped thankfully on to Jerry's chaise longue. It wasn't very comfortable, but it was, he'd always maintained, an antique, a bequest from his paternal grandfather, so I certainly understood his affection for the old thing. I felt the same way about Grandpère's chair.

Jerry busied himself brewing tea while I went upstairs to wash and change my clothes. When I came downstairs, cleaned up, a little, in a fresh shirt and my only other suit, they were sipping tea and engaged in polite conversation about the record business. Viv was telling him how much she liked Teresa Brewer, Rosemary Clooney and, of course, Dickie Valentine. Jerry was nodding thoughtfully, as if this was important information.

I asked Jerry if he had anything to eat, and Viv looked at him appealingly with big eyes. She hadn't even managed any breakfast before the Mountjoys had paid her a call.

Jerry glided off to his scullery, and we heard him rummaging in the larder. 'There's a tin of corned beef or a tin of pilchards,' he yelled.

So it was to be corned beef and Branston pickle sandwiches.

I took Viv up to my flat and found a clean shirt for her and showed her where she could wash. I was about to leave her to it when she put her hand on my arm.

'I'm really grateful to you,' she said, 'but this isn't finished.'

'I know,' I said.

'No,' she said, 'I don't think you do.'

I held my hands out, open-palmed, encouraging her to go on.

She coughed. 'The thing is,' she said, 'and I haven't told anyone this, but I think I know who killed those two kids.'

'Call the police,' I said.

'You're joking,' she said.

'No,' I said.

'Well, you should be. If I said anything, I'd have to go into hiding. Leave London. I couldn't be a witness or nothing. Anyway, all the cops I know are taking backhanders. They wouldn't be interested. Except to shop me to Mr Fitz. I couldn't risk it.'

'Fitz?' I said. 'James Fitzgerald? He did it?'

'Who else?' she said. 'Not him personally, of course. But it was his blokes, I'm pretty sure. And he set it all up.' She paused and ran her hands through her hair. 'The thing is, I was walking past the Frighted Horse, on me rounds, you know? And I saw some blokes leaving that alley where the kids were found. I don't think they saw me. They were black, like the guy you were talking to this afternoon. I don't know if he was there. Anyway, they weren't acting like they'd killed anyone. They were laughing, and one of them went back into the alley and he said something like, "That's a warning. Pass it on. Next time it's serious." When they'd gone, I poked me head round the corner and saw it was the nasty little oiks who'd been beating on your mate, the pianist. They were both struggling to their feet, so they were alive then. I didn't hang about and walked past, and about five minutes later I saw four of Mr Fitz's men heading that way.'

I was puzzled. I thought back to my first encounter with James Fitzgerald when he'd implied that I might know something about the missing drugs. And then Malcolm Booth had expressed his worries that some of his words might have been misconstrued.

'And you think . . .?' I said.

'Oh, come on,' she said. 'The boys weren't particularly careful. Mr Fitz knew they were setting up on their own. He shops 'em to the West Indians. They deal with 'em for him. He's in the clear. No gang war. They don't deal with 'em properly, he does, and the West Indians get the blame. As it happens, your mate is around and he's in the frame. So *everyone's* in the clear and Mr Fitz is owed a favour.'

'Oh,' I said, feeling way out of my depth.

'And Mr Fitz's boys saw me, and they tell Ricky Mountjoy's

family that I helped the pianist and know where their stuff is so they come and visit me.' She paused again. 'And the worst thing about that is what they don't know.'

'What's that?'

She shook her head vigorously, and her hair fell over her face. 'I don't know why I'm telling you all this,' she said.

'Maybe I can help,' I said.

She shook her head again. 'I'll have a quick wash,' she said, 'and then I'll come down for a sandwich. Thanks for the shirt.'

'What's the worst thing about all this?' I said.

She sighed deeply. 'The worst thing about this for me is that I ran away from the Mountjoys when I was fifteen and I've spent the last twelve years trying not to be found.'

I should have been happy.

I'd woken up that morning missing three people: Daff's daughter, Britain's pale imitation of James Dean and a piano player with some nasty habits. Pretty soon, I'd added a fourth to the list – Viv Laurence.

Now, it seemed, in a few short hours, I'd found them all.

Most of it was luck, of course, but all the same. If that's not the equivalent of picking the only eight draws on the coupon and scooping the pools, I don't know what is.

And though it is cheating to claim all four when two of them – Daff's daughter and Viv Laurence – were the same person, it's still not bad going.

But happy just didn't come into it.

Philip Graham was, I hoped, tucked up somewhere, safely out of harm's way, but Leroy Summers was banged up in chokey on a double-murder charge that he'd confessed to, and Viv Laurence was up to her rather sweet, if slightly worn, neck in ouble-tray.

The corned beef and sweet pickle sandwiches were not consumed in celebratory vein, and the lukewarm stewed tea that washed them down tasted just like lukewarm stewed tea. In fact, neither Viv nor I said anything as we worked our way through the entire plateful. We were both brooding.

Jerry located a jar of fish paste and smeared it on the last two slices of his Neville's loaf. He looked at me accusingly.

We'd just scoffed his tea. 'That's it,' he said. 'I hope you're not looking for breakfast tomorrow.'

'Breakfast's in Costello's. On me,' I said, which cheered him up a bit. Well, enough for him to put a precious Louis Armstrong recording of 'Basin Street Blues' carefully on the radiogram. Sadly, even that failed to lift my mood. I really was brooding.

I finished the last mouthful of my half of the fish-paste sandwich, licked my lips – not because it had been so tasty but to remove a few dry crumbs that had adhered to them – and realized it was time to be decisive. 'Viv,' I said, 'do you have anywhere you can go?'

She looked at me blankly

'Well, you can't go back to Old Compton Street, can you? Ricky can just pick you up again any time he likes. Best if you went absent without leave for a week or two. Till things sort themselves out.'

'I hadn't thought,' she said. 'Maybe I could stay here. Just for tonight.'

'Well, tonight might be all right,' I said, 'but the Mountjoys know this is where I live, and they might well pay me a visit. Which means it's not a long-term solution. So, any ideas?'

She gave a little shake of her head.

'That's fine,' I said. 'I'll give it some thought and make a call or two. See what I can sort out.'

I did have a couple of ideas. My brain had not been completely inert while I'd been eating. It was probably the fish paste. Good for the brain, fish.

The two bars of Jerry's electric fire glowed fiercely as the gloomy afternoon turned into a gloomier evening. The little rectangle of warm orange light on the radiogram beamed cheerfully at us through the increasing shadows.

Jerry stood up and turned on the harsh overhead light, then disappeared into the scullery, and I heard him feed a couple of coins into the meter. I followed him out and handed him two bob.

'Thanks,' he said. He nodded at his living room. 'You going to tell me the story?'

'Of course,' I said. 'Just not now.'

'All right,' he said. 'And I don't mind playing host here, but I am absolutely not putting on any Dickie Valentine. I hope that's understood.'

'Not even "I Wonder"?' I said.

'Especially not "I Wonder"!' he said.

'Thank God for that,' I said and punched him lightly on the shoulder. 'Can I use the phone for a bit?'

'Be my guest,' he said.

I wandered back through Jerry's living room and into the darkened shop.

I called Jeannie Summers at her digs, but her landlady told me she'd been out for some time.

I then called Les, but it wasn't my day. He wasn't there, but I left a message with the young woman who answered asking for Charlie and a car in the morning.

For the second night running, I slept in Grand-père's chair in my office. For all the events and people buzzing in my head, I managed to nod off quite quickly and stay nodded off for a good few hours.

The three brandies I'd swallowed down in short order at the Antelope probably helped. I'd thought the least I could do was buy Jerry a pint or two and a packet of Smith's crisps and a pickled onion, and all three of us – Viv swathed in an old black mackintosh borrowed from Jerry – spent a pleasant hour and a half in the pub.

The Antelope was always a bit subdued on a Sunday night. Even Mickey Morgan had forsaken the place, presumably for the delights of domestic bliss, so we had a chance to talk.

I asked Viv about her time with the Mountjoys, but she wasn't very forthcoming. She just said she'd had enough by her teens and the war had offered her a chance to escape and get out. Her especial dislike was reserved for the old boy, her grandfather, which made me think. She shuddered slightly at the thought of him and made a face and a sound that suggested she was smelling or eating something very unpleasant.

It turned out that she'd picked her new name by putting together the Christian names of her two favourite film stars, who just happened to be married to each other, the glamorous

Vivien Leigh and Laurence Olivier. She got the idea because someone had once told her she looked like Vivien Leigh in *Waterloo Bridge*. Maybe she had when she was thirteen, but she didn't much now. She had told us that with a big laugh and an, 'Imagine!', so I guess she knew she was far too blowsy and worn to be mistaken for the elegant and delicate Miss Leigh these days.

She was proving to be a resilient woman, though, and was obviously getting over her ordeal at the hands of the Mountjoys. She'd even suggested that there was a couple at the church who might be able to put her up for a few days. But I had what I thought was a better idea.

Anyway, we'd all, even Jerry, been tucked up in bed by half past ten, which in my case had been essential. I was knackered.

I awoke with a slightly stiff neck but surprisingly refreshed at about seven. The horse and cart from Heywood's Dairy was plodding past, crates clinking, Bob Heywood whistling and dumping bottles noisily on door steps. It was difficult to believe that I usually slept through all that, but apparently I did.

I got up, dressed and then tiptoed past a still slumbering Viv to the scullery where I splashed some water over my face and boiled up a kettle in order to shave and make some tea. The soft plop from the gas oven as I lit the ring was enough to wake her, and she joined me in the scullery, wearing my shirt and not a lot, if anything, else and yawning mightily.

'Morning,' she said.

'Morning,' I mumbled, trying not to stare at her slim, lean legs. 'Tea?'

'Please,' she said.

'Ah,' I said, remembering that I didn't have any milk. 'Costello's, the café over the road, is open. We can go there.'

'I'm parched,' she said.

'Sorry, no milk,' I said. 'Don't know why, but I haven't found much time for visits to the Co-op over the last few days.'

'I heard a milkman just now,' she said.

And so she had.

I didn't hang about and raced off down the stairs and out of the front door.

It wasn't a bad morning. A bit chilly, but there was no hint of rain in the high cloud. A couple of buses, full of bleary-eyed factory workers, trundled past, a solitary, old black Ford struggled around the corner into Lea Bridge Road, and four or five cyclists glided along, but I couldn't see any sign – apart from a few steaming lumps in the middle of the road and pints of milk, little silver tops winking at me in the early morning light, left on steps outside the shops – of Bob Heywood or his old nag. It did cross my mind to 'borrow' a pint from the boot and shoe repairer's three doors down, but the action could have been misconstrued by someone passing.

No, it was going to have to be Costello's.

I went back in and banged on the door that led off the corridor into Jerry's shop. For some reason, I borrowed Billy Cotton's catchphrase. And that was odd because I never listen to the show. It's not my kind of music.

'Wakey-waakey,' I yelled. 'We're off to the caff. You coming?'

There was a muffled murmur from inside, and then Jerry opened the door. He, too, was already up and about. 'On my way, my friend,' he said. 'I believe you mentioned that you were buying.'

'That's right,' I said.

'Then you will find me a valiant trencher man,' he said. 'I'll grab us a table.' And he was off and across the road before I was up the stairs.

Viv had pulled on most of her clothes by the time I got back, and she was buttoning my old shirt. Without any make-up she looked surprisingly vulnerable. She even looked a bit younger.

'You got anything else I can wear on top?' she said. 'It's probably a bit cold out there.'

I rummaged around in my extensive wardrobe and found an old grey pullover that I don't think I'd ever worn. It had been, of all things, a Christmas present from Bernie Rosen's Aunt Ruth, who I'd stayed with for a few winter months when I got back after the war. I have to say that it looked better on Viv Laurence that it would have done on me.

The kettle had boiled, and I shaved very quickly while Viv went out into the backyard to 'use the facilities'.

We were only a few minutes behind Jerry, but, even so, he was on his second cup of coffee and the always lugubrious Enzo (I don't know where the idea that all Italians are of a sunny disposition comes from) was busy complaining that we had come at his busiest time.

'What's the matter with you?' he said. 'You showing off to your lady friend? You never come in before half eight. Why you gotta come now when I'm rushed off my feet?'

It was true that the place was busier than I've usually seen it, but all that meant was that there were two weary-looking workers with leathery faces sitting at one table drinking mugs of tea and a ruddy-faced woman who worked in the Co-op around the corner tucking into beans on toast.

'Sorry, Enzo,' I said, 'but I'm making an early start this morning. Things to do.'

He took our order and, still grumbling, went off to attend to his sizzling frying pans and grill and pay homage to the coffee machine that was wheezing away like an old man with TB.

He must have felt he was busy because he wasn't fiddling with the dial of his wireless as he usually did. In fact, the wireless wasn't even on. He did, though, manage to find time to light a cigarette and take a few puffs on it before breaking our eggs into a pan.

I was sipping my third cup of tea, and Viv and Jerry were mopping up the last of their eggs with fried bread when I glanced out of the steamed-up window next to me.

Church Road was quite busy now with workers streaming off to the London Electrical Wire Company and the Caribonum factory and school kids dawdling along, bouncing balls and yelling at each other. Two of them even stopped to play conkers. That didn't last long. One skinny, crafty-looking boy obviously had a grizzled old fighter on the end of his string. Two hits and the shiny brown sphere dangling from the other boy's hand shattered.

But, even if the street had been even more crowded, I would still have noticed the red and white Ford Consul sliding to a halt

fifteen yards away by the bus stop. Another car stopped behind.
It was black and looked new. It could have been one of the recent
Austin Cambridges, but I couldn't see it properly.

George and his big mate got out of the Consul and stood
on the pavement for a few seconds, and then the doors of the
big black car opened and Malcolm Booth and his mate, Stanley,
got out. All four of them slowly crossed the road – Malcolm
a bit more slowly than the others. His ankle was obviously
still troubling him.

Jerry pushed back his chair. 'Better get off,' he said. 'Post'll
be here soon.'

'Have another cup of coffee,' I said.

'No, thanks,' he said.

'I think you should,' I said and waved to Enzo.

I glanced out of the window again. The four big men were
standing outside the entrance to the record shop now. George
was banging on the door.

Enzo came over to our table. 'Who's that, over at your
place?' he said.

'No one we want to see,' I said. 'Can we have some more
coffee and tea, Enzo, please?'

Viv nervously cadged a fag from Enzo. Jerry just looked
worried.

'Who is that, Tony?' Jerry said.

'They're looking for me,' Viv said.

'And it wouldn't be a good idea if they found her,' I said.
'We'll just stay here until they've gone.'

'And if they decide to come in here for a cuppa while they
wait?' Jerry said.

'They won't,' I said.

'What makes you so sure?'

'Enzo's coffee,' I said.

'Come on, the coffee's not that bad. Its notoriety can't have
spread further than Walthamstow.'

He was right, of course. We couldn't risk it.

'You're right,' I said. 'You'll have to go and talk to them.'

'Me!' he said. 'I don't think so. You're the one they're after.'

'Exactly, Jerry,' I said. 'You don't know anything. You're a
complete innocent. Just tell them you haven't seen me since

Saturday morning and you don't know anything about me or what I get up to.'

'And if they don't believe me?'

'Jerry, trust me. They'll believe you. You've got an honest face.' I smiled at him sweetly. 'And, Jerry, come back as soon as they've gone.'

He let out an exasperated sigh and stood up. 'All right, but I'm not risking my membership of the Holy Church of the Latter Day Cowards for you,' he said and moved to the doorway just as Enzo brought his coffee.

'He don't want this?' said Enzo.

'He'll be back for it in a minute,' I said.

Enzo shrugged and plonked the cup down. Between them, the shrug and the plonk had managed to tip most of the coffee into the saucer. Enzo licked some off his thumb and then went back to the counter, turned his attention to the wireless, to his third cigarette since I'd come in and the *Daily Mirror* that he'd been leafing through. The paper just happened to have a huge headline on its front page about a double murder in Soho.

I watched Jerry talking to the blokes over the road and wasn't too surprised when he opened the door that led to my flat and they all trooped in. As they did, something occurred to me.

'What did you do with your blouse?' I said to Viv who was smoking furiously. 'The torn one.'

'Oh, it was ruined,' she said. 'I left it.'

'Where?'

'I can't remember. In your room somewhere.'

I closed my eyes and tried to visualize my room, but I couldn't remember seeing the blouse anywhere. I could picture the book Ghislaine had sent me, lying by the bed, and Jerry's cat, the hefty and formidable Fluffy, had spread himself out next to it. But I couldn't see that damned blouse. Maybe George and Co. wouldn't either. Well, I could hope.

Then, while I stared through the window of Enzo's dark little café, the low, reassuring murmur of the wireless in the background, my stomach roiling with tea and tension, I had one of those rare moments of clarity in my chaotic life. I realized that it didn't matter whether they found it or not. They weren't looking for it. They weren't interested in Viv, except as a means to an end. And they weren't much interested in me, although I did have the distinct impression that Malcolm bore me a grudge for the bashed ankle and that George just bore me a grudge. They really were only after the 'goods' that had gone missing – Ricky's and Mr Fitz's. They thought Viv knew where they were, and they thought I knew where they could find her.

Well, they were right on one score.

And then I had another blinding flash of insight. I think the Bible calls them epiphanies. For some reason, recalling the details of my room had me thinking back to Saturday night and Miss Summers' dressing room. I hadn't been at my best then and probably wasn't thinking all that clearly, if at all.

Sometimes, things are every bit as simple as they seem.

Not that it mattered, but I also suddenly realized that I knew exactly where Viv's blouse was, and I for one wasn't going to risk disturbing Fluffy to recover it. Although, I did rather hope that one of the thugs rummaging through my things would. Fluffy is not a winsome, charming cat.

'Right,' I said decisively to Viv, because I suddenly had a plan of action, 'I'm going to find you somewhere to hide while I sort a few things out. Enzo must have a broom cupboard. With any luck, it'll only be for a few minutes and then I'll find you somewhere a bit more comfortable.'

She looked worried but stubbed out her cigarette and stood up.

Enzo wasn't happy but finally ushered her into a large storage room out the back, with strict instructions that she wasn't to muck about with anything. I couldn't imagine what he thought she was going to do with his priceless collection of tins of beans, but I promised him faithfully she wouldn't touch them. He didn't look convinced.

I stood by the door of the café for a moment. They'd been in my flat for nearly five minutes and that was more than long enough to ascertain that, as Jerry had no doubt told them, I really wasn't there. Even if they were feeling vindictive – which that might be – they'd also had plenty of time to break every one of my treasured possessions. All three of them.

I couldn't think what they had to gain by duffing Jerry up, but I was beginning to think they might have decided to do it out of straightforward badness when Malcolm and Stanley slammed the door behind them and strode – and in Malcolm's case limped – across the road to their car. A few seconds later, they pulled out in front of a bus, which gave full voice to its objections with a loud and strident blast of its horn, and drove off.

Almost immediately, George and his mate came out of the flat. I stepped out of the café and, hidden by the bus, waited for them to appear.

I'd been expecting them to go around behind the bus, but they dashed in front of it and saw me immediately. George was on me in seconds. He grabbed me by the lapels of my jacket and slammed me into the wall of the Gaumont cinema by the bus stop and hit me once in the stomach. I doubled over but he held me up. His mate stood behind him, ready to step in if he was needed. That didn't look likely in the immediate future.

'Where is she?' George said very quietly. 'Tell me or you'll really take a pasting.'

I sucked in air and coughed. George had hit people before. He was quite good at it.

'George,' I finally managed to squeak out, 'I know you don't like me, and I don't doubt your ability to work me over.' I nodded at his mate. 'Particularly with help.'

He smiled. 'I don't need no help,' he said.

'All the same,' I said, 'it might be worth you listening to what I have to say.'

He relaxed his grip on my jacket slightly, but he didn't step back. I took that as encouragement to speak.

'I know what you're looking for, and I think I know where it might be. You let me go, and I'll see if I can't get it to Mr Fitzgerald by this evening.'

He tightened his grip on my lapels, pushed me back against the wall and bunched his fist. 'Tell me where it is or I'll really let you have it,' he said.

'Now, now, George,' I said. 'I'm not going to tell you.'

He waved his fist in front of my face.

'George,' I said, 'once, during the war in occupied France,

I spent two days in a cell, a guest of our Nazi friends. Do you know what I told them? Nothing. And that's what I'll be telling you. If you do beat me to a pulp, I won't be able to follow up my guess and Ricky and Mr Fitzgerald will probably never see their stuff.' I paused and looked at him. 'I don't know what Ricky's like about his stuff, but I'm pretty sure that Mr Fitzgerald would much rather have his returned to him than see me plastered all over this wall.'

He still held on tight, and he really looked like he wanted to take another swing at me.

Then something else occurred to me. George wasn't in the first flush of youth. He'd been around a bit, was probably more than ten years older than me.

'How long you been with the Mountjoys, George?' I said.

He was slightly confused. 'Long time,' he said.

'Since before the war?' I said.

He nodded warily, unsure what I was on about.

'I'm sure you're a very loyal servant to the Mountjoys. And I'm sure you look out for old Mr Mountjoy, same as you always have. I doubt you'd want him caused any trouble at his age. But trouble could be caused, George, if Viv – or Jean, as you probably know her – decides to tell her story to the authorities.'

'No one would believe a tart,' he said.

'Maybe not, George, but I can think of a few briefs who'd love to give your old boss a difficult time. Interfering with young girls . . . It's not pleasant, is it, George?'

I could see the doubt dancing all over his face, and, again, he relaxed his grip.

'You vicious bastard,' he said. 'He's an old man, and he's not well. He's not right in the head these days. You wouldn't bring all that up again.'

'I will if you make me,' I said. He glared at me but I knew I had hit home. 'Otherwise, it's just between him and his conscience. Let me go to sort things out. And get Dave to keep Ricky on a tight leash on a permanent basis and it might all be forgotten. Otherwise . . .'

The look he gave me was not pleasant, but he let go and stepped back.

Loyalty's a funny thing.

From what little she'd said, I suspected that Daphne's daughter been used and abused by the old boy for years as a young girl. I'd just had confirmation. Clearly, George knew it to be true. But, in George's eyes, I was the villain of the piece for having the rank bad taste to mention it.

I straightened my tie and smoothed down my lapels. 'Thank you, George,' I said. 'Now, get off back to Dave and tell him this will all be sorted by tonight with any luck and Ricky'll have to see Mr Fitz for any compensation.'

He offered me another ugly look and lumbered off to the car. The other guy, who hadn't heard much of what had been said, looked very puzzled but followed him and climbed behind the wheel of the Consul. The car pulled out into the middle of the road and performed a U-turn at speed, surprising and scattering cyclists and pedestrians.

Ah, well, it wasn't exactly the end of another beautiful friendship. And, as long as the old boy was alive, I knew now that I did have something to hold over the Mountjoys.

Of course, that wouldn't stand me in good stead if Ricky decided to knife me one dark night in the alley off Grange Park Road or in the cemetery of St Mary's Church.

EIGHTEEN

J erry said nothing about the morning's little kerfuffle, after I'd rescued Viv from Enzo's stockroom and installed her in Jerry's living room, but he busied himself in the shop, performing such vital duties as moving invoices from one pile to another and counting the number of harmonicas in the window display in such a listless and martyred manner that I felt I had no choice but to return the two quid I'd borrowed from him in a vain attempt to cheer him up. It didn't work.

I was about to apologize to him and explain what it was all about when the little bell on the shop's door tinkled and Charlie Lomax came bustling in.

'Hello, Tone,' he said. 'The motor's outside as requested. The guv'nor says to try not to damage it too much.' He came closer and spoke quietly. 'He's in a bit of a two and eight over Daphne, you know. Took a turn for the worse overnight.' He sniffed. Daff didn't care for Charlie. She'd always seen him as complicit in Les's little liaisons. Which was hardly fair. 'Where to this morning?'

'I thought we might pop in on Daff,' I said. 'So Whipps Cross.'

'Right,' he said. 'I'll go and turn the motor round. I'll be opposite, outside the caff by the Gaumont.' He nodded at Jerry and left.

'Listen, Jerry,' I said. 'I'm really sorry about this morning.'

'It's all right,' he said. 'Just a part of life's rich tapestry.'

'Yeah, well,' I said. 'I didn't mean for you – and Fluffy – to be brought into this. Mind you, I expect Fluffy can look after himself.'

Jerry laughed. 'Meaning I can't, I suppose,' he said.

'I didn't say that.'

He gave me a dark look.

'Anyway, I've got to get off. Things to do and all that. I'll go and get Viv.'

She was sitting on Jerry's chaise longue listening to Frankie Laine belting out 'Cool Water' on Jerry's radiogram. She looked up at me and smiled as I came in.

I felt awkward. I just didn't know how to say what I needed to. Finally, I just came out with it. 'Viv, listen. Your real mum, Daphne, asked me to find you.'

She looked shocked. 'What?'

'Yeah. She's not well. In fact, she's in hospital. I thought I might go and see her this morning.' I paused. 'I wondered if you wanted to come.'

She didn't say anything, just stared at the floor. Frankie was singing the praises of cool, clear water, making me feel quite thirsty myself. Viv's silence went on until the record finished. I cleared my throat.

'No,' she said, without looking up. 'I'm not going to see her.'

I don't think I'd been prepared for a flat refusal, but, when I thought about it for a moment, it was understandable.

'Well,' I said, 'perhaps you can wait in the car, while I pop in. She's a nice lady. I'm fond of her.'

I was nearly as morose and thoughtful as Viv when I climbed back into Les's Roller in the car park of Whipps Cross Hospital after seeing Daff.

Charlie had been very pleased at having the old Rolls at our disposal and had been disappointed that neither of us had so much as remarked on being in the elegant old lady. She was Les's pride and joy, and he didn't let just anyone ride in her. So Charlie had been hurt at our lack of appreciation. And he was quiet and morose as well.

I'd had to wait half an hour for visiting hours to begin before I could get in to see her, and then she'd been so tired that I'd left after ten minutes, glad to be out of the overheated, stifling ward. Still, I'd told her I'd found Viv and that she was assimilating the news that her mother wanted to see her. Daff had completely understood.

'Must be difficult for her,' she said between wheezes.

I don't know what they were giving her for the pain, but she kept drifting off. Still, she was conscious enough to register what I said about Viv being in a little trouble and needing somewhere to hang out for a bit. I didn't even have to suggest it. She offered her little house.

'She might as well get her feet under the table,' she said. 'It'll be hers soon enough.'

Then she'd dozed off, and I left.

I told Viv about the house, and I directed Charlie there.

The curtains in the front rooms on the houses on either side started twitching as soon as the Roller swished to an elegant stop outside the quiet little terrace. And they continued to move discreetly as we all walked up to the front door.

The key was hanging from a piece of string behind the letter box, as Daff had said, and I fished it out and let us in, happy to be hidden away from the eyes of neighbours. I wondered if either of them would call the police. On balance, I thought not. Your average housebreaker doesn't turn up in an immaculate, if elderly, Rolls-Royce Phantom.

The cloying smell of dying flowers in the bright front room was overpowering, and so we went back to the neat, gloomy kitchen. Dishcloths, tea towels and a white tablecloth hung from the wooden rack suspended from the ceiling. Charlie turned on the light. Daff's sister had obviously cleaned it up before she left. Pity she hadn't thought to throw the flowers in the front room out. Maybe she couldn't bear to do it.

Viv looked around and then spoke for the first time since I'd told her about Daff.

'Is she really my mother?' she said. 'The woman who owns this.'

'I think so,' I said. 'It does say Eugenia Higgins on your birth certificate, doesn't it?'

'How would I know?' she said. 'I've never seen it. I was always Jean Mountjoy until I did a runner.'

'All the same,' I said. 'I think that's who you are.'

'Well, I always knew I'd been adopted. They never stopped telling me how they'd taken me in out of the goodness of their hearts, after me mum abandoned me.' She paused. 'Is she, you know, slipping away?' she said.

I nodded. 'Anyway, you'll be safe here for the time being,' I said. 'As long as you stay put.'

'I haven't got any of me stuff,' she said. 'I need me stuff.'

'What do you need?'

'Clothes, make-up, toothbrush. Bank book. I need me bank book. There was five quid in me purse as well. And some of the girls'll be worried. They'll need to know I'm safe. And me regulars.'

'Best not to let anyone know where you are,' I said.

'How can I? I don't know meself,' she said. 'Anyway, who am I kidding? The girls will have forgotten about me by this time tomorrow. And most of the regulars are, not to put a fine point on it, sleazy old geezers who can find relief somewhere else without too much bother. No one's going to miss me.' She thought for a moment. 'And I'm not going to miss them.'

'Listen,' I said, 'me and Charlie will pick up a bag of your clothes and stuff and Charlie will bring it back here. I'll look out some dosh for you, and anything we don't bring you can buy in Leytonstone High Road. It's only a hop, skip and a jump from here. All right?'

'I suppose so,' she said.

'Well, don't sound so enthusiastic,' I said. 'If you prefer we can take you back to your gaff and leave you to it.'

She sighed. 'I'm sorry,' she said. 'I am grateful for you looking out for me.' She looked around and smiled. 'And this is great. But me long-lost mum who abandoned me? That takes a bit of thinking about.'

I laughed.

'What's so funny?' she said.

'That's what she said,' I said. 'More or less.' I looked at my watch. It was getting on for twelve. 'I've got to go. Charlie'll be back later. All right?'

'Yeah,' she said. 'And thanks, Tony. I am grateful, really.'

Charlie and I walked out to the car. I could almost hear the neighbours' net curtains being pulled back for a better view.

'What's all that about, Tone?' he said.

'A dark secret in Daff's past,' I said. 'I'm not supposed to tell anyone – especially Les – but I don't see how I can keep it quiet, what with everything that's going on. Anyway, I'm not even sure that Daff wants me to. Now.'

'So, Daff had a daughter,' he said. 'Fancy that.'

I clambered into the front passenger seat of the Rolls and leaned back against the worn, comfortable upholstery.

'Right, James,' I said, 'Old Compton Street. And don't spare the horses.'

Charlie left me outside Pete's Place before swishing off to take the suitcase we'd packed to Viv back at Daff's house and then to report in to Les in Wardour Street.

I stood on the pavement for a moment or two and looked up at the dark window of the Acropolis. There were no twitching curtains here, but I still had the feeling I was being watched. Mind you, I'd had that same prickling apprehension almost all the time I'd been in France with Robert and the others, and there had rarely been any German officers with their field glasses trained on me. I'd just been a bit scared.

I couldn't see any noses pressed against the glass so I shrugged off the feeling as best I could and trotted down the greasy steps to the club.

The corridor smelt even damper and ranker than usual. I suppose the place had been locked up most of Sunday and the walls sweated.

I pushed the door to the club open and walked in. It was just a dark, smelly, shabby room with a bar, a low stage and a few chairs and tables. There was something very sad and dreary about it. No wonder Peter Baxter was so morose. The place needed music, clinking glasses, smoke and laughter.

There was no sign of Bill or Peter, but then it was dinner time and they'd probably popped out for a pork pie, a pickled onion and a pint somewhere. I would have been thinking along similar lines myself, only without the pint, if I hadn't still been digesting Enzo's eggs, beans and bacon. A little burp burbled up as I thought about all that fried bread.

My footsteps sounded very loud as I walked across the stage and along the back corridor. The dressing room wasn't locked, and I just pushed the door open and entered another sad, musty space.

The brown-paper carrier bag was still where it had been on Saturday night, tucked away beneath the little dressing table.

I'd noticed it when I'd been collecting Jeannie Summers'

things, and I'd mentioned it. She'd given the creased, greasy-looking thing a quick glance, and then she'd shaken her head.

'No,' she'd said, 'that's not mine. It must be Mr Baxter's.'

And we'd left it.

I hadn't thought about it at all until I'd suddenly remembered Ricky Mountjoy carrying something similar. I suppose I could be forgiven for not making the connection at the time – I'd had other things on my mind, and a recent lump or two on my body – but I'd been kicking myself ever since I had.

I knelt down and reached under the table to pull the bag out. As I grabbed hold of the string handles, I heard light footsteps resonating outside. I stood up, the bag in my hand, and turned to face the door. It didn't weigh very much, and I let it dangle from the end of my arm, the string barely cutting into my fingers. I peered inside. It was about a quarter full of small brown envelopes, like the ones people in gainful employment get their wages in at the end of the week.

The footsteps weren't heavy enough to be Bill's, and they lacked the slip-slap of Peter Baxter's old worn suede shoes. They stopped right outside the dressing room, and then I saw the doorknob slowly turn. The hinges groaned slightly as the big, red-brown door swung open.

I hadn't really known who to expect, so I suppose anyone, except Bill or Peter, would have been a surprise, but I certainly hadn't anticipated seeing Jeannie Summers come through the door, and I was a bit taken aback. I relaxed a little and was suddenly aware of just how tense I'd been. I rolled my shoulders.

'Tony,' she said, looking at the carrier bag. 'I suppose I should have known you'd be here.' She waved her hand at the bag. 'When did you guess?'

'Not long ago,' I said. 'When did you know?'

'Just now,' she said. 'Mr Perkins, the solicitor your nice Mr Jackson asked to look after Lee, arranged for me to see him this morning. I came as soon as I could after Lee told me about it and I'd spoken to Mr Perkins.'

'Where are they holding him?' I said.

'Pentonville,' she said. 'Horrible place. Smells of boiled

greens, feet, sweat and lavatories. And something else.' She
wrinkled her nose.

'How is he?'

'Not too bad. Considering.' She paused and waved her hand
at the bag again. 'He told me to get rid of that.'

She was looking a little drawn and pale, and there were
shadows under her eyes that her make-up couldn't hide. But
she was neat and tidy in a dark-grey jacket and skirt, and flat,
black shoes. She had tied a navy-blue scarf around her hair,
knotted under her chin.

'Mr Perkins explained to him that there's no such thing as
justifiable homicide in this country, and so he's planning to
plead guilty to manslaughter, claiming self-defence,' she said.
'That –' she pointed again – 'could, he thinks, be used by the
prosecution to suggest something else.'

'He told you all this,' I said, 'with a prison officer in the
room with you?'

She nodded. 'I don't think he heard anything,' she said. 'To
be honest, I don't think he was listening.'

'I wouldn't bet on it,' I said. 'So, Lee really did do it.'

'Of course,' she said. 'Why else would he confess?'

'I don't know,' I said. 'He might have fallen down a few
flights of stairs.' She looked puzzled. 'They might have
knocked him about a bit,' I explained.

'Oh, I see,' she said. 'No, I don't think so.'

I shrugged. Or, I thought, he might be protecting someone
close to him. And there weren't too many of those.

She inclined her head towards the bag in my hand. 'Will
you . . .?' she said.

'Of course,' I said. 'I was planning to deal with it, anyway.
The police won't get a sniff of it.'

'Thank you,' she said.

We fell into an awkward silence. I don't know what she
was thinking, but she raised her right forefinger to her mouth
and worried away at a hangnail.

I was thinking just how grubby, meaningless and confusing
my life had become. I tried to think of the decent things –
Paris, Mrs Williams, good wine, Jerry and jazz, Ghislaine,
even the old reprobate Les – but, somehow, they counted for

less than the criminals, the drunks, the vicious thugs and sporadic violence I'd encountered over the past few days. Even the jazz had been tainted. Pete's Place could never be quite the same for me.

Jeannie Summers opened her dark-blue handbag with a snap and took out a small handkerchief with a flower embroidered in one corner. She dabbed at her nose, mouth and eyes.

Then we both heard the sounds of people arriving in the club.

I put down the bag. 'Wait here,' I said. 'I'll just go and tell Peter and Bill that you forgot something on Saturday night and we came in to pick it up.'

She nodded slightly and then put the handkerchief back in the handbag.

I left her standing there, lost in her own miserable thoughts, and went out into the corridor, closing the door quietly behind me.

As soon as the wonky board on the stage groaned and creaked when my much-repaired good black brogues landed on it, I knew I was in trouble, with a capital TR.

The club was every bit as gloomy as it had been before. It wasn't just people it needed to cheer it up. It was the right kind of people.

Ricky Mountjoy, George and the other two heavies they had with them definitely did not count as the right kind of people. Particularly as the boot was very much on the other foot this time. Or, to put it another way, Ricky and George had the sawn-off shotguns.

'Oh, look,' Ricky said, 'it's wossname, the frog. Like a bad penny, ain't he?' He pointed the gun at me.

I assumed it was loaded and someone had shown him more or less how to use it, so I stayed where I was. Anyway, I didn't want to lead them back to Miss Summers.

'I didn't expect to see you here,' I said, although thoughts of bent screws, telephones and greasy fivers did flicker briefly across my mind. 'I didn't take you for a jazz fan.'

'Stop pratting about,' he said. 'Where's my stuff?'

'Sorry,' I said, 'I don't know. It's gone.' I just didn't want him to have it. And, apart from the simple pleasure I got from cheesing him off, I didn't know what the vicious little sod would do once he placed his grubby little mitts on it.

He took a few steps forward, his sharp, Italian, mohair suit a shimmering shiny blue with flecks of purple in the gloom. 'I won't ask you again,' he said.

I shrugged, and he jumped lightly on to the stage, which groaned again, and he thrust the gun hard against my stomach. He had a livid bruise on his left cheek that almost matched the colours of his suit, so I could see why he wouldn't be happy with me. Funny, though: they may have been similar colours, but the suit was pretty and the bruise was ugly.

I straightened up after the painful jab to the belly and shrugged again. I've always been good at dumb insolence, or so my old headmaster and one or two senior officers in the army had told me.

I saw the move early, so I managed to get my arm up as the barrel of the gun swung towards my head. Although I parried it a bit, I still took a nasty whack to the bonce and went down in a heap. My head hurt, but my arm didn't. It would, though, once the numbness wore off.

I lay there, pretending to be a bit groggier than I felt – though I felt quite groggy enough – waiting for Ricky to follow up by booting me, but he didn't. At first, I thought it was because he didn't want to scuff his new black suede shoes, but then I heard Jeannie Summers calling softly to me from the corridor off the stage.

'Tony, Tony, is everything all right?'

Ricky poked me in the shoulder with the shotgun. I wanted to rip it out of his hands, but my left arm wasn't going to respond until I got some feeling back in it.

He leaned down, his face only inches from mine. 'Tell her everything's fine and dandy,' he hissed at me.

Apart from a few blackheads nestling around his nose, his skin was surprisingly unblemished – thanks, no doubt, to the nightly use of Fuller's earth – and his hair was slick with Brylcreem, but he gave off a sharp, sour smell.

I was about to refuse to call her and was preparing myself for the blow that would follow when Miss Summers appeared at the side of the stage, the greasy carrier-bag in her hand.

'I found the bag,' she said, holding it out in front of her. 'Is this what you're looking for?'

Ricky reached out and snatched it from her.

'There's nothing in it,' Miss Summers said flatly.

Ricky stared into the bag. Then he crushed it into a ball and hurled it against the wall at the back of the stage.

'Where's the stuff?' he yelled at me. 'What have you done with it?'

I sat up and, as best I could with a reluctant left arm, gave him my best French shrug. Then I told him the truth. 'I haven't done anything with it.'

Instead of then asking me who had – which might have caused me more of a moral dilemma, though, admittedly, not much – he turned to George and the other blokes. 'Get back there and look for it.'

George waved the other two forward, and they both stepped on to the stage.

'That won't do you any good,' Miss Summers said. 'We've already looked.'

The two heavies hesitated and turned to Ricky for instructions.

'I'd be quick, if I were you,' I said. 'The owner, Peter, and his staff will be back soon.'

Ricky looked undecided and started to pace about the stage angrily. I hoped he wouldn't do anything stupid, but I wasn't about to rush off to Nobby Clarke and ask him to give me odds. Nobby would have smiled suavely and quoted me something like a thousand to one. And Nobby would have been right.

Ricky smacked the barrel of the gun against the old upright piano, bruising the veneer and setting the strings thrumming sweetly.

'George,' he said, 'put these two in the car and take Brian with you. Me and Steve'll have a quick look out the back and we'll be right with you.' He waved the gun at me. 'Any trouble from him and smack him one.'

I tried to look innocent of any thoughts of escape, but I must have failed because Brian, the guy who'd been with George earlier that morning, grabbed me by the arm rather more roughly than was warranted and hauled me off the stage and towards the door. George, rather more politely, took Miss Summers gently by the arm and helped her step down.

Ricky and the other one, Steve, nipped off the other way. I didn't know whether I hoped they'd find the stuff or not. Ricky didn't seem to be in a forgiving mood.

I blinked as we came out into the light and tried to slow Brian down by stumbling on the steps. He wasn't having it, though, and cuffed me on the back of the head. Once on the street, I searched for any potential sign of help, but although we did attract a few curt, interested looks, they were from bystanders who passed hurriedly on. No friendly face or strolling bobby appeared before I was bundled into the two-tone Consul parked right outside the Acropolis. I did cast one glance up at the restaurant, but the darkened window just reflected the sullen sky. In any case, I could hardly look for any help there. Malcolm Booth was probably peering out, cheering the bad guys on.

Miss Summers was ushered in next to me, and then came the big squeeze as George hemmed us in on one side and Brian on the other. We were packed as tight as sardines in a tin. Miss Summers leaned in to me, probably to avoid getting too intimate with George.

I was definitely getting feeling back in my left arm as I was only too aware of the soft weight of her breast as it pressed against me.

Brian lit a cigarette and breathed smoke all over me. I tried not to give him the satisfaction of coughing, but it was hard.

Within a matter of minutes Ricky and Steve jumped into the front of the car. They appeared to be empty-handed. Ricky looked very cheesed off and slammed the passenger door so hard that I assumed he hadn't found the heap of envelopes. I wondered what Jeannie Summers had done with them, and why, as the car roared off with a crash of grinding metal towards Shaftesbury Avenue.

NINETEEN

Although it wasn't actually raining, the scrap-metal yard in Temple Mills Lane looked just as bleak and dreary as it had on Sunday.

There were a few odd splashes of colour in the mounds of bent, crushed and rusting steel, but nowhere near enough to brighten the scene.

There was some movement, too, as a couple of men sorted through some bits and pieces. Ricky soon put a stop to that. He left the car, closely followed by Steve, strolled over to the men and told them to hop it for a couple of hours. They didn't hang about. That did not fill me with confidence. I could see no reason to look forward to the next hour or so.

George and Brian had climbed out of the car as well and stood by the open rear doors, looking relaxed. Why not? They were on home turf now. Even if I could outrun them, they knew I wasn't going to leave Miss Summers to their tender mercies, and her neat, stylish and quite tight skirt wasn't made for running.

Ricky sauntered over. He jerked his thumb at me. 'Out,' he said.

I slid across to the right, and Miss Summers manoeuvred her way to the left.

I hoped that I was the only one of us who noticed that she left her large, navy-blue handbag on the floor of the car. She very carefully shut the door behind her to stop George from seeing, and I did the same to keep the sight from Brian. Not that either of them were paying much attention.

Brian shoved me hard in the back, and I staggered towards the prefabricated grey office. I was beginning to resent the way that Brian was treating me, and I found myself itching to add to the kinks in his much-broken nose. The only thing stopping me was the thought that he'd barely notice and it would hardly ruin his chances with the ladies.

Well, that and the fact of the two sawn-off shotguns, both of which were pointed more or less in my direction.

I had a very nasty feeling as I went through the door into the untidy and dusty office.

Dave Mountjoy stood by a desk, drinking a large mug of tea, looking over the shoulder of a grey-haired middle-aged woman who was pecking away, painfully slowly, at a type-writer. Dave was looking very old and drawn. I suddenly realized his face had collapsed because he wasn't wearing his false teeth. Something must have cracked when the plates fell out of his mouth.

Ricky walked up to the desk and dismissed the woman with a peremptory wave of his hand. She looked up at Dave, who put his hand on her shoulder and nodded.

'Off you go, Glad,' he said quietly. 'Take the afternoon off.'

She, like the two men outside, didn't wait to be told twice. She just pulled her grey, shapeless cardigan from the back of the chair, collected her plastic mac from behind the door and scuttled off.

Dave Mountjoy waited until she had gone and then looked me up and down. 'You found him then. He have your stuff?' he said.

'No, he says he don't know where it is,' Ricky said.

There was a pale, yellow, unhealthy cast to Dave's face, and he was moving carefully. The bang on the head must have shaken him up. 'That his bint?' he said, pointing at Miss Summers.

Ricky shrugged.

The little office was crowded. It wasn't built to house seven people, a desk, five chairs and four overflowing wooden filing cabinets. Brian and Steve were standing shoulder to shoulder by the door. George, with his shotgun, was a looming pres-ence, just behind me.

Under the far window, the one I'd peered through the day before, a couple of piles of old papers were spilling over on to the floor. Judging by the thick layer of dust that covered them, they'd been there for quite some time. Who would have guessed the Mountjoys were such meticulous record-keepers? Not, I suspected, Her Majesty's Inspector of Taxes.

Ricky put his sawn-off down, on the desk, and turned towards me. Without any warning, he backhanded me across the face.

Jeannie Summers gasped, and I, surprised rather than hurt, fell against George, who pushed me back towards Ricky.

'Now, where's my stuff?' Ricky said.

There was a little trickle of blood coming from the corner of my mouth where his ring had caught me, and I dabbed at it with my left hand. Still, no real harm done. Yet.

I sniffed. 'As I told you before, I don't know,' I said.

He didn't give me an opportunity to elaborate. He backhanded me again. This time I was ready for it and swayed back. He barely made contact.

I did though.

I hit him full in the mouth with a short right jab hard enough to loosen teeth. He sat down with a startled look on his face just before George tapped me on the back of the head with the barrel of the gun.

I pitched forward and landed next to Ricky, but I didn't know much about it. I didn't come round for a couple of seconds.

When I did, George was standing over me, pointing the gun straight at me, with an ugly snarl on his face. 'You say the word, Mr Mountjoy,' he said, 'I'll do him now.'

'No, not just yet, George,' Dave said, putting a restraining hand on his forearm. 'Later, perhaps.'

Steve and Brian, the other two thugs, had crowded into the room and were helping Ricky to his feet. Ricky shrugged them off and spat blood on to the floor.

I sat up and shook my head. It hurt. A lot. I squeezed my eyes shut, but it didn't do any good. When I opened them, George was still glaring at me, blood was still dribbling from Ricky Mountjoy's mouth, Dave Mountjoy wasn't looking any prettier and my head still hurt.

'Get him up,' Dave Mountjoy said, and Brian and Steve each grabbed a handful of bunched-up lapel and shirt and hauled me to my feet.

To be honest, I was almost grateful to them. I'm not sure that I'd've managed the manoeuvre on my own.

'Now then,' Dave said. He was mumbling a bit, and little drops of spittle came out as he spoke. Without his teeth, he looked as if he had sucked his cheeks in. 'I'm fed up with all this. Tell the boy what he needs to know, and we can stop all this unpleasantness, and no one has to get badly hurt.'

He started quietly and slowly, almost reasonably, but by the time he was approaching the end of this little statement he was speaking quickly and loudly, his hands were trembling and I was under no illusions that someone – specifically, me – was going to end up hurt, no matter what.

I sighed deeply. 'Mr Mountjoy,' I said, slowly and deliberately, 'I can't tell him what I don't know.'

He took a step towards me and raised clenched fists. He held them either side of my face. I wasn't sure if he was daring me to respond or just trying to be threatening.

Either way, it didn't work. I couldn't be bothered to hit him – I'd just get another bonk on the bonce – and I didn't feel any more threatened than I already was.

After a few seconds of staring at me, his jaw as clenched as his fists, he relaxed and stepped back.

Then he did exactly what I'd hoped he wouldn't.

He turned towards Jeannie Summers and smiled.

She had backed up towards the far wall when the violence had started. The little bruise on her left cheek where Ricky had smacked her the other night stood out against her pale cheek. Her lips were a thin, red line, and she looked grim and scared.

Dave had an evil leer on his face when he turned back towards the rest of us. 'Hold him tight,' he said. 'He's a tough guy, a war hero. Let's see how tough he is when his girl starts screaming.'

'No,' I said, moving towards him. 'Leave her out of this.' But George and Brian grabbed me before I could get any closer. As they did, Jeannie Summers looked straight at me and gave a brief shake of her head.

George and Brian dragged me back a few feet, and Brian punched me a couple of times in my right kidney. But they were both half-hearted taps, and I didn't think I'd find any Burgundy in my pee in the morning.

But I was confused. I didn't know what Jeannie Summers was up to. She seemed to be telling me to do nothing, but that wasn't going to be possible if they started roughing her up.

'Leave her,' I said again. 'She doesn't know anything.'

'Maybe not,' Dave Mountjoy said, 'but a pound to a penny says that, if you do, you'll tell us within a minute of Ricky getting his razor out.'

This was no time for the red mist to descend. I needed a clear head. I took several deep breaths and tried to relax, but it wasn't easy.

Ricky spat out another mouthful of blood – that grubby floor would need the attention of a sturdy mop, buckets of clean water and a lot of elbow grease – and then he reached into his pocket and pulled out his razor. He opened it with a flourish and flashed me an ugly grin. His front teeth were outlined in blood.

I thought that George winced at the sight of the open blade, but, even if he didn't approve, I wouldn't bet on him intervening. He'd worked for the Mountjoys too long. And he'd probably seen too many nasty things to be overly bothered by one more. Scrap-metal merchants are not known for having bleeding hearts.

Steve moved away from the door and came alongside the rest of us to have a butcher's at the floor show. He, at least, didn't seem to have any qualms about what was going on.

I felt hemmed in but tried to relax again, reasoning that if I didn't struggle they wouldn't hold me as tightly and so when it came to the 'with one bound he was free' time I just might break their grips and do some real damage to Ricky before he could hurt Miss Summers. But I wouldn't be putting any of the folding stuff on me to manage that either.

For someone who doesn't have so much as a flutter on the Derby, I was spending a lot of time calculating odds that grim Monday afternoon.

I tried to look away as Ricky swaggered over to Miss Summers, but Dave Mountjoy noticed, placed a big, nicotine-stained finger along one side of my jaw and his thumb along the other and yanked my head around.

Miss Summers moved as far away from Ricky as was

possible, her body pressed right against the wall, but he just leaned right up to her, trapping her. She beat at him ineffectually with both hands until he grasped both her wrists in one large fist. Then he placed the flat of the blade against her face, much as I'd seen him do with Viv Laurence, and lovingly stroked her cheek with the cold steel a few times.

Then he stepped back and, instead of threatening to cut her, chopped off the top button of her jacket. He turned and leered at the rest of us before chopping off the second button. Her jacket swung open. He turned back towards us again.

'I think we should search her properly, don't you? Make sure she isn't hiding anything,' he said.

I wondered how far to let it go before giving it my one shot. Not very far, I decided.

'She isn't hiding anything,' I managed to squeeze out, in spite of Dave's hand being clamped to my jaw.

'Then she's got nothing to be afraid of. Have you, darling?' Ricky said, turning back to Jeannie.

He lifted the razor and ran it from her breasts to her waist, slitting open the white nylon slip she was wearing under the jacket. He took a step back again, presumably to get a good look, and grinned at the sight of the thin line of exposed white flesh.

She looked at him evenly and spat in his eye.

He started back, surprised, and let go of her wrists to rub her spittle off his face. She took full advantage of his surprise and shoved him hard towards the window.

He banged against it, and then all hell broke loose.

Steve ran over to help him, bashing his hip painfully into the desk on the way. Just as he got there, the window exploded inwards, showering the pair of them with shards of glass, and a half-brick landed on the back of Ricky's head.

I briefly glimpsed a dark face that I recognized as Clive's before a Tizer bottle smacked into the wooden filing cabinet next to Ricky's unconscious body and exploded with a loud 'whumpf', filling the office with petrol fumes.

In France, we'd heard about the improvised bombs the Finns had used against the Russians during the Winter War, but I'd never seen one used before.

They must have been effective.

Within seconds, the piles of paper and the filing cabinets were all ablaze and the place was alive with darting tongues of flame and dark roiling smoke. George, Brian and Dave all let go of me and just stood and gaped, presumably in some kind of shock.

'Out,' I yelled. 'Everyone get out.'

I pushed past George and Brian and stumbled through the already thick smoke to Jeannie Summers, who looked as shocked as the men. I took her arm and steered her towards the door, barging George that way as well. Steve, Brian and Dave Mountjoy had snapped out of shock and moved into full-scale panic-stricken flight, struggling with each other to get out of the door first.

The smoke was already catching at the back of my throat and making me cough, and I was aware of the heat at my back, but I tried not to add to the problems by rushing at the only exit – which was not easy – and waited while they all sorted themselves out and tumbled through the door in an untidy heap. George lumbered along after them, and then I ushered Miss Summers out as well and, with some relief, staggered down the step and on to muddy earth.

Out in what passes for fresh air in London, I doubled up and gasped and so did Miss Summers. I retched and coughed for what seemed like an age but was probably only a few seconds. I tried to spit out the taste of petrol and smoke, but it was useless.

Then, when I looked up, I saw that there was definitely a cliché involving frying pans and fires waiting to be coined because Nelson Smith and three of his mates, including Clive, were standing in a semicircle, looking at us. And they were all holding firearms of some sort.

Dave Mountjoy was wailing incoherently, and it was only when Nelson Smith shouted that I realized what Dave was saying.

'That's a warning for Ricky,' Nelson yelled. 'Tell him to stay out of my business or there'll be worse.' And Nelson and his boys backed away, still pointing their guns in our general direction.

I didn't wait to see what would happen next. I stripped off
my jacket and ran back through the doorway into the office,
holding the coat in front of me. Someone – I think it must
have been Charlie Lomax speaking about his experience in
the fire service during the war – told me that you should keep
low when entering a blazing building. It was something to do
with the way the smoke rose, I seemed to recall. So, I dutifully crouched down and waddled forward, my jacket, for the
time being, keeping the worst of the heat away from me. I'd
forgotten just how much noise a fire makes when sucking in
air. I couldn't hear anything above the roar and the crackle
from the burning wood. And I couldn't see anything through
the thick, black smoke edged with darting orange flames that
lashed the ceiling.

'Ricky,' I yelled, but there was no response.

I edged further forward and found myself next to the desk.
Inconsequentially, I found myself thinking of the unfinished
letter in the typewriter. Suddenly, Bix Beiderbecke was playing
in my head. I don't know if Bix was trying to tell me something, but he was tootling the chorus of 'There Ain't No Sweet
Man That's Worth the Salt of My Tears' for all he was worth.

I pushed feebly at the desk and moved it a few inches out
of the way, crawled a bit further and reached out with my
right hand. The heat was really intense. I was sweating like I
hadn't sweated before and felt my skin scorching even behind
the pathetic protection afforded by my jacket. I reached out
with my hand again and felt around. It brushed against some
fabric. It felt like Ricky Mountjoy's pretty blue suit. I grabbed
the collar and hauled.

He didn't move.

I braced myself and pulled again. This time he slithered a
couple of inches. I moved backwards, braced myself again
and pulled. I felt like my arm was going to come out of its
socket but he slid another six inches.

Painfully slowly, long darts of flame flicking out towards
us all the way, my eyes stinging unbearably, I dragged him
towards the door, inch by muscle-straining inch. I tried not
to think about the fact that the fire was probably travelling
faster than we were. And I tried not to notice when the desk

started to smoke and then burst into flame with a great crack as we came alongside it. I concentrated on other things. No one would, after all, have to clean Ricky's spat blood from the floor. Ricky wasn't going to stripe me or Jeannie Summers with his razor. And the great Bix was still belting away in my head.

You're right, Bix, I thought, but this is no sweet man, and I ain't crying for him, though, God knows, I am sweating.

If there's a world record for covering eighteen feet in the slowest possible time, I reckon I must have broken it. But, somehow, I made it, and we popped out of that doorway followed by a billowing pillar of thick black and grey choking smoke and the odd lick of flame.

George and Brian were standing just by the door, and they took Ricky from me and carried him ten feet away from the office and laid him down by Dave. I wondered if he was dead.

My sore and stinging eyes hurt so much that I could scarcely see, and the smoke felt like lumps of suet pudding in my lungs. I sat down and heaved and coughed and heaved and coughed some more. And then I heaved and coughed again.

Jeannie Summers suddenly materialized next to me and stroked my sweaty forehead. 'You could have been killed,' she said. 'Why did you do that for that animal?'

I couldn't speak so I didn't say, 'Don't ask me, I don't know,' but that's all I could have replied.

She leaned down and kissed my grimy, smoke-streaked, scorched cheek. I could feel that the skin was scorched, and I knew it must be smoke-streaked and grimy because hers was. I tried to smile at her, but I suspect it came out more as a grimace.

And then I laid down and passed out to the distant sound of clanging bells. Some observant railwayman from the shunting yards must have called the fire brigade.

I couldn't have been out for long because the emergency vehicles hadn't arrived when I sat up – though, judging by the noise the bells were making, they weren't far away. Funnily enough, I already felt better. There was a nasty taste in my mouth, and I thought I'd probably be coughing for a month, but, aside from the burgeoning bump on the back of my head from George's gun barrel and some nasty-looking blisters on the back of my right hand, I wasn't in bad shape.

Miss Summers was still sitting next to me, holding her jacket together in front of her breasts.

'Right,' I croaked – not everything was in full working order – 'let's retrieve your handbag from the car before the fire engine and the police arrive.'

She looked warily around, but Nelson and his boys had long since departed and Dave and the others were huddled around Ricky's prone body.

'How's he?' I managed to rasp out.

'Still breathing,' she said. 'And not too badly charred. More's the pity.' She looked down at me. 'You knew all along, didn't you? Where I'd put the drugs.'

'I guessed,' I said. 'Why?'

She sighed. 'Lee thought we could sell them. He reckoned there might be a few hundred dollars' worth. It would pay the solicitor.'

I coughed and tasted smoke. 'No,' I said. 'Bad guys want 'em back. I have to be straight with them. I can find some money for the brief. Silks are another matter, but we'll see.'

I struggled up and realized that my knees were creaking more than a bit. All that crouching and hauling had taken its toll. We both slowly walked, unnoticed, to the Consul. I reached in, pulled out the handbag and gave it to her just as the fire engine rattled around the corner and bumped through the entrance, across the muddy forecourt and slewed to a halt by the car.

The office was burning fiercely, and there wasn't much the firemen could do to save it. It would be a burnt-out shell before too long. But they rolled out their hoses, anyway. And they were all bustling activity and reassuring competence.

The second fire engine clanged to a halt behind the other one. It took about three seconds for the second crew to recognize they weren't needed. They hung about for a few minutes and then announced they were off.

I begged a lift from them for me and Miss Summers, and they happily agreed to drop us off outside the Gaumont. One of them did ask if I shouldn't wait for the ambulance that had been summoned for little Ricky and be given the once-over by the quacks at Whipps Cross, but I said I'd be as right as ninepence after a rest, a wash, an aspirin and a change of clothes. He didn't look entirely convinced but shrugged and helped me up into the cab.

The truth was that I wasn't entirely convincing because I thought that I probably did need a bandage or two for the hand, but I really didn't want to hang around and have to explain anything to the police should they turn up.

And, anyway, I'd wanted to ride in a fire engine since I was four.

If I was good, and I asked very nicely, one of the blokes might even let me wear his helmet.

I didn't bother to say goodbye to Dave Mountjoy and his boys.

It turned out that I'd overestimated my powers of self-repair and I felt more like a snide thruppence than nine bright pennies.

The wash helped a bit. And a couple of aspirin dulled some of the aches and pains. But my right hand felt like it was still in the fire, and the lump on the back of my head (lumps, if you counted the one from the coshing the other night) pounded away like the Light Brigade charging into the Valley of Death. Someone had blundered all right, and I had a sneaking suspicion that it was me.

And the change of clothes didn't help one bit.

I'd run out of suits, and I had to resort to the old brown demob number that I hadn't worn for eight years. It still fitted as well as it ever had, which is to say not at all, and I was definitely not at my dapper best. Maman would have tutted loudly, rolled her eyes and sent me back to my room to change. Papa would have rolled his eyes too, but that would have been at Maman. He would have been laughing at me.

I was also out of clean shirts and had to borrow two from Jerry. Miss Summers looked well enough in hers, but mine threatened to split across the back every time I laughed. Fortunately, I wasn't feeling all that jocular. I've always been a traditionalist, much preferring white shirts to grey.

Jerry made a big pot of tea, broke open a fresh packet of custard creams and listened with some attention as Miss Summers told him what had happened. I was still croaking too much for any extended conversation, and every time I coughed – which was often – I tasted smoke.

When she'd finished, Jerry asked a lot of questions she couldn't answer. They both looked at me from time to time, but I just pointed helplessly to my throat. So Jerry settled for shaking his head a lot, muttering something about mad buggers and asking me, I suspect rhetorically, what I thought I was playing at.

I told him it wasn't my fault. These things just sort of happened. He then asked me why it had just sort of happened that I'd dashed into a burning building to rescue some little toerag who'd shown a strong inclination to damage me badly. I told him I would take full responsibility for that, although Bix had something to do with the successful outcome.

He shook his head again and then smeared something cooling and greasy on the back of my hand and wrapped a bandage around it.

When I asked him, he found a recording of Bix Beiderbecke playing 'Mississippi Mud' and that worked its magic and bucked me up no end.

It was nudging on for six o'clock in the evening, and I was so restored and full of beans that I fell fast asleep on Jerry's chaise longue.

TWENTY

'**M**y, my,' James Fitzgerald said when I eventually tracked him down, which hadn't been all that difficult, 'someone's been in the wars. And,' he added with a malign smile after looking me up and down for a few seconds, 'been awarded a *costume civil* for his services.'

He was sitting behind a large, dark desk in a cluttered and gloomy little room at the back of a house in Romilly Street. The grimy window behind him looked out on to a singularly dispiriting and lifeless vista. The dismal back wall of the house behind, unrelieved, as far as I could see, by window or door, stood only a few feet away, like a large and impassive bouncer. With Harold standing behind me and the wall in front of me, I felt hemmed in. I stared at the wall, over Mr Fitz's head, for a few seconds. The mortar was crumbling away. It desperately needed repointing. Much as I felt, in fact.

I tore myself away from the riveting view and sighed. The irony of a man who looked a little like Alfred Hitchcock and who had the dress sense of Gabby Hayes commenting on my sartorial misfortunes was not lost on me.

'Yes,' I said, 'I had a little trouble yesterday.'

He tilted his head on one side and looked at me sympathetically. Well, it would have been a sympathetic gesture in almost anyone else. He could just have been laughing at me. 'Do go on,' he said.

I raised the carrier bag that was dangling from my good hand and placed it on a pile of papers on his desk.

He raised his eyebrows inquisitively and smiled at me.

'It's your "goods",' I said. 'I found them.'

'You just found them?' he said.

'Sort of,' I said. 'I suddenly realized where they had to be.'

He reached out one pudgy hand and pulled the bag towards him. He peered into it. 'Hmm,' he said, then he pushed the bag away. 'Well, thank you, Tony, that's very decent of you.'

'Well,' I said, 'I'd like things to be straight between us.'

'Oh, they are, Tony, they are. I know you're a decent sort, honest as the day is long and all that.' He drummed his fingers on the desk and hummed tunelessly. Suddenly, he looked up and smiled his vicious little smile. 'I wonder if I might impose on you to do something for me?'

I shrugged. It hurt a bit. The shoulders and neck were still sore. 'Sure,' I said.

'I'd be awfully grateful if you'd be so kind as to take these goods to my dear friend Nelson Smith. As a peace offering.'

I said nothing and stared at the wall. It just stared blankly back.

'You look puzzled, Tony,' he said.

'Well, I thought you wanted this stuff back,' I said. 'There was a certain amount of fuss about it.'

He waved his hand dismissively. 'The goods themselves are a mere bagatelle, Tony. Of very little value. But the principle is of the utmost importance. And the principle is that no one takes anything from me.'

'I see,' I said. And I did. I really did. I tried to keep any resentment at his cavalier approach to my life out of my voice. 'Do you know where I'll find your very good friend?'

'Oh, I don't imagine that he's left the leafy lanes of Ladbroke Grove yet, Tony, but, no doubt, he'll be out and about in an hour or two.' He looked at his watch. 'In fact, I have it on good authority that he may well be in the Frighted Horse at opening time. He is hoping, I understand, to meet young Ricky Mountjoy there. I believe he will be disappointed.' He smiled at me knowingly. 'Why don't you find a pastry and a cup of coffee somewhere? You look as if you could do with a sit-down.' He nodded at the looming presence behind me. 'Harold, show the gentleman out.'

I reached out and grabbed hold of the bag, and then a heavy hand fell on my shoulder and guided me away from the desk and on to the narrow little landing outside the office. The door closed firmly behind me.

I sat away from the window, in the shadows at the back of the Moka, and sipped miserably at my rapidly cooling coffee.

I felt very gloomy. It's just as well that no one had ever told me that life was going to be easy, or fair. I would have been forced to disagree strongly.

I looked down at the brown carrier-bag on the seat next to me and thought it would be just my luck for Inspector Rose, or his altogether less attractive sergeant, to turn up and ask to have a butcher's inside. Still, the bag itself wasn't as suspicious as the creased, greasy one the stuff had originally been in. This was a new one, acquired first thing that morning when I'd nipped around the corner to the Co-op in order to fill Jerry's larder with the staples he'd generously bestowed on me and my guests over the past few days. He'd been uncharacteristically moody. I'd tried to jolly him out of it by pointing out that at least I'd stopped maundering on about Paris. He'd smiled, but he'd said he actually preferred life to be a bit boring. I'd agreed with him and promised to be much more boring in the future.

I was startled out of my reflections by the sound of a cup and saucer being plonked down on the Formica opposite me. I looked up and saw Viv Laurence standing there.

'This seat taken?' she said.

'Be my guest,' I said, 'but what are you doing here?'

She slid on to the seat, brushed her hair back and then leaned forward and sighed. 'Got fed up,' she said. 'This isn't much of a life, but it's the only one I've got. Tucked away in that suffocating little house, nothing to do but listen to the wireless all day . . . "Woman's Hour", "Workers' Playtime", "Listen with Mother", "Mrs Dale's bloody Diary" . . . It's not me, Tony.' She picked up her cup and noisily sipped tea. 'We all hate the life. Of course we do. We all want out. But I don't know . . .' She trailed off and shook her head.

'This could be your chance,' I said. 'I think your mum's planning to leave everything to you. There won't be much, I don't suppose, but there's the house and a few bob probably. Why don't you come and see her before . . . You know.'

She shook her head, fumbled in her bag and took out a pack of cigarettes and a box of matches.

'I can't,' she said. 'I can't forgive her for abandoning me and leaving me in that place with that horrible old man.' She

actually shuddered at the thought of the old boy. She lit a
cigarette and drew on it. Her hand was shaking slightly.

'I think she wants to make it up to you, if she can. That's
why she wanted me to find you. She was very young, and it
wasn't her decision.'

She sat back and blew a thin plume of blue-grey smoke
towards the ceiling. 'I don't want her to make it up to me,'
she said.

'Come to see her. Tell her,' I said.

She shook her head firmly. Her hair fluttered about, and her
impressive cleavage trembled. For the first time, I could see
that she bore a resemblance to Daphne. She certainly had very
little of the Mountjoy look.

She smoked for a while, staring past me, and then she
suddenly seemed to notice me properly and leaned forward.
'Here,' she said, 'you look—'

'Terrible. I know,' I said. 'It's been a hard couple of days,
and the suit is an old one and the shirt's borrowed.'

'No,' she said, waving her cigarette about. 'You look a bit
like that Dirk Bogarde. Only older and a lot more lived-in.'

'Thanks,' I said. 'I think.'

I left Viv in the Moka. She was still smoking, still drinking
tea and still refusing to have anything to do with Daphne. As
I walked towards the Frighted Horse, the carrier bag clutched
tightly in my left hand, I realized that there was a bit more
of a spring in my step. Somehow, she'd cheered me up.

It was another dull old day, and the grubby streets of Soho
and the dirty buildings, streaked by pigeon poo, desperately
needed some sun, or a few of the louche, colourful characters
of the night.

I suddenly had that strange prickly feeling on the back of
my neck that made me think I was being followed. I sauntered
on for a few seconds and then stopped to look into a shop
window and cast a surreptitious look behind me. I didn't
recognize anyone, and there was no one acting oddly. Well,
no more oddly than was to be expected in Soho just before
opening time. A thin, frail, threadbare alkie in a greasy gaber-
dine mac stopped next to me and peered vacantly into the

window as well. There wasn't much there apart from half a dozen dead flies and a few paperback books with garish paintings of *femmes fatales* in various stages of undress on their curling covers.

'Spare a couple of bob for an old soldier, sir?' the alkie suddenly said.

I reached into my pocket and found half a crown. I dropped it into his hand.

'Thank you, sir, that's very kind,' he said and touched his right hand to his forehead in the sort of salute that would have had him on a charge in any unit I'd served in.

He drifted off, looking as if a gust of wind would catch him up and carry him gently across the road.

I felt slightly depressed again but still wary. That niggling feeling nagged at the back of the neck. It was probably nothing. Probably just residual anxiety.

But Big Luc had once told me that one should always follow one's instincts and that if you thought you were being followed, act as if you were. Better to feel a little foolish afterwards because there had been no one, than to be dead. An image of the big man sitting quietly with his back to an apple tree, sipping Calvados from his battered tin flask, his prized Luger next to him on the damp grass, flittered into my mind. I wondered if he was still alive.

My alcoholic ex-soldier had disappeared around the corner into Old Compton Street. I hoped he spent my half crown sensibly. Somehow, I couldn't see him wasting it on fish and chips.

There was a little light rain in the air, and a few shapeless, dowdy women of a certain age in cardigans and headscarves took pakamacs out of shopping baskets and wrestled their way into them before rolling off to the baker or the butcher or the greengrocer.

I sauntered casually along and, following the old soldier, turned into Old Compton Street, then I moved as quickly as I could until I came to the entrance to a drinking club I knew and stepped inside. The club itself was on the first floor, and I didn't venture up the stairs. I stood in the little corridor, pressed up against the clammy wall, and waited, smelling the

musty, damp odour of a sick and crumbling building, listening
to the creaks and groans. Occasionally, the pleasing smell of
warm, fresh, yeasty bread wafted in from the baker who had
the shop on the ground floor.

A couple of roly-poly women bowled past the narrow
doorway, and then I heard the heavy footsteps of a large man
hurrying.

He lumbered past, half running and half limping, and I
stepped out of the dark, dank corridor and into the street.

I was in no condition for any kind of physical confrontation,
but I had no intention of spending even a small part of my
life in hiding. It could so easily become a habit.

'Are you looking for me?' I called. As he stopped and
turned, I held the carrier bag in front of me. 'And this?'

Malcolm Booth bent over, his hands on his thighs, sucking
in air in quick little gulps. I was happy to see that he was in
no state to offer violence. After a few seconds he straightened
up and coughed. 'You, yeah. That, no,' he wheezed out. 'I
wanted a word.'

'I'm all ears,' I said.

An old woman came out of the baker's, a loaf of bread
poking out of her shopping basket. She looked at us warily
with rheumy eyes and then put her head down and trudged
stoically past.

'Let's walk and talk,' Malcolm said.

I nodded and turned back along Old Compton Street. He
fell into step beside me, and we ambled along, the light rain
drifting into our faces, tiny little drops sliding from his slick,
Brylcreemed hair.

'The other night,' he said. 'A couple of things ain't right. I
don't think that joanna player did for those boys. And I know
you think I had something to do with it, but I didn't.'

He gave me a quick little look, but I said nothing.

'The thing is, Mr Fitz set it up to warn that Ricky off. He
told the black boys what was what, time of the rounds and
that. But Mr Fitz didn't want things to get out of hand, so he
asked me and a couple of the boys to walk past, like, make
sure they was just warned.' He cleared his throat. 'Anyway,
we ran a few minutes late and it was all over by the time we

got there. The boys was stabbed. In the back, both of them.
The knife was still sticking out of Billy. But that Yank wasn't
up for that. He was huddled up at the other end of the alley,
hugging his knees, just rocking backwards and forwards.'

'So,' I said, 'what do you think happened?'

'Well, at first we thought it must have been the black boys,
you know. And we didn't think that Mr Fitz would want them
done for it, so Stan, he pulls the blade out of young Billy and
he gives it to the joanna player. And we shove off.'

We walked in silence for a little while.

'I didn't think about it at the time,' he said, 'but there was
a woman we ran into just before we got there.'

'Yeah,' I said, 'she saw you too.'

'Oh,' he said, 'you know about her then?'

I nodded.

'Right then,' he said and stopped. 'I'll leave you to it.' As
he turned to go, he added, 'Watch your step with the boys in
the Frighted Horse. Give them the stuff and get out. I wouldn't
hang about.'

'Thanks,' I said. 'I won't.' I cleared my throat. 'About the
ankle. I'm sorry, but you know . . .'

'It's all right,' he said. He looked down at it and moved his
foot a little gingerly. 'S'not busted. Painful, though. I wouldn't
have fancied facing you at Highbury in me playing days.' He
raised a hand in farewell and then, exaggerating his limp, he
walked away.

I didn't quite know what to make of that. Why follow me to
tell me something I already knew? After all, he'd taken me to
Viv's gaff. Either he wasn't such a bad bloke or else he had
something he was covering up. I'd suspected the latter before.
Now I was just plain puzzled.

I shrugged and shoved my way through the door of the
Frighted Horse.

It was the usual scene of genial hospitality.

Two tables were occupied by crumpled-looking middle-aged
men, who looked at me suspiciously. Well, the demob suit
was decidedly dodgy. My old soldier was standing at the bar.
The glass of whisky in his hand and the half pint of beer
standing on the deeply scarred wooden counter in front of

him, waiting to chase the whisky down his gullet, suggested he'd decided on a well-balanced meal. He offered me another of his shabby salutes. Maybe he thought I was good for another half crown.

I nodded to him and then made my way over to Nelson Smith, Clive and their mate, who were drinking glasses of rum in the corner. Nelson looked up at me and the mean little expression on his face suggested that perhaps he wasn't his usual sunny self.

'What you want, man?' he said. 'We ain't in a good mood wit' you.'

'Peace offering,' I said and put the carrier bag on the table. 'From Mr Fitz.'

They all looked at each other, and Nelson prodded Clive. He stood up, leaned across the table and peered into the bag suspiciously.

'What's in there, man?' he said.

'Like I said, a peace offering. Nothing too flammable. I promise.'

I backed away as Clive took one of the little packets I'd carefully packed into the bag, opened it, sniffed it and nodded approvingly to Nelson.

'Whoa. Where you goin'?' Nelson said to me before I'd gone a few feet.

'I got things to do,' I said.

'You don' wan' a drink?'

'No, I'm just the errand boy,' I said. 'Got other errands.'

He nodded. 'All right,' he said, 'just bein' friendly here.'

'I appreciate that,' I said, 'but I've got to go.'

Clive took the bag off the table and tucked it down by his feet.

They made no attempt to stop me, so I left.

I was back on Frith Street and well away when three things struck me:

First, maybe I'd misjudged Malcolm. He had done me a real favour. The two police cars that passed me going towards the pub suggested that James Fitzgerald was even more unscrupulous than even I'd suspected and would have had no qualms about seeing me arrested along with Nelson and his mates.

Second, I was getting very wet.

And third, of course, I'd been very, very stupid.

The Central Line train I sat in all the way from Tottenham Court Road to Leyton whiffed even worse than usual. The filthy floor, littered with cigarette butts and spent matches as usual, was wet from dripping umbrellas and raincoats so the fag ends were soggy and little shreds of brown and gold tobacco wormed their way into every crevice. The smell of damp wool added to the smoky miasma, but I suspected that much of that was coming from my antique suit.

I stared at my reflection in the grimy window opposite as we screeched our way under Holborn and Chancery Lane and brooded a little.

I'd learned in the war not to underestimate women.

Ghislaine, in her beret and Robert's big, worn leather jacket, had been as fierce as any of the men in our little group, as determined and every bit as brave. And there had been the tough, redoubtable and authentically dirty-minded factory girls, wearing trousers, their hair tied up in scarves.

All the same, I still found it difficult not to think of them as the gentler sex.

You opened doors for women, you walked on the side of the pavement nearest the road to protect them from splashes from passing cars, you raised your hat to women. You worked from half past eight until half past five to put bread on the table for the little woman.

Well, I didn't. But then I didn't wear a hat either.

The train clattered to the surface at Stratford in a rush of grey light. The bloke sitting next to me took out a pouch of Golden Virginia and a packet of Rizla and, with remarkable dexterity, quickly rolled a thin cigarette, spilling nothing in spite of the erratic motion of the train. He put away the makings, ran his tongue over the emaciated little tube and then tucked the roll-up neatly behind his ear.

A little cold fresh air blew in when the doors opened, and I shivered slightly. But at least it seemed to have stopped raining.

I yawned, stretched a bit and stood up when the train started again, grabbed one of the swinging straps above me and swayed along until we reached Leyton.

I'd made a decision. The damp, wrinkled suit had to go. I had a plan of action: fish and chips, cash a cheque at the Midland Bank and take a bus to the Bakers' Alms. Half an hour in Foster Bros should see me right. A new suit and a crisp white shirt and I'd feel fine. Well, as fine as anyone with a few bumps on the head and a burnt hand could feel. The shoes were old but not too shabby. They'd do for the time being.

Of course, I knew what I was really doing. Just putting off a little chat. But I'd have to buy a new suit sometime. I felt more cheerful.

There was a spring in my step, and I bounced up the stairs at Leyton station. Even the headline in the *Evening Standard* about troops heading off to Cyprus that I noticed as I passed the vendor on my way out didn't depress me.

Billie Holiday was singing 'Good Morning Heartache' when I clanged my way into the shop. (Jerry's bell didn't really ring.)

It was my day for peace offerings, and I handed Jerry the canary-yellow silk tie I'd bought him. But this peace offering was kosher. I didn't think the police would come crashing in. Unless it was to arrest him for crimes against conventional taste.

I had a momentary pang when I thought about Nelson Smith and Clive, but, if I'm honest, it was more a worry that they might have mentioned me to the police than concern about them being banged up. It did also cross my mind, not for the first time, that they could well be thinking that I'd set them up, which was probably what Mr Fitz intended. Still, they had more pressing concerns than that just at the moment. All the same, it would fester. I could always hope they'd get long stretches.

Jerry claimed to love the tie, and Jeannie Summers came out from his living room to admire it. And me in my new charcoal-grey suit. She hummed along with Miss Holiday.

Les had called an hour or so before, and I rang him back. It seemed that there was nothing much that the quacks could do for Daphne. It was just a matter of time, and she'd asked if she could go home. She'd be there the next day, he said, and her sister would be staying again to look after her. There was a catch in his voice. She'd asked, apparently, if I could visit and, perhaps, bring someone. She'd said I'd know what she meant. I said I did and that I'd see what I could do. If Viv Laurence hadn't pushed off and moved back to Soho, I wouldn't have had to. I pondered that for a moment after I'd manoeuvred the receiver back on to its cradle

A couple of customers – a boy and a girl of about sixteen – came into the shop, and I took Miss Summers off to Costello's for a cup of tea.

She was looking pale and tired but surprisingly elegant in one of Jerry's grey shirts and her blue costume.

The tea Enzo poured for us was dark brown and stewed. I put a couple of spoonfuls of sugar in mine. She didn't look at all interested in hers.

'Mrs Dale's Diary' murmured gently from the big, brown wireless behind the counter, and I thought of Viv Laurence and smiled.

'I wanted a quiet word,' I said.

'You've guessed, haven't you?' Miss Summers said.

'I suppose so,' I said.

'I love him,' she said simply.

'And he loves you,' I said.

She nodded. 'I knew that you'd understand. The French understand *l'amour*,' she said.

'I'm not really French,' I said. 'My parents were, but I'm not.' I paused and thought for a moment. 'Why didn't you take him with you, when you ran away?'

She shrugged. 'I don't know.' She waved her hands help-lessly. 'I was in a state. I just ran.'

I swallowed some tea.

'They were going for him,' she said in a flat monotone, like in the pictures when the broad finally confesses to the dogged flatfoot who's been pursuing her relentlessly. 'One of them had his cosh out.'

'They were going for him?' I said. 'But they'd just been set on themselves.'

'I don't know about that,' she said. 'When I got there, they looked all right. Except they were mean and mad and they looked like they were going to take it out on him. I saw the knife on the ground. One of them must have dropped it, I suppose. Anyway, I used it on both of them and ran. It was only a matter of a few seconds. They didn't yell or anything.'

I wondered if Viv Laurence had seen her. She must have done. Then why hadn't she mentioned it? Some sense of loyalty to her sex perhaps. Or maybe Miss Summers had arrived at the alley just after Viv. It was possible.

'Was there anyone else there?'

She looked puzzled.

'Did anyone see you?'

'I don't think so,' she said, shaking her head.

I wasn't sure I could face any more tea, but I had to do something to cover my silence, so I took another sip.

'What are you going to do?' she said.

'Me?' I said. 'Nothing. What should I do?'

'Tell the police.'

'Why would they believe me? They've got a confession. You and Lee can sort this one out between you.' Anyway, I had no intention of going anywhere near the good Inspector Rose if I could help it.

'What'll happen to him?'

I shrugged. 'I don't know. He might get away with manslaughter. But they were knifed in the back, weren't they?'

'You think they might hang him,' she said.

I shrugged again. 'Let's hope not.'

She leaned across the table and put her hand on mine. Fortunately, it was my left hand. Her touch was soft and cool. It felt good. It also meant that I couldn't lift the cup and so didn't have to swallow any more of Enzo's foul brew.

She looked thoughtful, but she still didn't drink any tea. A scum was forming on the surface of her cup.

'Do you think the judge might be more lenient with a woman?' she said.

'I doubt it,' I said. 'They just hanged Ruth Ellis.' A fleeting memory from my time at Church Road School came into sharp focus: Mrs Wilson's white hair the only bright spot in the

November-afternoon gloom of the dusty classroom as she says to my mate, Bob, 'No, no, no, Robert, meat is hung; men – and Dr Crippen was a man – are *hanged*.'

Jeannie Summers stared off into space for a few moments. 'Did you mean what you said about finding some money for the lawyers?' she said.

I nodded.

'I'll pay you back, of course. When I can,' she said. 'I don't know how to thank you.'

'There might be something,' I said.

She squeezed my hand.

TWENTY-ONE

I n the event, I didn't have to go to Inspector Rose. He came
to me.

It wasn't, he said, an official visit. To prove it, he'd left
the grumpy-looking Sergeant Radcliffe in the back of the
comfortable old black Wolseley. At least, I assumed that was
why he pointed it out to me as we stood on the pavement
outside the shop. The fact that it was ten o'clock in the morning,
rather than ten minutes before dawn, also went some way to
confirming the friendly and informal nature of the call.

After tea in Costello's, Jeannie Summers had made her way
back to the boarding house close to Marble Arch where she
still had a room. I'd slipped her a fiver to cover her immediate
expenses. And that meant that I'd spent the night in my own
bed and, in spite of the occasional nasty dream about fires,
I'd slept quite well. I'd also washed, shaved, breakfasted on
bacon and eggs and put on some fresh new clothes. I'd been
ready for almost anything – even the inspector.

I invited him up to my office for a cup of tea.

He sat on my grandfather's chair and fiddled with his pipe
while I went to the scullery to boil the kettle.

'That's a nasty wound,' he said, pointing the stem of his
pipe at my right hand when I brought the coronation coach
tray with teapot, milk bottle and cups on it and plonked it on
the worn old table that masqueraded as my desk.

I'd decided to take the bandage off, and the back of the
hand really did look raw and angry. It still hurt too.

'It's nothing,' I said. 'Burnt myself.'

He nodded sagely.

He was looking his usual dapper self in a smart blue suit
set off by a dark-blue bow-tie. I wasn't sure about the brown
shoes, but I didn't say anything.

'So,' I said, pouring tea, 'what can I do for you, Inspector?'

'Well,' he said, 'your name came up this morning, Tony.'

'Really?' I said. 'Sugar?'

He shook his head and took the cup and saucer I offered him. 'Yes,' he said. 'At least, one of my colleagues was asking if I knew someone called Tony. Apparently, the name was mentioned by some unsavoury types he caught red-handed, with the goods.'

I sat down on the wooden chair behind my desk and drank some tea. 'That's odd,' I said. 'I don't really know any unsavoury types. Must be some other Tony.'

'Hmm,' he said.

I watched him as he tried to juggle pipe and cup and saucer. Eventually, he admitted defeat and slipped his pipe back into his jacket pocket.

'That's what I said,' he said. 'The Tony I know wouldn't have anything to do with anything crooked. He's a decent sort. But I also said I'd check with you. Just in case you know something.'

'Can't help, I'm afraid,' I said.

'So,' he said mildly, 'you weren't in Soho yesterday around midday?'

'Well,' I said, 'Hoxton Films has an office in Wardour Street.'

'And you went there yesterday at, say, twelve? And Mr Jackson of Hoxton Films will confirm that?'

'Probably,' I said. 'If he remembers.'

'Fine,' he said. 'I'll take your word for it, and I'll tell my colleague these unsavoury types are all either mistaken or it's some other Tony.'

I didn't know whether to believe him or not, but he was definitely marking my card and I'd better ring Les and fix a story with him.

We sat in silence for a few minutes, sipping tea.

'You know,' he eventually said, 'that the "jazz" musician confessed to murdering those boys.'

'I heard,' I said.

'Sergeant Radcliffe's cock-a-hoop. It's a very nice result all round. Very satisfactory.' He leaned forward and placed his cup and saucer on the desk. Then he retrieved his pipe and started playing with it. 'For me, though, it doesn't add up. I'll live with it, of course, unless there's any evidence to the contrary – I wouldn't want to upset the sergeant – but it's not quite right. The lad can't remember how come they were stabbed in the back when he claims they were attacking him. It's curious that. And both of them had just the one knife wound. Slipped straight into the kidney. Ouch!'

'I heard they were pretty cut up,' I said.

'No,' he said. 'Journalistic exaggeration. Just the one wound. Nicked a number of important organs, apparently. Lot of blood, of course.' He clenched the pipe between his brown-stained teeth. 'You don't know anything about that either, I don't suppose. Only, I know you've been comforting the singer, his wife.'

'Just seeing what I could do,' I said, wondering if he was suggesting something. 'She must have told you what she's told me.'

He nodded. 'Just thought I'd ask,' he said. 'It'll take some pretty fancy footwork from a silk to keep him from swinging.' He stood up and stretched. 'Always good to see you, Tony.' He looked at my desk and saw the letter from Ghislaine that had arrived that morning. I hadn't opened it yet. 'How's that French friend of yours? The one you went to see in Paris.'

'She's fine,' I said. '*En pleine forme . . .*'

He chuckled. 'Going back to see her soon?'

'No,' I said.

'Thanks for the tea. It's back to the grind for me. There are a lot of bad people out there, Tony, doing bad things. A police-man's work, like a woman's, is never done.' He walked to the door and then turned back. 'If you do think of anything – on any of these matters – you know how to get hold of me.'

'Yes,' I said and got up and walked down the stairs with him to the door.

We stood on the pavement, and he ostentatiously offered his hand. I pointed to my burnt skin and awkwardly took his right hand with my left.

'You ought to get that seen to,' he said. 'Nasty things, burns. In fact, I heard that a lad who shows up as a green blip on my radar screen every so often had a lucky escape from a fire the other day. He's in hospital recovering, but he probably won't be troubling me for a few weeks. He comes from around here, I think. But I don't suppose you know him.'

His driver had hopped smartly out and opened the rear door of the Wolseley for him. He waved his pipe at me and then slid on to the back seat.

I watched as the car pulled smoothly away and wondered why nothing was ever neat and tidy, why nothing was ever really resolved. Somehow things were never like they were on the silver screen or in books or on the wireless.

But I didn't have time to reflect on life and its vagaries for long because my second unexpected visitor of the morning turned up while I was standing there.

The red and white Consul slid to a halt by the bus stop opposite, and Dave Mountjoy and the redoubtable George both struggled out and lumbered across the road.

My right hand started to sting, and I tucked it behind my back. I hoped I wouldn't have to use it. And I hoped the new suit would survive this encounter intact. But I braced myself. Suits can be replaced. Hands usually heal.

A number fifty-eight bus turned off Lea Bridge Road into Church Road and roared past me, the gritty draught whisking my tie after it. I tucked the tie back in place and smoothed it down just as George and Dave scurried across the second half of the road in front of another number fifty-eight determined to catch the one ahead.

George stopped on the kerb and let Dave come on alone, which was encouraging. I could take Dave with one hand tied behind my back. Which was just as well since I did have one hand behind my back.

Dave still didn't have any dentures in, and his collapsed face made him appear older than his father. He peered down at the cracked paving stone he was standing on and shook his head. 'Look,' he mumbled, 'I didn't like your dad, and I don't like you. And those black devils wouldn't have been anywhere near our place if you hadn't brought 'em, so I'm not saying this is over. But you didn't have to drag Ricky out of that fire. So –' he looked up at me with tired, bloodshot eyes – 'thank you for that. You saved his life.'

'Anyone would have done it,' I said.

'No, they wouldn't,' he said. 'I didn't.' He jerked a thumb at George. 'He didn't. Nor did Steve or Bri.'

'How is Ricky?' I said. 'I heard he's still in hospital.'

'He's not so bad,' Dave said. 'Lost some of his hair, and he's going to have some scars, but he's not so bad, considering.' He hawked up some phlegm and spat. 'Won't do him any harm to spend some time at home with the new missus. Might just have learnt a lesson about going up West as well.'

I nodded. 'Might be best if he didn't. Not for a while.'

'Now,' he said, 'we do have a bone to pick with your black friends. So, give me some names.'

'I don't know their names,' I said. 'Ricky might. He's the one who stepped on their toes. But, in any case, they got nicked yesterday. So they're off the streets for a bit. No point in going after 'em at the moment.'

'How do you know?'

'I was just talking to a policeman from Scotland Yard,' I said.

He gave a phlegmy laugh. 'Yeah,' he said, 'of course you were. Seriously, how do you know?'

'Seriously,' I said, 'this inspector dropped by to ask me about it. But I couldn't help him because I don't know anything.'

'Of course you don't,' he said.

My tongue worried at the chipped tooth for a few seconds. 'It's worth bearing in mind,' I said, 'that some of what I don't know anything about involves Ricky. I hope he's learned not to play with the big boys just yet.'

'I doubt it,' Dave said, 'but I'll try not to let him out without George to keep an eye on him. Worships the boy, George does. And it's worth you keeping *that* in mind.' He spat again. 'Anyway, thanks for what you done.' And he held his hand out.

I risked the pain and took it in my right. To be fair to him, he saw the ugly red wound and his grip was loose and brief. It was a symbolic gesture for George's sake. The Mountjoys and the last remaining representative of the Gérards had negotiated an uneasy truce.

I sat at my desk and stared at Ghislaine's letter.

So, for the time being, I was safe from reprisals from the Mountjoys and from Nelson Smith and his boys. Well, for as long as Ricky remained sick, and for as long as Nelson and his crew stayed in custody. I was hoping for a decade or two, but I didn't suppose I'd be that lucky. James Fitzgerald didn't give a monkey's about me, and I seemed to amuse Inspector Rose. If I kept my head down for a while, I might get away with it. A two-year holiday in some inaccessible spot, like Timbuktu, might do the business.

I ran my thumbnail along the edge of the flimsy envelope and took out the letter.

As I'd suspected, she'd changed her mind about going back to Robert. He was, after all, an unfeeling pig. Did I think it was a good idea for her to visit London again?

I decided that it was difficult for me to hold a pen in my right hand for longer than it took to write a cheque, so a letter was out of the question for at least, oh, another week or so. She might not change her mind about Robert again, but giving her a little time to do so wouldn't hurt. And, anyway, there was Mrs Williams – Ann – to consider. For all my faults, I'd been scrupulously faithful to her for years, whatever Jerry and Inspector Rose thought had taken place during my holiday in Paris.

I went down to the shop and telephoned Les.

I asked after Daff, and he gloomily said she'd be back home that afternoon. Then I asked him where he'd been at twelve o'clock the day before.

'Where would you like me to have been?' he said.

'In the office,' I said, 'with me, if anyone asks.'

'That sounds right,' he said. 'I think that's what it says in the diary. We probably discussed Philip Graham. I probably told you I was fed up to what remain of my back teeth with him, his unprofessionalism and his petulance and I was cancelling his contract. I probably also told you I'd send Charlie round with the car to pick you up to see Daff about four this afternoon. Is that what you remember?'

'Yeah,' I said, 'that's what I remember. Thanks for reminding me, Les.'

'What are mates for?' he said. 'Did I ever tell you the story that Diana Dors tells about the vicar's speech when she was opening a fête in Swindon, where she comes from?' He didn't wait for a reply, which would have been yes. 'You probably know that her real name's Diana Fluck, and she told the vicar that over lunch. He got really worried about mispronouncing it, and when he got up he was so flustered that he introduced her as "the local girl we all knew as Diana Clunt". Brilliant, eh?'

Les seemed to have recovered just a little of his usual *joie de vivre.*

He'd lost it again later that afternoon and was attempting to hide his dismay at the sight of Daff by being ridiculously solicitous, asking if she was comfortable every minute or so and if there was anything she needed every thirty seconds. All of which got right up her nose. She retaliated by asking him about the office and the progress of all the current films. After about twenty minutes she told him that he was needed back there to run things and that she wasn't planning on giving him the satisfaction of pegging out just yet. He left, promising to return later with anything she wanted. He said he'd send Charlie back for me and 'the girl' in an hour or so.

Daff rolled her eyes. 'I thought the old bugger would never go,' she said.

She was lying on a little bed in the front room I'd seen her in before. The old flowers had been cleared out, and there was only one vase of red roses – from Les, of course – on the mantelpiece. I guessed that Viv Laurence had thrown the dead ones away. She'd left the alabaster Alsatian with its loving master where it was, though. Pity.

Her skin had a yellowish hue, and she'd lost weight in the last few days. But her eyes still had a little sparkle and said there was life in the old dog yet.

She held out her hand, and her nightgown rolled up, showing how painfully thin her arm was. Jeannie Summers stepped towards the bed and took her hand.

I'd spent a fruitless half hour trying to persuade Viv Laurence to visit her mother, and I wasn't proud of resorting to a lie. I told myself it was a white one and told for the best of reasons, but I still felt guilty.

In fact, it turned out to be a lie only by implication. Daff didn't ask any questions at all, and Jeannie just stood by the bed holding her hand until Daff told her that she needed a private word with me. After she'd left the room, Daphne asked me to write down the name she went by and her address so she could change her will and her solicitor would be able to get in touch. I'd carefully printed out Viv's name and the Old Compton Street address on a sheet of paper from a red Woolworth's notebook, and I put it in her hand. She fell asleep clutching it.

Jeannie Summers and I waited with Daff's sister in the kitchen until Charlie returned in the Roller to pick us up.

We were all in sombre mood, and I wasn't sorry that he dropped me off first. Jeannie Summers kissed me on the cheek and said she'd telephone the shop.

I felt the soft touch of the kiss as I opened the door to the flat. I tried not to think what was likely to happen to her and Lee over the next months. And then, as I climbed the stairs, I felt my eyes prickle a little when I thought of what was going to happen to Daff.

Jerry had left a letter on my desk. It must have come in the four o'clock post.

It seemed that James Fitzgerald was not as indifferent to me as I'd thought. He wanted to see me. He had a proposal for me. Malcolm, apparently, spoke highly of me. He thought he could use someone of my background and initiative. It would, he said, be mutually beneficial.

I sat in the shadows of my room for a few quiet moments looking at his elegant, flowing script. Then I forced myself to move.

I raided my larder and found some Wall's pork sausages and a tin of Crosse & Blackwell beans. I took them down to Jerry.

While I fried the sausages, warmed the beans and listened to an Artie Shaw recording of 'What Is This Thing Called Love?' Jerry reverently placed on his radiogram, I told him most – well, some – of what had happened in the last few days. He didn't say anything until we sat down to eat.

'You know, my friend,' he said as he picked up what he always called his eating irons, 'your life sometimes reminds me of something a great German poet called Goethe once said.'

I looked at him over the forkful of sausage I was about to put in my mouth.

'He said, if I remember it aright, "Everything is both simpler than we can imagine and more entangled than we can conceive."'

Jerry sometimes comes out with stuff like that. It's what he salvaged from a privileged education.

I tried to look thoughtful, as though I understood what this Goethe chap was going on about and was considering it, but, apart from a poem about daffodils, the truth was that we'd gone for the more martial stuff at Church Road School: boys on burning decks, cannons to the right of him sort of thing. Ghislaine, of course, had sent me a couple of books of French poetry, and I had found some of the pomes almost interesting, although what I'd seen of M. Apollinaire's *Alcools* I'd have to say I found not altogether comprehensible. I prefer stuff with *virgules* and the occasional *point d'exclamation*.

'Well,' I said, dipping my sausage in bean juice, 'look on the bright side, Jerry. I haven't mentioned Paris once in the last five days.'

Later, before we strolled down to the Antelope, I went back upstairs and tossed James Fitzgerald's letter into the rubbish.